FANG

VOLUME 9

Edited by Ashe Valisca

Bad Dog Books

2019

FANG Volume 9
First publication 2019

Edited by Ashe Valisca

Cover by Donryu

Published by Bad Dog Books
www.BadDogBooks.com

An imprint of FurPlanet Productions
www.FurPlanet.com
Dallas, TX

TABLE OF CONTENTS

Preface

I want to thank all of the authors for FANG 9. Every year I give them a theme and every year they surprise me. I have never received such a diverse collection and such a broad interpretation, and I am proud to present this collection to you. Remember the stories contained herein are fiction and no actual fursons were harmed in the creation of these narratives (they legally require me to say that.)

-Ashe

To Sparf, Syr, Jaden Drackus, SignificantOtter, and Alkani Serval for all the helpful feedback. This story wouldn't be where it is without you.

Summer Camp Showdown, Tuesdays at 8e/7c

by Skunkbomb

I was only acting. "Reality" was part of the name, but reality competition shows were always scripted at some level. I had survived six eliminations and I'd seen plenty of manipulation from behind the cameras. 'Hey, that guy was talking shit about you. Go confront him.' 'That chick you hate is talking with your alliance. Go check it out.' Sure, Summer Camp Showdown was pretty scripted, but my student loan debt was real. Plus, the prize money would easily allow me to move to Los Angeles to pursue an acting career.

I would have preferred to be acting in some artsy indie film or a gripping television drama, but there have been a few contestants from reality shows who have used their fame to build successful acting careers. I could make this work. After I was officially cast on the show, I made sure to watch as much of the previous seventeen seasons as possible. From my research, I had to do three key things to stay on the show: be interesting, stick with a majority alliance, but most importantly, don't get romantically attached to someone. That's when most people start acting dumb. Well, dumber. After college, I'd done everything that was in the best interest of becoming an actor in Hollywood. I'd gladly play my role as the token gay guy for a chance to make my dream happen.

The thing is, I didn't think I was the only gay guy here.

Gabe was one of the last of our teammates into the cafeteria. I usually imagined reindeer wearing thick jackets and sweaters (or belled harnesses). Seeing him in a button-up t-shirt (how else would he wear shirts with those antlers?) and shorts made him look like a young dad coaching his kid's basketball team. His shirt was sleeveless, showing off his toned biceps and broad shoulders.

The reindeer sat down with a bowl of oatmeal. "Morning, Clark."

I held back a chuckle. "Sit still for a second, okay?" I didn't have to pretend to be gay, but I didn't want to come off as a stereotype. For me, playing the token gay guy was all about little comments and, if I could tell they'd be okay with it, little touches. I placed one hand on Gabe's shoulder while I brushed white paint chips from his antler tips. He squirmed.

"Are they sensitive?" I said, grinning.

"A little," Gabe said. "Those shower stalls aren't built with antlers in mind. I can barely move around in there."

I had heard the show does stuff like that on purpose: low showers to mess with tall species, high shelves to irritate short species, and cramped cabins to mess with species with sensitive noses and ears, such as foxes like myself. "If it's that tough on you, next time you're in the shower, take a seat and I'll wash your back." My tail swished slowly. A cameraman was shooting the whole scene. This would make it into an episode for sure.

"Thanks for the offer," Gabe said, rubbing the back of his neck, "But I think I'll manage."

I shrugged and sat back down. "Suit yourself." We ate in silence for a few minutes. "Clear morning today. I'm betting it'll be just as nice tonight."

Gabe nodded, but he didn't look up from his oatmeal.

I rolled my eyes. "I'm glad they have sausage rolls today. I've been craving them." God, I hoped that line didn't make it into any episodes.

The reindeer finally looked up.

I slipped the end of the sausage into my mouth a little slower than usual before biting.

Gabe nodded. "Oh, right, tonight. Yes, tonight should be good."

He was handsome, but he sure wasn't that quick on his hooves.

"What's tonight?" Cassie sat down next to me, swinging her ringed tail over the bench.

"Elimination, if we don't win today," I said. I'd tell the raccoon afterward, but I wasn't about to blurt out how Gabe and I were going to fuck tonight.

"Good morning campers!" Our host, Ryan Sullivan, blared into a megaphone. I folded my ears back. The weasel stood on an unoccupied table in front of each of the two teams' tables. "I hope you're all fueled up and ready to go, because we're kicking off today with a little surprise. Reach underneath where you're sitting. You'll need it for today's challenge."

I reached under me and pulled out a yellow bandana. For a second, I was confused. I already had a yellow bandana since I was in the yellow cabin.

Gabe held a green bandana.

"That's right everyone," the weasel squeaked into his megaphone. "It's team swap time! We'll move your belongings to your new cabin after the challenge. Everyone follow me to the playing field!"

This was all wrong. A team swap wasn't supposed to happen for another two episodes. A team swap this early hadn't happened since season six. Two teammates chatting with each other wasn't too suspicious, but two members on opposite teams just saying hello was almost a one-way ticket to getting voted out. I took a deep breath. I could make this work, because I was more than the token gay guy. I was a fox.

"Tonight," I hissed at Gabe before he got up.

He nodded, pulled off his yellow bandana, and tied the green one around his wrist.

***

I had claimed a bottom bunk near the door. It minimized the number of teammates I had to pass and squeaky floorboards I had to step over to sneak out. It was helpful for late night strategy sessions, but it also came in handy for a midnight sex rendezvous.

There was a wooded area near the lake. It was far enough away from the cabins that no one would hear any moaning, the foliage would conceal us, and we could clean up a little in the lake. My tail swished and my pants tightened a little. Or maybe fooling around in the lake could be our foreplay. No, the splashing could make too much noise.

After twenty minutes, Gabe still hadn't arrived. I caught myself chewing my claws. Our team had won the challenge earlier that day where we caught rings while sliding down a slip and slide, so Gabe's team had to vote someone out. Maybe he got sent packing. Less than 24 hours ago, he was a member of the yellow cabin. The other green cabin members could have suspected he was still loyal to everyone on the other team. I'd seen it happen plenty of times in previous seasons.

I curled my tail around my legs. I'd wait another ten minutes, and if Gabe still didn't show up, I'd head back to my cabin. Someone could wake up and notice if I was gone for too long.

Sticks crunched underfoot and Gabe pushed a low branch aside. He brushed pine needles from his shoulder. "Sorry. Duncan was mumbling. Had to make sure he was just talking in his sleep."

My tail relaxed as I helped brush the last of the pine needles off the reindeer. "Glad to see you're still here. It would have been hard to have sex with you while you were in the loser's lodge."

Gabe rubbed one of his antlers. "Are you sure there aren't any cameras around?"

I shrugged. "Even if there are, they air this show at 8 p.m. on Tuesdays. They aren't going to show two guys fucking at that hour." I slid my hand down his shorts, fondling his hefty balls.

"Oh, wow—" the reindeer said as he stiffened in more than one way. "So, we're going to, um, how are we…?"

"Clothes off so we don't get jizz on them," I said. I worked my thumb over the head of his shaft. "I'll take you in my muzzle. It'll be less messy than if you took me in the ass. If we get cum on ourselves, the lake is nearby. Get as little of yourself wet as possible so that you don't come in soaking wet, because that'll look suspicious."

Gabe shuddered as I traced my paw pad down his shaft and back up. "How long have you been planning this out?"

"Since that first challenge when I caught you staring at my ass," I said. I unbuttoned the top button on his shirt. "As much as I'd like to savor this, we should get going before someone notices we're missing."

Gabe was still fiddling with the last couple buttons on his shirt by the time I'd stripped naked. Were his nerves getting the better of him or was he staring at my cock peeking out of my sheath? It was probably a little of both. I grabbed the waistband of his shorts and yanked them down. He wasn't rock hard, but he was past half-mast.

I knelt down and brushed my nose between his balls. His musk was strong, but nowhere near intolerable. "Try not to make any noise."

The reindeer nodded.

I started slow. I needed to warm up my jaw and not gag myself right away. That, and the hiss from Gabe made it clear he was more than a little pent up. I wanted this done quickly, but not immediately.

Gabe braced himself against the trunk of the tree behind him.

He wasn't the largest guy I'd blown, but he was easily in the top five. The saltiness of his cock mingled with the pre leaking from him.

When I finally eased myself down to the hilt of his cock, I drew up ever so slowly, tightening my sucking. I was used to fucking guys with longer tails, but I couldn't see Gabe wagging. Did reindeer wag? Sucking cock is fun, and it's not hard to get a guy off, but I wanted my partners to enjoy it.

Gabe's grabbed my head and pushed it down. "That, but faster."

I did as I was told. He rewarded me by rubbing one of my ears. When I teased his head with the tip of my tongue, he tightened his grip on the back of my head.

"Fuck," he groaned. He bucked his hips, almost gagging me. I was happy to take the lead when it came to sex, but bottoming was my true love. It was more of a thrill for me when whomever I was fooling around with took the reins and used some force. Getting drilled against the wall, the floor, or, in this case, his hand, got me harder than anything. I reached between my legs and stroked myself.

In between his grunts, Gabe asked, "Mouth or face?"

I pointed to my mouth, which I hoped he understood because I wasn't looking forward to cleaning jizz out of my fur.

The reindeer almost knocked me off my knees with his last thrust. Salty tang coated the back of my throat, and I swallowed as quickly as I could. A few strokes of my cock, and I was painting the pine needles beneath me.

"Damn, I needed that," Gabe panted.

"Me too."

"Do you need me to…?"

I showed him the streaks of my seed. "No, I'm good."

The reindeer nodded silently, not meeting my eye.

I patted his ass. "You can help me with that next time." I stood up and grabbed my clothes. "Come on. Let's get cleaned up."

Jumping into the lake, while fun, was out of the question. A washcloth was more discreet than bringing a towel. I washed my hands and ran the washcloth around my muzzle and along my cock. I handed the washcloth to Gabe. When he balked, I snickered. "It's your cock and jizz. What are you worried about?"

The reindeer sighed, took the cloth, and cleaned himself up. "Tonight was fun. I really needed that."

I licked my lips. "Yeah, I could tell."

He chuckled. "Right, but about what you said earlier about next time. You were the one who said we had to be careful. Maybe we should hold off. We don't want to get caught and get targets on our backs."

"True," I said. "But that only really applies now that we're on separate teams. In a few episodes, the teams will dissolve and it'll be everyone for themselves. Once we form a majority alliance, we should be safe enough to try this again."

Gabe nodded and handed me the washcloth. "That could work, but what about at the end of all this? What happens if we make it to the final three?"

I gave the reindeer a friendly push. "Geez, I like to think ahead, but even that's going a little far. Let's just try not to get voted out, okay?"

Gabe smiled, if only a little. "Okay."

I pulled on my underwear. "You get going first. If anyone sees us coming back at the same time, it'll look suspicious."

I didn't have a mint or gum, but I had snagged a granola bar from breakfast. I hoped the oats would cover the smell of reindeer in my mouth. Tonight was great, but I didn't love Gabe. Still, as far as I was concerned, this was just a job, another stepping stone to landing more acting roles, and work wasn't always fun. There were some nice people in the competition, especially Cassie, but having a physical release was just what I needed to ease the tension for a little while. Gabe was worth keeping around.

After about twenty minutes, I walked back to my cabin. I'd have to be careful how I opened the door since the hinge squealed. If I wasn't careful how I walked on the wooden floor, my claws would tap against it. I hoped my teammates would be heavy sleepers. God, I was ready to conk out. My jaw ached. My tail swished.

As I made it to the cabin, my tail stilled. Joanna was leaning against the door, eyeing me like she was ready to pounce. Instead, the lioness tilted her head left. I nodded, and we walked together away from the cabin.

Once we were far enough away from the cabin, I spoke first. "I needed to clear my head. Well, more like my nose. I swear Kevin's feet smell worse each day no matter how much he bathes."

"I saw Gabe walking past our cabin," the lioness said. She wrinkled her nose. "And your breath smells like… you know what. You would have to be blind or dumb not to see those eyes you two make at each other."

I sighed. "Look, the only scheming we were doing was how to find ten minutes on this camera-filled campsite to get off. I wasn't trying to be some sort of double agent."

"I believe you."

Even though I wanted to relax, if this was the end of our conversation, we could have done this back at the cabin.

"And I think I can use the two of you to my advantage," the lioness added. "I found the map to the hidden immunity bracelet, but when I got there, it was already gone."

Lucky lioness. If only she had been quick enough. No one could get voted out as long as they were wearing that. All they had to do was reveal it at the elimination campfire and all the votes against them would be voided. Too bad it only works for one elimination. "I don't have it if that's what you're implying."

"I know you don't," the lioness said. "I already went through everyone's bags in our cabin, and you obviously don't have it on your person. I even interrogated our new teammates, but they're clueless. The bracelet has to be with someone in the green cabin. That's where Gabe comes in. Have another one of your midnight meet ups with him and pump him for information."

"If the former green cabin members don't know about who has the bracelet, I doubt Gabe would know," I said. "And if he snoops and gets caught, he'll get voted out for sure."

Joanna shrugged. "Not my problem. If he fails, I'll tell the team I caught you collaborating against us. Maybe we'll throw the immunity challenge just to go to the elimination campfire and vote you out."

She had me by the balls, but at least I had a chance to save myself. I just wished Gabe didn't have to get roped into this mess. "I'll need to get him alone somehow to give him the invitation."

"Figure that out on your own," Joanna said. "I've got enough work on my hands keeping this team together." She purred lightly as we returned to the cabin. "Let's get some rest. You've got a busy day tomorrow."

***

"What a fucking hoe bag," Cassie said to me over breakfast the next morning.

"Careful," I whispered. "You'll be next on her shit list if someone in the alliance hears you."

Cassie stabbed at her eggs. "As much as I want to hear every detail of you and Gabe making sweet backwoods love with each other—"

"It wasn't lovemaking."

The raccoon waved me off. "We have to vote that tyrant of a lioness out or she'll control everything. Between you, the former green cabin members, and me, we could make a run at voting Joanna out at the next elimination campfire. Hell, there's probably one or two people in Joanna's alliance that are sick of her enough to flip sides."

My ears folded back. "She could have those former green cabin members under her thumb by now. The best strategy is to wait until we all merge into one cabin and we pick off the remaining members outside of Joanna's alliance. Then we turn on her."

Cassie rolled her eyes. "She'll only get more powerful the longer she stays here. Be honest with me. If you and Gabe find out who in the green cabin has the immunity bracelet, do you think that'll be the end of it? You really think Joanna will just leave you alone?"

I couldn't answer, partially because Joanna sat down at our table, but honestly, I didn't know how far Joanna's plans for me went. I just had a plan to survive until the next elimination campfire.

***

I lucked out at the immunity challenge. It was a one-on-one competition where you raced your opponent along a rock wall collecting flags. Up high on the side of the cliff, no one could hear me whisper "tonight" to him. The poor reindeer was so flustered that he dropped one of his flags. He still grabbed more flags than me, so he won his round, but our team won the challenge. Gabe most likely wasn't going home tonight.

My fur was on end, and I couldn't stop pacing in the confines of the evergreen trees. I could just tell Gabe the position he was in since we were caught. Sure, he could be angry, but at least we'd be on the same page. But what if this went even more downhill? If he were clueless to what happened, the blame would be on me, not him. God, since when was getting some cock so complicated?

Sticks and leaves crunched underfoot as Gabe ducked into our little prison. "I thought we weren't going to risk it for a few eliminations."

I snuck a hand under his shirt. "I couldn't get my mind off last night. Something about the outdoors is really getting me going, you know?" The muscles under his shirt were firm and smelled of the "mountain mist-scented" soap the show gave us.

Gabe grabbed my hand. "Look, I had fun last night, but I still think this is a bad idea. We should be playing it safe."

"Planning ahead is fine," I said. "But we're not going to get what we want unless we take some risks."

"First you want to use caution and now you want to take a risk?" Gabe said. "What the hell do you want?"

I grabbed the reindeer by the front of his shirt and yanked. "I want you to be the reason I'm sore in the morning. Now get undressed and fuck me in the ass." He didn't immediately return my kiss, but when he did, he picked me up and slammed my back against the tree. We weren't going to be so quiet tonight.

I pulled away from the kiss long enough to say "pants." I shucked off mine, and when the reindeer took his off, his musk was like a slap to the face. There was nothing like a little roughness to get the musk flowing. I braced myself against the tree as the reindeer spit into his hand and jacked himself. My tail swished high and slow, giving him a full view of my asshole. The both of us were already panting and the real fun hadn't even started yet.

"What are you waiting for?" I asked. "Take it."

The head of his shaft pierced me. I gasped. Normally I would have insisted on some more lube, but it was enough to get the job done. My ring burned by the time Gabe had me all the way to the hilt. I pressed back against him, begging for every fraction of every inch he had. Then he thrust.

Gabe was by far the stronger of the two of us, but I was expecting to at least hold myself still. He may have wanted to be cautious, but his thrusts bashed me against the tree shoulder first. He wanted this just as bad, if not more so, than me.

"Like this?" He grunted.

I teased his chin with the tip of my tail. He yanked my tail and clamped it under his arm. Maybe I was biting off more than I could chew, but I was ready to test my limits. Each of Gabe's thrusts threatened to buckle my knees. Yips belted out of my mouth.

Gabe's thrusts quickened, but with no less intensity. He leaned in close, and the rough exhalation from his nose brushed the back of my neck. "Come for me."

"Almost there," I grunted.

Gabe reached between my legs and squeezed my balls. I had been flirting with the edge of the cliff, but that launched me off it. My seed coated the side of the tree. My moan turned into a yip as he grabbed my head and pushed it against the tree. Heat soaked my ass. One, two, three squirts coated my insides. Any strength I had to hold myself up escaped me when he drew his cock out.

I collapsed on the ground and panted. Gabe did the same, forming himself into the big spoon. Pine needles stuck to my fur, but at least I could brush those off, unlike the jizz.

"Not exactly covert this time," Gabe said.

I shrugged. "I don't think we made that much noise, right?"

"Oh shit." The reindeer touched my shoulder. "Damn, you're bleeding."

I ran my hand over my shoulder. Blood stuck to the pads. "It's not as bad as it looks. It's just a tiny scrape. Let's wash in the lake and dry off..." I sighed. "with the washcloth I forgot to bring. Okay, we'll just drip dry. It's not a cold night."

No lights were on at the cabins across the lake. I wanted to wash up quick and hurry back, but I still had some snooping to do. Hopefully the orgasm made him more compliant.

"I'm sorry about your shoulder," Gabe said, splashing water on his armpits. "I shouldn't have gotten so rough with you."

"Hey, I wanted it to be rough," I said. "Besides, it was the tree that did the damage, not you. Honestly, I'm more surprised at how pent up you were after last night. You don't have anyone back home getting you off on the regular?"

"Well, my wife and I had a healthy sex life."

I stopped scrubbing under my tail. "Please tell me I didn't just help you cheat on her."

"No, no!" Gabe said. "We're divorced."

I sighed. "That's good. Not that you two broke up, but you know."

The reindeer chuckled. "It's fine. We had plenty of sex when we were together. We were both always thinking of the now. As long as we were both happy, who cared what the future brought?" He shook his head. "What we just did, that was lovely for right now. I just hope it doesn't hurt our futures."

I opened my mouth to chime in, but Gabe kept going. "Becca and I never really thought about the future until Annie was born. Then we realized neither of us could think ahead for shit. It strained the marriage. We divorced before Annie made it to middle school.

"Now Annie's almost done with her junior year and Becca and I don't have nearly enough money to get Annie through college. I was watching this show with Annie on one of my weekends with her and I decided, 'why not try it?'" The reindeer brushed lake water from his face, but I didn't remember him dunking his head underwater.

I patted his shoulder. "Hey, it'll work out. You just have to start thinking how people like Joanna think ahead and then think one step ahead of them."

The reindeer shook his head. "Not everyone can do that."

"Not with that attitude," I said. "Maybe you can find the immunity bracelet."

"Too late," Gabe said. "Duncan has it."

Even though I was clean under my tail, I kept holding it so it wouldn't wag. "Is he like the green cabin's version of Joanna?"

"Less intelligent, but more paranoid," Gabe said. "But yes. He's not subtle about it either. He knows he's leading the cabin and that everyone else is either too scared to challenge him or dumb enough to be loyal to him."

"If I had to bet," I said, stepping out of the water, "he'll hold onto that bracelet until the merge. Then he'll either use it early on if he feels like he doesn't have a strong enough alliance or throw himself into a new alliance or he'll be in the majority, knock out the competition, and use it when he feels like his alliance is ready to turn on him. In theory, your cabin could try to overthrow him before the merge, but it sounds like no one's going to step up, at least certainly not without the majority of the cabin behind them." I shook water off myself.

Gabe climbed back onto the bank. "I think you could win this thing."

I snorted. "Please. I'm surprised I made it to the cabin swap."

"Just promise me you'll keep me around until the final three, okay?" Gabe said.

I tickled his inner thigh with the tip of my tail. "I'll think about it."

"Really, I'd get on my knees and blow you now if that's what it'd take," the reindeer said with a shaky chuckle. "I'd do it every night."

"God, if you suck cock like you plow ass, my balls will be all shriveled by the end of all this," I laughed back, equally as shaky. All I could hope was that the information I had now was enough for Joanna, and that Gabe and I could make it to the cabin merge.

***

The next morning, both cabins competed in a game that mixed dodgeball and archery. I think I spent more time paying attention to my teammates than the green cabin's players on the other side of the field. Every nose that wrinkled and every ear that twitched set my fur on end. One of my teammates had complained they had trouble falling asleep last night because apparently some production assistants were making a lot of noise. I laughed and managed not to sound guilty.

And then someone shot me in the ass with one of the foam-tipped arrows, and I yipped. After last night, I didn't need anymore throbbing back there.

One of my teammates who was out of the game asked about my shoulder, but I had a lie prepared.

"Nicked it on the top-bunk's ladder getting up this morning."

Kevin, a maned wolf, sniffed. "Why do you smell like the lake?"

"Why do your feet smell like you wear skunks for slippers?" I said. And then everyone laughed and before Kevin could say anything else, our last teammate got nailed with an arrow.

Someone in the yellow cabin would be going home tonight.

Cassie gave me a quizzical look when Joanna pulled me into her canoe after the challenge, but I did my best to look confused. Joanna and I kept our voices low as we paddled back to our cabin.

"Duncan has the immunity bracelet," I said to the lioness.

"I'm not surprised. He's more paranoid than I am. Good work."

I let my tail slack a little, hoping it didn't brush up against her. "No problem."

"There's just one more little thing I need you to do."

Of course. I curled my tail around myself again.

"A little bird told me Cassie's been talking about trying to vote me out," Joanna said. "I want you to vote her out tonight."

I forced my ears to stay up. "Why waste your time with her? I doubt she has the support to actually vote you out. We're only a couple eliminations away from both the cabins merging. Why not get a head start on voting out someone strong so you don't have to go up against them in the individual challenges?"

The lioness leaned in, her whiskers brushing my ear. "I think you're someone strong. Remember that when we're at the elimination campfire tonight." I was so focused on her that I didn't notice we were at the dock until we bumped into it.

***

The elimination campfire was just a big decorative campfire the campers sat around, but it wasn't the campfire that would be lit. When it's your time to vote, you go behind a curtain, take a stick, and place it onto the little campfire that has the name of the person you want to vote out. The one with the most sticks on their campfire gets their sticks lit and is officially eliminated.

When Joanna went up to vote, Cassie whispered to me, "I think we've finally got her. Everyone I talked to was on the same page with me about Joanna being a total tyrant. Don't worry, I didn't tell them about you and Gabe hooking up."

"Thank you," I whispered back.

After Joanna rejoined everyone, our host, Ryan Sullivan, stood in front of the curtain blocking the voting booth. "All the votes are in. After tonight, someone's summer at camp will come to an end, and the yellow cabin will be short one less camper. The yellow cabin was doing so well. Joanna, what do you think happened today?"

The lioness shrugged. "We all have our off days. All we can do is pick ourselves up and try again tomorrow."

"But not everyone will have the opportunity," Ryan said. "Someone has to go home tonight. Cassie, do you agree with Joanna?"

"No, I don't," the raccoon said with a smile I didn't like. "Because it wasn't an off day. We threw the challenge on purpose."

Joanna kept her face neutral as she looked to the rest of the campers in our cabin. "Is this true?"

There was a lot of paw shuffling, ears folding down, and tails curled. No one met Joanna's gaze.

"We're all tired of you bossing us around, Joanna," Cassie said. "It's time for you to go."

Joanna looked ahead to Ryan. "We'll see."

"Wow, who knew there was so much tension in the yellow cabin?" Ryan said, looking at the camera with bewilderment that wasn't fooling anyone. "Clark, care to comment on this?"

"I think whatever happens tonight will change the course of the game."

Ryan pushed aside the voting booth curtain, revealing a second curtain blocking each of the mini campfires from view. "And with that, it's time to see which camper will be going home tonight."

I could already imagine the drum roll from the TV show whenever the votes were revealed. I clinched onto the edge of the stump I sat on.

The weasel pushed the curtain aside.

A single stick lay on Joanna's campfire. Cassie had a bundle.

"Cassie, your fellow campers have spoken," Ryan said. Cassie's campfire ignited.

"I already heard about your plan," Joanna said, "so I went along with it to lull you into a false sense of security. I already knew how everyone else would vote."

"I'm sorry," I said. It was what was best for me in the long term. She would have had to turn against me eventually, at least that's what I told myself when I cast my vote.

"Yeah, I bet you are, you motherfucker!" Cassie said, standing up. "I trusted you!"

"Cassie, your summer at camp is over," Ryan said.

The raccoon tore off her yellow bandana and threw it into the main campfire. "Clark's working for the other cabin!"

I bolted up. "What?"

"He meets up with Gabe in the middle of the night to plan against us," Cassie added while giving me the finger. She pointed her middle finger at Joanna. "She caught him and did nothing. I bet she's planning to jump ship and screw over the rest of you after the merge."

"Why would I abandon this alliance?" Joanna said, still cold and collected. "We have the majority. Even after the merge, as long as we function as 'us-versus-them', we'll pick them off one by one." She glared at me. "But if I'd known about Clark's little midnight outings, maybe we would have voted differently tonight."

"These are lies from a sore loser," I said, forcing my tail to stop twitching. "I'm sorry, I really am, but I'm just playing the game."

Cassie flipped us all the double bird as she walked toward the pathway leading to a motorboat that would take her to the loser's lodge. "I hope you all lose! If any of you make it to the final three, none of you will get my vote!"

As Cassie finally left, Ryan took his place back on center stage. "Wow, and I thought her campfire was fiery! Folks, this is by far the most explosive elimination we've seen all season, and we haven't reached the halfway point. Join us next time for another explosive week at camp."

Someone off scene called the cut.

"Someone get me a beer," Ryan said. "I'll be in my trailer."

I had made a terrible mistake. How would Joanna realistically know if I voted for her? Someone else could have just as easily voted against her, which I could have told her if I hadn't betrayed Cassie. I couldn't help but feel this would be the final week at camp for me, and maybe for Gabe too.

***

I didn't have any chance to talk to Gabe the next day, but he had to have noticed Cassie wasn't with the yellow cabin anymore. In a way, luck was on my side. I was expecting Joanna to have the rest of the cabin throw the challenge on purpose so they could vote me out, but the game was literally just picking rocks that had numbers under them. There was no way for Joanna and her alliance to throw the challenge. They had been shunning me since Cassie got voted out. With any luck, Gabe and I could join Duncan's alliance.

Around the time of the elimination campfire, a production assistant collected the yellow cabin members. As she led us closer to the elimination campfire, I knew some bullshit was about to go down. The yellow cabin and I arrived as Trevor, a goat who had been in the green cabin since the beginning, walked out looking like someone told him the tooth fairy wasn't real. Poor guy. I didn't know him that well, but he excelled in the puzzle challenges.

"And with Trevor's elimination, you've all made it to the halfway point of Summer Camp Showdown," Ryan said from the stage. "Give yourself a hand." Applause broke out from the green cabin members, some more enthusiastic than others. The P.A. with us held a finger to her muzzle and shook her head at us. My tail curled around my legs, and my fur was on end.

"Of course, with ten campers remaining, you know what time it is," Ryan said. He waved to us, and the P.A. ushered us by the elimination campfire. "Everyone remove your bandanas. As of right now, you're all one cabin competing individually. And your first challenge for individual immunity starts now."

And there was the bullshit. Cameras zoomed in on us, trying to capture the best facial reaction to use for when the television broadcast would cut to commercial.

After someone off set called cut, Ryan hopped off the stage. "Give them their bandanas and set up the challenge," the weasel said. "I've got a date planned with Ben and Jerry."

After we got our new purple bandanas, Gabe pulled me over to the far corner of the set. "I flushed out Duncan's immunity bracelet."

I opened my mouth to speak, but his words caught me off guard. Before I could get any words in, the reindeer continued. "I've been thinking about what you said about planning ahead, and after I saw Cassie got voted out, I knew I had to make a big play to keep us in the game until the end. Trevor and I were talking and decided to blindside Duncan, but I guess he found out because he played his immunity bracelet. All the votes against him didn't count, and the other half of the cabin voted for Trevor, so he's out now, but I think Duncan knows I was planning against him because he was giving me some sort of death glare."

"So what you're saying," I mumbled. "Is that there's no chance of us joining Duncan's alliance?"

"I doubt it," Gabe said, rubbing one antler. "So, what happened with Cassie?"

"You screwed us!" Fellow campers and workers on set were looking at us now. A camera on my left zoomed in. There wasn't any point in being quiet anymore. "Joanna caught me coming back from seeing you. She's had me in her pocket ever since. Cassie was going to go after her, so Joanna said she'd vote you and me out if I didn't help her vote out Cassie. Then when Cassie got voted out, she flipped and told everyone about you and me meeting up at night. The whole yellow cabin is against us at this point!"

I could see the gears turning in the reindeer's head. "We can start a new alliance. There were some people on the green cabin that helped me vote for Duncan."

"Oh, sure," I laughed. "Who wants to join an alliance with two campers with the biggest targets on their backs and zero power?"

He grabbed me by the shoulders. "We can make this work. We have to make this work. We have to."

"Everyone take your places behind the tables," a P.A. announced. The cameras were pointing back at the tables and the main stage, and Ryan had returned. I silently took my place behind one of the tables.

"What summer at camp is complete without arts and crafts?" Ryan said. "In tonight's challenge, you'll need to take the materials we've provided and build a tower two feet tall. Sorry, we were in such a rush to get this together that we forgot to buy any proper stacking materials or glue. We raided all the cabinets around camp and found a nice assortment of knick-knacks like coins, pens, used popsicle sticks, and whatnot. Anyway, good luck!" He honked an air horn.

I took a moment to study my materials. I had a pencil that looked like it had been chewed on, an old bookmark, a few pieces of uncooked pasta, a piece of saltwater taffy, a spool of thread... I could use the thread to tie everything together.

"Gina's is looking very much like that tower in Pisa," Ryan said. "Oh!

There it goes. Gina's back to square one. Speaking of squares, Kevin is folding that granola bar into a square structure. If he doesn't win, that's a waste of a perfectly good breakfast substitute. And Gabe's tower falls for the third time! He's a stacking machine, but where's the strategy?"

With all the materials on my table, if I stacked them on their sides, they wouldn't reach two feet, but if I created a base and then stood one or two longer items upward, I could have a chance. I started with making a large base. Then I set up the chewed-up pencil and a couple of pens into a teepee-like structure. All I had to do was secure the top of the teepee so the pens and pencils wouldn't slide away from each other. I unspooled a foot of thread and reached for the sci—

I didn't have scissors. Fuck.

I chewed and yanked on the thread, but it wouldn't break. I chucked the spool of thread to the floor.

"Watch out for flying art supplies!" Ryan said. "I can see Clark's tail bristling from here. Keiko's got all of her supplies stacked, but no, it's still too short. Toby appears to have confused arts and crafts with snack time. He hasn't even bothered to stack any of his materials and is just eating his Limited Edition Midnight Dark Chocolate Cocoa Koala Bar. In stores now. Let your taste buds indulge in their dark side."

Snack. That's it! I opened my saltwater taffy and chewed. I pasted chewed up bits to the tips of the pencils and pens and to the bottoms of the uncooked pasta, forming a smaller secondary base. I only had a tiny bit of taffy left in my mouth by the time I grabbed the bookmark. The paper crinkled at the edges and wavered in the slight breeze. If I could get it to stick tightly for long enough—

"One, two, three!" Ryan honked the air horn. "Joanna has won the season's first individual immunity challenge!"

The lioness let out what sounded like a combination of a laugh and a roar. Duncan pushed his tower over and snorted. Gabe gripped his antlers, his head resting against the table. I could smell the dread around the campfire. I was sure some of that odor was coming from me.

The tables were cleared away, and a few campers left to do confessionals. I couldn't spare the energy to do one. There was a knot in my gut, and if I opened my mouth, I could have puked. There was the possibility that Joanna could instruct her alliance to vote for Duncan to blindside him. Honestly, he was the bigger threat. But for sneaking behind our respective cabins, neither Gabe nor I was trustworthy.

When a P.A. herded us around to the elimination campfire, I was seated next to Gabe. Neither of us said a word. He didn't look at me.

"And now it's time for the second elimination of the night," Ryan said. "When it's your turn, drop your sticks down the tube belonging to the camper you wish to send home. Clark, we'll start with you."

Inside the voting booth, I picked up the first stick. I considered tossing my stick into a random tube, but that would be a waste. Whether I accepted the inevitable or held out hope, I wanted it to be a calculated decision. Gabe and Duncan's tubes were next to each other. Every first episode of a new season, as a bonding activity, each camper was instructed to decorate his or her tube. Duncan just pasted his name in red construction paper to the tube, though he did add a couple dots in the circle of the D to vaguely look like a pig snout. Gabe's was painted like him, minus the antlers. A few bells were pasted to it. Something black and square-shaped was wedged in between his tube and Duncan's. I tugged on it just a little, but it came loose. While I tried to wedge it back into place, yellow letters caught my eye. *Do it for Annie.*

I dropped my stick into Duncan's tube. Maybe Gabe or I would be voted out tonight, but at least if I voted for Duncan and he won the grand prize at the end, I could hold that over Joanna's head. Not that I'd ever see her again. I walked back to the campfire and took my seat.

I didn't remember the voting process taking this long. I just wanted Ryan to pull back that curtain and reveal our little campfires so my gut could unclench.

Finally, Duncan, the last person in line, came back, and Ryan stood in front of the curtains.

"This has by far been the most eventful day of camp this season," the weasel said. "I'm sure everyone's looking forward to getting some rest, but someone around the campfire won't be sleeping in their bunk tonight. It's time to reveal the votes."

He drew back the curtain to the voting booth and held onto the second curtain blocking the tiny campfires from view. To the viewer, it looked like he was looking at us, but I know for a fact he was looking at a P.A. who magically determined how much tension to built for the sake of ratings and Jesus fucking Christ my tail was wound so tightly around my leg that I think I was losing circulation and I could barely breathe this felt like murder.

Ryan drew back the second curtain.

A couple sticks sat on Duncan's campfire. Gabe and I each had a small pile.

"Ladies and gentlemen," Ryan said. "We have our first tied elimination campfire vote of the season. Clark and Gabe each received four votes. In this situation, everyone but Clark and Gabe will go back and vote again, but you can only vote for either one of them. We'll give each one of them a minute to make their case as to why they should stay in the competition. Clark, you're up first."

Standing in front of the other campers made me feel like I was back in high school trying to remember my lines for the school play. What were my lines? There were no lines or scripts. I just had to take the facts and do what I felt was best.

"I'm untrustworthy," I said. "I was dishonest, and I even voted one of my friends out of the competition. I'm not surprised to be where I am now."

Gabe's mouth opened and shut. God, I hoped he just stayed quiet and let me say what I had to say. He was playing for his daughter, so maybe he deserved to stay here more than me.

I turned away from the reindeer. "And that's why you should keep me in the competition." I tried not to notice the camera zooming closer to me as I continued. "The winner is determined by three factors: Individual challenge wins, vote from the eliminated campers, and America's vote. I'm not bad at puzzles, but I'm not great at them. As for physical challenges, I'd be lucky to outlast half of you. After all this betrayal, none of the eliminated campers, let alone anyone in America, will want to vote for me to win the million-dollar prize. If you take me to the final three, it'll essentially be a final two vote. I'll be a non-factor."

Gabe was giving me some sort of look when I sat back down next to him. There was pain, but maybe a bit of understanding to it too? Maybe if we ended up dating, I would have learned what that stare meant, but that was never happening. I didn't love Gabe. If I won the grand prize, which was doubtful at this point, I could give him money to send his daughter to college, but I had student loans of my own to pay off, and moving to Los Angeles to pursue an acting career wasn't cheap.

"Thank you, Clark," Ryan said. "Gabe, it's time to make your case."

Gabe stood in front of the crowd and cleared his throat. "There have to be parents here, right?" After a few of the other campers nodded, he continued. "I'm a parent too. My daughter's name is Annie. She's 17 years old, she's got an encyclopedic memory of all rom-coms, and she thinks rocks are just the coolest things. She wants to study geology, but my ex and I don't have nearly enough money to send her to college without a mountain of debt. I'm not asking to win the grand prize or even make it into the final three, but I know there will be some opportunities to win a little money from individual challenges. I can't leave here empty handed. Please just let me stay a little longer. Please." Gabe wiped at his eyes as he sat back down.

"Thank you, Gabe," Ryan said. "It's time for the vote. If you don't want to change your vote, go into the voting booth, shake your head at the camera, and walk back out. If you want to change your vote, nod at the camera in the voting booth. We'll start with Duncan this time."

As the boar walked into the voting booth, I pinched the bridge of my muzzle. "Gabe, you're an idiot."

"I'm not the one who got us into this mess in the first place," the reindeer said.

"You made yourself sympathetic."

"And how is that a bad thing?"

"Because sob stories go a long way in the final vote," I said. "No one will want to risk you making it to the final three."

Gabe glared at the camera that was zooming in on us. "You're telling me no one here has an ounce of sympathy or pity or mercy or anything like that?"

I pointed at the camera. "You know what makes better TV than sympathy? Betrayal. Backstabbing. Selfishness. Reality competition shows don't recruit saints."

Gabe turned away from me. "I think I learned that the hard way."

"Just promise me you'll start a PleasePayMe page for your daughter," I said. "The show will give you nationwide publicity. Use it to your advantage."

"Why should I listen to you?" Gabe said. "Look where that's gotten me."

"And the votes are all in," Ryan said. "After looking at the footage, I can confirm that someone is about to leave camp for good tonight. We've placed sticks in the eliminated player's campfire. It's time to reveal whose campfire burns."

The weasel pushed the curtains out of the way. A bundle of sticks ignited on Gabe's campfire.

"Gabe, your fellow campers have spoken," Ryan said. "Your summer at camp is over."

The reindeer buried his face with one hand, but it wasn't enough to cover the tears rolling down. A camera zoomed in closer to his face.

Maybe I should have pushed the camera away. Maybe I should have hugged him or patted his shoulder. I didn't deserve to do that now. He was right. This was my fault.

***

I sat outside the cabin unable to sleep. Each side of the porch had a wooden seat on chains so you can swing. Gabe and I sat with each other on them the first day of the competition. One of his antlers got caught on the chain, and once I made sure he was okay, we laughed. Would that make it into the show? What would Gabe's daughter think seeing me flirt with her dad while knowing what I'd do to him later? Why did I have to ruin their lives?

Joanna walked out of the cabin and sat down next to me.

"I'm not in the mood," I said. "If you're going to convince your alliance to vote me off, just do it."

"Well, if that's your attitude," the lioness said, kicking back so the chair would swing. "Maybe I shouldn't have changed my vote to save you."

I tried to keep my outward appearance calm, but holy shit, what? "Why save me? I thought I was done being useful to you after I voted out Cassie."

Joanna shrugged. "I thought so too, but you brought up a good point in that little speech of yours. I didn't have time to tell my alliance to change their votes, so I went against them to save you."

"And what's the price for you keeping me around?"

"Well, I hope you'll vote along with my alliance," the lioness said. She sighed. "Now that the cameras are off, I'm going to stop talking to you as Joanna the competitor and talk to you as Joanna the parent who has had many lovers in the past along with a goal. You came onto this show because you had a goal, right?"

I nodded. "Take care of my student loans if I can, but it was mostly for exposure so I could add to my acting resume. I want to be on the red carpet."

"And how long have you had that goal?" Joanna said. "The acting part, not the student loan part."

"Most families talk or put on the news at dinner," I said. "My parents always put on a movie. It was usually classics, even black and white stuff. When I was younger, I thought the actors behaved like their characters in real life, but my parents told me that wasn't the case. That just made me admire actors more. It's amazing how they can just shut out everything and become this new person. I'm still learning how to do that."

Joanna nodded. "And if that's your goal, why are you getting beat up over a man you've only known for a couple weeks and will never see again after the show is over?"

"I ruined his life, and the life of his daughter."

"Says who?" The lioness said. "If she's as smart as he claims she is, she'll think of something. There are scholarships, and that PleasePayMe idea you had sounded good. Besides, they're not your responsibility."

"I thought you were talking to me as a parent."

"I am," Joanna said. "Trust me, I sympathized with Gabe, but I have three sons. They'll always take priority over anyone else's cubs. My parents told me I was the brightest of their five cubs. They couldn't understand why I didn't pursue a career after college. It was because above all else, I wanted to be a mother. When I had that goal, I let nothing get in my way. Sure, you'll make mistakes and trust the wrong people. I certainly did, but if you continue working toward your goal, I'm sure I'll be taking my sons to one of your movies in the future."

I nodded. "Thanks for the pep talk. I'll be more inclined to believe it if I survive an elimination campfire or two."

"Shouldn't be hard if you vote with the alliance," the lioness said as she stood up. "I have your vote, right?"

I grinned. "As long as it's my best option."

Joanna opened the door slowly so it wouldn't creak. "I'll be sure to keep my eyes on you." She walked back into the cabin and shut the door slowly behind her.

I looked out at the water. The moon and stars reflected off the surface. Maybe I could win this competition. Maybe I could act like someone who could.

To my family and friends, who helped me.

Silk and Amber

by Quincy Connally

The lounge was a mild buzz of movement and chatter from my father's guests, patriarchs accompanied by their wives and children in their dress coats and hoop skirts. Corrina Hamilton, a grey wolf like myself seated next to me on the sofa, sipped her Petite Vidure and watched the activity, while a short distance away I spied her father speaking to mine. I couldn't hear nor imagine what they were talking about; their business and interests, most likely, after which Mr. Hamilton would complement the function whereupon my father would modestly obfuscate the expense to which he had gone to set it up. It had been at a party like this one that I was introduced to Corrina. Centuries ago, both of our families had been among the gray wolf packs that established dominance in the north of England, but since then my lineage had come down to my father, the Lord Ellis, whose wife, my mother, had died giving birth to a litter of which I was the only survivor. It was for this reason that I bore the totality of my father's hopes for the future of our family.

After the wine, we moved to the main hall, where my father had arranged our day's entertainment. Chairs were aligned across from an as-of-yet unoccupied temporary stage. The guests didn't know what was planned, but I happened to be aware that a few days prior an Irish music and dance troupe, just arrived in the county, had approached my father and requested to perform for us. I expected him to turn them away, but I suppose he saw the opportunity to host a crowd-pleasing affair at a manageable cost. I took my seat next to Corrina. Presently the violinist appeared at stage left, a wolf in a long blue gown, and with her a stag carrying a set of pipes the likes of which I'd not seen before. The piper began first, filling the reservoir of his instrument with air from a bellows under his arm. A set of drones produced a continuous tone, which he allowed, for a measure or two, to fill the room with a melancholy tension before he began to play the chanter. The tune was strange to me, a sort of slow air of spacious notes rolled with warbling movements of the hooves over the chanter's holes. The notes, lacking regular meter or rhythm, seemed to be held for whatever length felt natural in the moment. It had an overall calming effect, and invited those listening to stillness and introspection.

Four dancers, a male and female wolf and two female cats, entered the stage and stood all in a row. They were still for the duration of the piper's tune, but as he resolved to the tonic, the violinist joined him with low, pulsing movements of the bow over one string. The dancers in synchronicity lifted one foot and set it back down. On their feet were hard shoes that with each step produced a sharp, kinetic tap, and in the same moment as that first step the musicians launched in duet into a new tune altogether, a fast-paced, adventurous reel of richly ornamented quaver rhythm, here building tension with droning of the low notes and there releasing it with wondrous movement to exciting highs and lows. The dance consisted of many quick steps and created a rapid percussive rhythm in time with the music. Nearly all the dancers' movement was in the legs, while their upper bodies were held tall and straight. It all came together into a mesmerizing display, a full-bodied orchestra.

The second part of the tune pushed itself to even greater heights. The dance took on even more extravagant kicks and jumps, until the final measure wherein the musicians brought the number to a rapid conclusion as the dancers placed their final step. The dancers cleared off, and it was then that a red fox, clad in a brilliantly-dyed green shirt, leapt upon the stage. His feet hit the wood at the very instant the next tune began, roughly double the tempo of the first and reaching new levels of ambition and virtuosity. The fox engaged in a solo dance of stunning dynamism, tapping the surface with such speed and ferocity that it was at times difficult to tell where one step ended and the next began. While keeping to this extremely fast rhythm, he moved all about, leaping, prancing, and spinning such that he appeared to me almost like a flame set on the floor. I was transfixed. As he paused for a moment on the final beat of a line, in the interval of less than a second, his eyes met mine, him smiling with the purest joy before the next measure began and the dance continued.

The others returned to the stage, the five together dancing the last movement and arriving at a spectacular finish. I was taken with an urge to howl and cheer, but in a moment I caught Corrina in the corner of my eye and remembered to restrain myself. The show went on with a variety of tunes and dances. The cats removed their shoes and proceeded with a softer, silent dance to a tune in triple time. The female wolf sang a vocal solo, a lament in the Irish language, moving though I couldn't understand it. Even the violinist came center stage for one of her most virtuoso pieces of the night, in which she played while dancing almost like a fairy. However, my attentions remained on the fox, whose most captivating moment came when he danced to no music whatsoever, such that the only sound was the rhythms of his toes resonating throughout the hall. The show concluded with a grand finale involving all five dancers and both musicians. When it was over, they bowed and disappeared from the stage.

I left the hall paw in paw with Corrina. As we walked through the lounge where the guests were mingling, I overheard her father speaking to mine.

"A fine display," her father said. "I find it very impressive the energy and liveliness exhibited in these folk dances."

My father answered, "Impressive, if only in its capacity to entertain with a small showing of wildness. In that sense it's fortunate that the wild energies of the Celts, particularly Celtic foxes, can be channeled into something of value to civilized society."

Dinner was served, followed by dessert and tea. It was late in the evening when Corrina left with her father, she giving me a polite farewell as she went. I retired to my chamber, but settling into the sheets I found my thoughts returning to that frenetic music, the quick, percussive steps of the dancers, and in particular the wild, prancing form of the red fox.

The excitement was over, however, and in the morning I submitted myself to my lessons which occupied the bulk of my daylight hours. In the afternoon, I was afforded some freedom to visit the market and strongly advised to purchase a gift for Corrina in the meanwhile. I settled on an amber brooch set in gold, with bark and fur immersed in the gem giving it an appearance something like a forest in microcosm. I had intended to return home after that, but as I left the shop, I was stopped by the sight of the red fox, the very same who had performed at my home the previous night, and with him a wolf and two cats from his troupe. He was examining a scarf from the next door clothing stand, which he, now dressed more simply in a white shirt compared to his colorful performance attire, playfully threw about his neck. I was possessed with the urge to approach him, yet I could not. What had I to say to him? Surely, he had plenty of admirers. I hid my face and endeavored to pass as quickly as possible, and I might have gone by never speaking to the fox had I not heard him call: "Lord Ellis?"

I looked over to see he had spotted me. There was no possibility of evading an encounter, so I turned and approached.

"Sure, it's good seeing you," he said. "You were at our performance last night, were you not? How'd you find it?" His voice possessed a gentleness and musicality that I found rather pleasant.

"I enjoyed it," I said.

"Grand. 'Twas a fierce pleasure to play for ye all."

"Thank you," I said.

That was all we could think to say to one another. We stood in silence for a moment, until one of the cats spoke up and said, "Are you quite finished acting the cod then, Aidan?"

Acknowledging his companion, he bowed politely to me, and they turned to leave.

"Just a moment," I said. "May I ask your name?"

"Certainly," the fox said. He put a paw on the shoulder of the wolf to his left. "This here's Eveline." Then he turned to the cats and said, "And these're Maeve and Grania." They curtseyed their short gowns. "And I, as you may have heard, am Aidan."

"My name is James," I said.

"James," he said, stretching the name with a bit of playful pomp. "It's been grand meeting you." They again turned to leave, but suddenly Aidan turned back and said, "Actually, would you care to be joining us for a night?"

I hadn't expected an invitation, and I wasn't quite sure what he meant. "Joining you?" I said. "What for?"

My tone may have come across harsher than I intended, for his expression turned dour as though he were less sure than a moment ago that he was pressing upon the right course. Committed as he was, he continued, "I apologize if I'm acting bold. The fellows and I'll be visiting a number of pubs tonight, singing and dancing and the like. I thought you might enjoy yourself is all."

"Where, and at what time?" I said.

His smile returned. "Will you meet us here at six bells?" he said.

"Very well," I said.

He returned the scarf to the rack and departed along with his companions. Out of their sight, for reasons unexplainable, a weakness came over me that nearly caused me to be sick. I was forced to lean on a nearby wall until I regained my composure.

When I returned at the break of dusk, Aidan alone was there waiting. We greeted each other, then he led me to what would be the first of several stops that night. His companions were already seated at the pub, and with them were a few musicians from about the town. Their instruments were tucked beneath their seats; for the moment, they sat and drank beer as though that were their only design. Aidan leaned to me and pointed to the male wolf of their group. "Fillan," he said, "is mated to Mairead, our fiddler. They're parents of a sort to our group, although Osheen, the piper, is the oldest of us. Mairead is also the sister of Eveline, who you met earlier, and Maeve and Grania are also sisters."

When they had finished their pints, the musicians retrieved their instruments and made their way to the head of the room. The rest remained where they were, still drinking. The musicians sat in a circle, facing each other rather than the room, and conversed as they made ready to play. Mairead quickly adjusted the fine tuners on her violin while Osheen set his pipes upon his lap. With them were a couple of badgers, male and female, playing lute and dulcimer, along with a moose on crumhorn.

They started with a reel, the town musicians following along with the Irish players. In the pub as opposed to the performance hall, their music was more informal and improvisational, each musician reacting and adjusting to the others, almost seeming to play for each other rather than anyone else in the room. The bar patrons drank and talked as though the music were incidental. As the first set came to an end and the next began, the rest of my group, sufficiently fortified with alcohol, stood and gathered near the center of the floor, where the space was most clear. They stood in a square, facing each other, and danced in a set about the center, at times all linking arms, and at times each taking it in turns to pair with the others.

The music came to an end, the musicians began to pack up, and soon we departed. We traveled directly from one pub to the next, where we were joined by another set of musicians. Again they filled the place with music and dance, then set out for another location, and another after that. At each stop we were served beer, until it was decided we were too drunk to go on, and so after our last performance we settled to chatting.

Aidan and I moved to our own table in order to escape the din of the rest of the group.

"Savage fun crack, wouldn't you say? Right langered, I am," he said.

"Right," I responded. "You and your, um, your group… You're from Ireland?"

"We are. County Sligo."

"What brought you to England?"

"Sure we love our homeland. We traveled around Ireland for a time, doing much the same as we're doing now, but when our earnings grew slim, we crossed the sea for the sake of our survival. Here the barmen'll pay a good price for our sort of music and dance, and they'll usually throw in a rake of pints on top of it, but we'll be getting on eventually, and someday we'll return home."

"How did this group of yours come about?"

"I don't rightly know. I was just a kit when I joined them."

That seemed to be all he cared to say on the subject. We sat and drank in each other's company until our pints were finished, and I was just about ready to order another round when Aidan looked to the others and said, "Well, Osheen's there carrying poor Maeve and Grania, which is usually when they're after drinking their fills. I suppose it'll be time for us to be going then. Thank you for being my guest tonight, James Ellis."

He joined them, and the seven all left together. I remained in my seat and looked into my cup for a moment. Then I had it filled.

In the days that followed, I found myself unable to quit the thought of Aidan. The sensation was confusing to me. I had known friends, friends who had been dear to me, friends with whom I'd had great fun in the past, but they had not occupied and dominated my mind as Aidan now did. I found myself recalling wistfully his dance and music in those cramped pubs, and the gentleness of his voice as we drank and talked. One evening, I returned to the pub, but without music, it seemed dull and empty. At another table, I spied a group of three wolves, commoners by the looks of them, and in celebratory spirits. I saw them together turn their heads to the ceiling and let out a joyous howl. I felt the urge to join them, to add the sound of my own howl to theirs, but I did not.

On the next afternoon, I returned to the marketplace, not sure what, if anything, I expected to find. It seemed almost miraculous, then, that there I felt a tap on my shoulder and turned to see Aidan.

"I was starting to think you were avoiding me," he said, smiling.

"Of course not," I said. "Where's your group?"

"Off doing as they like, to be sure."

"And… yourself?"

"Well, I was just after seeing more of ye'r markets, but I'm fierce pleased to have run into you now."

We walked the market streets for a time. I noticed that though he stopped to examine many of the items on display, he bought nothing, and as he didn't ask me to buy anything for him, I didn't think it appropriate to offer. When the both of us tired of walking, we stopped at a fruit stand, where I bought two apples and a basket of blueberries. These I shared with him. He bit into his apple quite noisily, letting the juice run down his chin.

"I envy you," I said at last. "I'm bound to remain here, to learn and then carry out the duties of a Lord. But you and your troupe are free to go where you like, to other lands if you wish, and you dance and play music wherever you go."

"You're flattering me," he replied. "Sure I can't imagine the pressures you're under, and I understand your frustration. But the truth is I'm disposed to envy you myself, so I am. I've never known what it's like to come home to a warm fire and a cooked meal. We travel, but we can't always be going where we like; we do be making our living performing, so we have to be going where there's people willing to pay for us. And even if we're enjoying ourselves someplace, we can't always be staying as long as we'd like to. Here, for instance, we make a fair bit playing at the pubs every night, but sooner or later the interest drops off and they won't be willing to pay as much or as often. And there've been hard times before when we didn't earn as much as we really needed."

We chomped our fruit for a time until he decided to change the subject. "Y'know, I've always wanted to explore the mountains here. Could you tell me a bit about them?"

"Mountains? You mean the Pennines, to the west? I'm afraid I can't say anything in particular. I've never been myself."

"Never? They're quite close to where you live."

"I suppose I've never had the occasion to go."

"Shame. Would you like to go together so? It'll be a new experience for the both of us."

"I—er, certainly, of course I would."

"The sunrise from out there must be beautiful. Might you be willing to go tomorrow morning?"

"I believe so," I said.

"Come here tomorrow just before dawn, and be ready for a hike. I'll be waiting for you."

He left. At home, I moved to assemble the things I'd need so I would be ready to leave immediately upon waking: a good sturdy coat, woolen stockings, and boots. It was while I was searching the cabinet that my eyes fell upon the amber brooch I'd bought days prior. It occurred to me that Aidan had gone to some effort to entertain me, and politeness dictated I return his kind gesture somehow. I regretted missing my chance to buy him something at the market, but a trinket from my home, which would remind him of me when he saw it, struck me as suitable. I took the brooch, considered, then placed it in my coat pocket.

I went to sleep early and awoke shortly before the sun. Aidan was waiting as promised, dressed in his usual white shirt and no shoes, a knapsack on his back. We went west, passing through the flat farmland of the vales until we entered the Pennines, rolling grassy hills broken by rock formations. Much of it was gentle enough to walk over, but some required dexterity to navigate. Aidan's lithe body negotiated the steep stones without much trouble, but I was forced at times to stop and consider my path. Roughly three quarters of an hour after we had first set out, we came upon the edge of an outcropping, the steep face of which dropped some distance to the fields below.

Aidan sat on the open stone, and I next to him. The spot offered a wide view of the eastern horizon, far enough that the town and farmland looked small before us. Aidan produced from his knapsack a small wooden flute, which he put to his muzzle. He blew a few lazy notes, testing the sound.

"Do you play?" I said.

He chuckled. "Only a little. I've not practiced in ages. When I was young, I thought I'd play flute for our troupe, but I took better to the dancing. Do you play music, James?"

"I've had some instruction on piano and violin, neither of which I had any aptitude for. My instructors deemed me a lost cause and gave up."

"More's the pity."

He returned his attentions to his flute and played some short phrases. From there he went on to a slow air, rolling his paw pads over the holes so that each note seemed to resonate into the space around us. He went from this to a reel. For all his modesty, he was really quite adept; his fingers darted rapidly over the instrument, and his playing took on an airy roughness owing to the sharp breaths he blew into each note. He made errors, but always either corrected himself straight away or played through. He went from one reel to the next, and henceforth into whatever tune seemed to come to mind, ranging from the quick and jolly to the low and suspenseful to the slow and mournful. He actually seemed to forget I was there, so lost was he in the music he was making, but I didn't care to remind him. It was pleasurable enough for me to sit and listen.

"It's quite beautiful," I said, when he finally stopped.

"Thank you," he said.

In the east, the first traces of sunlight were showing over the horizon. We watched the sun climb slowly over the mountains, turning the countryside a shimmering gold. Then, the two of us side by side, Aidan started to sing, softly as though to himself, a gentle, soothing melody that hung in the air:

***

Siúil, siúil, siúil a rún,
Siúil go sochair agus siúil go ciúin,
Siúil go doras agus éalaigh liom.

***

He looked out at the land for a moment, pensive.

"A ballad from back home, I suppose?" I said.

"It is," he said. He placed his flute aside and continued, "Right, I've had about enough of that. Will we dance, James?"

"I can't dance," I said, "not in the same way as you, in any case."

"Sure it's no obstacle. It's not hard to learn a few steps."

He extended a paw toward me, but I hesitated. "You mean, well—certainly I couldn't—I couldn't possibly—"

With a smile he said, "I do insist. I'll not have you sitting it out like you did the other night."

My nervousness was not assuaged, but as I didn't seem to have a choice, I took his paw and rose to my feet. Paw in paw, he brought me to stand beside him.

"Place your right foot in front of your left, turned sideways such that they're crossed like so."

He did this. Though I tried to imitate him, already I found it difficult to keep my balance. He helped to steady me through his grip on my paw.

"Lift your right foot and hold it behind yourself." He curled his leg back, but I found it even more difficult to balance on my left foot alone, now my only point of contact with the ground. I was forced to replace my right foot in order to avoid falling, but Aidan waited patiently, still standing on one foot, offering himself as a pillar to keep hold on. I lifted my right foot and found a shaky balance.

"Now hop on your left foot, then place your right foot in front of your left where it started." I at this point began to suppose he was making a fool of me, but though I didn't look graceful, I managed the step all the same.

"Now pick up your left foot and tap the ground. Now tap with the right foot. Now lift the left foot, hop on the right, and place your left foot in front of it. From here we do the same sequence, but on the other side: hop-left-right-left, hop-right-left-right, you got it!"

I didn't feel that I had gotten it, clumsy as I was, but Aidan's encouragement was warming nonetheless. "Now," he went on, "I amn't supposing you're wanting to do a hop-shuffle-hop-back next."

With a bit of time and patience he was able to show me a few more steps. Once we had a working vocabulary, we were able to do a simple sequence in rhythm, first slow, then faster. As we acquired the rhythm, Aidan began to vocalize a tune in a rather strange way. He made a sequence of what sounded like nonsensical syllables, each flowing into the next via natural mouth movements. As his excitement grew, he began to mix in faster and more complicated steps, and he didn't seem to mind when I quietly broke off to watch. His vocalizations ceased as he put the entirety of his efforts into the dance, his toes tapping at full speed, his whole body moving about the stone.

The sun was high over the mountains when he finally tired. He sat and pulled from his knapsack a portion of bread wrapped in cloth, which he set on the ground and cut in two with a knife. He then placed before himself a copper jar, which showed to be full of blueberry jam. He took the knife and applied the jam generously to both pieces of bread, then gave one to me.

As I finished the bread and licked the remnants of jam from my muzzle and paw pads, I remembered the jewel in my pocket. But now that the moment had arrived, I found myself paralyzed. Was I certain such a gift would be appreciated, or would it be seen as a flaunting of my wealth? Having finished his bread as well, Aidan was enjoying the sunlight for a moment more before undoubtedly we would be rising to go.

"Aidan, I—" I stopped, breath caught, and swallowed. "I've—I mean—I wish to present you with… with a small token of my appreciation. For your entertainment these last few days."

He looked to the jewel in my trembling paw. "You've brought a gift for me?" he said, but when he took the jewel, I could see the glint of warmth and joy in his eyes. "'Tis a powerful beauty, that is. Thank you."

"Would you care to, um…" I gestured toward my own neck. "…try it on?"

"I would, of course."

He clasped the brooch to the collar of his shirt, just below the chin. The amber matched his fur, and a glint of sunlight reflecting off the jewel looked heavenly.

"How do I look?" he said.

Stunning, was what I wished to say, but instead I said, "Very good."

We picked up our supplies and started our trek back to town. We parted ways at the marketplace. As I entered my home, the servants informed me I had a message in my chamber. There I found a letter addressed to me from Corrina, formally inviting me to dinner and a dance at her home that evening.

I put the letter aside. In that moment I could not think of a single thing I wouldn't do but that I didn't have to go to a party at the Hamiltons' that evening, but neither could I think of a way to refuse or ignore the invitation. The messenger had almost certainly shared with my father the purpose of the letter, and soon the servants would be expecting to help me prepare. I spent much of the remainder of the day being bathed, and having my outfit selected from among my finest silk garments. I departed at dusk in a carriage. When I arrived at the mansion, the servants brought me to the lounge which was already filling with the Hamiltons' guests. Corrina spied me at once and bade me sit next to her.

She sipped from her goblet as we watched the guests move and chat. I took a goblet as well; it was a deep red, a variety I didn't recognize, probably from a select vineyard somewhere. After a time, we moved to the dining room, a dizzyingly enormous space barely occupied by the great pine table. Dinner was brought out in several courses: stew to start, followed by roast duck and chicken, with fruit tarts for dessert. More wine was served as well. As we ate, the ensemble began to take their place in the nearby stands, an impressive group of strings and woodwinds. They started on the first movement of a sonata, and the guests began to rise. Wine flowing through my veins, I offered a paw to Corrina. She took it.

The ensemble went through the three movements of the sonata and proceeded to the cotillion. Corrina and I were joined by other couples, some married, some young hopefuls like ourselves. We got in formation, and the first part of the tune began in cut time. I knew the steps of most of the French styles due to the instruction I'd received. We danced the main figure, then initiated the periodic changes which broke formation, and in the excitement I saw a delighted smile come to Corrina's face. I had to admit the joy was contagious. She really was a fine girl, good-humored and well-mannered, and the dance to the beautiful music was profoundly pleasing. Directly after came the graceful and ceremonious minuet, to which couples were invited to dance close to their partners. I took Corrina in my arms, and with our attentions solely on each other, we drank in the other's movements, her scent, the sheen of her fur, and the joy in her eyes.

"I must admit I've been worried," she said in my ear. "You've seemed more distracted than usual lately."

"I apologize," I said. "A number of matters have occupied my attention."

"Well, I'm glad you weren't so busy as to miss coming tonight. Shall we make the announcement, then?"

"Announcement?" I said.

She laughed, believing me to be feigning confusion. "I should think it's been more than enough time that the announcement of our engagement is expected."

Engagement. I had always known that to be the end toward which our courtship progressed, but now hearing it spoken aloud, I felt as though the ground were shifting underneath me. Corrina must have noticed the change in my demeanor, for her eyes took on a look of concern, and she said, "Lord Ellis?"

"I—I beg your pardon, I've only been taken with a momentary dizziness. I'll have a brief rest, if you permit it." Then, not waiting to hear her response, I made my way back to my seat at the dinner table. I finished what remained in my goblet, then ordered it filled.

All seemed to be in a haze. The conversations of the others at the table seemed distant, and of even the music I could scarcely determine one crotchet from the next. At length Corrina returned to the table as well. I apologized again, whereupon she took her seat. An old badger across from us attempted to engage us in conversation. He talked with Corrina for a while, but when he turned to ask my opinion on whatever matter was at hand, on seeing my face, he said, "Lord Ellis, are you quite…"

I remember little of what followed. The taste and smell of vomit in my mouth. Scurrying. Two servants reported to carry me, one at my arms and the other at my legs. Beyond that is an incomprehensible succession of images and sounds, but what is clear is that my participation in this party was at its end.

I was placed in my carriage, taken home, and taken to bed. The lecture I received from my father the following morning was among the most severe in memory. The two of us rode to the Hamiltons' mansion, where I gave a formal apology for my behavior. Corrina said nothing, but her father expressed to mine that there would surely be a way to move past this affair. At home, I was plunged back into my lessons from morning to night.

One evening, after supper, when I had retired to my chamber, I was startled by a rapping at my window. I drew the curtain to find Aidan there, he having climbed the two stories up the sheer east wall of my home and now grasping quite uncertainly the windowsill beyond the glass. I opened the pane at once and let him inside.

"What the devil are you doing?" I said.

"I've not been able to find you in town," he said.

"I've not been able to go to town. And I'm afraid I've no ability to go out with you tonight. I've gone and gotten myself in a bit of trouble. But that's no concern of yours."

"I'm sad to hear it," he said. "The truth is I've been desperate eager to find you. Tomorrow morning we're to break camp and move on from here. I should very much like for you to spend our last night in the region with us."

I was taken aback. I had put his imminent departure out of my mind, but I of course wished nothing more than to spend his last night with him. Yet I was apprehensive. What would my father's reaction be were he to discover my having stolen away under cover of night under these circumstances? The consequences were unimaginable, yet to refuse was harder still.

"We should find it impossible to leave by any of the doorways," I said at length. "Even if we were to avoid the sight of any servants still about, the doors have almost certainly been locked."

"Are you supposing there's a problem leaving the same way as I came?"

Dread seized me as I realized what he meant, but lacking any alternative, we absconded through the window and descended carefully to the garden. We exited the grounds and made our way through the fields to the south, all the way to the river, along the banks of which the Irish rovers had made camp. They appeared to possess a single ox and a wagon, around which were pitched several tents.

The others welcomed us; they seemed to have expected Aidan to return with me. Osheen built a fire, around which we were soon joined by Maeve, Grania, and Eveline. Fillan emerged from the wagon and tapped a small cask on a stool. He and Aidan filled several cups and brought them to us, and Mairead was soon out to join us as well. The drink turned out to be sweet mead. Osheen and Mairead readied their instruments and began to play, everyone drinking and talking as they went through their first set of tunes.

On the next set, all but Aidan and myself rose to dance. The two wolves and two cats took their square formation and danced about the center, though they looked quite comical with the wolves being large enough to lift the cats clear off their feet. Though Aidan and I remained seated, we drank our mead and enjoyed the energetic music and dance in the flickering firelight. Then Aidan stood and took me by the paw. To my surprise we slipped away from the camp entirely, crossed the river by a footbridge and proceeded south into the levels. We walked until we were such a distance as to no longer hear the music, whereupon Aidan lied down on his back, and I next to him. The sky stretched above us like a great dome punctured by its many bright stars.

"Is every night like this for you?" I said.

"Like this?" he repeated. "Nah. If I'm for being honest, I think they're having a bit of a ceili for your sake. 'Tisn't often we have guests, and it's rather exciting all around."

I had the notion that there was a great deal I needed to say to him, yet I could articulate no words. I only turned my head in his direction. He turned in mine. The tips of our snouts came in contact, and we recoiled, startled; but in the next instant our lips were joined, we each lapping the other's mouth with our tongues at first tentatively, then with increasing vigor. At length we pulled apart and caught our breath, then he climbed on top of me, straddling me about the hips. He leaned forward to kiss me once more.

When he lifted his head again, I said, "I don't..." I was going to say *understand*, but the objection died in my throat as I realized I wanted nothing more than to continue. I pulled him into another kiss. He began undoing the buttons of my waistcoat, while I unclasped the amber brooch from his neck and unbuttoned his white shirt. He lifted his shirt up over his head, the soft white fur of his belly exposed to the chilly night air, then he pulled off my waistcoat and my shirt. We grasped each other tightly, pressed our bare fur together, and kissed yet more; until he slipped a paw beneath my breeches, and I felt a jolt of pleasure and excitement at his touch.

He pulled my breeches and my pants down below my crotch. My tip had already begun to press itself out from its sheath, a trickle of fluid escaping it. He slickened his paw and ran his fingers gently up and down my shaft. I gasped and growled involuntarily. With his other paw he gently pressed upon my sheath until the knot came free.

He stopped to pull my pants completely off from my legs, then removed his own garments and positioned himself over my midsection. He stroked his own shaft until it was free from its sheath, slicked his paw again with our combined fluids, and reached back to apply this directly below the base of his tail. Then he lifted himself on his knees slightly, aligned himself, and carefully pushed me inside of him. We both took in a sharp breath as I entered. His warm flesh enveloping me felt intoxicating. He took me up to the top of my knot and was still a moment, allowing his body to adjust. He looked into my eyes, and we both smiled.

He began to rock himself back and forth, both paws on my chest while his legs did the work. He went slowly, teasing the reactions out of me, but in time increased his speed. Our breath became heavier. I could feel a buildup of pressure in me.

Suddenly he stopped and pulled off of me. I was confused for a moment before I saw him turn around and position himself on the ground on all fours, his backside toward me. I understood at once what he meant me to do. I mounted him. My claws dug into his thighs and my teeth bared as I pushed in and out of him with an ever-harder rocking of my hips. I was in a state of instinct. I did not waste time teasing him, but went at once at speed that progressed into full-forced thrusting.

The pressure reached its apex and crossed the threshold into satisfying release. My knot entered and engorged within him, tying us together as my seed slowly filled him and began to trickle out. He had finished as well, his seed forming a pile in the grass. We collapsed onto our sides, curled together, both breathing thick, foggy breaths into the night air.

After a time, my knot began to shrink, until I was able to pull out of him. We lay together, I holding him in my arms, my nose buried in the back of his neck, taking in his musk. There, lying in the grass, I found the courage to say what I meant to.

"I want to go with you."

He turned, puzzled. "I beg pardon?" he said.

"When you leave tomorrow. I want to go with you."

He placed a paw behind my ear, but already my heart was filling with dread at what I knew would be his answer. "James... You know that's impossible."

What he said had of course been the sensible thing. Where I was, I had security, safety, but were I to go with him, my survival would be dependent on the whims of fortune, as his was. All the same, I felt as if I had gained something of a greater importance than anything previous in my life, and that it was now about to slip away from me after remaining all too briefly. I truly would have given anything, up to and including my home and my family, to hold onto what I had in that field. I felt a welling of emotions the flow of which I was unable to stem, and when he detected my unseemly outpour, he again extended a comforting paw.

"Ah now, sure it's not as bad as that, is it. I'll be back, I'll make sure of it. For all the time I'm away, I'll be fierce eager to see you again." Then, after a brief pause, he started to sing softly:

***

Siúil, siúil, siúil a rún,
Siúil go sochair agus siúil go ciúin,
Siúil go doras agus éalaigh liom.

***

We slept there, naked in the wilderness. As the first rays of light shone over the hills, roughly an hour or so before dawn, Aidan crept up and began to dress. He clasped the brooch to his shirt, then I noticed that something seemed to have caught his attention over the fields, something he was desperate to identify. I looked out and saw figures in the distance which I realized were horsemen. Aidan was prompted to hurry back to camp, I not far behind him.

We arrived no sooner than the horsemen. Eight riders, each with a loaded musket, quickly surrounded the camp and rounded the seven Celts plus myself into the open. They stood in a perimeter around us, guns at the ready, while one rider made his way toward me and dismounted from his horse. It was my father. Though I had hastened to dress, it was plain to him what I had done: the fox's scent was all over me, as was the grass and dirt of the field we had slept in. He considered this for a time before he found words to confront me.

"I struggle to imagine," he went on at last, "what could possess one such as you to leave the fine home I've provided you, the land our family has lived on for generations... Everything you could want I gave you... And a fine, well-bred lady you were to marry... Two nights ago you slept in a plump warm bed of soft sheets and blankets, but I see you prefer to lie in a cold open field, rolled around with the... vagabond..."

He was unable to say any more with any coherence, so given over was he to his apoplexy. I had not words to raise against him, but only kept my head cast toward the ground. When my father had said all he meant to say, he mounted his horse, pulled me onto the saddle with him, and commanded the others be arrested.

All of us were brought back to town. At home, my father had me placed forthwith in my chamber, instructing that I was not to be let out. There I remained for days, with no ability to learn where Aidan and the others had been taken or what was to become of them. After a time, my father did let me out, whereupon we affected something of a return to normalcy. But he never spoke of Aidan, and it wasn't until sometime after that I heard, from scattered utterances about the town, of the seven Irish vagrants who had been tried and accused of abducting the Lord Ellis' son, and whose bodies had hung from the dule tree, all in a row. That night, after I snuffed the candle and plunged my chamber into darkness, I climbed into my soft, warm sheets and wondered if anything in the world could be beautiful to me again.

To Kim who is quietly supportive even though she doesn't read my furrotica and my dog Whiskey, who winks too often to not be.

I WENT BACK FIFTY YEARS AND KILLED THE EVIL TYRANT ALDON HOWLETZ AND ALL OF YOU ARE WELCOME♦♦♦

by Slip Wolf

It makes sense that you can't know what came before, I can't fault you for that. That said, it still stings sometimes. I just wish Leonard would see the truth in me now that he's looking so great again. That beige fur is sandy over the milky sheen of this throat. The smell of him, it slips in and paints every stick of furniture he rubs past, lounges on, leaps out of when I bring the bad times up again. He gets mad because he thinks I've completely forgotten, but never will.

As much as it pisses him off, I can't help remembering him as he was before my powers came and went, before I saved him and you and everyone we've all ever known. I still remember the smudges of coal mine dust over haggard mange, the overwhelming gloom of despair. Every day he'd pleaded with the merciless consignment gang-leads to let him reduce his fifteen hour shift to just ten with his bad leg and was refused each time.

But not anymore. Not in this reality, the only one he knows or remembers. Here he puts silk ties around that slender throat to prep for work, narrows golden eyes at me, and asks me, "When are you going to get out and get a job, Gale?"

I had the most important job in the whole world, I want to say again. I did the work that saved us all. But he's not convinced, and like I said, it stings sometimes. I swish my butterscotch tail with barely contained anxiety. "I've got leads. I just have to make a few calls."

"Did you take your pills today?"

The pills that he thinks makes this cat better are the pills that stop me from shunting back again. But he doesn't know that. I only just figured it out recently now that I can't do it anymore. That's okay. The world only needed saving once. I think. "Yeah. They're... helping."

Leonard seems convinced.

"I love you." I add, smiling beatifically.

My fox's return smile has a crack in it. He doesn't know if he has what he wants. Or if he wants what he now has. "I love you too." He says. He leaves for the train and the silence in the apartment is deafening to my twitchy feline ears.

So I make my calls that go nowhere and take a bagel out to toast. The burning scent brings back another defunct memory, that of a place that no longer exists.

Since there's nobody else to tell the story, have a seat.

In another world next door to this one, a world that no longer exists, you were either a collaborator, or a slave. Or, if you learned concepts like proletariat or fifteen minute coffee break and ever said them aloud, dead. Factories churned out war machines and munitions and black smoke. You either toiled in them under the gun and lash, or held that gun or used that lash. All this shit went on under the decree of the fourth Emperor, the Wolf of woe, Jibrul the second, who waged war on the pockets of resistance throughout an impoverished world that was all you or anyone ever knew.

Until it wasn't. Until the Emperor wasn't. Or, more accurately, he never was. That's where I came in.

The power that I had, that I still have in dormancy really, came to me from a laboratory accident, as they do. Biological material that I was ordered to clean up without the right tools infected me with a miraculous-yet understandably horrifying-brain parasite. I could see visions of the past, periods and places I'd never known or would ever dream of knowing whenever I managed to stop throwing up. I saw places and times that never were and wonders that were yet to be between waves of nausea. From a stained cot where I was left to die, I saw all the permutations of a multitude of existences in threads unspooled cruelly like a lawn-mowed sweater. This was the first key event in—

Hear that bell? My bagel's ready. I like mine with cream cheese, personally, which in this world I've always loved, and in the last I'd never known existed. Imagine being able to discover all the things you've ever loved for the first time again. This world was amazing when I finally "returned" to it, let me tell you.

I make another phone call and finally manage to score a job interview at a bookstore on eleventh and Gillsbury tomorrow. Victory, though small, makes the bagel even more delicious.

I text Leonard the news and twenty minutes later I get a thumb's up. I want to imagine he's smiling at his desk downtown, but I think he's just relieved.

I do some house chores, tidy up, and dust a bit, taking a full minute to get stuff out of the crevices of the model planes and tanks I've got on the shelf, painted with defunct totalitarian logos that nobody in this shiny, perfect world even knows existed. This apartment is my whole world right now. It's cozy and familiar.

And I made it exist.

I go out for groceries with the meager amount of cash we have, making sure to thank the otter who wraps the strip loins that Leonard loves so much. I'm going to make them for him tonight.

Bumps on the road under the bus punctuate the monotony of all the lives that roll ahead without care or worry of anything dire and I quietly bask in my handiwork until I get my bounty home. I rub in a little soy and garlic and wrap the steaks back up. I should do more job applications online, but the descending sun brings wistful quiet, and I just take some time to breathe before taking another pill. Two a day. Calm floods in. The slight blur on my thoughts smooths out and I fold my tail around me on the couch, where I let the television blink things at me.

Back to what I was saying before, I guess. Remember the worst fever or migraine in the world? I was half there in that cot deep in the slums of the sixteenth Undercity of Jibrul's Empire. Loving, haggard, thin-as-a-waif Leonard was there as often as he could be, giving me half his rations since the foreman had cancelled mine. As he begged me to stay with him, those threads of existence looped back over one another in the cavernous capacity of my mutating mind, and I inevitably thought things I was not permitted to think. This sucked. Dying like this was awful, and I'd give anything, *anything* to make the world a better place where people didn't work every waking moment and suffer and die for one dynastic overlord's pleasure.

I found that thread, saw that line of causality when my sense of the world and Leonard's weeping were all but invisible to me in my last living moments, and I grabbed it.

It was obvious what had to happen.

But we'll get to that later. In this world it's ten minutes until Leonard arrives. Time to put the steaks on. We'll have a great dinner, cuddle on the couch and then watch a documentary on Netflix, something about the Last Great War that was mysteriously won forty or so years ago, wink, wink.

He's my whole world, and I'm his, and there's nothing I won't do to please him. In a bit of quick thinking, I close the patio door to the barbecue. I don't want a drifting smell to ruin the surprise.

When the door to the apartment opens and his keys hit the copper dish on the small table, it's like a Pavlovian response in me. I'm there, tail swishing and whiskers perked. His own lifts from its limp position to wag once. "Hi Gale," he says tiredly, one claw loosening that tie around his neck.

I take a step forward and put a hand on his shoulder, which gets a tired glance back before I bring my muzzle up to his and kiss him. There's the locked-lip huff of a tired laugh, but then he goes with it and we trade air for just a few seconds. He takes a deep sighing breath when we part. "I'm really tired, Gale."

"Then let me help you relax."

An eyebrow goes up on his copper-furred brow and he lets me take his paw and lead him to the living room couch.

Leonard rubs his temples and blinks bleary eyes. "When do you have that interview, Gale? I'm thinking—" He makes a surprised noise as he feels my paw down below, massaging the crest of his slacks.

"Stop thinking for a bit," I suggest with a toothy smile as he settles into the couch. I rub concentric circles under the spot where his pants are already tenting a bit. His own paws are over mine at first, but then hastily start working on his belt.

I know what my fox wants. I help him slip the slacks off, leaving his briefs tented and wet at the crown. His gaze goes distant, golden eyes half-lidded as he forgets all his concerns and melts into the moment. I trail my claws away and both hands slip around his briefs to undo the tail button and then tug them down. He obligingly raises his hips, dick poking up above the waistband trailing slickness, and the underwear joins the slacks on the ground.

I get down next to them, my blue-jeaned knees on the carpet and tail swishing round as I get a palm underneath his balls, his legs now yoga-spread for my access and the other around his warm cock, redistributing the slickness.

He makes deep growling vulpine noises, rising to squeaks before he gets control of himself. His dick is all the way out now. A couple fingers under his balls tickle him to coax his rump forward. My nose is in and under his tail, and damn that musk is good, pure and heady. My tongue finds that white patch just behind his balls, One long drag massages his sack upward, then lets it spring back into place with his gasp as I roll that tongue up the underside of his hard cock and then work everything back in the other direction. Fox claws knead the carpet and he grunts, his arms spreading back over the couch's banks, spread eagled in bliss. He sure wasn't expecting to come home to this.

His silk tie on his still-buttoned shirt touches his wet shaft and I flick it away to keep it from getting wet. Leonard moans and then helps, gets a claw under the tie, and pulls it loose enough to drag over his head and muzzle and it sails towards the dead TV. His arms return to a V of victory as I've pulled his ass almost off the couch to tease at the dark space between his buttocks with ice-cream licks, fast enough to catch a melting soft-serve in summer. He gasps twice and bucks his hips, and I take my cue, dragging my tongue across those engorged balls one last time before leaning back and taking him all the way in my mouth. He's hot as a fired pistol in my cheeks, and works himself in and out while I all but hold still and control the wet slide with my tongue. He rides my mouth for a short while, gasps getting closer together, then he stops. "I want…"

My eyes rise to the underside of his white throat, his voice distorted by the loll of his tongue out one side. "Wha?" I ask around him.

"I want to finish," he gasps "in you."

I can't smile or I might bite him. My jeans have no belt and are shed while I'm sucking him, then I pull out and spin, tail high and proud. He's already wetter than April. It won't hurt any more than I'm ready for.

I face the TV, watching his inky silhouette loom over me in the dark screen. Leonard slips off the couch and spreads my ass with kneading claws. His dick finds me quickly, painting wetness on me. One thrust slips with a hot tickle, the second brings the welcome violation of the first stretch, then in a few more presses he's inside me, boiling musk through every pore and grunting like the animal I love. I see his reflected silhouette in the eerie blackness of the screen, bucking like he's working a lathe of flesh, hackles static round his neck and the friction and heat is amazing, tightening with every thrust as his knot forms up. He's locked me, restricted the range of motion and with nowhere left to go, he grunts and unloads with fast short bucks. My own dick is hard and weeping onto my own splayed jeans as he all but falls across my curved back, panting on one ear.

One paw weakly comes round and grasps my cock. I smile as I hold up the fox's weight enjoying the slick action of my member being stroked when I hear him sniffing at me.

"Is there something wrong," I say dreamily. "I did shower today..."

"It's not you," Leonard says. "Is there something burning?"

"What could be burn—?" The scent then hits me too. I recognize charring beef immediately.

"Oh shit, oh shit." I scramble up, but Leonard is on top of me. "I have to get outside."

"I'm still knotted, Gale. What's wrong, is that—?"

"It's our dinner! I bought it special for you today. We have to get to the patio."

"What? You put something on the barbecue and just forgot it?"

The cock inside me is like a hot shackle now as I push off the carpet, the fox's arms still around me. "Yes," I gasp.

"Dammit Gale—?"

"Later!" We're both up. Even being close to the same height he's slightly taller and hunched over me. A dribble of cum kisses the back of my scrotum and then drips to the carpet. We hurry-shuffle towards the closed patio door, spunk pearling a trail behind and Leonard crying out at least once as the base of his shaft under the knot is tugged hard in a stumble. "We can't go out there, we'll be seen by any of a hundred people."

"We will for sure if you shout!" I hiss back. I grab the throw blanket off the back of the chair by the door and wrap it around us. The blinds that gave us privacy turn out to have damned us when I see the drift of smoke outside. Patio door open, the smell hits us both. Charred beef is a truly rank thing. I have to crab-walk us another few steps to get to the propane tank and, bending forward in a way that makes Leonard almost stumble again, I spin the line closed. We're both all the way outside now,

Leonard cursing because he's stubbed his toe. "I'm sorry," I mutter and throw open the barbecue lid. The contained grease fire lets loose, and flames leap high from the two carbonized bricks that not a half hour ago were two mouth-watering, herb-rubbed fillets. My first useless impulse is to blow it out, but heat and smoke fill my nose and Leonard's over my shoulder. We both use both paws to cover our watering eyes.

And the blanket protecting our modesty falls to the patio floor.

"Woo!" The wolf whoop comes reedy on the wind. Our apartment building, one of three, is visible from two other ranges of open matched patios going up another several floors. On one a timber wolf stands with a beer in paw, leaning out over the railing to leer at us. The smoke must have drawn his attention but now he's rapt, eyes roving downward at what's visible through our own railing. "Holy shit!" He fumbles for something in his pants pocket.

"Just let it burn out, get us back inside!" Leonard shouts plaintively and uses arms and cock to drag me back in where we fall together on the parquet flooring just inside the patio stoop. Leonard kicks the sliding door shut with a few frantic kicks, and I realize that without the falling sun glare to save us, the wolf would have a zoomable phone photo of our matching ball sacks, which in a distant part of my mind are equally terrifying and funny.

Life could be worse right? We already covered that didn't we?

We lay on our sides and I can only imagine Leonard's left flank will have the same bruise under the fur that mine will as he breathes raggedly at the back of my head. Ten silent minutes later, the smoke has dwindled outside, and I feel him slide free of my ass with a grunt. He rolls, curses at any number of hurts he's sustained and gets up, storming away to the bathroom and slamming the door.

I'm down for a few minutes more, weighing in my head all the way this perfect evening has gone wrong before it's even started. Even with the fire out, dinner is now ruined. All I have is some mushrooms with butter to sauté waiting their turn to join the crematorium outside, and not enough money left from the meager grocery allowance to buy more steaks.

I still don't have my pants on when I go to the bathroom door. "Leonard, dear, I'm so sorry."

"Don't talk to me," he snaps in reply and I can't guess which wound he's administering to. Most likely his dick is throbbing the worst after all that yanking.

"I wanted this to be a perfect night. I didn't mean for it to go this way. Len?"

No answer.

"It could be worse, Leonard. There are good times ahead and we've got a lot worse behind us."

The door opens so fast the draft raises my fur off my cheeks. "What, in your fantasy horror show, Gale? We going to deflect from your incompetence with that bullshit again?"

I'm cut, sudden and hard. "That's not fair, Leonard. I was going to suck your cock and then turn the steaks over. I just mistimed things"

Leonard takes a deep breath, then another, getting centered again. When he speaks again, he's devoid of emotion, a picture of detached calm. "I'm sorry, Gale," he says curtly. "I shouldn't be mad. You obviously tried hard to make this a good night and I snapped at you. I just," he winces, "goddam my dick hurts after you pulled like that."

"I'm sorry, Len."

His face screws up for a moment as though he's biting back a retort, but he throws sand on it. "Mistakes happen, I get that. I just wish you'd please quit bringing this time-travelling thing as excuses for them. It's just—nevermind. I guess I'm worried that wolf snapped a photo of us and if it goes online and I'm recognized then I could lose my job and we'd be really fucked then, wouldn't we?"

He doesn't say it, but it wouldn't matter if I was recognized. I have no job to lose and am nobody in the grand scheme as far as the working, living free world is concerned. It hurts to have that rubbed in, even if Leonard doesn't seem to be aware he's doing it. "Yeah we would," I reply in a whisper.

"I have a meeting really early and I'm not that hungry anyway. I'm gonna grab a protein bar and get some rest." Leonard's eyes dart to the bedroom door.

"I'll join you soon, I just need to clean up." I hear my voice in a monotone and wonder if the silence that falls after is a curse or a blessing.

Leonard gets his bar and goes back to our room. I clean up and heat up some leftovers that are on the brink, eating in silence.

Now's as good a time as any to catch you up.

Like I said, I've seen Leonard this way before in the place that no longer is, back on a cot that no longer roughs up my back, in a world that Hell itself only knows. With the gift in full bloom, on the verge of death itself, something happened that can never be explained. As my grasp on the strands that formed the universe took hold and the strands of Leonard's bedside sanity unraveled, they came for me.

Reclamation crews with their guns and stretchers arrived with their orders. I was to be euthanized both to free me from pain and to provide the military with roughly sixty-five units in protein rations, minus whatever was corrupted by the ailment wasting away. They had no idea what was brewing inside me, not one clue of the potential unlocked by that spill so many days ago. I could see further on the thread as they approached and held my wailing, loving Leonard back, the cold knives, the squirt-loaded ration packs, the soldiers on forward patrol and enslavement detail complaining about how gamey my meat was and wondering how much of it was D-grade horse or goat again.

The moment of truth came in which my body meant nothing, and my inner essence meant everything. I'd stumbled upon the universal truth of transcendence and time and space and mind over all matter.

And now I needed to kick ass.

Strength returned to my body on that cot and I clutched a gun right from one of their surprised limp fingers. "What in the Emperor's name?" The racoon exclaimed.

"Great question," I told the flabbergasted death squad. "I'll ask."

And I shunted. With the same effort that you expend wrinkling your nose, I shifted myself through the worm's eye that is time and space and causality and the slick membrane of tenuous, easily negotiable fate. Back forty years when the war was on that changed the course of everything, back when, as the resistance told us in flyer drops and radio signal spikes, it all went to shit.

We'll get back to that.

I wake up at about seven thirty, here in the mundane, familiar world that none of you can ever truly appreciate, and hear the front door close. I could chase after Leonard, wish him a good day, but it seems futile. I've only got one shot at pleasing him today and not burning dinner won't cut it. Sometimes being a hero means doing the small things right. That will depend later on preparing a dinner that I can put on the stove with a timer so accidents don't repeat. It will depend right now on getting set for my job interview in a few hours. I borrow a tie of his, powdered blue and conservative and tuck in a white dress shirt so that one pasta stain I can't get out doesn't show.

The bus ride is long and made arduous by anxiety, my brain seeking ways to flub the questions and my tongue roving my teeth for that bit of something unsightly that absolutely must be there. Maybe I just won't smile. Do bookstore employees stereotypically smile? Or are they always dour and serious like stereotypical librarians? My last brief job as a teller failed to prep me for this and my near-fatal job in alternate reality as a toxic materials sanitizer in the weapons test factory would be no use either. The only thing I got out of that job was a much better world. Yeah, I know you want me to get to that, but honestly, the past is the past, especially when it didn't happen anymore. Let's get this job taken care of and then I'll regale you with why you don't have to wear a shock collar if you fail to make night-fall curfew more than twice in a month.

I spend some time watching another cat like me work the cowlick off her kitten's head after removing a baseball cap and think on how easy life is for so many of us now. I'm trying not to stare because I don't want to be a creeper, but I can't help pondering the possibilities ahead for everyone on this bus with me, hurtling towards wherever we've chosen to go. Two more stops, one transfer then four more and I'm off. Just a block's walk south on eleventh and I can see the sign; Red's Rollicking Reads. A caricatured red panda floating cross-legged in space balances a tottering pile of books on an expansive, cushioning tail and their nose disappears into one cracked open in his paws.

Under this are more signs covering the windows in blocky script that don't make sense; 'Final closing, All must go, Up to 80% off.' There's a pit in my stomach that rises as I find the door, unlocked and enter confines that have been allowed to go dusty. Musty ancient paper and the onset of mold find my nose. Book racks recede into murky half-light. The bored mouse at the Formica counter doesn't look up.

"Um, hi." I say.

His eyes dart up, then down to the sheet at his elbow by the register. "Gale Quint. Interview, right?"

"Uh, yeah. I applied for a job here. Are you guys…"

The mouse's eyes dart up again and his nose crinkles. "You're at the right place. We're looking for someone to help us with inventory."

"But you're—"

"Closing yeah. It's gonna be a big undertaking. We've got about twelve thousand books to box up on two floors that are going to be shipped to a couple other second hand-places. We need help."

"I was told there was a fourteen dollar an hour job."

"That's right, it's a contract, two weeks to get all the work done. Red's throwing in a small bonus for every day that we shave off, but he wants to keep that on the down-low cause he's worried somebody will throw their back out getting the boxes on the truck too fast."

"Then what will I be doing? When the packing and moving is done?"

The mouse blinked at me like I was an idiot. "Looking for your next job?"

The rest of the interview went fast. Even though I'm a bit of a wiry cat who doesn't look that ready to lift heavy boxes, I got it. As a bonus, I was given a thirty dollar voucher to buy any books off the shelf I liked, to be set aside and collected when the job was done.

Numbly, I wandered the history section, slipping past the only other patron in the store, a sweater-vested weasel who was checking the spine quality on some fantasy novels. I found a book on the last great war, conspiracy theories on the coup that felled the rising evil Empire of the National Anti-socialist Aldon Howletz. I flipped it open to one captioned photo spread that covers two pages, a veritable cradle of stolen, palatial wealth centered around one dark spot of history altering ruin.

That would be good for a laugh wouldn't it?

"You've got another twenty bucks to spend," the mouse says as I hand it to him.

"I'll find something that grabs me as I go. See you Friday."

The bus ride back is long and senseless. That's it? A two week contract job? Fuck, Leonard is gonna flip. How can the Universe be this unfair to someone who's done so much in so little time with a time-travelling brain parasite and some honest world-saving gumption? In what world am I gonna get the thanks I deserve for fixing all the shit? I think back to that picture in the "history" book, the sheer scale of what one devious ruthless soul could accomplish, and how one little change could upset that.

To be perfectly clear, I hate guns and always will. But action movies tell us that the big stuff in history always gets one in there somewhere. I wish I could have brought in beer and some takeout pizza and hashed out a better world with the most hateful dog in mammalian history, but sure as my left ear is crooked, Aldon Howletz was pure, un-distilled evil. So, let's get back to that. You've been patient enough.

I came to from my shunt back forty years off course. By off course, I meant in the next room of the Parliament building that Howletz had turned into his palace when he'd liquidated the heads of all rival political parties all those years ago. I could hear the live orchestral strings played, hear the cries of someone being playfully tortured and opened the ornate chamber doors to the inner sanctum with a kick, locked and loaded.

Most history changing heroes get time to practice their big moments. The first words spoken on the moon or at the top of the highest climbed peak took months to perfect for the historical record. In the heat of the moment I came up with; "Surprise, asshole!"

The black Sheppard snarled as he turned towards the interruption, self-bestowed epaulets and medals jingling, the sherry in his glass tipping out onto the carpet. My first two shots were perfect. The two present members of his Death's Head guards went down immediately. The third and final made it all count. There was no head on Aldon's gilded shoulders in the next instant, just a smoking croquet hoop with ears. The bare-backed dissident bleeding on a whipping post gasped. The guard in the hood holding the whip made a run for it. I didn't shoot that guy. There are photos taken a few months later that I've seen in which he and dozens of other collaborators and torturers and yes-mammals got theirs after the post war trials, so don't worry.

In the meantime, with the musicians also fleeing in chaos, I untied the badger who's back was still bleeding profusely and passed him the rifle I stole from the future. "You need to bring this whole thing down," I slurred muddily. At that moment, my brain was starting to wobble in its bone house as memories started melting like confectionary under a heat lamp. That was the crux point. History itself was reforming into something new. Memories merged and kneaded with abused causality and things got confusing. "I'm gonna have to get going. My work here is—"

A thread I was still tied to was drawing me back, not to a cot where I was dying though. To a… city street intersection? The inside roof of an ambulance in motion. I was wearing leathers and stiff boots. It made no sense at all, which in that moment was saying something, wasn't it?

"Who are you?" The dissident asked from one tiny corner of existence that was fast slipping away. He becomes politically important later in his life but at that moment he was just a spark of possibility, one among millions being put on a different path.

"My name is…" I couldn't remember, couldn't feel, couldn't be. Darkness brought a soft blanket.

So yeah, you're up to speed. More or less, that's how that happened. Next came a hospital bed, a scolding from Leonard and a few weeks streaming movies with cans of chocolate ensure for company. A whole new, cozily familiar world.

One with its own problems. I head home and tell Leonard the news when he arrives. At first he says nothing, then asks the only question on his mind. "Then what. Are you already looking for the next thing after this two week thing is up?"

"Of course, I just need to refine my resume some more and get it back out there. Of course, we'll have half of all that money I make for groceries, which should be good for a couple more weeks."

Leonard gave me side eye as he removed his tie. "Why just half that money? You've been living rent free since the accident and I've been covering everything, groceries included, for most of that time."

I swish my tail and immediately try to still it. "Oh, right. Sorry, I was just setting a bit aside for the night course."

"What night course?" He's massaging his temples again as he sits down. The remote is in his paw but he's not turning the TV on.

"It's a history course with the local college. I thought I'd talked to you about that."

"You mentioned you were interested in a course. Are you looking to get some job associated with this?"

"Uh." That cold feeling when somebody catches you flat-footed is always a bad one, regardless of whether it's a curfew patrol or your significant other. I pull through this, though. Don't worry. "It could have job applications I think." Why didn't I prep myself for this question earlier? That's right, I thought I was going to get a full-time job and this question wouldn't be asked at all. I was prepping for the wrong interview.

"What kind of History? Western? Political? A night course on something this broad specializes in something." He has a dubious aspect, he eyes narrowed, ears at the half cock. I'm feeling the fear burgeon and my overtaxed brain stalls on its way to a lie. "Mili-uh, military."

He winces and he fumes. I can practically hear a well-trod straw snap inside him and know before the next words spoken that my time-travelling brain has fucked up the simplest of tasks. "No. Not this shit again. Second Great War I'm guessing? Do I have that right, Gale?"

I lose my voice entirely. My whiskers twitch but my mouth doesn't move for an eon. "Uh…"

He throws his fox arms up in the air and chokes off a laugh. "When are you going to let this fable go, Gale? You did not fucking time travel back to kill some evil world dictator and you know it! The guy's own guards killed him while our grandfathers were fighting in Europa. Why won't you—"

"They *think* his guards killed him. I took them out too! First I span left and potted the Rottweiler with a—"

"I don't fucking believe this is still going on!" He's shut his eyes so tight it's like he's trying to swallow them. He thinks he's shut in with a lunatic. Doesn't he fucking realize just how hard it was to take out so many bad guys in like, three seconds?

Something in me snaps along with him. "You can't believe it because you don't know what came before, Leonard! That's what's so relentlessly frustrating. I killed the worst tyrant that ever existed and changed the course of history! Prior to that you fucking crumbled boulders with a defective jack-hammer for a living and felt like shit all the time." I want to add he looked like it too but that won't help a situation that is rapidly spiraling away from me.

"No, you didn't, Gale. You didn't Doctor Who your way out of anything! You had a moped accident followed by a delayed seizure from brain swelling and nearly died. The whole thing was in your head." He's turned away from me, pacing around behind the couch. He wants to slap me and after all that he can't remember we've been through I want to slap him too.

"Then explain why nothing else is different and nothing else is wrong with me, Len. I've got no tremors. I have all my motor coordination, perfect reflexes, don't slur a word, and remember everything just as well as I always have, save the occasional steak when I'm getting fucked in the ass. Who doesn't? Why would I have this one elaborate delusion in the middle of my whole life that gives me overlapping memories for everything before the event and nothing else beyond a scar on my temple?"

"I'm not a shrink, Gale. You're messed up. You need serious medical care."

"What I need is someone who loves me and understands."

Silence falls like a hot blanket. I'd kill five more tyrants just to fill the empty echo that's rapidly filling the room between us. Leonard's next words change my mind. "Have you been taking your pills, Gale?"

"I—what? You're going to make it about that?"

"It is about that. It is most definitely about that. Don't change the subject. Are you?"

"No! I'm tired of feeling like my own emotions are high up on shelves where I can't reach them. I hate feeling like I'm just an empty shell that's gonna crack when it collides with anything at all. I don't deserve that.

Not after what I've been through. Not after what we both went through."

Leonard growls and snaps at that moment, turns to the shelf and grasps the model tank on it tight enough to crack it before he whips it across the room. Polystyrene parts shower the book-case. He keens, long and hard like he did for me on my deathbed when the shadows came for me with their guns and paperwork. "Look what we're going through right now!" He screams and he's actually crying. "You don't get to pretend this is something we're doing to *each other*, Gale. I want to love you; you make it impossible. You're not getting better, and I don't think you ever will."

He doesn't want me. I can see that right now. He wants the confused, aimless me, the perpetually fogged cat who is lost in himself. I wonder if part of him can remember me dying in that cot after all.

I wonder if part of him misses me being that way. "This isn't fair, Leonard. I've done all this for you."

"I know, Gale. And that's the scariest part. You really do think you have done all this. In spite of what I'd hoped, that this was something you would pull yourself out of and move on from, you just won't. I can see that now. It just makes this so much more tragic because you won't get the help you need."

"I love you." With my voice cracking, the words sound insincere, plucked carelessly from inventory. This thing that can't be happening is really happening. "Len you're everything to me."

Anxiety is buzzing low like a plane about to crash as he says nothing, nostrils flaring. I want to kiss him, grab him in a hug, and do anything. But just like before everything changed, I'm powerless, grounded in the horrible now.

"I want to love you too, Gale. I really do. The whole time I've known you, Gale, you wanted to be something better, wanted to be someone more. You've told me this so often. It hurts so much that this is all you'll give yourself, a fantasy you concocted to make yourself seem so much more important than either of us really are. You only needed to be important to me, Gale. You only needed to find yourself in the real world."

I know this is true. We have had this talk. When I was dead-tired from cleaning chemical spills and he was all but falling over after a stint in the Emperor's mines and we dared to dream of a better world, together.

Leonard's next words are eye-of-storm quiet. "But you never took that step, Gale."

He's wrong and has no way to know it. This fox I've loved my whole adult life has no idea that the better world came true. I'm just not—

"This has to end, Gale."

I'm just not a part of this world. And now I can truly feel it.

"I can't do this anymore, Gale. I can't keep enabling something so destructive. I have to do this for your sakes as well as my own."

I can't be here anymore, not in this paradise I've made for him, for all of you. The sensation of something slithering in my head comes back again, for the first time since... "Don't do this, Len."

His tear-streaked eyes, drained of all but pity, tell me it's done. "If the real you wants to come out and talk, I'll be here, Gale. But I won't wait forever. That wouldn't be fair to either of us."

The floor falls out from under me and I growl and spit my answer. "Fuck you. I'm as real as anyone you've ever been able to love. You just don't understand me because you just might have to appreciate me for just once in this mess of a relationship."

The furious words we trade are a flurry. I blink. Time's missing again. I don't remember if I screamed at him till the very end, cursed him even more or just cried and walked out. The air is cold on my face even though it's late spring and there are twinkling phantoms in the corner of my vision swimming with the dozens of people passing by me, all on borrowed time, borrowed lives.

None of you appreciate them either. So, fuck you too.

The pills are in my pocket, jingling like jailer's keys. I lob them as far as I can in no direction in particular, feeling the swell behind my temples that will melt suns themselves out of their erratic orbits, dissolve time itself down a black hole to oblivion. The power knows it's needed again. I can feel the static of the universe dragging its feet on the carpet.

"It's about time," I say and the rabbit couple passing look at me funny before going on their stupid mutually-affectionate way.

All I did was for nothing, thankless and soon to be forgotten, all for someone whose love I'd assumed unbreakable. Fate didn't tie us together; we were just particles careening off one another in the whole sordid mess that is existence and I was too stupid to see it. My whole life will shortly be boxes in a lobby if they aren't already.

Well that shit won't happen again. If romance was a person, I'd go back as many thousands of years as I'd need to kill the motherfucker.

It was a mistake to give my love to someone so fragile, so weak and inflexible. That haggard, hopeful soul who threw himself in front of the reclaimer's guns was dead and I killed him with a love that should never have been so unconditional.

So, I'll have to start again. I can already feel the slide of my interdimensional gift creating the necessary friction inside my brain, see the threads dangling loose where I'd cut them.

I'll go back even further this time, find a younger Aldon Howletz and have a pizza and beer with him and talk about exactly what destiny was best for the world. Maybe I'll figure out what made him go bad and channel that somewhere more constructive and less genocidal-evil. Didn't he paint or something?

That'll be me, Gale Quinte; sympathetic ear to victims-turned perpetrators of the cruel universe, now finally and justly serving myself. Don't worry all you out there in this wonderful taken-for-granted wonderland of opportunity and workplace safety considerations; Even broken hearted and betrayed by every single one of you I'm not stupid. I'll bring something sharp along just in case I fuck this up too.

Though you're unlikely to appreciate this either, in advance, you're welcome.

Special thanks to my fetish wear and death metal consultants, who should know who they are, for their help making this story happen.

Swipe Right, Now What

by MythicFox

'there in a few, just get me a beer'

Frank glanced at the message again as he tried way too hard to relax at the corner table. Two draft beers sat in front of him, their foam heads fizzling into nothingness, and he checked the timestamp. Six minutes? Was that long enough to think he'd been stood up?

The sabretooth lion reached up and ran thick fingers through his mane, finding it still a little damp from the shower. After the busy evening he'd had, he definitely needed to clean up and get properly dressed, but he was mostly pleased with the results. The blue shirt he wore, button-down because his fangs got caught on anything pullover, went well enough with his golden-tan fur in the bar's light coupled with a pair of plain-ish black pants, and like a lot of morphs he went barefoot. Part of the idea was not to stand out.

The thick-rimmed glasses he wore gave him an AR display keeping him up to date on his tab at the bar—*just the two drinks*, local sports scores—*who cares*, and the weather outside. A widget in the corner of his vision had the picture of the guy he was meeting, right from the dating app, next to the message about the beer. Eight minutes, now. He slowly turned his full mug of beer around so he could fidget with something without necessarily taking his phone out.

Just as Frank had reached the point of talking to himself about how much he hated this, he spotted his date. He sat up straight and found himself self-conscious about the sudden movement. He decided against waving. Not that the guy needed the help to spot him, with the small lamp hanging off the wall right next to the table. Frank hadn't intended to sit someplace so *'spotlight-y'* but it worked.

The white ferret's ruby-red eyes gleamed in the bar light as he slipped through the crowd with stereotypical grace and flexibility. His flannel shirt was unbuttoned halfway down his chest, letting creamy chest fur shine through, and the baggy jeans he wore made him look a lot more rugged than the gym locker room photo he'd sent Frank.

"Jack?" the cat asked with a smile.

"Yup. That means you're Frank, then," he said as he sat down and took a drink of the basic, not-trendy domestic beer waiting for him.

"I didn't know what you'd like, you just said 'a beer,'" Frank said. He dismissed the message and the picture from his glasses with an eye-twitch.

"Well, I wanted to see what you'd get if you didn't have any better ideas. It's… informative," Jack said as he licked his lips, tongue running over needle-pointed fangs.

"Oh?" Frank raised an eyebrow and drank some of his own, suddenly aware of how parched he was. "And what does that tell you?" he asked when his mug returned to the table.

"I have no idea," Jack laughed nervously. "I read it in a dating advice thing and well—."

Frank smiled brightly with relief, reassured that he wasn't dealing with some social predator. His inexperience with dating apps left him open to that sort of thing.

"The teeth tell me more, actually," the ferret commented, and Frank froze slightly. "Fan of the band?"

"You mean the metal band with the sabrecat singer?" Frank asked, taking another drink of his beer to cover up whatever face he might have been making.

"*Off the Pink.* Yeah, them. I know they were at the Arena earlier to-night." Jack gave Frank a once-over. "Aside from the fangs, you don't look much like the mosh pit type."

"Mosh pits ain't my thing," Frank said, suddenly wondering if he'd said that too quickly. "I got the teeth done in college. I thought it made me look cool playing soccer; my folks thought it was pretentious as hell." He cleared his throat and affected a falsetto. "'*Oh Frank, you're already a lion. Do you really have to look that much more dangerous?*'"

"'*Jeez, ma, I'm a fearsome predator, and I'm gonna be treated like one,*'" Jack said in a mock-deep voice, playing along.

"Yeah, yeah, that was me," Frank said with an awkward chuckle as he chugged more of his beer.

"You're probably the first guy I've met with a 'sabretooth' mod who's not into the band's music—"

"It's not that I'm not into their music, *per se*. I just said mosh pits aren't my sort of place; I'd rather just relax on the couch with some ear-buds in." Which, Frank figured, was technically true.

"So, you *are* a fan?" Jack asked, raising an eyebrow.

"Yeah. I'd just rather not be right in front of the speakers at one of their concerts, or the theatrics." Frank took a sip of his beer and realized this conversation was headed a dangerous direction. "What sort of music do *you* like?"

"I like something with a beat. I guess I'd say I'm into EDM, techno, old school hip-hop remixes. All that."

"Did I pick a bad spot for us to meet up?" Frank took some comfort that his instincts were right in finding someone who wasn't a metal fan.

"Nah, here we can talk. Better to talk here and move to a club than try to talk in a club and then move someplace to have a conversation while we're half-deaf and sore."

"Sore, huh? Expecting it to be that sort of meeting?" Frank asked, grinning and exaggeratedly raising his eyebrows.

Jack almost did a spit-take with laughter at the look on Frank's face. "I wasn't going to get my hopes up," he said with a cryptic smirk.

"Don't worry, everyone, it's okay," came a big, booming voice from the door. "I'm here now!"

Frank recognized the voice, and his ears reflexively flicked back. *Oh no.*

Everyone in the bar turned to look at a huge, muscular tiger morph. He had the arms and torso of a dedicated bodybuilder and was decked out in a leather trench coat, shirt, and pants underneath—all of it slightly shredded, like he'd just had to climb through a barbed wire fence. The ensemble covered gene-modded blood-red and black fur. He had a VIP pass-wearing groupie under each arm, both slender cat boys; the tiger had a type. The crowd parted to make space for him at the bar. He held his phone over a receiver and thumb-swiped to start a tab.

"Whiskey for me and my comrades, and a round of drinks for the room!" he boomed out again, like he didn't know how to talk at a conversational tone. A cheer went up in the bar at the tiger's generosity. "We're celebrating!"

"What's he celebrating?" Jack asked Frank under his breath as he stared at the tiger.

Before Frank could answer, the tiger held up his drink and bellowed "To one more day keeping ahead of *The Man!*" before downing the drink and pouring himself another from the bottle left for him. Because Jack was still staring, he missed Frank silently mouthing the toast in perfect time.

"There you go," Frank said, shrinking a little into his seat. "That's Nohar. He's from—"

"—OtP, yeah, I recognize him. Guitar player. You're kinda expected to know *Off the Pink* when you're a morph, so you at least pick up the lineup."

"Fair enough." Frank bit his lip and resisted the urge to point out that Nohar's real name was Nick and he's a nightmare to share a tour bus with. "Hey, you wanna get out of here? I like the band, but that doesn't mean that I want to spend however long watching..."

Frank trailed off and gestured to the bar where Nohar was trying to get into a drinking contest with his groupies—the two of them sharing a drink for each one of his, to keep it fair.

"Besides," the sabrecat continued with a grin. "I believe there was some discussion of talking and then clubbing?"

Jack, who'd looked a little unsure, brightened up at that. He took a moment to finish his beer while Frank brought up their tab on his phone, found that Nick's round had been applied to the drinks he'd already bought, and decided to take the win. He chugged his own drink, subvocalized to his glasses to find him a nearby club, and slipped out with Jack without the spectacle at the bar noticing.

The last thing Frank wanted, after all, was to be dragged into the limelight with his bandmate in front of everyone. Especially tonight of all nights.

***

Frank had only the one beer so far, but that and escaping from the bar was enough to help him relax. He and Jack found a club with a dance floor where they could unwind in some ways and get wound up in others. It was kind of an industrial place, but the DJ could get a decent beat, a happy middle ground between their musical preferences.

Frank wasn't dressed for dancing; not that Jack's flannel shirt was much of a 'clubbing' outfit either. The ferret had unbuttoned it the rest of the way to flaunt his wiry build; the white fur shone under the lights highlighting his gym-toned body with each movement. The sabrecat thought it spoke well of Jack's character that he was more interested in talking to someone he was hooking up with, because it'd be all too easy to enthrall someone once he got that shirt flapping and his body moving.

The lion's own movements were more subdued; moving with the beat. His tail flicked back and forth behind him as he tried to at least keep up though fatigued from performing. He slipped a strong arm around the ferret's waist and ground against him, feeling a tent in Jack's jeans press against his own. He shivered and his chest rumbled with a purr that he knew could be heard even over the music. Jack slipped his arms around Frank's neck and pulled himself in, nipping at the edge of Frank's ear. "Let's go sit down," he whispered. "Take a break, grab a drink, and maybe a bite, hmmm?"

Jack nipped at that ear again and slid away from the sabrecat. Frank followed close behind, not thinking about whether anyone could spot the erection barely concealed in his pants. Jack slid into a seat at an empty table and pulled out his phone to order something from the bar. Frank sat with him and angled his ears to better hear Jack if he said anything.

While Jack fiddled with his phone pulling up the club's menu, Frank tried to relax by focusing on the display in his glasses. It kept up a real-time listing of what song was playing, who the original artist was, and convenient links to services where he could stream the album. Below was a link to look up the DJ's social media. He tried to dismiss it with a well-practiced eye-twitch, but it kept coming back every time the song changed.

"Split a sandwich?" Jack asked, getting Frank's attention. He held up his phone to indicate the bar's menu. Frank just nodded, already salivating. The ferret's pink fingers picked something off the menu and gave Frank a look before ordering a couple of drinks as well.

"What was that?" Frank asked, an eyebrow raised.

"Just trying to pick a beer for you, is all," the ferret said with a toothy smile. "So, I never asked, what do you do?" He scooted closer so he wouldn't have to fight as hard to talk over the music, and also so he could squeeze Frank's thigh.

"I'm an actor," he blurted out as he felt the hand on this leg. "Stage, mostly. Unless you're a theater nut you probably wouldn't have seen me in anything." Technically true.

"Oh yeah? And what do you do to keep the lights on? Barista?

Waiter?" Jack asked with a chuckle.

Frank frowned defensively at that one, and before he could stop himself his ears laid back. Jack's smile faded a little bit when he recognized his misstep.

"Sorry, sorry," the ferret said, clearly mistaking the lion's reaction for embarrassed confirmation of the white lie.

"It's okay, just—let's just say my stage work pays the bills well enough." He placed a hand on Jack's and gave it a reassuring squeeze. "What about you?"

"Marketing," the ferret said, punctuating the one-word statement with an eyeroll that just screamed *ugh*. "I design ad campaigns, deal with picky clients who suddenly decide everything has to be purple and then it's *'just not right'*, and so I switch them back to the pre-purple design they originally hated, and they love it and call me a genius."

"Still a creative job, am I right?"

"Within constraints, yeah. Some days it's like someone keeps shoving their favorite coloring books in front of me and expecting me to turn it into fine art, but—they've just started me on storyboarding commercials instead of designing ads, and that's a lot less frustrating."

"Commercials, nice!" Frank said, impressed. "Anything I'd have seen?"

"Your ad said you're just passing through, so probably not. I do a lot for local companies."

"Try me, just in case." Someone from the bar came by and dropped off two glasses of a deep stout beer accompanied by a substantial BLT.

"How about..." The ferret thought a moment, his hand just resting on Frank's leg now that he was distracted, "the vid-board for the SUV dealership on the edge of town."

"The one where the guy slides back the sunroof and hangs out of it like he's in a convertible?"

"Yeah, that one." Jack gave Frank a warm smile and squeezed his thigh before releasing it. "It's ridiculous, but you don't get noticed being mediocre; especially in this business."

"Fair enough," Frank took a sip of his beer, so thick he was pretty sure it'd get stuck in his teeth. "Wow, that's something." He stared at the beer for a second.

"Local microbrew." Jack grabbed half of the BLT and took a big bite out of it. "Might be heartier than the sammich," he said around a mouthful.

"Not good?"

"The sandwich is fine!" Jack chewed and swallowed. "I'm just pretty sure you could stand a spoon in the drink, is all."

"Breakfast of champions," the sabrecat said with a grin as he took another big swallow, enough to drain half of it all at once. He grabbed the other half of the sandwich and took a bite, pretty standard BLT, definitely lighter than the beer.

Frank found himself surprisingly hungry after earlier and inhaled the rest of his half of the sandwich. He jumped slightly when he felt Jack's nimble fingers running along his pant leg again. He took a deep breath or two and tried to keep himself calm while he sent another swallow of beer chasing after the sandwich. He so rarely got to date properly; he wasn't sure if this was the sort of place where he could get away with encouraging the groping, or if he even should, or—

Okay, no encouragement necessary, Frank thought to himself. The ferret's fingers kneaded the front of his pants and traced the bulge of his length down the pant leg. Frank, thankfully, wasn't in the middle of swallowing anything at the time or else that could have been awkward or messy; probably both.

Of course, if he keeps that up, then the issue of 'awkward and messy' will be out of my hands. So to speak. He gripped the edges of the table as subtly as he could, and kept his visible reaction to slitted eyes, flattened ears, and some panting. He tried to put the club out of his thoughts, tried not to think about the fact that either the ferret was trying to jerk him off in his pants, or he was trying to provoke the lion into dragging him away someplace.

Frank took a deep breath and opened his eyes. He caught a familiar scent on the breeze of the club's A/C, even over all of the sweat and musky aromas in the club. His hardon wilted a bit despite the ferret's careful stroking.

"What, is something wrong?" Jack asked.

No, no, no, no, Frank thought to himself, looking around.

A short distance away, he could see where the dance floor crowd was parted to watch a shirtless black panther morph in camo pants dance with a small crowd of admirers.

"Max," Frank hissed. Jack followed his gaze to look at the panther.

"Oh, that's the, um… new bass player, right?" the ferret asked. "These guys are all over the place."

"Yeah, tell me about it," Frank said flatly. "Hey, y'know, once word gets out that he's here, this place is gonna be swarming with people trying to get pictures. Maybe we should get out of here."

"You think it's gonna be worse than Nohar back at the bar?"

Frank considered his answer carefully. "Nohar doesn't have alleged amateur porn videos circulating. With Max, everyone hopes they'll get lucky and see him naked to see if that's really him in the video."

Jack gave Max another look and Frank suppressed a groan, having seen far too many people mentally undressing Max right in front of him.

"Also," Frank said, annoyed. "He's not the *new* bassist. He's been with OTP longer than the original guy."

Jack stopped and looked back at Frank; his train of thought derailed.

"I didn't follow them after the first album, why'd they drop the first guy?"

"I'll tell you on the way out." Frank got up to leave, now annoyed with himself for bringing it up. Jack followed and fastened a few shirt buttons, a spring still in his step even after everything. Frank was a little envious of the ferret's energy, but then he hadn't played a concert at the Arena earlier.

"So, why'd they drop him?" Jack asked once they were outside and wandering through the late bar crowds.

"Jim, the wolverine they started with, took the morph supremacy thing a bit far."

"But isn't that their thing? 'Escaped super-soldiers fighting back against the human authority' and all that?"

"They dialed back the anti-human emphasis pretty quickly." Frank tried *very* hard not to sound defensive. "Attracted the wrong crowd, and the wrong bass player. They're still all about pushing back against 'The Man'; it just so happens most of the military is still human-run. Jim actually wanted to hire human guys to get the crap beaten out of them on-stage."

Jack stopped, eyes wide. "I never heard *that*."

Frank repressed a wince. Why had he mentioned that? Was he just that pissed?

"It's not well-known," the lion simply said, and sighed. "Hey, look, I think I took this night off the rails, if you wanna call it I'll understand."

"It's fine, it's fine. But where do we go now?"

"Well… I know a place. It's off the beaten path, but it might make it up to you." He grinned.

"I thought you were passing through."

"Doesn't mean I didn't do my research." He reached out with thick fingers to take the ferret's slim, pink hand. "Come on."

***

Frank led Jack off the bus, into an alley, and behind a closed restaurant to find a short line of people in front of a set of stairs leading down. At the top and the bottom of the stairs, a pair of muscular humans tried and failed to nonchalantly loiter in jackets that clearly marked them as bouncers. No signage marked the door at the bottom of the steps, but the line and bouncers spoke for themselves. Jack's pink eyes widened when he realized what Frank had meant by 'off the beaten path.'

"'Did your research,' huh?" the ferret whispered.

"Yup. Now let's see if I can do something about this line. Wait here, and I'll be right back."

The lion left Jack at the end of the line, his tail twitching thoughtfully, and approached the first bouncer. The man was human, black, muscular, in his mid-20's, with a shaved head. He carried himself like a football player, maybe someone who played college ball but never went pro. At the bottom of the stairs his lighter-skinned counterpart was just as broad, but shorter and slightly less imposing.

"So, what's your story?" the man at the top of the stairs asked Frank.

Frank took his glasses off for a moment and gave the bouncer a predatory grin that emphasized his fangs.

"Lieutenant Fury from Off the Pink would like to come in, discreetly," he said under his breath, affecting the growl he put into his singing voice when he was on-stage.

The man stared at him for a moment, nonplussed, but then glanced down to his partner at the bottom of the stairs. They shared a quick subvocal conversation on implanted throat mikes, and the bouncer turned back to him and nodded.

"Thanks," Frank said in his normal voice, handing the man a pair of bills.

Skipping the line was one thing, but he didn't want anyone to think he was a cheapskate.

Frank replaced the glasses and waved Jack up. The ferret gave the lion a curious, slightly confused look as he led him down the stairs, past the other bouncer, and into the dark club beyond. Frank tried not to relish the grumbling from the people who were still stuck in the line outside.

"What did you do?" Jack asked.

"I saved up for this vacation," Frank instantly said. "A hundred for each of them doesn't take too much out of my budget."

Electronic music, the kind that suggested there was an actual DJ at work producing a continuous track instead of simply playing songs, pounded through the small underground club. Dim lights marked a couple of hallways, one of which had the bathrooms, and another led to a couple of sitting rooms and a dance floor. The club smelled of sweat and alcohol, and if the silhouettes in the near-darkness were any indication it was an even mix of humans and morphs.

Frank slipped a strong arm around the white ferret's shoulders so as not to lose track of him as he went up to what passed for a bar and spent way too much on a couple of drinks in plastic cups. On the way his augmented reality glasses kept trying to identify the music, and the faces in the crowd, and so on. He just took them off and tucked them into a pocket rather than deal with the distraction.

"Let's find a place to sit down," Jack said to Frank, almost having to yell over the music, as he sipped his drink and grabbed a fistful of napkins.

Frank would have suspected from his tone that his date was annoyed by the music, but he could feel the ferret's slinky body wriggling against him to the beat. He curled his tail around Jack's waist, as much to keep it out of danger than anything else. *He'd definitely be popular on the dance floor in a club like this,* the sabrecat thought. *If this date doesn't work out, at least I introduced him to this place.*

The room they found was dimly lit in red. People clustered in twos and threes in the corners and on vinyl couches. The size of the room kept them close enough together that they may as well have all been sitting together. The pair of morphs could easily still hear the music well enough as Frank sat down and guided Jack to sit next to him. At the last minute, the ferret's lithe body moved to straddle the lion's lap where he pressed his muzzle to the big cat's.

Jack's tongue tasted like the beers they'd been drinking on and off all night in addition to a hint of the drink he'd just gotten him. Frank shakily secured his grip on his beverage without spilling it or crushing the cup, and he wrapped his free arm around the ferret's body. A tent in the ferret's pants pressed against Frank's abs and he ground his own arousal back against Jack.

The moment was unexpected but seemed natural as he made out with Jack, his tongue dancing with his date's. The tension from earlier went away and he finally managed to set his drink on a nearby table—next to Jack's, he noticed—instead of one of the couch cushions. He was worried for a moment about anyone giving them grief for making out in the club like this, but the husky, aroused voice whispering in the back of his mind reminded him that this was half the point for this type of club.

Jack shifted in his lap, moving with the music, pressing the warm bulge in his pants against the lion's. Frank gasped into the kiss when he felt Jack unbuttoning and unzipping his pants to wrap those pink fingers around his hard cock. Frank let out a kiss-muffled groan when he felt that grip on his prick, smearing drizzles of precum over the sensitive flesh. The lion panted into the kiss and he closed his eyes to focus on the sensations rather than thinking about how many other people were in the room, some of whom were likely doing their own share of groping.

His strong arms wrapped around the white-furred ferret's narrow body, pulling him in against his hardon. Frank's broad hand fondled Jack's groin, teasing his erection through his pants, but the ferret seemed more focused on curling his fingers around the lion's cock than pressing against the sabrecat's fondling. The lion groaned into the kiss as he felt the pink fingertips working at his prick, finding the spots that made him squirm and the spots that led to his hands squeezing at parts of the ferret's body.

Frank 'mmmmph'ed when he felt Jack slide a hand down to caress and fondle his balls, bringing him dancing up to the edge. Despite himself he couldn't help but lightly thrust into the ferret's grip, hampered only by the weight of the body on his lap, but he was big and strong enough that Jack wasn't that much of a hindrance. After the interruptions they'd already had that night, Frank was all too eager to lose himself in Jack's ministrations and the taste of booze on his tongue.

Before he knew it, Frank felt himself cross that line of orgasmic inevitability, that point where his climax was definitely a 'when' and not an 'if.' He broke the kiss to warn his date, but the words were quickly overtaken by a near-roaring groan, a siren announcing his orgasm.

There was a rustling noise and Frank felt napkins pressed against the head of his cock, catching the sticky eruption before it could get on their clothes, the couch, or worse—their fur. As he came down, panting, he realized that Jack must have planned this from the start when he swiped the stack of napkins from the bar. The ferret's grin, easy to see on his bright muzzle in the dark room, shone with excitement.

"Holy shit," Frank whispered as Jack looked around and found a trash can to toss the wad into.

"You're welcome," Jack chuckled. "Now tuck yourself back in, we're gonna dance and then you're gonna return the favor."

Jack got up off Frank's lap, once again squirming with the rhythm of the music. Frank's legs were a little shaky from his orgasm and having had the ferret sitting and grinding on them. The lion managed to get himself back into his pants and get them zipped back up without incident. Before he could get up, a couple of bodies flopped down onto the couch, just a couple of cushions down.

"Oh, you've gotta be kidding me," he muttered to himself.

A blue-furred, lop-eared rabbit was making out with a scantily-clad human woman with long black hair and—as near as Frank could tell in the dim light—Asian features. The woman held a leash that led to a tall snow leopard guy standing next to them. Specifically, the leash led to a leather bondage harness that complimented his latex sleeves and leather pants. He wore a collar that was a single steel ring. Frank noticed that the woman was wearing a leather corset and thigh-high boots that matched the snow leopard's outfit.

But the important thing is that the rabbit, even with the woman in his lap, was immediately recognizable as Chad, Off the Pink's drummer (and, as he often joked, 'token prey species'). The sabrecat remembered the rabbit saying something about hitting the town with a couple of fetish models after the show.

Frank quickly got up and took a few steps away to follow Jack. He heard a snap of furred fingers and glanced back, afraid that he'd been recognized until he realized it was Chad getting the leopard's attention, indicating the floor in front of the couch with a gesture. The leopard immediately got on all fours, taking his place as a footstool. Frank quickly turned to Jack.

"I think we should get out of here," the lion hissed in the ferret's ear when he caught up to him on the dance floor.

"What the hell? What, did something happen?" Jack bared his teeth with frustration.

"I just saw something that really put me off this place," Frank said as he turned to go.

Jack quickly followed, glancing in the room they'd vacated when they passed it. "Hey, is that the—"

"Yup!" Frank said as he all but fled out into the alley.

Jack followed close behind, his red eyes seeming to blaze with anger.

"Okay, what the hell?" the ferret asked.

Frank stopped to catch his breath and gather his words. The alley felt a lot cooler now than it had when they went in, and he admitted he found it a bit refreshing despite the circumstances.

"It just—it just got too weird for me," Frank said, which wasn't entirely false. "If you wanna just call it, I'll understand."

"Well, first, just answer one thing for me," the ferret snapped.

"Sure," Frank said as he rubbed his face. They weren't yelling, but they were definitely close enough to the club that people were staring and listening. Ears swiveled in their direction and Frank was pretty sure that the bouncer he'd revealed his identity to was smirking at him.

"Why are you so focused on ditching the rest of your band?"

"It's not that, it's—wait. You know!?" Frank asked, his voice raised.

The ferret just stared him down.

"Fuck me, okay, okay, just…" Frank ran his hands through his mane and made a frustrated noise. "Let's sit down someplace where we can get some food and coffee and discuss this calmly."

***

Frank and Jack stepped in from the outside, noted the 'Seat yourself' sign, and made a beeline for a booth. The restaurant was typical chain diner fare, the sort of place popular with people who live on the road because the food at each one is identical to the food at each other one. The sabretooth lion took off his AR specs and dismissively set them on the table with a clatter. The ferret sat down across from him, and they both waited for a human waitress with red hair and a name tag that read 'Nadine' to come and take their orders for coffee and an appetizer sampler. They waited until she was gone before they got down to it.

"So, I lied by omission," Frank said. "Well, at first. And then…" He looked at his hands as if he had notes or something, but none materialized. He just rubbed them together and wished he had something to fidget with. "Anyhow. I'm the lead singer for Off the Pink. 'Lieutenant Fury.'"

"We know that," Jack said with an unreadable look. "But let's start there. Why didn't you just say so?"

"Because being the front man for a popular band is exhausting. Because unlike my other bandmates, I don't like to unwind with just drinking or sex."

"Which is why you met a guy on a dating app and invited him to a bar to hook up?" the ferret morph said.

"Touché, I'll give you that. But no, it's because… meeting someone, getting together for a drink, hoping something happens… it's normal. It's a break from being in-character all the time. And I like the others in the band, I really do…"

He trailed off, looking for the words, and out of his eye he spotted a badger morph in a leather biker jacket and her human boyfriend, a black guy with short hair and a couple days of stubble, at another booth. Kristen, the other guitar player from the band, gave him a sheepish smile and a wave. Her boyfriend (whom Frank had met a handful of times, but damned if he remembered his name) turned, spotted him, and waved as well.

"Because of course," Frank chuckled with a smile as he waved back. Jack turned and looked, and nodded at the pair.

"So, do we have to go again?" the ferret asked with deserved bitterness.

"No, no, just… let me finish. I like the rest of the band. But most of them like to unwind by partying. In-character, if possible. But I like being normal. Doing normal things like going on dates, meeting people…" He hesitated as their coffee and a basket of nebulous fried shapes arrived. "…you get the idea. Kris is the same way." He nodded to the badger.

"I don't think I know her," Jack quietly admitted.

"She joined up during production on the second album. Nick— Nohar—had to leave the country for a while. Family emergency. We needed someone to sit in for him for a couple of shows, and met Kris. And she worked well with us, so we rearranged the band to keep her around."

Jack opened his mouth as if to make an observation, but stopped and shook his head. "We're getting off-topic."

"Right."

"Why didn't you tell me who you are and that you were in town for a show?"

"Because… because I love performing, but 'the Lieutenant' is just a character I play. And especially when we're on tour, I really need to be able to just break character and be a normal guy for a while."

"To the point of saying you're not a fan of your own music?"

"Hey, I admitted to enjoying it. I just said I wasn't the mosh pit type, and that I'd rather relax on the couch with earbuds. Which is absolutely true. I mean, I'm not proud of the little white lies or the omissions, but it's the best way to get a break."

"And the band doesn't know that you do this?" Jack asked, understanding.

"Not really, no. They know I like to drop character and go out as just myself, but they don't know specifics. Nick, Max, and Chad are big on spectacle. Kris isn't. And Ronnie, well… not even I know what Ronnie gets up to when he's away from the band."

"Ronnie?" Jack picked up a fried cheese stick and chewed on it.

"'Ronin.' The keyboard player. White wolf, comes out streaked in fake blood for every show."

"Right."

"But I know I can trust Kris to not make a big deal out of seeing me here. Nick and Max, even if they get that I'm 'undercover,' are still likely to find some excuse to mess with me. I just wasn't expecting to run into someone in the band every place we went tonight!" He nervously chuckled and ran his fingers through his mane.

"So, you do this a lot? Pick up guys after a show?"

"Almost never," Frank was quick to say. "Sometimes I just really need to unwind, and want to do it as myself, and apps give me a way to dodge the sorts of fans who would spot me even like this. It gets weird if they recognize me, because I'll never know if they're into me or into the character or into the fact that I'm kinda-sorta famous." Frank grabbed a bottle of ketchup to apply to the onion rings, and dipped and ate one. "What about you, though? You were on the app, too."

"Well, like you said, sometimes you need to unwind." Jack dipped the rest of his cheese stick in the marinara, finished it, and then gave the marinara a sour look. "It's easier to meet people if they're not staring at you because your fur stands out. Helps me feel someone out before I feel them up."

"I'll drink to that," Frank said, lifting his coffee mug and clinking it against the ferret's. "Marinara not good?"

"Nope."

Frank grabbed a cheese stick and all but inhaled it.

"So where to from here, then?" Jack asked after nibbling on something that turned out to be a fried pickle. "After we get out of here, I mean. I know we're not fleeing into the night from another of your bandmates, but it's not like we live here." A thoughtful gleam shone in the ferret's pink eyes.

"Honestly, I dunno… I mean, I don't really have anyplace peaceful to go back to, and honestly it might be a little late to head back to your place at this point."

"It sucks when you don't just whisk someone off to a hotel room, doesn't it?" Jack said with a wink before continuing in an overdramatic voice. "You have to *talk* to people, and people just talk *forever*. It's a wonder that *anyone* gets laid."

Frank rolled his eyes. "Okay, then, smartass. I've been dragging us around all night. You sound like you've got a place in mind."

"I do. But first, we finish eating. And maybe introduce me to Kristen before we go."

"I can do that," Frank said as he plucked another onion ring out of the plastic, paper-lined basket. "In fact..." He waved over at the other table and gestured for Kris and her boyfriend to come over.

The badger raised an eyebrow, tapped her boyfriend on the arm, and they got up to cross the room to where Frank and Jack sat. Kristen silently mouthed something at him, and he didn't quite get it until she arrived. 'LT or Frank,' she was trying to say, looking for a sign as to whether this was in-character.

"Jack, this is Kristen and her boyfriend whose name I've sadly forgotten because I've met him like three times," Frank said, just leaning into the awkwardness at this point. The badger shot Frank a dirty look.

"Kurt," the man said as he reached out to shake Jack's hand.

"Yes, Kurt, thank you, sorry about that," Frank said. "Kristen, Kurt, this is Jack."

Kristen shook Jack's hand, his pink fingers disappearing into her broad, black-furred grip. "So, this one fer the orgy later, then, luv?" she asked in a thick, obviously fake Cockney accent.

Jack suddenly looked a little concerned, like this had all been a setup. Kristen burst out laughing.

"She's messing with me for forgetting Kurt's name," Frank said as he shot her a look. "This is why I don't tell you people where I go after we play."

"Pleased to meet you, Jack," she said through her toothy grin, the accent vanishing. "How's your guys' night been?"

"Awful," Frank said, simultaneous with Jack replying "Just fine." They glanced at each other.

"Every time we went somewhere tonight, one of the guys showed up," Frank said, clarifying. "Nick at the bar where we met, Max at the club we went to after that, and as we speak Chad's probably bending over a snow leopard in another club bathroom while his mistress watches."

"Well, that's at least two videos for the net tomorrow," Kristen sighed. "No sign of Ronnie?"

"Never any sign of Ronnie."

"For the best, probably." She stuffed her hands in the pockets of her jacket. "You know how it is, it's always the quiet ones."

"It hasn't been *that* bad, once we cleared the air on what was going on," Jack insisted. "How about your guys' night?"

"Pretty straightforward," Kristen said with a shrug. "Cleaned up after the show, met Kurt, and we fooled around a bit." Kurt blushed as she continued. "Best advice ever: Fuck first. Better to work up an appetite than try to screw when you've got a gut full of road food, are too drunk, or both."

Nadine the waitress showed up at *just* the wrong moment to refill Frank and Jack's coffees.

"Hey, you movin' over here?" Nadine asked, annoyance seasoning her voice.

"We're just saying hi," Kristen said to her. "We'll be back over there in a minute, we don't need anything."

The waitress nodded and backed off, somehow managing to vanish into thin air in the half-empty restaurant. She muttered something under her breath that the morphs around the table pretended not to hear, rather than start trouble.

"So is your advice to fuck first a knock on us about letting the guys waylay us all night?" Frank asked as he added cream and sugar to his refreshed coffee.

"Now there's a choice phrase," Jack chuckled.

"I like him," Kristen said. "But no, no, nothing like that. Well, maybe a little."

"Not to brag," Frank said, giving Jack an awkward glance. "But given what we do and how popular we are I could get hot and cold meaningless sex on tap if I wanted it. Which, quite frankly I don't."

"So what, did I jerk you off in that nightclub for nothing?" Jack asked, getting a sputter—almost a spit-take—out of Frank. Kristen and Kurt both burst out laughing.

Frank grabbed some napkins to get coffee out of his muzzle fur.

"I like him, too," Kurt said.

"So glad he gets your approval," Frank muttered through the napkins.

"And with that, we should probably go," Kristen said, slipping an arm around Kurt's waist. "Leave you two be. Nice meeting you, Jack."

"Nice meeting you, too," the ferret said as they left, still chuckling at Frank as the lion grumpily chewed on one of the fried pickles. "Oh, what?"

"Nothing, just..."

"Just what? Spent all night running away from your bandmates, and now you feel like you finally got trapped by the sort of thing you've been afraid of?"

"Yeah, actually." Frank grabbed another cheese stick and chomped it down.

Jack grabbed the plastic basket and pulled it away before Frank kept eating out of frustration.

"How about this," the ferret said with a smile. "Like we said, the night's kinda winding down, and we're probably not gonna have time for something more... intimate. So, let's go somewhere else, somewhere specific, and get a *decent* cup of coffee to cap things off. I think you'll like it."

"And where's that?" the sabrecat asked, raising an eyebrow.

***

"How late is this place open?" Frank asked as Jack led him into the coffee shop. By now it was coming up on 4am. The display in Frank's glasses immediately brought up the hours for the coffee shop, and the lion suppressed a groan and put the specs away without looking. In the back of the surprisingly-crowded coffee house, he heard the strumming of an acoustic guitar. The tune sounded vaguely familiar, but he couldn't place it.

"Bar hours during the week, 24 hours on weekends," Jack said. "They've got booze, but when the bars are supposed to close they put it away. And even if that weren't the case, I think we've had enough to drink."

"What, a couple of beers and whatever the hell it was they were serving at the underground place?"

"Says the big, rough, sabrecat," the ferret teased. "Look at me, get one more drink into me and you can just pick me up and wring it out of me like a towel."

"Good point. Coffee it is."

Jack got a couple of coffees. They weaved through the crowd and found a seat in view of the small stage area. A white wolf sat on a stool, playing an acoustic guitar. His eyes were closed but he still paid attention to the crowd with tall, swiveling ears. One ear twitched in Frank and Jack's direction when they sat down, and he went back to focusing on the room. After a few moments, Frank realized why he recognized the wolf, why he recognized the tune, and how he knew that he was paying attention to the acoustics as well as the crowd.

"Yeah, that's him," Jack said softly. "Your jaw dropped, you're not exactly subtle."

"You knew?" Frank asked, all but whispering. "You knew Ronnie comes here?"

"A couple of times a year, he drops in, yeah. White wolf, brilliant musician. Always appears after Off the Pink does a show in town. I don't think anyone notices because he plays keyboard on stage but guitar here. Also, he doesn't do the fake blood here."

"He's the heart and soul of the band," Frank said. "I mean, I'm the front man, I do the singing, I came up with the foundation of our gimmick, but…" He gestured to the wolf with his coffee cup. "Without him, we'd probably just be recording variations on the same three songs over and over again. That song he's playing? That's something we've been working on for the next album. Or at least what it would sound like if we played places like this."

"You should do that sometime. Do what my grandpa called an 'Unplugged' show."

"Hard pass. Some metal guys can really sing, but not me—all I've got is leveraging a lion's roar into…" He dropped his voice into the lower register he used on stage. "…my death growl." He put his voice back to normal. "And that just doesn't work with acoustic."

At that point, Frank glanced back at Ronnie up on stage, who'd opened one eye and noticed him. Frank just gave him a thumbs-up, and the wolf smirked and went back to focusing on his music. Frank sipped his coffee as he and Jack listened to the performance.

"So, got any wacky trivia for this one?" the ferret whispered.

"He's pretty scandal-free, and a very private person," the lion said as he took another sip.

"What, come Monday I'm probably gonna be in the background of a video of a panther getting ready to publicly strip, your drummer is banging fetish models in a club bathroom, and I don't get anything juicy about the keyboard player?"

"Honestly, Kris' comment earlier about 'the quiet ones' aside, Ronnie's probably the most normal of us," Frank said after a moment's consideration. "Maybe after Kristen. Kind of a toss-up. Besides, after playing heavy metal, he comes here and plays guitar for—apparently—a couple of hours. Not to mention what he does in other cities. And he tests out material we're still working on. That isn't juicy enough?"

"I'll give you that," Jack said with a thoughtful nod.

They listened and watched for another couple of minutes, scooting closer in their seats, sipping their drinks. Frank tried not to 'hear' the band's normal music style in the tunes that Ronnie was playing, and appreciate it on its own merits. He'd gotten so used to hearing the wolf compose and play on the keyboard, that he'd forgotten that he could play anything else.

Time got away from Frank and Jack as they just quietly enjoyed each others' company. Maybe twenty minutes passed, but it felt like they'd been there an hour—but in a good way, like they had plenty of time instead of having to call it too soon. At one point they'd started holding hands, but couldn't say when or who initiated it. But after a few more songs, Ronnie started packing up and Frank glanced at the clock and realized it was time to get back.

"So tonight was kind of a wash, wasn't it?" he asked Jack with a sigh.

"Not too bad. Bit of an adventure. Wasn't at all what I was expecting when I swiped on your profile."

Frank laughed out loud despite himself, his laugh heartier than he'd intended. He drew a lot of stares and covered his muzzle with a hand to finish chuckling into it.

"That… is an understatement," the lion said with a bright grin. "But y'know, I'd take the night we had—frustration and all—over all of the quick meetup sex in the world."

"Wow, was that handjob in the club *really* that bad?" the ferret asked.

"I thank you for not waiting until I was mid-drink to say that this time," Frank said with a smirk.

"What's this about a handjob at a club?" Ronnie asked as he hauled his stuff over to their table.

"I'll tell you later. Ronnie, this is Jack. Jack, Ronnie." He lowered his voice. "Or, y'know, 'Ronin.'"

"Pleased to meet you," Jack said, shaking hands with the white wolf.

"Pleasure's mine." Ronnie replied. "And as much as I'd hate to break up a cute couple, we probably should get back to the bus. I only mention it because I've already got a car coming and we can share a ride back."

He held up his phone.

"He's right," Frank sighed. "Ronnie, give us a second and I'll meet you outside?"

"Sure. Just don't take too long, you know how the auto-cabs get when you make them wait." Ronnie shouldered the strap on his guitar case and shuffled out to the door.

"Sorry I screwed up your night," Frank said.

"Pfft. It was plenty entertaining in its own way. Just too bad we can't get a do-over tomorrow."

"No, but…" Frank thought a moment, pulled his phone out, and brought up a list of dates. "Look, here's the tour route we're on. We'll be on the road all day tomorrow, but…" He scrolled down the list. "Yeah, here we go. Next week we loop around and come back this direction and we'll only be about an hour and a half away for this show." He showed Jack the date and location. "Think you can make that? I'll make it worth your while. Free tickets and VIP at the will call kiosk. I might even let you blow me." He winked.

Jack laughed now, his own laugh high-pitched and a little squeaky.

"Y'know, I bet I can do that," the ferret said. "No promises, but we'll see what happens." He pulled his phone out and three or four swipes of his thumb later, he nodded. "And there, you should have my regular contact info."

"Thanks." Frank trusted him enough at this point not to check the phone.

He and Jack got up and the lion wrapped his arms around the slim ferret, hugging him tight. He pressed his muzzle to the ferret's in a soft kiss—soft, sweet, more of a 'see you next time' kiss than a 'knock your socks off' kiss. But it felt nice, in a way that Frank hadn't gotten to experience in a while, so it was only with reluctance that he let Jack go once the kiss broke.

"So, this is it?" Jack asked.

"Until next time," Frank said with a nod.

"Still nothing juicy about Ronnie?"

Frank eyerolled. "Actually, well… there is one tiny thing."

"Oh yeah?"

"You know, the band does the whole 'genetically engineered super-soldiers' schtick and all that. Most of us are really second-gen morphs. Only Nick and Ronnie are actual Converts. Which is *really* funny if you know the old novels where Nick's stage name comes from."

"I'll notify the tabloids at once," Jack said dryly, though the gleam in his pink eyes suggested he was intrigued.

"And with that…" Frank pitched his voice into the death growl again. "Lieutenant Fury, out."

He finger-waved at the ferret and stepped outside to where a cool breeze, his bandmate, and a self-driving car awaited him. Somewhere beyond that: tour bus, stages, hot lights, sore throats, and if he was very lucky in a week's time, a sexy ferret.

For my own orca, who has always encouraged me to fly among the stars.

CROSSCURRENTS

by Jaden Drackus

Above the blue orb hanging against the backdrop of stars, the blocky shape of the United Terran Federation Starfighter Carrier *Intrepid* slipped into high orbit as the other ships of her task force assumed standard diplomatic formation. A few moments later, escorted by a pair of starfighters, a dropship departed the *Intrepid* and headed for the surface.

"Questions?" Admiral Boyd asked the three pilots in the passenger compartment.

Colt, seated nearest the hatch, said nothing as the wolf looked around. The silver vixen next to him elbowed him in the stomach.

"I see that twitching. Ask," she said with a grin.

"I'm just a pilot. I don't get to question admirals."

"You're also a Viper now," Boyd replied. "And elite squadrons get certain privileges. Like asking questions of admirals."

"Feels like that should be the commander's privilege," the otter murmured.

The third pilot, a wolfox, stirred at the comment and met Colt's gaze. He smirked. "I already get that by being the *Intrepid*'s wing commander. Ask him, Colt."

"Why do you need us with you on a diplomatic mission, Admiral?" The otter asked after a pause.

"By request of our hosts," Boyd answered with a sniff. "Relations between the Terran Federation and the Chanthu Imperium are reaching the boiling point. In an effort to avoid conflict, we are conducting joint exercises to prove that we can cooperate. But we are also demonstrating Federation abilities. That's why I brought the Vipers. I want the best of the UTN starfighter forces with me to show the Imperium just what they will be facing if they go to war."

Boyd checked his watch and then nodded to the pilots. "I have to give the recognition codes. I'll leave Drake to handle further briefing."

"Chanthu Prime is an aquatic world," Drake said as the door closed behind the admiral. "The land is almost exclusively small islands. You're never more than a mile or two from the ocean."

"Sounds great," Colt commented.

"Says the otter," Silver quipped. "Sand in your fur doesn't bother you."

"Not when you can just hop in the water."

"We'll have time for that later," Drake said, adjusting his uniform. "Diplomacy first."

The wolfox turned to the viewport, watching the accompanying fighters. Silver did the same. The otter let out a jealous sigh. He knew what they were looking at: Wash and Crimson where flying escort—Drake's boyfriend and Silver's husband respectively. Colt wondered what he had to do to find someone for him.

"What're they like? The Chanthu," Colt asked.

"Inward looking. To the point of xenophobia. Didn't look at the briefing?" Drake chuckled. "I figured you'd love the pictures they included in the data files."

"I. Uh. Really wasn't expecting to be picked for this," Colt replied as he tried to sink into the bench.

"Well. Because their world is aquatic, they are as well. You know the whales and dolphins back on Terra? They look like bipedal versions of those."

Colt's ears perked. "So is that why I'm here? To be the token Terran aquatic species?"

Drake's ears and tail flicked as his gaze returned to the viewport. "That and I thought you might like seeing an aquatic world after so long on duty."

"Oh," Colt said, feeling the heat of embarrassment in his ears. *Don't assume.*

"Don't worry Rookie," Silver assured him. "Good commanders, like that one, make it a principle to take care of their people."

Now it was Drake's turn to be embarrassed, if his ears and tail were anything to go by. He didn't reply, and kept looking out the viewport. Colt hid a smile behind his paw as the shuttle entered the atmosphere.

***

Admiral Boyd moved towards the hatch as soon as the shuttle touched down. His adjutant fell into step behind him and the Vipers followed suit, with Colt taking up the rear.

"Is language going to be a problem?" he whispered to Silver. He thought he'd asked too quietly for the wolf to hear, but Boyd's ear twitched anyway.

"Not really," Boyd said over his shoulder. "The Chanthu language *is* extremely complex. I'm told if you know Ancient Japanese, you might have some luck—minus the clicks and whistles. We're still having trouble working out the subtleties of the harmonics. But Terran Common isn't an issue for them. I hear that most of the population speak it."

"Oh good," Colt replied as he tried to hide behind Drake.

"Relax," Drake said. "And if you can't do that, then remember you're the face of the Federation."

"Right," Silver whispered. "No pressure there."

"Well if he's going to be pressured no matter what I say, he might as well have some real pressure."

"Well, you all are going to have to deal with that pressure now," Boyd put in. "Best behavior—we're trying to ease tensions here."

The Vipers straightened as Colt tried to look around the canines to see what was ahead of them without being obvious about it. The Chanthu reception consisted of five members: two in flowing robes that the otter guessed were diplomats, and behind them three others in military uniforms. Drake described them as bipedal dolphins or whales, and Colt had to agree with that. The two civilians and two of the military officers resembled dolphins of various species—the only variations being in snout size and markings.

It was the last officer that kept Colt's attention. He was slightly taller than the other Chanthu—perhaps as tall as Admiral Boyd—and a bit more thickly built. His snout was shorter and thicker than the others, and he had black and white markings like a Terran orca. He wore a similar cap to Terran uniforms, which rested against a small, crest-like fin at the back of his head and neck. A thick fluked tail swept the tarmac behind him. Colt recognized the air of a fellow fighter pilot. As they approached, he saw dark purple eyes watching them. The otter swallowed and let out a soft squeak.

"He told you you'd like them," Silver whispered, her tail swishing in amusement.

"Just keep your stallion in your pants," Drake murmured. "With tensions as high as they are, showing how much you might like them isn't a great idea."

Further discussion was cut off by the Admiral coming to a stop in front of the diplomats and bowing. The Vipers followed his lead. Out of the corner of his eye, Colt saw the orca smiling as he straightened up.

"Greetings, honored representatives of the Chanthu Imperial Court," Boyd said. "I am Admiral Boyd of the United Terran Federation Ship *Intrepid*. With me are Wing Commander Jason Horn and two members of his fighter squadron, the Vipers." Boyd introduced the rest of them in turn.

"We extend to you the greetings of His Majesty and of the Chanthu Imperium and welcome you to Chanthu Prime," the lead diplomat, the one in the red robe replied in Terran Common. "I am called Khili'ckazth'ic. As your kind do not grasp the full subtleties of our language, you may call me Kaz."

Colt stared at the dolphin, his eyes widening at the pronunciation of the Chanthu name. It did sound like the clicks and whistles of a dolphin back on Terra. He frowned—there was disdain in Kaz's voice when he offered up a Common style name for them to use. And if an ambassador looked down on them—what would the average Chanthu be like?

Boyd continued the diplomatic pleasantries, thanking the envoy for being so accommodating. Colt tried not to fidget in boredom as they continued. Finally, Kaz gestured to the orca, who stepped forward. He gave a half bow to Boyd, but his eyes never left the Vipers.

"This is Starfighter Commander Tic'thi'chil. If my knowledge of your military ranks is correct, he is equal to your Commander Horn. He is eager to converse with your pilots."

"As I'm sure my pilots are eager to speak with him," Boyd replied, returning the orca's bow. "They have been looking forward to these exercises for weeks now."

"As am I," the orca replied. "Are those the Gryphon-class fighters I have heard so much about?"

They followed his gaze to Wash and Crimson's fighters settling to the tarmac. The orca looked ready to run up and start examining them. But Kaz let out a snort, muttering something about how ugly the angular delta shaped fighters were.

"They are indeed," Drake responded with a grin. "We're looking forward to showing you what they can do, and to see how they match up against your Tangos."

Kaz's snout dropped open at the mention of the UTN code name for the frontline Chanthu fighter, but Boyd stepped in to cut off any outburst from the dolphin.

"Perhaps it would be best to leave them to that while we continue our own discussions, Ambassador."

"An excellent suggestion Admiral," Kaz replied, not quite hiding that he was glaring at Drake. "Now if you will accompany me, I will escort you and your adjutant to meet the rest of the delegation."

With that, the dolphins moved down the tarmac, leaving the orca with the canines and the otter. His beak parted in a smile as he offered another bow.

"I know the admiral introduced you, but what are your 'real' names?"

"Call signs are Drake, Silver, and Colt," Drake said with a grin as he indicated who was who. "How about you, what's your call sign?"

"More unpronounceable to you than my regular name," the orca said with a laugh. "Perhaps 'Tic' would be the best."

"Needs work," Colt murmured.

"Oh? I am open to suggestions."

"Well, on Terra, call signs are jokes or references. Silver's refers to her fur. Mine is a mythical creature. Colt's… is a dirty joke."

"Interesting," the orca mused, studying the otter. "My insignia is one of our legendary creatures. But maybe something about my background would be easiest. I am from one of the major spaceports in the… East Isles, they translate to. I am a senior commander. I have flown for almost ten years and have twenty victories."

"Sounds like Saburo Sakai," Colt put in.

"I am not familiar with this name," the orca admitted.

"He was a famous Japanese pilot in the mid-Twentieth Century," Drake said, rubbing his chin. His whiskers twitched in concentration. "If I remember my Ancient History courses, he was Japan's leading ace in the Second World War and had a background very similar to yours."

"Ah. I have read of this conflict. The Japanese Empire reminds me very much of the current state of Chanthu." He looked back towards Boyd and the diplomats as they disappeared into a building. "Not all of which is positive."

Colt followed the orca's eyes and wondered how much was meant by that comment. He thought he caught a great deal of disapproval in the other's tone.

"But this Sakai sounds like an interesting individual," the orca mused.

"Then how about that as a call sign?" Drake asked.

The orca mused, chattering and whistling to himself. After a moment, his snout parted in a smile.

"I like this."

"Excellent," Drake said as he returned the smile. "So Sakai, what is on the agenda?"

"I would like to see your fighters," Sakai replied, taking a step that brought him closer to the otter. "Is one of these yours, Colt?"

"Not one of these," Colt replied. He fidgeted a little at being the center of attention all of a sudden. "They're bringing it down tomorrow. But it's a Gryphon, so all the same."

"Ah. I have many questions about your fighters. Will you show me them?"

"Sure," the otter replied.

***

Hours later, Colt tossed his duffel onto the bunk and looked around the room. It was sparsely furnished with a simple desk and chair, dresser, bunk and a night table—all of which had a rounded look to it, as if it had been grown out of coral. To the right, a door lead to a private head. Windows dominated the wall across from the door, though with the curtains drawn he couldn't see out. The feature that most intrigued him was the wall by the bed, which was a tiny waterfall enclosed by glass. It gave the room a watery feel, filled with the babble of running water. Colt grinned: it felt homier than any Terran quarters he'd had for the past ten years.

He poked his head into the toilet and was delighted to find not only a shower, but a tub as well—one big enough to stretch out in. The otter smiled. A real bath would be nice after almost a year of nothing but sonic showers. He returned to the bed and began unpacking.

The hours after they'd met their hosts were busy ones. Sakai had a lot of questions about the Gryphons, and always addressed them to Colt first. Since many of them were concerns a fellow aquatic might have— like how his thicker tail fit in the cockpit—the otter answered most of them. When Sakai satisfied his curiosity, the orca had suggested drinks and a meal to get to know each other better. He'd continued directing his questions about preferences to Colt, and the otter had suggested seafood before the orca checked with the others. No one said anything about it, so the otter let it go and just assumed that he was flying lead.

Afterwards, Drake interrogated the otter as the commander walked him to his quarters. From the tone of his questions, Colt got the impression that the wolfox thought they weren't very welcome. But his questions kept coming back to Sakai: Drake wanted to know everything they'd talked about, how the orca seemed to fit in with other Chanthu, what Colt thought of him as a person, and as a pilot. The otter admitted that he hadn't gathered enough information to form an opinion. Drake told him to keep his eyes open. Colt said he would, and offered to keep flying lead. The wolfox agreed, and left Colt for the evening with his tail swishing in a way that left no doubt what he and Wash would be doing.

Which wasn't a bad idea, Colt thought with a smirk. A little self-care would do him some good too. He stripped out of his uniform and hustled into the head.

By the time he got to the tub, his cock was half way out of his sheath. He reached a paw down to caress the pink shaft, but paused as he realized he'd have to figure out the strange controls for the tub. That turned out not to be a concern: someone had put a card with Terran translations next to the tub. A moment later, he had a few inches of warm water—just enough to take the chill away from the porcelain, or whatever it was. Colt grinned and hoisted himself in. His mind flashed back to the last times he'd done this in his parents' tub as he settled into the water.

He sighed and squirmed to get comfortable, the water level was perfect: just up to his sac. His paw worked its way down his stomach to take hold of his shaft. He closed his eyes and caressed his balls before moving further down. This wasn't the most comfortable position, but it would work fine.

He stroked his shaft, bringing himself fully erect. He thumbed his tip and worked his way down to his base. Meanwhile his other paw explored the sensitive area under his balls, drawing a moan. Fingers massaged his taint and sought out the ring of his hole.

Over dinner, he'd finally gotten a look at the files Drake had mentioned. They'd included medical images of both male and female Chanthu, which helped the otter imagine Sakai joining him in the tub. In his mind, he could imagine the weight of the orca settling against him. He gasped as he slid a finger inside his ring, imagining it as the other's shaft. He added a second finger and resumed stroking himself. Already, he felt the pressure of an orgasm building in his loins—he wasn't going to last long. He picked up his pace, splashing water on his stomach. A moment of hesitation—it felt almost a little taboo to be fantasizing about someone that could be an enemy. Ultimately, lust won. The otter moaned as the wave of orgasm hit him.

"Oh, Sakai..."

***

The next week was a blur to the otter: a constant grind of lectures, evaluations, and flying against the best pilots in the Chanthu navy. Colt lost track of the number of simulated dogfights he'd taken part in. The otter continued to lead in socializing with their hosts—as Drake hinted, they did seem to respond better to a fellow aquatic. He returned to his quarters each night; dreams filled with their orca guide. He considered complimenting the orca on his appearance and seeing what the reaction would be. He held back, warned by instinct that Chanthu culture wasn't the most gay-friendly culture in the galaxy. A few hints from Sakai had reinforced this.

Two nights before their stay on Chanthu Prime was scheduled to end, Drake led Colt and Wash back to their quarters. As they approached Colt's door, the wolfox stopped and smiled back at the otter. Colt frowned at his commander, puzzled.

"I was thinking," he said. "Time for... local studies is running out."

"Yeah," Colt agreed. "But all my reports are in, so I'll be okay."

"Not what I meant," Drake returned. "I meant any *personal* studies you might want to engage in."

"What did you mean?"

"Damn rook," Wash put it. "You haven't noticed?"

"Noticed what? Goddamn, I've only been out of your sight when we're sleeping, it's not like I could've seen anything the two of you couldn't have."

"Oh. We noticed alright," Wash said with a snicker.

Colt stopped and stared at the raccoon, his whiskers twitching in frustration. Wash's muzzle was parted in a huge grin. Colt opened his own muzzle to snap back a retort, but was halted by Drake's raised paw.

"Take it easy, Colt. This isn't something to get angry about," the wolfox said.

"Still don't know what you're talking about, sir."

"Well, next time we're back at base put in for repairs," Wash huffed. "Your 'gay-dar' is broke."

"What?" Colt blinked, then looked between both of them.

Wash chuckled again and Drake sighed. The wolfox reached out and put a paw on his shoulder.

"I think our guide might be interested in spending some time with you."

"Me?"

"Yeah. You," Wash put in, giving Colt a playful shove towards their quarters.

"I don't see it," the otter said. "He's hot, but I didn't get a gay vibe from him."

"Oh you didn't see how he stayed closest to you? How he also lined up behind you in formation? Or how he always got your opinion first?" Wash asked with a grin.

"Or where he asked *you* specifically about how much Terran pilots tended to sleep around?" Drake added.

"I... okay. I don't remember it that way," Colt said. "He just was more comfortable asking an aquatic."

"Different question," Drake replied as they came to a stop in front of Colt's room. "As your friend, not as your commanding officer: would you be interested in finding out if he was interested?"

"Didn't you tell me it was a bad idea to get involved with one of them because of the volatile political situation?"

"Yeah," the wolfox replied. "But I never said you shouldn't. Now would you like to know if Sakai is interested in you?"

"Yeah," Colt responded after a long moment, his ears on fire. In his mind, he went over the past few days and saw it all in a different light. All the things he'd seen as just being a good host became signs of genuine affection from the orca. He turned and put his keycard up to the sensor, cursing himself for letting so many opportunities go by.

"Good," Wash said giving the otter another shove into his quarters. "Cuz he's under the impression you want to go out for drinks with him privately."

"What?" Colt all but shouted.

"He'll be here in ten minutes," Drake put in. "Get yourself together and have a good time. That's an order."

"I didn't agree to this!" Colt shouted after the retreating duo. They were laughing as they made their way down the corridor. He sighed and went back into his quarters to prepare himself for his first date in a year.

An eternity later, there was a knock on his door. Colt took a deep breath to steady himself before he touched the control to open it. Sakai stood there, holding a bottle and two tumbler sized glasses. Buy the sweep of his tail, he was nervous. He was also wearing his work uniform, while Colt had put on his dress blues. Silently, the otter cursed himself. Sakai smiled.

"Ah. At this time of the evening, most taverns are crowded. I thought we might have a more pleasant time at your quarters."

"I'm sure we can," Colt replied with a wince. He motioned for Sakai to enter. "Excuse me."

"Certainly," the orca replied. He stepped in and set the bottle and glasses on the nightstand.

He was moving the table over to the bed as Colt darted into the head. When the otter emerged a moment later in one of his own work uniforms, he found that Sakai was pouring a purple liquid into the second of the tumblers. The orca smiled at him as he capped the bottle.

"That is much less formal," Sakai chuckled. "Would you prefer the bed or the chair for a seat?"

"I'll take the bed," the otter said, climbing on the bed and seating himself cross-legged. He accepted the offered drink with a smile.

"If I may say, I was somewhat surprised by your invitation. You had been reluctant to have social engagements without your fellow Vipers."

You and me both, Colt thought. "Yeah. This is my first time with a non-Terran culture. I've been a bit nervous."

"I see," Sakai said as he took a sip of his drink. "I am pleased that you overcame your nerves."

Colt took a hasty sip of his own drink, and found it to be the Chanthu equivalent of whiskey. It had the same smoky flavor of the Terran version, but whatever aquatic plant gave it the purple hue left a slightly salty floral taste to it. He licked his lips and worked to come up with a response.

"Yes," was what he managed.

Sakai stared into his drink, swirling it as the silence lingered. Colt waited—it was clear the orca was working through something in his mind, so the otter let him think. Finally, he looked up at Colt.

"I have been thinking that I wish to ask you a thing."

"I'll answer anything I can," Colt said.

Silence returned as they both sipped their whiskey. The orca continued to study the table. As Colt watched him, all of Drake's insinuations returned to the otter's mind. He smiled into his tumbler. He recognized the nervous twitch of the orca's tail, the lack of eye contact, and the nervous snout motions. He'd made them too when he'd first expressed interest in another male.

"Would you be offended if I asked a personal question?" Sakai murmured.

"Is that the thing you wanted to ask?"

Sakai's head snapped up, and the white portions of his face turned pink. The otter was fascinated that on the furless Chanthu embarrassment was a visible emotion like that. He smiled broadly, and Sakai took the hint.

"Oh. That was a joke?"

"That was a joke," Colt agreed. "To answer—no, I won't be offended." *It would be kind of hard to be after pawing to the thought of you.*

"I have been reading. And I am curious about Terran attitudes towards a certain topic. One of relationships."

"Alright. Please go on."

"I am interested in the attitude towards… Relationships between two males."

"Sexual relationships?"

"Yes."

"I see," Colt responded, taking another sip of his drink

"Forgive me. My asking feels… forward. In our culture, this is not something that is discussed often—if at all."

"Your society frowns on same sex relationships?"

"Before it was simply private, but since the Than'kink ministry and the death of the old Emperor they have become much more 'frowned on' as you say. But I guess from your question that it is not so in Terran culture?"

"It was—long, long ago. Now? They are still uncommon, comparatively, but are an accepted type of relationship."

"Ah. How uncommon are they?"

Colt looked across at his guest, who was studying the table with rapt attention. In his mind, he heard the beep of a starfighter launch warning. However he answered that question, there would be no going back. He hesitated. What if Sakai was simply curious about something that was unusual to him? Or worse, what if he was looking for some reason for his government to discontinue ties with the Federation?

Colt looked at his drink. Drake hadn't thought the orca was up to something like that. If he'd smelled something off, he wouldn't have pushed the otter into this. Colt swallowed, caught between his doubts and his commander's assurances.

His trust in Drake won. He downed the rest of his whiskey, took a deep breath, and hit the launch button.

"Fairly uncommon. But, if you want to know more about them, you're in luck. Drake and Wash are a couple."

That brought Sakai's eyes off the table up to meet the otter's. Colt smiled at the orca.

"I also prefer males."

Sakai said nothing, staring at the otter as his tail swept the floor behind his chair. The dark purple eyes blinked repeatedly, but no words escaped the orca's snout. Or at least Terran words: a low whistle followed by a clicking sound did come out. Colt's whiskers twitched as he resisted the urge to let out a nervous chitter of his own. Sakai finally let out something resembling a snort and finished his own drink. He set the glass down and reached for the bottle. He took it and offered the otter a refill which Colt accepted.

"That is… interesting," Sakai finally said.

The awkward silence reigned as both took long pulls on their drinks to cover it. The otter recognized that the orca was as nervous as he had been his first time—perhaps even more so. But that was expected from someone who'd grown up in a less gay-friendly culture than Terra. Colt waited, his own stomach doing flips. Would Sakai actually be interested in him specifically? What if he just wanted advice on how to approach someone else? The otter's thoughts were broken when he realized that Sakai was looking up at him.

The orca's snout opened and closed a few times without saying anything. He stared at the table again, and muttered something in Chanthu before his eyes again returned to Colt.

"Then you would not be offended if I said that you were attractive?"

Colt's heart leaped into his throat. Heat rushed into his tiny ears and he fought the urge to hide his face behind his paws.

"Not in the least," he said after an eternity.

"You thought about that for a moment," the orca remarked, turning away from him. "I—"

"No!" Colt lunged forward, splaying across the table and seizing Sakai's wrist. "It's not that. I just. I. Uh. Would you be offended if I said that you were attractive too?"

Sakai stared down at him. A look of sheer joy threatened overwhelm his face. Finally he laughed, and Colt felt his heart flutter at the sound. He let go of the orca's wrist and pushed himself off the table. Sakai stared down at him. A look of sheer joy threatened to overwhelm his face. He laughed, and Colt felt his heart flutter at the sound. He let go of the orca's wrist and pushed himself off the table. Sakai reached a paw up and wiped away a tear.

"Ah. What fools we are. Like, what is the Terran word? Teenagers experiencing romance for the first time."

"Yeah," Colt responded with a chuckle of his own. "I remember my first time asking another guy if he liked me. Almost threw up on him, I was so nervous."

"Well, it seems mine is going better," Sakai responded. "Although my stomach is unsettled."

"This is your first time?"

The orca nodded, the color of embarrassment still on his furless cheeks. Colt studied him. He looked so different from Terran species, and yet in many ways he was just like they were. The otter hopped off the bed and walked over to the other, taking Sakai's cheek in his paw and gently turned the orca to face him.

"I'm flattered that you chose me. I'm honored. I'd love to show you just how much."

"Are you sure? Our governments will not like this."

"I don't care what they think or like. I care what *you* think and what *you* like. And if you'd like to do this, then I want to as well." Colt locked eyes with Sakai and let his defenses down so the orca see that he was serious.

Sakai broke away first. "You have the advantage on me. I have never done this before."

"It's easy. Like swimming in a river: you just go with the flow."

With that, Colt leaned in and touched his nose to Sakai's snout. The orca hesitated a moment, but followed the otter's lead and rubbed his nose against Colt's. Colt gave him a playful lick before backing up and smiling. Sakai blinked and stared down at his snout, much to Colt's amusement. Colt pressed forward and locked muzzles with the orca. It took a moment, but the last of the Chanthu's resistance shattered and he let the river guide him.

He lunged forward, pulling the smaller otter off his paws and into a tight embrace that sent shivers down his tail. Sakai's scent filled Colt's nose, evoking memories of sun on the sand and a salty ocean breeze. The orca was wearing a deodorizer that added a layer of a citrus-like fruit. Colt threw his arms around the bigger male, holding the kiss for as long as he had breath. When he withdrew, a new scent had filled the air—almost fishy, but somehow warmer. He guessed that was what an aroused orca smelt like. He giggled as a new pressure against his leg added more evidence that he was correct.

"So," Sakai said. "Where does the river take us?"

"Uh. Heh," Colt replied. "To start, have you ever bottomed before?"

"I am not familiar with this term," the orca said with a frown. "But as I said, I have never acted on my attraction to males before,. but I have been with females when I was trying to convince myself otherwise."

"Ah. Well. I guess that's me, then. Now let's take a look."

Colt reached out to the collar of the Chanthu's jumpsuit. He took hold of the zipper and looked up for permission from the orca to continue. Sakai nodded, and Colt unzipped it to the bigger male's crotch before reaching up to the other's chest and pulling back the fabric to expose him.

Colt chittered in delight at what he found. As expected, Sakai was lean, but with muscles prominently displayed due to his lack of fur. Like Colt himself, the underside of his chin, his throat, and the front of his abdomen were all white. The black skin of his back crept around his flanks around the middle of his abs. His pectorals looked especially round, an effect the otter guessed was heightened by the fact that Sakai's arms and shoulders were mostly black. As his eyes dropped, he found that the orca was wearing a pair of tight-fitting briefs that were struggling to contain Sakai's excitement. Colt let his eyes trace the silver lines of decorative markings on Sakai's arms and flanks and let out a whistle.

"Do. Do I please you?" Sakai asked.

"Very much so." Colt replied. "You are quite attractive."

Fingers reached out to take hold of the otter's zipper. Colt looked up at the orca and gave a nod to his silent request for permission. The zipper slid down the front of Colt's jumpsuit. He shifted his shoulders to let it fall away, leaving him exposed.

Sakai let out a low whistle and a series of clicking sounds. Colt's ears heated again as his whiskers twitched. For the first time in months, he considered what he looked like to someone else. He was average size for an otter, which left him a head shorter than the orca. He had an otter's slim build, but the outline of well-toned muscles were visible through his brown fur. He also wore a pair of briefs that bulged with his excitement. Bulged quite a bit. Sakai whistled again.

"I think you are bigger than me," he said, his tone clearly impressed. "I was not expecting that on a smaller body like yours."

"Yeah," Colt said, fidgeting under the orca's scrutiny. "That's how I got my call sign: I'm hung like a horse."

"Horses are known for their large… what is the euphemism?"

"'Equipment?' Yeah," the otter confirmed. "You wanna keep going?"

"I would. I assume we both fully remove our clothes?" Sakai asked with a chuckle.

"Yes. Oh shit! I forgot something!"

Colt looked towards his bag, but knew it was futile. He didn't have what he wanted. His mind raced, and it dawned on him who would have it. His paws darted down to pull his jumpsuit back up. He zipped up and darted to the door.

"Be right back!" He called over his shoulder.

He dashed down the hall and skidded to a halt in front of Drake's door. He hammered on the door before he remembered that the rooms had a doorbell. He was just reaching for it when the door slid open with a wave of de-scenting spray that made Colt cough.

He looked up to see Drake standing in the doorway, dressed only in boxers… and a black leather collar. The wolfox's fur was matted, especially around his face and neck, and his expression hovered halfway between annoyance and concern. Colt winced as he realized what he'd interrupted. Drake glared at the otter.

"I thought I ordered you to have a good time. You're too damn pokey to have followed that. What the hell did you do wrong?"

"I. Uh. Could I borrow some lube?"

"You didn't bring lube?" Wash's voice called out from the room. "Why the fuck not?"

"Look, I wasn't expecting anything like this and it's my first time away from the fleet in a while and I wasn't sure if there would be bag checks—"

"Alright, alright. Calm down," Drake interrupted with a wave of his paws.

"Don't suppose you'd have a condom too?" Colt asked sheepishly as Drake turned back into the room.

Wash replaced the wolfox in the doorway, dressed only in a towel with his ringtail still soaking wet. The look he gave Colt made the otter want to shrink into the floor.

"You know I've been with the same guy for almost six years now, right?" He asked, skipping the obvious statement that none of Drake's condoms were going to fit the otter.

"Oh."

"Relax Colt," Drake said as he returned and held out a small bottle to the otter. "I did the reading. Their biology is different enough that disease transmission should be difficult. But you'll be reporting to sickbay when we get back to the ship."

"Yes sir," Colt replied as he took the lube.

"Good. Now get back in there."

The otter saluted and took off down the hall. As he reached his room he heard Wash ask Drake,

"Were you wearing your collar the whole time he was here?"

***

Colt grinned at the orca lying on his bunk as he brandished his prize. Sakai smiled back and chuckled.

"I guess that is lubricant? I am surprised you did not have any."

"Yes, well. I wasn't expecting this situation," the otter replied as he padded over to the bed.

"I see," the orca replied. "I may not have done this before, but I have read much. Perhaps intercourse would not be wise then?"

"I'll be fine," Colt reassured him as he set the bottle on the table. "I'm not that out of practice."

"Very well. If you insist."

"I do," the otter said as he unzipped his jumpsuit and let it fall to the floor before he crawled onto the bunk. "Now. I want to see what my new friend has to offer."

"I hope it is to your liking," Sakai chuckled as he lifted his hips to allow Colt access to his briefs.

The otter hooked a couple of fingers under the orca's waistband and slid them down his legs. They came off easily—Sakai had undone the fastener above his tail while he was waiting. The orca squirmed a little as he was exposed, reminding Colt that Sakai was experiencing this for the first time. The otter smiled and chittered to let him know he liked what he'd uncovered. Liked, and found rather interesting.

Unlike Terran mammals, Sakai didn't have much in the way of external equipment. His crotch was smooth, with only a slit to mark where his cock would come from. Or was coming from—the orca's pink shaft was still peeking out, much to Colt's delight. He leaned in, pressing his nose close, and taking in the warm ocean scent. Sakai let out a gasp that became a moan as the otter's breath played over his shaft. Colt giggled as he watched the orca twitching.

"Been a long time since I had sushi," the otter muttered.

"What? I am a mammal not a—Oh…"

Sakai's question was interrupted by the otter's warm tongue running up the underside of his maleness. Colt squeaked as the rest of the orca's shaft launched like a missile from his slit to full arousal. Sakai's erection was rather different from his—it was almost tentacle like, thicker at the base and tapering to a point, but with a distinct head that was already leaking clear pre-cum. The otter watched as it wiggled in the orca's excitement.

"Impressive," Colt chittered, giving it another lick. "Been a while since I played with one this large. Let's see."

Sakai let a few clicks and whistles, but didn't manage anything in Terran before the otter gripped his shaft teasingly took the tip into his muzzle. He worked his way down the orca's length, taking his time and massaging the underside with his tongue. Colt saw Sakai's head back, his eyes closed as little squeaks and clicks of pleasure escaped his snout. The otter moaned around the thickness filling his muzzle, part of his mind analyzing that the orca didn't really taste different from the Terran guys he'd been with. He swallowed a few times as he worked down the orca with a steady pace, easing his way along until his nose crested on the shore of Sakai's crotch. The orca let out a contented sigh as the otter began to bob his head.

Colt took it slow his first few times, making sure he was comfortable with the warm thickness in his muzzle, but soon he was working with the rhythm of an incoming tide. Sakai's shaft throbbed against his tongue, letting out a spurt of pre almost every time the otter hilted him. Colt slowed his pace—he might be curious to know what Sakai's seed tasted like, but he wanted a different hole filled right now. He was just about to pause his attentions when the orca let out a cough. Colt looked up the orca's torso to meet his eyes.

"You are still wearing your underwear," Sakai said.

Colt released him from his muzzle. "So I am."

"Perhaps we should fix that problem?"

Colt grinned and pushed himself up off the bed. His paws dropped to his waist. But before he could hook his thumbs into his waistband, Sakai was shaking his head. The orca made a casual "come here" motion and patted the bed. Colt grinned, but pointed to the floor. Sakai nodded and rolled onto his side as the otter slid off him.

Sakai leaned over and pulled the otter's briefs down to the middle of his thighs. Colt shimmied to let them fall to the floor while the orca stared at why the otter had earned the nickname "Colt." He let out a low whistle, provoking an embarrassed chitter from the otter.

"That is quite lovely. And impressive. What is this under your penis?"

"We call them 'balls' generally." Colt replied, feeling his ears heat up.

"I see. May I touch them?"

"You have permission to touch anything you wan—oh..."

Sakai's paw gently taking hold of his sac broke the otter's train of thought. The orca caressed his orbs, running his thumb along them and giving them a gentle squeeze before exploring up the otter's sheath to his erection. Tentatively, his fingers traced the otter's hard-on before forming a ring and giving it a few strokes. Colt shuddered and let out a squeak as he closed his eyes and let the pleasure fill him. Too soon, the paw on his cock vanished and he opened his eyes to find Sakai looking up at him with crimson cheeks and a sheepish smile.

"I do not think I am prepared to return the favor from earlier."

"Don't worry about it," Colt said taking hold of the orca's wrist. "For now, as your liaison, it's my duty to teach you how to fuck this ass properly."

He playfully yanked on the orca's wrist as he spoke. Sakai chuckled and slid off the bed. Colt grabbed the lube off the table and guided his partner to the wall at the head of the bed. There he popped the top and squeezed a bit onto his paw before passing it to Sakai. As the orca lubed himself, the otter reached under his tail and rubbed, fingers tracing around his ring before he slid one inside, followed by another. He rotated them, making sure everything was slick. His shaft throbbed with the attention.

Satisfied that he was ready, Colt withdrew his paw from his rear and gave Sakai a smile. The orca was smiling as well, his nervousness faded as his instincts took over. The otter turned and slapped his paws against the glass in front of the waterfall. The babble of running water filled his ears as he wiggled his hips at his partner.

"So hot shot, think you can find the target?"

"I think so," Sakai chuckled. "Though, guidance would be appreciated."

He stepped closer, getting a moan out of Colt as the firm pressure of his erection squirmed between the otter's cheeks. Colt reached his right paw back and took hold of the orca's shaft, leading it to the goal. He aligned the tip with his hole, letting it rest teasingly against his ring. He fought the urge to slam his rear against the orca's hips.

It's his first time—you need to be an instructor. A really horny instructor.
"Got it from here?" He asked with a wiggle of his hips.

Sakai chuckled as he placed a paw on the otter's hip and pushed into Colt's waiting entrance. The otter gasped as the biggest thing he'd taken in months slid past his ring. Sakai stopped and pulled back before an otter paw landed on his rump with an audible *smack.*

"You're… oh. Keep. Going," Colt stammered.

He shuddered in ecstasy, his eyes closed as he moaned. He'd missed this so much—the feel of another inside him. He played with toys– but it just wasn't the same. His cock throbbed, and he felt himself beginning to leak.

Sakai hesitated too long and the otter shoved himself back against the orca, taking his full length all at once. The orca staggered, but managed to keep himself under the otter's tail. Colt braced himself against the glass and rocked his hips, riding the bigger male even though they were both standing. Sakai was ready, and held his ground as the otter slid up and down his length.

Colt was in heaven. The orca's shaft throbbed each time he reached the other's hips, and his own cock pulsed in time with it. Sakai let out a clicking sound that was absolutely adorable. He wondered what the orca thought of his own chittering as he kept up his pace. They changed to a surprised squeak as he felt the orca's cock wiggle—just enough for him to notice. The sunny beach scent of Sakai's musk filled the air, mixing with the otter's own somewhat earthy scent. Colt sighed in contentment, but already felt the pressure building in his loins. *Damn, not going to last long.*

As the thought passed through him, Sakai leaned in close and whispered in his ear. "May I take lead?"

"Go. Uh. For it."

"Alright. Have you ever done this underwater?"

"Not in a long time. But I like it."

"Then you may love this…" Sakai leaned forward and reached out to press the control next to the waterfall. It was the one control in the room that wasn't labeled, so Colt hadn't touched it. The orca tapped two buttons and chuckled.

Without any other warning, Colt's paw sunk into the "glass." The otter barely had time to gasp before his arm was submerged and the water splashed down it. Sakai leaned in, the taller male's head covering him just enough that the water ran over Colt without giving him worries about accidental drowning. Sakai had a blowhole and no such concerns. The water poured over them, cool at first but quickly warming with their body heat. Colt loved it.

"Please," Sakai whispered through the babble of water. "Tell me if I must stop. But I am afraid I will not last much longer."

"Me either," Colt replied, leaning up to nuzzle the underside of the orca's chin.

"Do you wish me to finish inside you?"

"Mmm. Fill me up, handsome."

There were no more words after that—just the grunts, moans, and other sounds of mating. Sakai took the lead, pressing against the otter and working his hips to work Colt's rear. His furless thighs slapped against the otter's rump, splashing water over the tiled floor. Colt leaned forward under the pleasurable assault, putting both paws against the wall as the orca's tempo picked up to rapid storm waves. Over the rush of running water, Sakai panted as the orca quickened his pace to a frantic sprint towards climax. The pressure inside the otter built with each of the orca's thrusts, threatening to burst and send him over the edge. Colt wondered if this would be the time that he finally went hands-free.

He didn't find out. Sakai let out what sounded like the recordings of whale songs Colt had heard and slammed himself one final time against the otter. The orca's shaft throbbed as Sakai released deep inside him. For a heartbeat, he thought he felt himself swelling as spurt after spurt filled him. The orca shuddered and collapsed against him, blocking the water from flowing over him completely.

Sakai didn't neglect his partner. Even as the orca's weight settled against him, a paw slid around the otter's waist and took hold of his cock. Colt squeaked in surprise, which shifted to a moan when the paw began stroking him. It took only a moment to get the otter panting and pressing himself tight against the warm muscular wall of orca behind him. Sakai took the hint and stroked even faster, nuzzling the otter's tiny ears as he went.

Colt let out a groan and shuddered. He shaft throbbed and erupted in a fountain against the wall. Sakai paused as he spurted again and again, then released the otter's shaft to take hold of his chest as Colt's knees gave out with the bliss of his climax. He opened his eyes to see the last of his seed disappearing down the waterfall drain.

Sakai chuckled and lifted the otter back to his paws. The orca had slid out of the otter sometime during his orgasm. With a grunt, Sakai pulled Colt to the bed and they fell in it together. Colt summoned up the energy to roll into a position where they both could lay comfortably and the orca down next to him. Colt smiled and put a paw on the orca's chest.

"For your first time, that was pretty good."

"Thank you," Sakai replied, mirroring Colt by placing a paw on the otter's brown furred chest. "I am happy to have such a skilled teacher."

Colt winced at the joke being brought back up. For a long time they lay there in silence, and Colt almost dozed off. Sakai's voice brought him fully awake.

"I would be willing to do this again, if you are also willing."

"I'd like that," Colt replied.

"But I should tell you something."

Uh oh. Colt looked up at him. "And what's that?"

"In Chanthu culture the…" He trailed of, then shrugged and said something musical in Chanthu. "That is everything."

"Was that the word for family?"

"That would be a possible translation. It is more complex than that, and encompasses more."

"On Terra, some species—like wolves—have the concept of 'The Pack.' I think you're talking about something similar. We call a 'pack' of whales a 'pod.'"

"I see. 'Pod.' Such a simple word for something so important. But my point is that by tradition, certain things are shared only with the pod. What we just did is one of them."

Colt blinked and stared up at Sakai, his whiskers twitching. The tip of his tail smacked the bed behind him.

"Traditionally, such activity… consummates a relationship."

"Did we just get married?"

"No!" the orca laughed. "It has not been that way for centuries. But usually, it would make us… I do not remember the Terran word for males in a committed relationship."

"Boyfriends?"

"Yes, thank you," Sakai rubbed the otter's chest. "I did not mention this because you were enjoying yourself, and have said this is not the case on Terra. But. Even in the brief time I have known you, I feel that I would be willing to engage in such a relationship. I do not ask for it though."

Colt was silent for a long time as he thought. He knew the answer should be "No," this was a one night stand with an attractive guy because he hadn't gotten any in almost a year. And yet, a lot of that was his own choosing: Wash and Drake had made an open invitation to him as the other gay guy in the squadron to help him blow off steam. He hadn't taken them up on the offer, but had thrown himself at Sakai. Perhaps there was something more to this than he understood. He chittered and licked his muzzle. This wasn't going to be easy—not with possible war clouds brewing.

"I don't know if we're boyfriends. But if you want to keep up a relationship, I would like that."

"Do you believe we can make this work?" Sakai asked after a moment, pulling the otter close. "It will be a long time before we can see each other again. If at all. There are elements in the government that continue to call for breaking ties with Federation. Some even go so far as to suggest hostilities."

"I don't know," Colt replied. "But I know I want to try."

"Then, I will try with you," the orca said, pressing his snout between the otter's ears. "The entire galaxy cannot wish to keep us apart."

***

Outside his cockpit, the world turned to flame.

Colt ignored that, focusing on the readouts of his fighter—the otter knew that if he panicked now, he was dead. Ejecting was bad enough in the vacuum of space—doing it in a planet's atmosphere was another layer of difficulty. His eyes danced over his displays as he fought the control stick to keep his crippled craft on something like a proper reentry vector.

"Seal cockpit pod. Prime evac boosters," he called out, glad for the second time in his career that someone had had the bright idea to give the Gryphon voice commands for the eject sequence. A pilot's paws tended to be a little busy when they were crashing.

For a heartbeat, Colt wondered how his squadron mates were doing out there before he snapped his attention back to Gamma Caninari. Drake had made it clear before the battle that the Federation couldn't afford any losses. Colt had failed to save his ship, but he could still save a pilot. A ping in his helmet speakers snapped his attention back to his own situation: he'd gotten the Gryphon into proper ejection orientation. He took a deep breath, reached up to tap his helmet seal activation in case the pod's failed, took tight hold of the control stick, thumbed the confirmation button, and focused on keeping his tail still.

"Eject!"

Even braced, the otter was surprised by the rapid change in his situation. One second, he was in his dying fighter alarms wailing over the roar of improper reentry; the next, everything was silent as he drifted down towards the planet. Looking past his knees, the Gryphon rolled over in its death dive. Then it was out of sight, leaving only a contrail to mark its passage. For a moment, everything was peaceful.

A timer appeared on his HUD, counting down the time until the pod touched down. He grimaced—almost ten minutes. He sighed and flipped his comms back on just in time to hear Drake order the Terran fighters back to their new home at Walcott Intrusion.

"*Intrepid* just went to FTL," Crimson said. "We're committed."

"We knew the deal," Drake reminded him. "We're going to do our part to hold off anymore attempts on the base."

"Besides," Wash put in. "We gotta pick up Colt."

The otter coughed. "Would be nice."

"Good to hear from you," Drake quipped. But there was no mistaking the relief in his voice. "Oh, eyes up. The Tango that got you is crashing in the same sector."

On cue, the Chanthu fighter streaked past, flames enveloping its aft section. Colt winced—he couldn't tell if the pilot had ejected or not. Sakai said that atmospheric ejections were so tricky in the Tango that it was almost better to crash. The otter didn't know if he hoped the pilot had ejected or not.

"Anybody catch the name of that 'phin carrier? Was it one that tore the fleet up at Perseus Halo?" Crimson asked.

"Translator program is still chewing on it," Silver responded. "But the profile suggests it wasn't."

"They only have six carriers," another Viper put in. "Was it that one that we tangled with six months back? The *Glorious Dawn*? Is that the one here?"

"Don't think so," Wash said. "Glyphs are different. Could be the other one. The…"

"*Concordant Waves,*" Colt whispered.

"That's it," Silver agreed. "She's the one we're up against."

Colt winced and stared past his legs at the column of smoke rising from the forest. He looked back up at the purplish-blue sky as fear turned his stomach to ice.

"Have we gone up against that one before?" Drake asked. "Some of those fighters' moves seemed familiar. I'm sure I've seen the one that got Colt before."

The unease growing in the otter became crystal certainty. He hissed. "Boss. We got the second wave of fighters?"

"Yeah," the wolfox responded. "We got their best pilots. Probably the wing commander too. Why?"

Colt didn't answer—he slapped the controls on the arm of his seat, bringing up the limited scanners and maneuvering thrusters. He tracked the Tango's trajectory and probable crash site. He edged the pod in that direction.

"What the hell are you doing, Rudder?" Drake's voice returned over his headset.

Colt looked up and saw they were on his private channel. "I have to know."

"If it's him?" Drake asked. "It's been a year and a damn war. And what if it is? What then?"

"And if the ground pounders get to him first?"

Silence confirmed what the otter had already guessed—if the Army found the downed enemy pilot first, he was dead.

"I can't let them do that, boss," Colt pushed the button to mute all his comms and pushed the pod's thrusters as hard as he dared.

***

It took an eternity for the pod to thump to the ground. If he was going to investigate the crashed Chanthu fighter he had to move: his escape pod was automatically broadcasting his location for rescue.

When he got the all clear, he jerked off the restraints, popped his helmet, and slid out of the seat barely trying not to catch his tail on anything. He turned back and reached for the survival pack under the seat. As he pulled it out, his paws brushed the pistol attached there. He hesitated. Shooting down another fighter in combat was one thing, but shooting another being face to face... Could he do that? And if his hope/fear about the crashed Chanthu pilot's identity was wrong...

Colt snatched the pistol, checked the charge, and shoved it into his belt. He shucked the survival pack, checked his coordinates on his wrist-mounted datapad, and headed off in the direction of the other fighter.

***

Colt finally saw the wreckage through the trees and hesitated. The ship was surprisingly intact. He swallowed and wondered if that would be a good thing or not. Was he being a fool? The odds of that being Sakai in there were astronomical. Even if it was, it was unlikely that the pilot had survived the crash. Compared to his Gryphon a Tango was positively primitive—especially when it came to crash safety equipment.

The otter sighed. Above all that, other concerns filled his mind. What if it *had* just been a fling for Sakai? Yes, they'd kept in touch in the twelve months since they'd met, yes they'd sent encrypted videos of them enjoying some "private" time to each other—but that didn't make it love. The videos had stopped after four months, and the messages all but stopped a month before the attack of Perseus Halo. Did that mean the orca wasn't interested in Colt anymore? And yet… The last message he'd received from Sakai had been the one that tipped the Federation off to the location of the Black Star pirate base—information that had sent the *Intrepid*'s taskforce out to investigate and kept them from being caught in the Chanthu attack. Would Sakai risk treason to protect someone he didn't really care about?

Colt broke into a sprint, dropping his paw to the pistol in his waistband. His heartrate spiked as he recognized the symbol behind the cockpit: a winged serpent type creature similar to the dragon that Drake used. The snake was a mottled black and white, like cub storybook cows—or an orca. The otter groaned as that realization sank in, and the pistol fell to the ground as he slammed into the still warm fuselage of the fighter. His fingers traced over the kanji-like glyphs, looking for the one that Sakai had pointed out.

He found it, dug his fingers into the slot, and yanked on the lever contained there. The cockpit canopy shot open, knocking the otter to the ground. He scrambled back to his paws, and took a hesitant step forward.

Another step brought him close enough to see a black and white snout peeking out from the helmet. He swallowed again as he stepped up onto the wing of the Tango, trying to get his heart out of his throat. The last doubts fell away: Colt could see the unforgettable silver of the orca's neck tattoos through the visor of his helmet.

The otter shook as every possible emotion hit him at once: fear, hope, recognition, despair, joy, anger. But two questions overrode every other thought and emotion: was the orca still alive? And did he still care about Colt? He had to know. The decision made, all the emotions drained out of him—he knew what had to be done. He hoisted himself up to the cockpit, prepared for the worst.

As soon as his muzzle was fully inside the cockpit, he noticed the smell. Mixed in with the reek of hot metal, spilled lubricants, and burning wood was another subtle but distinctive scent—pine needles. Colt's heart stopped as his brain processed that. Pine. In Sakai's cockpit. He hadn't seen any evergreen trees around here, and this had a slight chemical tinge. Chanthu's climate meant that there were no evergreen trees on the planet. The only way for a native of Chanthu Prime to be smelling of pine...

Was for him to be wearing the deodorizer that Colt had given him as a parting gift.

Colt lunged forward, doubts gone. At long last he saw the slight rise and fall of the orca's chest. Sakai was breathing. The otter whispered a prayer to whatever deities there were in the universe while he ran his paws along Sakai, checking for obvious injuries. He couldn't find any, aside from the fact that the orca was out cold. Colt rocked back, sitting on the console as he tried to remember his emergency first aid training.

Moving Sakai was likely a bad idea. Going to get help was probably the best thing to do... if there was actually help to get. No, the only chance for Sakai would be for Colt to be there when he was found, claim the orca was a defector: that had given vital information to the Federation. But even that might not work.

I don't know. The words drifted up in his memory. *But I know I want to try.*

Then I will try with you.

His paws darted to the releases on Sakai's restraints.

The shuttle caught up to him ten minutes later—half carrying, half dragging the orca back to Walcott Intrusion. It took another two minutes for the shuttle to find a clearing and settle down. Colt stopped and waited, putting all his effort into not falling over with Sakai on top of him. It didn't take long for the rescue team to come bolting out of the trees: a couple of bulls and rams with rifles pointed directly at the orca.

"He's a defector!" Colt cried. "He's given information that kept the Navy in the fight!"

They didn't fire or tell him to get away from Sakai, but they kept their guns on him. They parted to allow a stoat in a corpsman uniform and another figure to pass: an orange furred wolfox in a pilot's jumpsuit.

The universe wasn't done with miracles today: the one person who could and possibly would keep Sakai from getting executed had come to pick him up.

"Colt!" Drake called out as he rushed ahead of the army soldiers, his tail wagging furiously. "Stand down, you four."

"Hey, boss." Colt sank to a knee under his load. "Can I get a paw?"

Drake slid to a halt and stared at the otter and his companion. His tail stilled and his ears folded. "That's him?"

"Yeah. What are the chances of that?"

Drake's eyes narrowed. "Colt. He's the one that got you."

"It happens," the otter replied with a chitter. He locked eyes with his commander, a silent prayer in his gaze. "Boss. Sniff him."

Drake took a few steps forward and did so. His eyes went wide. "Pine…"

"I gave it to him," Colt said.

Drake paused, then took the remaining three steps to the otter and helped him lift Sakai up. He turned back to the stoat. "How's your Chanthu biology?"

"Not great," the corpsman replied as he pulled his pack off his shoulders. "I can give a look and probably get him stabilized. But we'll need to get him back to base for a full work up."

"For a 'phin?" One of the rams asked. "Why waste time? Shoot 'em and be done."

"No," the wolfox said flatly. "This *orca* is the reason we're standing here. He's coming back with us."

They accepted that and turned their guns to the forest as the corpsman ran a medical scanner over Sakai. A moment later the stoat declared him fit to move to the shuttle. The two bulls snorted and took the orca while the rams covered them. The stoat followed after, talking into his comm. Drake followed after, with Colt in tow.

"What the hell are you getting me into this time Rudder-Tail?"

"I don't know, boss." Colt replied. His eyes followed Sakai as the UTF soldiers laid him on the shuttle floor and the stoat began doing a more thorough examination. "But I know we'll be doing it together."

To Adelio, for having the patience to put up with me while I'm working.

Painting the Prince

by Reverie

Marcoh sat outside the small cottage that served as his studio and living space, feeling flushed not only from the warmth of summer but from his rush to get the inside impeccably clean and organized for his guest. Contrary to the stereotype about boars or artists, he couldn't stand clutter, and this wasn't just any old visitor. No, today was Thursday, and like every Thursday for the past three months Marcoh's day would be spent with the most important client he had ever worked for in his entire career as a painter: Prince Reed, heir apparent to the throne of Cheyet. If ten years ago someone had told the painter he would be commissioned by the royal family themselves he would have laughed them off and shown his worst still life as proof of his unworthiness. But while he was no celebrity, word had spread about the obscure but breathtaking paintings of a boar living in the hills just outside the castle town walls. Be it a genuine appreciation for his work or a pompous desire to "discover new talent," someone at the castle had taken notice and sent Marcoh a request to paint a portrait of the prince in recognition of his 20th birthday. Somehow that news had spread quickly, and for the first time Marcoh found himself having to turn down clients to avoid overworking himself.

A bead of sweat crept towards Marcoh's eye from his brow, which he wiped away with the hem of his shirt, briefly exposing his potbelly. He was about to head back into his studio to escape the harsh sunlight for a moment when he saw a trio of figures come into view over the hills. Even at a distance he could immediately make out the black and white fur of a badger adorned with violet and blue garments only worn by the royal family. This was Prince Reed himself, being escorted as usual by two guardsmen, a black bear with a stern face and a grey wolf who panted miserably as they marched in the summer heat. Standing up, Marcoh dusted off his trousers and adjusted his shirt in a half-hearted attempt to look more presentable, which was difficult as he was in his paint-stained work clothes. As the prince and his guards approached Marcoh bowed and waited to be addressed, as was proper. The wolf guardsman stepped forward to speak, but had not caught his breath yet and merely wheezed as he struggled to form the words. Grunting in annoyance, the bear spoke instead.

"Marcoh the painter, I announce the arrival of Prince Reed, heir to the throne of throne of Cheyet, to your place of business for the purpose of continuing work on the official portrait of His Highness as agreed upon."

"I once again welcome His Highness to my humble studio," Marcoh replied, having learned his part by rote. "Would he like a refreshment while I finish setting up?"

Prince Reed himself spoke now; "I do not need any water, although it seems one of my guards would appreciate the hospitality." At those words the wolf guardsman stopped his panting and looked away in shame. Marcoh stepped inside and filled a mug with well water he had drawn earlier that day and offered it to the wolf, who quickly lapped most of it up before pouring the remainder onto his head.

"Forgive me for my rudeness," Marcoh said, "But there's only a few hours left of daylight, so I'd like to get started soon."

"Of course," Prince Reed replied. He then turned to his guards to speak. "You may return to the town for now. As always I'll be ready to be escorted back at sundown."

"If I may, Your Highness," the bear spoke up, "I think we should stay this time." The prince frowned.

"Did my father order you to say that?"

The bear hesitated. "His Majesty finds it odd that it has taken months for this portrait to be completed."

"My father is no artist." Reed looked over to Marcoh. "Good art takes time, doesn't it? The boar had often thought of himself as a slow but meticulous painter, but simply nodded, not wishing to get too involved in the dispute.

"I just think—"

"You're too uptight," the prince said, cutting off his guardsman. Reaching into his cloak, Reed pulled out two small purses that jingled with the sound of coinage. He tossed one at the wolf, who fumbled a bit but managed to catch it, and held the other out to the bear. "Why don't you buy yourself some company for the evening? It'll do you good." The bear stammered for a moment, then took the purse and walked away wordlessly. The wolf followed with his tail wagging, no doubt at the prospect of an evening with a lusty wench. Marcoh silently chuckled at the scene.

With the guards now departed Marcoh led Prince Reed into the small but mostly empty studio and got to work on preparations, setting up his easel along with a small table for his bushes and paints. He carefully pulled the half-finished portrait of Reed from the wardrobe he was storing it in and set it on the easel, then grabbed a chair from the corner of the room and set it against a wall he had painted off-white. "Now if Your Highness would sit here as I adjust the mirrors for light," Marcoh said with his back to the prince, "I think I can get the shading on the face done before it gets too dark, but—" Marcoh turned to look at the prince and was met with the sight of a pantsless badger standing with his legs spread, his manhood proudly displayed for the painter's viewing. Marcoh chuckled, dropping the facade of professionalism. "Already, Reed? You know, I would like to actually get some work done this time. Last week I didn't make a single stroke with my brush while you were here."

"I remember you were stroking something quite a bit," Reed responded cheekily as he made his way across the studio and embraced the boar. Marcoh put his arms around Reed and caressed his back, then brought his and Reed's lips together to share a more passionate kiss as their tongues danced together. Pulling away, Marcoh looked into the badger's obsidian eyes.

"You've got a lusty gaze about you. Don't want me to accidentally paint that, do we?"

"No, that would make for an inappropriate royal portrait. But I can't control how I feel about you, my big, strong boar."

"Well," Marcoh let out an exaggerated sigh of resignation, "I suppose I should help alleviate that feeling or we'll never get your expression right." At this Marcoh got on one knee, putting himself eye-level with the prince's now erect member. The tip brushed against his snout, which took in the familiar scent of Reed's arousal. "I can tell this won't take long anyway."

Reed started to retort when Marcoh leaned forward and took the entire length into his mouth in one motion, his lips forming a seal at the base as he ran his tongue along the underside. Whatever utterance the prince had made quickly became a gasp as he placed his paws on the boar's broad shoulders for support. With a free hand Marcoh gently handled the furry pouch between Reed's legs and bobbed his head back and forth. By now the boar had gotten plenty of practice stimulating the prince, and knew exactly where along the shaft to apply pressure with his tongue to get the best reaction out of him. It took only a few minutes of this before Marcoh could taste slightly sweet pre-come oozing into his mouth. Sure enough, Reed started to buck his hips in rhythm with his partner's motions. Gripping Marcoh's shoulders tightly, Reed silently urged him to go faster, and he obliged, a slurping sound escaping his lips as he pressed the badger's cock against the roof of his mouth. Over the sounds of flesh rubbing together Marcoh could hear Reed muttering incoherently, only catching a few words like "good" and "almost." Moments later Reed's bucking grew into outright thrusting, and Marcoh relaxed himself, allowing the prince to set the pace. With a sound that was somewhere between a growl and moan, Reed pushed himself as far into Marcoh's maw as he could before forcefully climaxing, his salty and slightly bitter come splashing onto the boar's tongue and against the back of his throat.

Marcoh allowed the badger seed to pool at the back of his mouth before swallowing and pulling away from Reed's fuzzy loins. Reed's slicked member was already shrinking as it slid out from between Marcoh's lips, and the boar couldn't help but chortle when he saw Reed's blissful expression. "That should tide you over," Marcoh said.

"For now, yes," Reed replied with a wink.

Marcoh shrugged as if to ask what he would do with the lusty prince. "Take your seat, Your Highness."

***

Reed sat in the chair as Marcoh painted him, partially dressed although he had declined to don his trousers. Instead he wore a confident smile, still feeling pleased from the oral stimulation Marcoh had given him. Marcoh saw this and thought back to Reed's first visit three months ago. At that time the prince was quiet and barely spoke, and when asked to smile could not do so convincingly. He kept letting his gaze become unfocused and allowed his pose to go lax. Marcoh had found this aggravating and after having to tell Reed to sit up straight and face forward countless times he felt a headache coming on and excused himself. He had contemplated heading into town and finding a tavern with a water pipe to indulge in, but decided the repercussions of abandoning the prince were not worth a moment of peace, so he walked around his studio a few times to calm himself before returning.

He stepped through the threshold and froze at the sight of what he found inside. Apparently, the prince had decided to nose about and stumbled across some old graphite sketches Marcoh had done when he was still living in town. He used to frequent the taverns and talk other men his age into following him to his place to pose as nude models. A few were tame enough that they could pass as simple anatomy studies. The majority, however, featured subjects in very explicit positions, often sporting erections or presenting their rears. Marcoh had bedded many men in his early 20s this way, but he had grown out of that, only keeping the sketches because he hated to discard his work even if he did not consider it his best. That, and to help himself remember the touch of another male during dry spells.

"You did all these?" Marcoh hesitated, and then nodded.

"My prince, I know the crown has outlawed such debauchery between two males, but a peasant can only ignore such impure desires for so long. Please understand." Marcoh's heart raced, thinking about the potential punishment he faced.

"These are… arousing." Reed traced a finger along a sketch of a horse gripping his own shaft with both hands.

"…I beg your pardon?"

"I'm no stranger to craving the companionship of another male. Your secret is safe."

"Thank the lord," Marcoh muttered under his breath, the weight on his heart lifting so suddenly he very nearly fell as he sat on the dusty floor.

"This one looks a lot like my teacher," Reed said calmly, holding up a sketch of a fox sitting in a chair—the same chair Reed was sitting in now—legs spread, sheath exposed, arms folded around the back as though he were tied up. "I was fond of him," the prince continued. "In my teen years when we were in the study together, no one else around… leaning over me as I did my arithmetic… I would often wish…" he trailed off and Marcoh noticed a swelling between Reed's legs. "I wonder if this is him."

"I wouldn't know," Marcoh answered. "This was about 5 years ago. I didn't ask many personal details, and probably couldn't pick him out of a crowd today." Seeing the disappointment in Reed's face, he added, "Did you and he—your teacher I mean, did you ever tell him how you felt?"

Reed shook his head. "As much as I trusted him, I never had the courage to talk to him. When I became an adult, his service was considered complete and he left the castle. I haven't heard from him since." The prince's expression soured a bit. "Just as well. I was too young for him; he probably didn't feel the same way."

"He might have called your feelings immature or misguided," Marcoh suggested. "I remember being young and lusty, seeing a handsome male and feeling like he was the one I'd spend my life with only to feel stepped upon when he left the room without even noticing me. A sad truth in life is that few if any fall in love just once." Reed pondered this and nodded in agreement.

"Since he left, I'd often find myself falling for total strangers who visited the castle." Reed laughed at himself a bit. "Here I am at 20 years of age and feeling as desperate as I did at 13. I may never enjoy the touch of another male. I envy you, really. You might not be royalty but that leaves you free to bed whom you please without scrutiny."

Marcoh bit his lip. If the prince was trying to flirt, he was terrible at it. Normally he'd just give the young badger a pat on the back and end their interaction with that old and oft-repeated advice, but he felt an aching in his own loins. Lust is a terrible thing, he thought as he stood, his slacks failing to hide his intentions. He placed a hand on Reed's shoulder, causing the badger to look up at his face… and then down at what was before him

"That doesn't have to be true."

***

Before long the sun was beginning to set, and there was no longer sufficient light coming into the studio to continue painting. "Alright, I think I've gotten a good amount of work done today." Marcoh looked over the portrait. Not bad for two hours of work, he thought to himself. Most of the shading on the face was now complete, though the eyes looked a bit dull. From a distance the portrait might already look presentable, but there was still a lot of detailing needed before it was truly ready. He picked it up and turned it around to face Reed, who stood up and beamed as he examined his likeness on the canvas.

"It looks like you're nearly done."

"Not quite. Look at those soulless eyes."

"You've made me look like I've seen a ghoul," the prince joked.

"I need to make the fur stand out a bit more, and I haven't really done much with the clothing. See? There's no shading there yet. It really sticks out. I also need to add a more defined background, though that part can be done without you"

"Ah, right." Reed tugged lightly at a patch of white fur on his cheek, as though testing the length. "If you had to estimate, how much longer would this take?"

"Well, working on it just once a week like this, probably another month. Though I could probably do a bit of work on my own time and cut that down by a week."

"Trying to finish sooner? Have you tired of me already?" Reed teased.

"Not at all! But if I get ahead maybe I can afford more time for you next week." As Marcoh said this he stepped up to the prince and took hold of his exposed length, feeling it twitch and begin to swell against his palm.

"Oh! I do like that idea," Reed said, placing a paw on Marcoh's stomach and sliding it down until he was caressing the boar's sack through his trousers. "Although that reminds me..." Breaking away from Marcoh's grip, Reed allowed his coat to fall to the floor and pulled his tunic over his head, fully exposing his naked form. The prince padded over to the wall behind the chair with a slight sway in his hips, wordlessly beckoning Marcoh to follow as he braced himself against the white surface and stuck his rear out with a playful wiggle.

Barely two seconds had passed before Marcoh had loosened the cord around his waist and dropped his slacks, stepping out of them and kicking them aside while his growing erection bobbed in the open air. Reed looked over his shoulder with a grin as he watched the pantsless boar trot to another corner of the room and kneel down to remove a loose floorboard. From this compartment Marcoh retrieved a medium-sized bottle of a substance officially marketed as an aromatic salve but was known in some circles to have a different, more pleasurable application. Pouring some into his hand as he made his way to the awaiting prince, Marcoh set the bottle down in the chair for easy access if they needed more, then squatted down and lifted Reed's short tail out of the way. Rubbing the fragrant ointment between his fingers, Marcoh watched with a perverted glee as the badger's sphincter relaxed without needing any preparation, a far cry from four months ago.

"A bit eager, I see." Marcoh ran his slick finger along the rim of Reed's hole teasingly, eliciting a pleading moan.

"It's been a long week, and I've been counting the minutes till today."

Slowly, Marcoh plunged his middle finger into the prince, twisting as he went deeper. Again, Reed moaned, reflexively clenching on the invasive digit briefly before giving way again. Marcoh pushed until he was knuckle-deep inside the badger. The tip of his finger found the prostate within, and Marcoh pressed upon it, causing Reed to whimper. Pulling out slowly, Marcoh rubbed down his own length with the rest of the slick ointment in his hand, then took his shirt off and wiped off the remnant before tossing the garment aside. He pushed his tip past the prince's fuzzy buttocks, prodding his hole teasingly. Reed decided that was enough build-up however, and pushed himself away from the wall, taking Marcoh into himself with a stifled murmur.

Marcoh grunted at the sudden warmth enveloping him. Truly the prince was no virgin anymore; this is what he wanted, and Marcoh would certainly give it to him. Grabbing Reed by the hips, Marcoh pulled himself partway out, only to ram himself back in, making the badger cry out in surprise. Leaning forward Marcoh held himself close to Reed, the coarse yet sparse fur on his stomach pressing against the softer grey fuzz on Reed's back. Again, he grasped at Reed's manhood, feeling the swollen organ in his calloused grip as he gave several quick thrusts into him.

Reed let out a whine as his body was shaken. "Please," he gasped, "use me... claim me..."

Marcoh bucked his hips roughly, each motion making Reed more and more vocal. Soon he had the badger pressed tightly between himself and the wall, a long and sustained moan coming from Reed as the boar's shaft was plowed into him. The two breathed heavily and in sync with each other as Marcoh's climax welled up. Although he personally wasn't fond of it, Marcoh bit into Reed's shoulder, knowing how it affected him. Sure enough, Reed's moan went up an octave, and the sound of the prince's unfathomable pleasure rang in Marcoh's ears as he hilted himself, releasing a flood of come into Reed's innards. Marcoh lost all sense of time as his orgasm peaked and slowly ebbed, but eventually the heat dissipated and the two stood there against the wall, sweat and seed dripping to the floor as they basked in each other's presence.

***

Marcoh looked outside and frowned slightly upon seeing the fading orange glow of the sun as it dipped below the horizon. "The guards will be back soon, won't they? We should make ourselves presentable."

"I suppose so," Reed replied forlornly. As the two went through their usual clean-up routine (a damp rag under the tail, burning foreign incense to hide the smell of sweat), the prince sighed and spoke up. "I don't want to stop seeing you."

Marcoh paused halfway through pulling his shirt on. "The painting probably won't be done for another month, remember?" He wanted to say something reassuring, but didn't know what else he could add, so he merely continued getting dressed.

"Normally there wouldn't be anything stopping me from continuing to visit you as an acquaintance after the portrait is finished." Marcoh scratched his chin. The thought hadn't really occurred to him, although he could tell there was a "however" coming up. "If I really wanted to," Reed continued, "I could even see about having you moved into the castle as an attendant. Lord knows there are documented incidents of the royal family having consorts live in the castle under the pretense of being servants." Reed's lips formed a crooked smile at that thought. "I once found some old letters that indicate my own great-great-grandfather was involved with the captain of the guard even as he sired 5 children with his queen. I could be married and stay with you. There is precedent."

"What's wrong then?"

Reed finished getting dressed and meticulously examined his tunic for signs of creasing to delay his answer. Finally, he spoke. "I'm to be married by the end of the year."

"Oh." Marcoh's reply was flat, and he felt like a hole had opened up in his chest. "I hadn't heard."

The prince looked at Marcoh, but averted his gaze and stared down at the floor. "The official announcement won't be until this autumn, but I'm being married to a princess from Myelan.

"Myelan is a nice kingdom." Marcoh found himself struggling to keep the conversation going to avoid any uncomfortable silences. "Is she pretty?"

"We haven't met. I don't even remember what her name was. I'm told I'll grow to love her. Perhaps I will." Reed gazed out the window although there was little to see in the dying light of the day.

"I feel like I'm supposed to congratulate you, but that seems inappropriate."

"Arranged marriage comes with being royal. It's rare for any of us to choose our spouse. I always knew something like this would happen, and really, I might not mind too much if I could keep you nearby."

Marcoh was about to ask what the problem was then, but changed his mind and instead asked, "Is there a different reason why you don't feel comfortable with the arrangement?"

Reed finally looked back towards Marcoh. "It's all a political ploy. My father wants to forge an alliance between our kingdoms."

"That's not, erm, a bad thing, is it?"

"Not by itself. But my father's real goal lies with Esche."

It had been a while since Marcoh looked at a map, but he remembered that the Esche Republic was a small nation south of Cheyet and west of Myelan. "What's in Esche?"

"Did you know that Esche used to be a Duchy under our kingdom's rule until about 80 years ago?"

"Yeah, I've heard as much." Like most common citizens Marcoh lacked an extensive education but he remembered how as a piglet his bedridden grandfather occasionally spoke of the "traitors" in Esche.

"My father wants to use the alliance with Myelan to cut off Esche's eastern trade routes and cripple their economy."

"Why?" Marcoh suspected he already knew the answer but didn't want to jump to conclusions.

"To pressure Esche into reunifying with Cheyet." Reed's voice trembled slightly with restrained rage. "Esche didn't rebel, they negotiated for their independence. My father doesn't understand that because he refuses to read any of our castle's records. And now he's marrying me to a woman I don't know at all because he feels entitled to land that hasn't been part of our kingdom since before even my grandfather was born." Reed stood up and paced impatiently about for a few seconds. "I just can't stand by and watch a whole nation be subjugated in such a way."

Marcoh didn't understand much about politics, but wanted to offer some kind of advice. "I'm sure there's something that can be done." Reed did not look convinced. "Maybe you can—"

A knocking sound interrupted Marcoh's thought. He got up and opened the door to see the two guards. Judging from the faint smell of perfume and sweat on them and the bear's softened demeanor, they had indeed purchased the time of some women in town. To Marcoh's surprise, this time the wolf spoke up. "We're here to escort His Highness back to the castle."

"Of course," Marcoh responded. "We were just waiting for your return." Looking back towards Reed, who now made his way to the entrance, Marco added, "I bid you safe travels on your return, Your Highness."

"Until next time," Reed said with a somewhat distant expression. The prince stood in the threshold momentarily, then added "actually, I'd like to come by tomorrow as well."

Marcoh and the guardsmen looked at Reed with puzzlement. After a moment the bear spoke up. "Your Highness, that's not on your schedule. The agreement was that you'd come only once a week to avoid taking all of the painter's time."

"I am aware," Reed said, "but Marcoh here told me he just needs to put the last touches on the portrait before it's ready, and if it's alright with him I'd like to go ahead and get that out of the way."

Marcoh was taken aback by the claim. What could the prince be playing at? Was he tiring of his visits, or could there an ulterior motive? The boar locked eyes with the badger, looking for some kind of unspoken message. He decided to play along for now. "Yeah, it's nearly done. Don't wanna keep the royal family waiting."

"That settles it," Reed declared, clasping his paws together. "Father certainly won't mind if it means getting the painting sooner than expected."

The guardsmen exchanged glances but said nothing. The four stood in uncomfortable silence until Marcoh interjected with "alright! I'll see you tomorrow, Your Highness. Same time as today."

"Of course. Until then, farewell." Reed and his escorts turned to leave. Marcoh watched for a bit as they disappeared into the night, then closed the door and turned the latch on it. As he prepared for sleep, Marcoh kept wondering why Reed would want to see him tomorrow. Dozens of ideas ran through his head, some bordering on paranoia.

Marcoh did not sleep well that night.

***

The following day saw Marcoh waiting outside the studio again. There was no need to tidy up again and so he sat calmly by the door eating a fig as his lunch, trying to push the sense of dread he had been feeling toward the back of his mind. There were clouds in the sky and so the weather felt fairer than yesterday. Eventually the familiar trio of Reed and his guardsmen came into view over the hill, although this time they paused before coming any further. Reed seemed to be saying something to his escorts, which Marcoh couldn't make out from where he sat. The exchange went on for a few minutes before Reed made his way forward, leaving the guards behind. Had it happened any time in the past Marcoh might have been relieved to not have to interact with the guardsmen but now it made him feel uneasy. Reed was smiling as he approached however, and Marcoh felt some of his discomfort ebb. Perhaps a good night's sleep had done the prince well and cleared his mind.

"Hello," Reed said with a cheerful tone. He looked back over his shoulder and waved the guards away. "Sorry for imposing on you like that last night."

"It's no problem," Marcoh replied, deciding not to mention how worried he felt about the prince's actions. He opened the door to his studio and as the two entered, he added, "I think we should get started right away if they think the portrait is almost done.

"Oh, don't worry about that. I admitted that I was saying that just to get out of the castle today." Even more pressure had been taken off Marcoh with those words, and he felt he could breathe more easily.

"I guess there's no rush then?"

"None at all. In fact," Reed stepped closer to Marcoh and placed a paw on the boar's hip, a sultry expression adorning his face. "I want you to take me before we do anything else."

Marcoh was a bit unsure of leaving things as they were for the moment, but Reed's paw worked its way to his loins and lust soon clouded the boar's judgement. Moments later two sets of clothing lay in a heap by the door. The pair had retired to Marcoh's bedroll, where Reed's legs were draped around Marcoh's waist as the boar plunged his girth into him from above. Marcoh could feel his climax building and tried to shift his posture to allow a more vigorous reaming, when a bead of sweat that had been hanging on his brow fell into his left eye. He grunted in discomfort as he reflexively winced, causing the other eye to be hit with the salty drippings as well. Marcoh tried to keep going despite this but the burning sensations had killed his orgasm.

"Your eyes are closed."

"Huh?" The sudden comment made him pause mid-thrust. He forced his eyes open, though the stinging had not yet subsided.

"Just felt like… never mind," Reed said a bit flatly. "Should we change positions?"

"N-no," Marcoh wiped at his eyes with his forearm. "Just got some sweat in my eyes; it burns a little…" the boar looked at the figure underneath him and saw that Reed's erection had waned. "Are you alright?"

Reed unbound his legs and allowed them to rest, which Marcoh took as a sign to pull out. He helped the prince sit up and the two sat there for a moment in silence. Finally, Reed spoke.

"I'm leaving."

"Leaving? Back to the castle?" Marcoh's heart sank, wondering if he had done something wrong.

"No, I mean… Tonight I'm leaving Cheyet."

Marcoh felt as though his innards had frozen. He opened his mouth to say something, but he had too many questions and struggled to utter anything coherent. Finally he managed to meekly ask, "why?"

"I can't be a part of my father's plans." Reed stood up and began to pace around.

"Did you try just talking to him?" Marcoh knew that was a ridiculous question to ask.

"Of course I did!" Reed's words carried a bite of rage with them, but he paused and composed himself. "He's long since made up his mind, stubborn as ever."

Marcoh thought carefully before making his next suggestion. "Well, you are in line for the crown. Maybe you could wait until you become king and work to reverse the damage done to Esche?"

Reed shook his head. "My father is king for life. It could be decades before I succeed him. And what if he is successful in forcing reunification upon Esche? Would I, as king, simply turn them loose again?" He paused to allow Marcoh to think but could read his response on his face. "True, some would see it as a kind gesture, but others would at best think me sanctimonious, or protest to me giving away land."

"Are you just," Marcoh cringed at the thought of what he was saying, "abandoning Cheyet? If the only prince disappears into the night, what will happen to the throne? Won't others challenge for it? There could be a civil war. Not to mention how Myelan might react to your engagement to their princess being called off." Marcoh examined Reed for some sign of remorse at his plan, but it seemed the prince was fully aware of what may happen.

"My father fancies himself a genius; I'll leave him to deal with the consequences." Reed's expression softened, and he looked at Marcoh the way he often did in their intimate moments. "Marcoh, do you love me?"

Love wasn't a word the boar liked to use lightly. "It never seemed like anything more than a pipedream, but I did often find myself thinking of a future with you."

"Then come with me. We could go anywhere, as long as it's away from here. I don't want to be your prince anymore; I just want to be yours."

"I…" Marco felt as though he were choking. He took a deep breath. "I want to follow you…" Reed smiled, which only made what Marcoh said next more painful. "But Cheyet is my home, the only one I've known. I'm not a young boar anymore. I don't have the courage to strive for a new life. Even to spare another nation from suffering I couldn't abandon the land of my birth."

"What about to spare me from my suffering?"

Marcoh was silent. Several minutes passed, neither of the pair uttering another word. Eventually, Reed gathered his clothing and dressed himself.

"What now?" Marcoh asked.

"I'm returning to town. I'll tell the guards you weren't feeling well and couldn't work anymore." Reed turned his back and headed to the door.

"Is that really where you're going?"

Reed glanced back, but returned his gaze to the entrance. "I won't allow them to suspect you had a hand in any of this."

"You still intend to leave then?"

Turning around, Reed looked Marcoh in the eyes one more time. He was trying to appear stoic, but Marcoh could him struggling to fight back tears. "You were the one part of my life I wasn't ready to leave behind." Before Marcoh could react Reed composed himself, giving the painter a stern look. He turned on his heels, and padded outside, the door slamming shut behind him.

Marcoh stood alone in the dimming light. He moved as though in a trance before sitting in the same chair Reed would occupy as he was being painted. Would he really leave Cheyet tonight? Maybe the Reed that Marcoh knew months ago wouldn't, but in that short period of time the young prince had grown into a different badger. If he said he would leave, there was no room for doubt. Wondering what news would spread throughout the land tomorrow, Marcoh looked upon the unfinished portrait of Reed, its dull, unlit eyes now perfectly matching the prince's own as he left.

For Othello Rysingson, who has supported me for many years and through many late nights.

SILK AND SWORD

by NightEyes DaySpring

The silk is smooth in my paws, its dark lustrous nature beautiful, its allure appealing, and its shame upon me unmistakable.

"I thought you would want something appropriate for tomorrow."

I look up at Usman. The cheetah's expression is apprehensive, and I know why. Men do not wear silk; it is taboo. "It's beautiful," I whisper, trying to keep my emotions in check.

"I hope it fits right. My wife got the fabric from Hafiz last month. He said the silk would go well with your fur coloration. Farida cut and tailored it just for you."

I look down at the fabric. Holding it in my hands, the dark green silk contrasts well against my sandy fur. To wear this will mark me as less than a man, but is that not what I am becoming?

"Zayn?"

I look up at Usman again. We are standing in his market stall in the caravanserai, tucked in the back under the arch of the nook it occupies, away from the bright light of the courtyard beyond. Ceramic cooking vessels and plates are stacked up around us along with a couple of sun-bleached carpets tucked against the back wall. A collection of iron cooking utensils sits out front on a rug along with some colorful plates that catch the sun outside. It's a setting I know well, but today it feels different.

"Sorry, just admiring her work. Thank you." I manage to get out.

The cheetah wrings his hands together. "Do you want to try it on?" he asks me cautiously.

I gulp and nod. "Yes."

"Then let's go somewhere private," Usman suggests.

***

We jackals have a proverb we tell our children: opportunity, like a good meal, does not last. Both my parents were fond of this saying, and those words have been on my mind a lot during the last month. This is a great opportunity for me, and also the crux of my descent.

We have retreated to an alcove inside the caravanserai where goods are stored. A half dozen large, clay, water storage jars sit on one side while some baskets are stacked on the other. By shimmying between them to the back of the alcove, there is some privacy behind the baskets where they obscure the view from the main hallway. Only a little mid-day light filters in through the high-cut windows, but even here in the shadows, I know I can't hide my shame.

The dark green fabric, with bits of emerald green thread interwoven into it, is soft against my golden pelt. I would not have thought it a good match, but wearing it I realize why Hafiz selected it. Even in the low light of the alcove it shimmers.

The cut of the skirt is excellent. It drapes off my hips while leaving the front open and my tail free. I must give Usman's wife, Farida, credit for this. Her craftsmanship is impeccable. She has even sewn a line of small beads on the hem and provided fabric for me to tuck under myself to cover my maleness. She has completed the look with a simple top that covers only my upper chest, leaving my stomach and arms exposed. The top is a little loose, but I'm sure I can have her adjust it. Included in the clothes is a scarf of sheer dark blue fabric to dance with.

Of course, all her expert work still doesn't change what is happening to me and instead reinforces it. Now that I'm wearing this, my manhood is truly gone. My father died by the sword out in the desert, cut down by raiders. I am to be pierced by a different kind of sword.

"Well?" asks the cheetah.

"Farida does good work," I manage to get out.

"She does, and Hafiz was spot on about the fabric. You look very striking in that."

My ears fall back. I know why Hafiz knew the fabric would look good on me. He regularly comes to sell here, and I've caught him staring at my tail before as I go about my odd jobs. He knows what I am be-coming. The fact I fit this new position in life so well concerns me. Have I always been destined to do this?

"Zayn," says the cheetah, obviously picking up my hesitant feelings, "you don't have to go down this path. We'll think of something else for you."

I close my eyes. "I can't keep borrowing money from you, Usman. I still don't know how I can repay you for this."

"Don't worry about that. The cut of your earnings is enough."

"Right." On top of his normal work as a trader, Usman arranges the dances, and each dancer pays a small bit of their purse to him. I will do the same, just like the other girls. From his fee he pays the musicians and earns a few coins for himself.

He sighs softly. "You've been practicing your footwork, like I suggested?"

"Yes, Usman," I say, with a bob of my head. For the last two months, whenever they do the dances, I follow along on the roof of the caravanserai, letting myself twist and twirl through the darkness of the night just like the dancers in the courtyard below, trying to fix the beats in my head while the girls earn their keep.

He nods and runs a clawed hand through the fur on top of his head. "Then tomorrow, I will debut you. I have clients willing to pay good coin for one of your proclivities."

I nod and start taking the outfit off. I don't want to be reminded of my shame right now.

"Zayn?"

I stop and look up. "Yes?" The skirt falls to the ground, but I resist the urge to pick it up. I need to get comfortable being exposed now.

He wrings his hands. "Your father would be proud of you. Both your parents would be actually."

"What?" I glare at Usman and then gesture down. "Proud of this? Of me?"

He looks away from my nudity. "Yes," says the cheetah. "You're stronger than anyone else I know. It takes courage to do this, especially for a man. One does not simply lie there and take it without suffering the scars of their profession. Your father was a survivor, no matter where the rains fell. You have to be here in Zaptu. He always kept his ears up for trades to make and goods to transport. He didn't go down in that raid without first taking a number of the attackers with him. Few would notice, but I see that same steel within you."

I don't feel any steel inside myself right now. I feel only the crushing sensation of what I'm undertaking. My mind wants to cry out in panic, but I am holding it down. Maybe that is my strength in this. "Thank you."

The cheetah claps a hand on my shoulder. "I try and make sure all my dancers earn good coin. I will do my best to make sure you do as well, so you can retain your family honor."

I nod, and he walks off then, leaving me to take the top of the silk costume off in private. Slowly I pull it off and carefully fold it up.

Since Hafiz chose the fabric I'll be wearing, I can only hope that means he is looking to buy my attentions for the night. He knows what I'm going through. He has always treated me well, and I know he shares my proclivities. I'd like my first night to have some meaning. Amare, a wolf a few years older than me, has told me about his times with Hafiz, so perhaps tomorrow I'll finally get the chance to experience it firsthand.

That hope helps stills some of the dread inside of me.

***

I remember when I was young and my parents' house had furniture in it. My father worked hard as a trader and caravan master. Like most homes here, it's made of mudbrick, but its two small rooms are comfortable. We had wall to wall carpets, wooden chests to keep our cookware and clothes in, and a divan. My parents even had a bed, but when father died, my mother slowly had to sell off the furniture to make sure we could eat. When she died, I sold the rest of it. Now the two rooms are empty save for one carpet, my sleeping mat, and a chest that was too battered to fetch much money.

Before me is a small plate of dates, the only food I could afford in the market today. These dates are overripe and past their prime, but I used all the coin I had left to buy them. Odd jobs around Zaptu are hard to come by, and I owe the Emir taxes. It's only a few dinari, but if I don't pay soon, he will lock me up and give my home to someone else. Usman can't afford to employ me as an apprentice, and while he has been able to kick me some work, I cannot rely on that.

My father's sword and one of my mother's shawls sit on the carpet across from me. These are the last personal effects of my parents I still own. Next to them, the silk outfit is also sitting on the carpet, waiting for me. A small clay bottle of olive oil sits on top. I'll need that once my client for the night pays for my attentions.

I pick up a date and chew on it, letting the sweetness play across my tongue. There is a sourness underneath the sugar, but these will give me the energy I need for tonight. I've already brushed out my tail, but I couldn't afford a bath today. Water is scarce on the edge of the dunes, so the bath I took two weeks ago will have to do.

There comes a knocking that pulls me out of my thoughts. Getting up, I go and unbolt the worn wooden door. "Yes," I say, swinging it open, letting the bright light of day flood over me. Outside is a jackal with a pelt darker than my own.

"Oh good, I was hoping to catch you at home, Zayn."

"Hafiz! I did not expect you to come by." We exchange formal cheek kisses. "Come in, come in! My home is your home."

"Thank you," he responds, and when I gesture to the carpet, he goes and sits down.

"Would you like a date?" I offer, reaching down and lifting up the plate. Even though it is all the food I have, it is customary to share my meal. Even in my growing poverty, let no one say a guest in my home was mistreated.

"Just one," he responds, taking a date and tossing it into his muzzle. He cringes as the taste hits, but he swallows. "Thank you."

"Things go well?" I inquire, walking over to the chest to pull out my battered kettle. "I can brew tea."

He holds up a hand. "There is no need. I wasn't planning to stay long." He gestures to a spot across from him, so I can join him on the rug. "I need to get back and help pack up my stall. I have my two assistants already doing that."

"You are leaving?" I say surprised, as I sit across from him. He generally makes the three-day journey south to Zaptu once a month to sell for a week. He only came into town two days ago.

"Tomorrow. Sales are slow, and while two caravans just came into town, they don't trade in cloth. I'll return north and see how things are going back home. I'll be back through next month."

"Well that is sad news, but you are coming to see me dance tonight?"

He flicks his ears. "You are doing it tonight?"

I wave my paw over to the silk. "Usman gave me the outfit yesterday. I've been practicing."

His gaze follows the motion of my hand. "Farida is quite the seamstress I hear."

"And you have quite an eye for color. It matches my fur well."

The other jackal smiles. "Excellent," he remarks, "I look forward to tonight then."

My tail wags. At least my first customer will be someone I care for. "I can show you a preview, if you wish."

"Oh no. I'm happy to wait till tonight. Plus, I don't want to disturb your preparation."

143

"Sure," I say, with a little regret. I forget to keep my ears up.

"Oh, don't be so disappointed," chuckles the other jackal. "You need to be focused on tonight. This is your big moment. I did want you to know though, I'm not going to be through this area much anymore."

"Why not?"

"Trade has been shifting south, and most the caravans are heading straight for the Sultanate of Khalin. Plus, the local Emir has raised his taxes to compensate for a lack of income. My trip next month may be the last trip I make in a while. Unless things change, I'm not going to stay and sell."

The markets in the city of Aksu are said to overfill with goods, enriching the Sultan who rules on the other side of the mountains.

"You'll need to go to Kantara to buy fabric, won't you?"

"Only for the silk and cotton I can't get locally. I'm considering making a trip to Aksu next year to buy fabric. I sit on too much of the high-priced stuff now."

"Ah," is all I can say.

"But tonight, is your night. I can't wait to see it." He leans forward to give me a cheek kiss. "I will see you later."

"Of course, Hafiz."

He gets up, and I lead him to the door to let him go. I watch from my doorway as the other jackal strides out into the bright light of day, heading back to the caravanserai that dominates this small town. I guess I should finish getting ready for this evening. Tonight with Hafiz will be bitter-sweet, but this is my life now.

***

I leave home just before the sun touches the horizon. It is still hot out, but it will quickly cool once the sun sets. I have the silks wrapped up in a bundle of cloth I carry under one arm. At my hip, I have my father's sword, its presence reassuring. The eyes of my neighbors flirt over me, but do not linger. No one says hello either, and that surprises me.

Zaptu is a small village of mud brick homes clustered around the stone walls of the caravanserai. Nestled in a little valley among the foot-hills, the entire town spills out from the caravanserai's main gate. To the west lie the mountains and to the east the great sands stretch out to the horizon and beyond. Trade is the lifeblood of our little town, otherwise this place would be little more than a well and a palm tree grove.

Life here is always hard. There are years it doesn't rain, years where the only grazing for sheep and camels is far away. The shepherds some-times have to travel quite a distance to feed their herds on what little vegetation the dunes and hills can provide. Only by offering a good re-spite from the elements for those weary souls who reach our home are we able to survive out here.

The caravanserai is the center of life in our little town. A square stone structure with high walls, it shelters the travelers who pass thru here. The interior of the building hosts a grand courtyard with nooks off it that traders can rent to sell their wares. Spread around the building are the baths, storerooms, and sleeping quarters that serve the weary. Our Emir also makes his home here, along with the treasury of the village. A single gate controls access to the fortress.

Once inside those stone walls, I run into Amare. He has set up a small stand to sell kebabs near the gate where he is cooking over a camel dung fire. The wolf is bent over the coals, carefully tending the meat when I walk up, so I have to call to get his attention.

"Hey, how are sales tonight?"

He looks up at me and quickly glances down. "Good."

"I'm surprised you are in here," I say, coming around to the side to talk to him. "Are you moving over from the village square permanently?"

The wolf looks up at me and slowly stands up. "Zayn…" he says softly.

My ears splay confused. "Yes?"

He glances around. "We can't—" he stops to gulp, "we can't be seen together anymore. You know that, right?"

"What!" I say shocked.

"With you taking up the dance, I don't want anyone asking questions they shouldn't." He bends back over the fire.

"Amare, we're friends," I hiss.

The wolf's ears flick at the sound of my voice. "Do you wish to buy a kebab?"

Is that it? Are we no longer friends? "Amare…"

"Do you wish to buy a kebab?" he repeats, not looking up at me.

I stand there gawking at the wolf. I have not yet stepped out wearing the silks, and already I am unclean? It can't be the act of sex with a male either that turns Amare away from me. I know what his heart desires, but to admit that in public is anathema?

I turn and slowly walk away into the crowd milling about the court-yard, the parcel carried under my arm. Glancing around, I can see fa-miliar muzzles turn away when I meet their owner's eyes. I don't want to be here now if this is how I am to be treated. Already my shame is known it seems. I am only to be an object to be desired, and no longer a presence to be acknowledged.

"Zayn!"

I stop. Usman is coming up to me through the crowd. He puts a hand on my shoulder as I turn to meet him. "Once they've finished lighting the lanterns, the crowd will begin assembling for the dances."

I want to speak, but my throat is tight, so I just nod.

Even though dusk is falling, my limp tail and stiff posture is unmistakable. "Are you going to be ready?" he asks.

"Usman, by doing this, am I unclean?"

He blinks and pulls his hand back. "Who said that?"

"Amare won't talk to me anymore."

The cheetah rolls his eyes. "Amare thinks no one knows what he does in the stable at night with the visiting camel drivers. I have heard stories."

"Yes, but… am I unclean now?"

He glances around. "I never said this would be easy. You know that," he says, so only I can hear him.

"That still doesn't answer my question."

"Because only you can answer that. Only you can feel the shame others might try and force upon you." He looks around the courtyard, and in that moment, the cheetah looks older. There is gray fur around his eyes and flecks of gray in his hands. "But no matter what they say, only you will feel the hunger in your belly," he adds.

And then I realize what I should have known before. Usman doesn't run the dances because he wants to see young woman sell themselves out. He runs the dances because he knows from experience what drives someone to this point. I have seen the way some of the older adults of our village treat Usman and give him a wide berth. I thought they had disagreements that dated to before I was born, but now I see it was more.

"You've done this yourself, haven't you?"

The cheetah nods.

"Why did you never tell me before?"

He tilts his head and chuckles. "Because you must make your own decisions. It was years ago also."

"And yet some remember, don't they? They still think you're less of a man."

He shrugs. "Some will never forget, but time heals many wounds."

He stops to take in a breath. "Do you wish to still take up the mantle?"

I don't have to do this, but I can't expect Usman to support me either. He has a wife and two young kits now to feed. He's done all he can do for me without me doing something for myself.

I suck in my breath. "Yeah."

***

The lantern light is low, but I can see the other dancers getting ready as I pull the top over my head. The silk garment falls neatly around my shoulders, and I tie it into place. The fabric is velvety against my paw pads. It has a heavenly feeling to it, a far cry from the rough wool and cotton I normally wear. I check the skirt to make sure it is lying right. My maleness is covered by the fabric, but its presence can still be seen in the bulge it produces. I close my eyes for a moment, just letting this sink in. It's too late now to turn back.

A good dancer can earn up to four or five silver dinari a night if they're lucky, although two or three is common. The dancers usually perform twice a week at the caravanserai, although many do private engagements. Work follows the rhythms of the caravans, and tonight we have two new ones in town. It looks like we'll have a good crowd tonight, so everyone should get a buyer for the night.

"Do you have your routine down?" one of the other dancers asks me.

I open my eyes and look at who addressed me. A jackal named Nawra is standing before me. She has red silk draped from her hips, and a heavy, silver necklace hanging from her throat along with silver bracelets at her wrists. Her breasts are left exposed.

"Yes. I've been practicing it as often as I can."

"Good. Now don't focus on any one person too long. The more you flirt, the more tips you'll get. You never know who might want to bid either." She points to the sword on top of my clothes. "Are you doing a sword dance?"

A sword dance is dangerous. Dancers have been known to cut themselves on their own blades. "I hadn't thought about that, but I could try. I brought it more for moral support."

She shakes her head. "If you have not practiced it, do not attempt it. Later, after you've danced a few times, I can teach you how to do that."

"Thanks," I mumble as she looks me over.

"Do a quick twirl for me," says Nawra.

I oblige her and perform a twirl.

"Good, but you need to watch how you let your tail flow." She demonstrates for me. Her tail neatly whips around behind her as she turns. "Now you try it."

I repeat the motion for her.

"Again," she barks, "and be mindful of your tail."

I do it again, trying to keep my tail from flying everywhere.

"Better. You'll need to work on that, but it will work for the moment. Good form can earn you some extra coin."

"I'll try and keep that in mind. I'm kind of nervous about tonight."

She smiles. "Usman will make sure you earn well."

It's more than just the dinari, at least for tonight. Next time, it will just be for the coin. "I think I know who will bid on me tonight."

She quirks an ear at me. "Don't ever count on that. You earn your keep by pleasing the whole crowd, not one person."

"You have your admirers, don't you?"

She shakes her head and claps a paw on my shoulder. "I haven't earned as much silver as I have by being anyone's favorite. Sure, some will take a liking to you and come back, but it's never a sure thing. Every good whore knows that if you ever fall in love with one of them, they'll end up breaking your heart."

My ears fall. I know Hafiz will only be here for tonight, but surely some of the girls have stable clients.

"It's a tough lesson to learn," adds Nawra. "It took me a while myself, but do not despair. We look out for each other, and that will include you, Zayn."

I don't know Nawra that well, so I just nod. She lets go of me, and before I can dwell on her words, Usman comes in to make sure we're ready.

After Usman collects our personal effects for safekeeping, we wait inside the caravanserai until Usman returns to get us to begin the night's festivities.

The troupe comes out of the building in a procession to yips and growls from a raucous audience happy to see us. The nine of us take seats on cushions next to the musicians beside the small area that serves as the stage. They place me in the center of the group, signifying that I'll be in the middle of tonight's program.

As I'm taking my seat, I see Hafiz in the audience, who smiles and waves to me. I flash him a smile back, and he bobs his head in response.

Usman steps forward and gives a short spiel to the prospective buyers. Then the first dancer, a lioness who has been doing this for a number of years, gets up, steps out, and begins her routine as the musicians start to play. The ney, with its soft whistling notes, and the oud, with its plucked strings, combine with the beating drums to create a tapestry that tickles the fur in my ears and entices the body to move.

When the lioness finishes, the bidding is quick and with a seductive flash of fangs from her, her attentions for the night have gone for three and a half silver dinari. The next dancer then steps up and takes her turn.

Nawra goes just before me. "Watch my tail," she advises as she gets up and she steps out in front of the audience, a set of zills in each of her hands.

Once the music starts, Nawra's movements are smooth and fluid, as the drums beat out a quick tune for her. She follows along with the zills, using the finger cymbals to accent her movements. She is graceful, her hips mesmerizing, and indeed Nawra does place her tail carefully as she moves, her spins and shimmies expertly executed. Her body responds to every note of the music, the drums driving her forward. The audience is enraptured by the thrust of her hips, and even I can appreciate the sensuality of her movements.

When she is done, she takes a bow, and Usman steps up to begin the bidding for her attentions. The calls are quick, and Nawra walks away with four silver dinari and three coppers to a caracal trader. He grins toothily at his prize as the money exchanges hands and then leads her away.

With Nawra's dance complete it is now my turn. I get up and smooth down my clothing before walking out carrying the sheer blue fabric Farida provided.

There are some hoots, but the crowd is quieter than it was for the other dancers. Still, I smile to the audience and bob my head respectfully, not looking up to meet anyone's eyes. My role is to be the receptive partner, so I don't want to look aggressive. It is time for me to offer my wares.

"And now for a treat we haven't had here in a while," calls Usman to the audience, "may I introduce our newest performer, Zayn."

There is muted applause and Usman steps back, leaving me alone in the middle of the circle. If I wanted to back out, it's truly too late now. The whole town can now see my new role. My heart beats fast, but I keep my body still, waiting. It feels like forever before the music starts.

Finally, I hear the first notes for the song I asked for, my song for tonight. I spring into action then, placing my feet as I have carefully planned out as the ney begins the song, followed by the drums.

At first, I feel stiff, my motions nervous. My footwork is sloppy, and I find myself out of sync with the drums. I have to pivot faster than I intended to catch up, and that leaves me with more momentum than normal. A second correction, and I drop back in sync, getting the carefully practiced stomach roll right.

Slowly I'm able to loosen up. Having watched the other dancers up close, I'm aware how much better I could be. I can only hope that my hips, stomach, and ass offer something alluring to these men that they haven't had a chance to bid on in a while and that covers up some of my missteps. I do my best also to control my tail, just like Nawra suggested, but I can tell I will need to practice these motions later.

At one point, while doing a hip motion with my left side, I catch Hafiz watching me in the audience. Eye contact is brief though, and it's impossible to keep my focus on him. I also remember I'm supposed to please the whole crowd, so I let my gaze wander through the audience.

Near the end, I have my steps in sync with the drums and ney, and I finish on a high note. I take a quick bow as people clap. It sounds like I've won over some doubters with the response I get. I pant and wag my tail; I've done it, and now it is time to bid for my attentions. In that break, I glance over to Hafiz again who smiles, still clapping. Usman steps up and nods to me before he turns to the audience. "An excellent first dance! Now, who would like Zayn's attention tonight?"

There is a murmur. It has been quite a while since a male has performed here, so I don't know what to expect.

"Half a Dinari," calls out a voice I don't know.

"Half to start. Do I hear three quarters?" responds Usman.

I look toward Hafiz, who smiles back at me. He hasn't placed his bid yet.

"Three quarters!"

"A full silver!" retorts the first voice.

This is good, but I hope they won't try and outbid Hafiz. I glance around to see who is trying to buy my attentions.

"Excellent," says Usman. "Anyone else?"

There is a murmur of voices from the crowd, but no on one else speaks up.

"A silver Dinari going once! Going twice!"

Why hasn't Hafiz bid? I glance back toward the jackal, but I can see him talking to someone now.

"A silver dinari it is then," calls Usman, the cheetah rests a paw on my shoulder. "Good luck, Zayn," he says softer, just to me, as he pulls out from under his kaftan the small bottle of olive oil he's holding for me.

"Thanks," I whisper. I turn and walk to the side. I can see a leopard coming over to me. Through the crowd, I glance toward Hafiz, but the other jackal is gone. He never planned to buy me attentions, did he? My heart falls at the thought.

"One silver dinari," says the leopard, holding up two half dinari coins, now that he is within earshot. I don't know who he is, but I think he's one of the merchants who came to town today. This isn't who I was supposed to be with tonight. This isn't who I wanted to be with tonight.

"Yes, sir," I manage to get out. I hold out my hand for the money, trying not to let it shake. He drops the coins into my palm, and I quickly pocket the coins into a pouch in my dancing outfit where I've tucked the bottle of olive oil. I try and smile to welcome my customer. "And where shall I entertain you this evening?"

The leopard grins. "Come. I've rented a room here tonight that will be comfortable. I trust you can provide all services?"

"Of course, from now until dawn."

The leopard smiles, a smirk creeping onto his muzzle. "Excellent." He turns. "Come then, let us take our leave."

Dazed, I follow him into the inside of the caravanserai. As I walk away from the crowd, I glance back toward Usman. He's just introduced the next dancer and is stepping back. I will have to ask him tomorrow how he came to do this. I want to look for Hafiz, but I have to keep up with the leopard. My time for the rest of the night is no longer my own.

We enter the building and he turns toward where the rooms rented to travelers are. I follow the leopard down the hall, my mind racing, trying to make sense of what just happened. Did my dance displease Hafiz? Did I go for more money than he expected? Surely, he must have known I'd command at least a silver dinari. Many of the other dancers go for much more.

In my dazed reverie we turn a corner, and I'm forced to look up. There is Hafiz, talking to one of his assistants in the corridor. I let out a soft bark and stop dead in my tracks.

The other jackal looks up, then quickly turns back to his assistant, and keeps talking louder than before about some wool he sold earlier in the day. I step forward and stop. His ears twitch, but he does not glance my way.

The leopard turns to me, having gone a few steps further. "You aren't going to keep me waiting are you," he asks, tapping a foot.

"Coming," I say through gritted teeth, walking past Hafiz. The other jackal doesn't look at me as I pass, and each step is like a stab in my heart. In my new role, like Amare, he will not associate with me now.

Down the hall the leopard stops and takes out a key to unlock his room. As the leopard opens the door to his rented quarters, my blood pounds in my ears. He takes a lantern hanging against the wall in the hall and lights it before he ushers me into the room. Then he hangs the lantern on an iron hook in the room before he closes the door behind us.

"Undress and get on the bed."

I gulp. This is it. This is who I've become. This is what I do now for a living.

"Yes sir," I whisper, slipping the silk off, after taking out the small clay jar of olive oil. I let the silk fall to the ground, and I force a seductive smile. As I get on the bed, I can hear a low contented rumble from my client. I do not care what his name is; I just hope that he will be gentle.

For my incredible friend Jelly who puts up with all my nonsense. I would not be half the writer I am today without you.

FLY TRUE

by Significant Otter

"I love you, Sidney," my porcupine said.

"Love you too," I said back to him. He didn't notice that my voice was hollow.

When he leaned forward to press his short, bristly muzzle against mine, I held back a grimace. The kiss was gross and wet. I didn't like the taste of his spit and wanted his muzzle to be out of mine as soon as possible. Luckily, his hardness pressing against me through the fabric of his boxers served as a good distraction. I latched onto the sensations of heat and pressure until his lips seemed so distant.

Ken always talked about the wispy fluttering butterflies in his stomach. I'd felt that with my anxiety, but never in a good way like he talked about. His heart was larger than life with such a capacity for love. I didn't deserve it.

I swallowed hard and smiled at Ken—a big buck-toothed smile pasted over top of my insecurities like only a groundhog can make. Against my instincts, I leaned in and pecked another kiss on his chin. That was better than on his lips, way less gross.

I mouthed, I do deserve your love. He couldn't read lips, though.

I knew I loved him. The feelings weren't what he described, or like what I saw on my sitcoms, but he was so good to me and I liked him more than I liked other people. That's what love was.

"I already said I love you, Sid. You don't need to go whispering it," the porcupine said, teasing a claw down my side. It hit a spot near my waist that rattled my body with a fur-raising shiver. "I don't mind when you do though."

I did need to say it. I worried about myself. I forced those thoughts away to make everything okay again. I didn't like kisses or care about hand holding or anything, and that twisted up my stomach into knots. I looked up into his smile and faked my own smile. I shuddered. Those

155

thoughts weren't good.

No, we were okay. I repeated that in my head. Everything was okay. Sure, his affection went further than it would in my ideal relationship, but that affection made him happy. I liked to make him happy, even if it meant enduring him getting all gooey when I just wanted to watch a movie. I had to re-watch so many on my own just to figure out what actually happened in them.

"Can't have myself forgetting." I winked at him, then buried my next kiss in the ragged fur near the base of his neck.

I lingered there before I pulled away. His warm paw ran a last circle through the fur of my chubby belly. He knew what it meant for me to get up right then—right after that tenderness. His paw had been adventuring down my thigh, and his eyes flicked between mine and the strained fabric of my boxers. His own warm understanding rested against my leg as I stood up.

Walking to the light switches, I sneaked another quick look at my porcupine laying there on his bed, waiting for his groundhog to come back to him. He offered a narrow-browed devious smile that I returned wide with the added intensity of my two big front teeth.

In a flip of the switch, the lights snuffed out and I was safe.

The first few times I turned the lights off, it was just due to anxiety. I knew back then that I couldn't go forward with sex with Ken, even though I had wanted to. It would have been nice to let him see the pleasure he was causing me through the expression on my face, but I feared that he would notice there was nothing more. No spark.

I could never get his expressions out of my mind when we were having sex. He made these hilarious, unintentional orgasm faces that I caught glimpses of through the moonlight that shone through the thin shades over his window. Of course, I made them too. We poked fun at each other for them in our afterglow. However, what really hit me—the reason I turned the lights off after the first few times we had sex—was a certain shimmering sparkle in his hazel eyes that mine didn't have. He looked at me with intense adoration. His smile bunched up like mine did when I was a kid on Christmas and I saw the box I knew had my new Game Boy in it. Only, his was like that all the time. I did my best to treasure him. He was an awesome dude. But that adoration that I saw in his eyes made me feel like I was playing an amateur league while he was off competing in the Olympics of love.

I was hard for him. He made me feel so good. Still, something in my mind said he'd be devastated if he ever realized that my love wasn't as strong as his.

I lay down with my back to Ken. His arm found my side and he pulled me to his chest. It was easier this way. The second time we had sex, I wrapped him up in my arms and spent the next hour in the emergency room. I had been too terrified to pull the dozens of two-foot-long needles from my forearm myself. We still had accidents of course, but they were fewer with time and familiarity.

His shorts were gone. A slim, lengthy line pressed against my boxers. God, I wanted to shuck that fabric right off and bury him sheath-deep inside me. But I took my time. The anticipation made me so wonderfully jittery.

He slipped his paw down into my boxers and wrapped soft fingers firm around my shaft. I felt where his pads slicked with the pre that I'd drooled in anticipation as we cuddled earlier. The rest of them were rough. Unlike those first few handjobs he gave me, he moved with a gentle, practiced ease. He tugged just right to draw my ears back and open my muzzle into an involuntary pant.

I slid my hand behind me to feel him. He wasn't hard to find. The pressure against my ass drew me right to his length. I knew what it wanted. It knew what I wanted.

My other paw awkwardly shuffled out from underneath me and patted the bedside table for the lube that always seemed to be set down in the last unchecked corner, no matter which that was. My cock was screaming at me to hump. My ass was demanding to be filled. My brain was simultaneously playing babysitter to both my ass and cock while hopelessly directing my paw to flail wildly in search of lube to make everything as it should be.

When I found it, the first squirt of lube shot straight over my hand to hit the bed. I swore under my breath. That was going to be a bitch to clean. I adjusted my grip so the second and third landed square in my palm.

That paw stuffed down my boxers first. I slicked the tip of my cock and the wiry porcupine paw wrapped around it. Pleasure prickled up my body, but not to half the extent it did when Ken's paw twisted it around to spread the lube in long, hard strokes.

Ken whispered in my ear, "You like that, groundhog stud?"

I groaned in response. I was quiet during sex, but Ken didn't mind. He taunted me and teased me, and I enjoyed every minute of it. When

157

I nervously made excuses after the first time we had sex, Ken just said, "You said all you needed with the way your tongue was lolling out of your muzzle." And he gave me a grin that told me I didn't need to worry about it at all.

I squeezed his shaft again with my lubed-up paw, and it was the hottest and the throbbiest and the shape the most perfect it had ever been. Somehow that was the always the case. It was like I got to see my favorite movie again for the first time. My paw slipped along its whole length, feeling every vein, dip, and ridge. I tried to picture it's each and every contour. My own cock throbbed. Ken stroked his paw down hard, tugging against my sheath, and I breathed his name.

I guided his tip between my ass cheeks and then tried to press back against him, a difficult task when we were already so close together spooning. My boxers stopped me anyway. I never took them off. I'd been so wrapped up in the sensations of feeling him and him feeling me that even that simple detail had escaped my single-minded attention. I felt like an idiot, but tried to play it off by dragging his tip slowly up and down along the crease of my ass. His breath caught. When the fabric's friction against his tip became too much the whole bed rattled from his convulsing shiver. That brought a big smile to my muzzle.

After shuffling my boxers down my legs and off my feet, I collected another squirt of lube on my paw before reaching back around my side and returning my touch to his slick cock. I turned my head to offer him an embarrassed smile, but I don't think he saw it very well in the dark. He leaned forward over my shoulder to nuzzle my cheek with the cool, wet tip of his nose. With us both on our sides, he was able to rest his muzzle light on my cheek. I tensed for a moment, wondering if he was about reach up to cup my muzzle and pull me back into a kiss. He didn't though, and that was nice.

I pressed my back to him with short jerky shuffles that worked his length up under my frizzy tail. The nudging of his tapered tip at my ring brought me to a stop. Anticipation rippled down my spine. My body was eager to have him.

I let go of his shaft and ran my fingers up to his waist. I didn't need that hand posing a barrier between us. His free hand slid under the crook of my neck and pressed the bristly pads of its open palm to my chest. I sunk against him. I felt so close. His body was warm. His fur was so soft.

Then, he pressed into me. I focused on relaxing my muscles to let him in, even though I wanted to clench tight around him. His grip tightened around my cock. His hot breath exhaled onto the base of my ear. The moisture curled my fur. I moaned. Neither of us made much natural noise during sex, but I wanted to let him know how good I felt.

He shifted lower, angling himself to press against my hole better. I lifted my leg higher to help ease him in. His thickness spread me out. A sharp slight pain rang inside me after each push, but that dulled into a thudding pleasure that made me want to thrust myself forward into his paw and heighten the sensation to the extremes that I knew it could reach.

God, he felt so good. His paw stroked my cock. That little bit of lube transformed rough pads into slick, sensually textured bliss. He knew how to give a hell of a handjob. With that throbbing length spreading me out and steadily rocking inside of me, that hell of a handjob felt like a cloud of electric euphoria that floated up and down and up and down.

"There you go, Sid, let all of the stress out for your tournament," he cooed into my ear.

Anxiety flashed across my vision and left a chilly aftershock in my chest. I forced a smile, though. He meant the best. He didn't need to know how terrified I was that I wouldn't do as well as all my friends expected me to.

I shuddered. "Keep this up and I won't be able to stand, let alone shoot a bow!"

He laughed. I felt the vibrations through his whole body. That returned some of the warmth.

His chest was so cozy. It helped me feel better. People thought of porcupines as bristly all over, but that wasn't true at all. Ken's soft, fuzzy chest begged me to melt into him. I did. That had the added benefit of sinking his warmth even deeper which radiated pleasure up through the rest of me.

"You are going to be so fucking amazing out there," he whispered. "First place barebow, for my sexy bareback groundhog." He thrust again.

I didn't answer. I thought of saying "shut up and fuck me," but I didn't want to accidentally sound too harsh. Instead, I blotted the thought out of my mind. Ken was amazing. He made me feel amazing. I loved him. I definitely loved him.

My legs strained. Even the raised knee tensed as my toes curled. Every part of my body wanted to participate, contorting in just the right ways to maximize my sensation. My paw on his thigh carefully slid fingers between quills. The claws lightly dragged against his soft skin. His strangled gasp of breath reaffirmed my touch. He moaned and thrust again.

Everything built up like cracks of pleasure chiseled into a glass. Any moment the whole thing could shatter in beautiful, euphoric bliss. I felt that moment coming. I saw it right in front of me and strained to reach it. My feet arced flat until they hurt. I balled my fingers into fists and squeezed my porcupine's hip as it rolled into my own like a powerful tide.

His fingers burned pleasurable fire along my shaft. I could barely tell he was stroking. My cock buzzed and throbbed with constant feeling. I was so close.

He squeezed me to him and rocked his hips fast against mine. His hand sped to a blur. He knew my breathing patterns so well. He knew I was at the precipice. Those fingers toyed with my tip even as they slid along my lubed length, coaxing moments of back-arching bliss that carried me those last few yards to my climax.

The cracks of pleasure finally splintered. For a second, I was on top of the world, breath caught in my throat. Then, all that pleasure came crashing down into my throbbing cock which rattled wave after wave that shook the rest of my body. Hot cum burst from my tip to splatter over the side of the bed and Ken's carpeted floor. He stroked his paw up and caught the next burst full on in between two pads, gooey, white, and dripping from short strands of fur.

I paid little attention. I kept riding that cock in my ass, trying to coax every ounce of pleasure I could from my intense orgasm as a few smaller spurts of seed left my pulsing thickness. However, everything was falling, the pleasure, the strength of the orgasm, and the breath caught in my throat. I swallowed, then exhaled.

He kept thrusting for another minute after my orgasm faded. I rode him a bit, but mostly took the time to hold him to me, feel his paws on my chest, smearing the now cool results of my climax into my fur. I didn't care. His touches felt nice.

"God, Ken, you're incredible," I gasped. His length felt a bit uncomfortable inside me now—and I could tell he was taking it slower because of that—but I wasn't about to tell him to stop. I shuddered as he finally emptied inside of me. He held me close. He made me feel so good, and I wanted to offer him the same.

He loved me so much. I wished I could love him too.

***

There were only so many times our archery club could stomach watching Robin Hood. However, we make it work. It wasn't about the movie after all—the half dozen of us stuffed in the hotel room knew it by heart. It was about the camaraderie and excitement before our big event.

Registration wasn't until Friday, but our team had bussed out on Thursday. We could relax right now. We would be rested and wouldn't have the lag of a long day's travel behind us. All of Friday we could train and acclimate ourselves to the campground. On Saturday during the competition, the teams and individuals who hurried in late the night before would have a sag in their tails and a droop in their ears.

I was already under the covers in the queen bed closer to the wall. I was clothed, though. Anthony, my stoat best friend from the team was on the other side of the bed. He was laying down as well, but outside of the covers. He periodically splayed his arms and legs out in this faux-selfishly wide way, then grinned at me and said, "Whoops, forgot you was there, Sidney!"

I knew what he was saying. Make some noise! Have fun! Everyone's chiming in at this shitty movie, and I wanna rope you in too! But that was alright. I was enjoying everyone else's jokes and laughter, and mine wouldn't be too funny anyway. I appreciated his support, though, so I scooted a bit closer to him and he gave me a thumbs up.

"Oi!" a rat called from his spot leaning against the AC unit. I didn't know him too well, but he was a nice guy. "Get a room, you two!"

Dan and Marissa were deep in each other's muzzles. In tandem, not even opening their eyes, both beavers each raised a middle finger in the rat's direction. They cranked it up another notch with an exaggerated sloppy end to their kiss which had me fidgeting and wanting to be in another room. It elicited hoots and hollers from everyone else, though. I tried to focus back onto the movie, but I was the only one.

"We paid for the fuckin' room. Get your own!" Marissa said. She reached behind her to grab a pillow that she whipped forward smack-dab center into the rat's face. He was cracking up for the whole thing, even harder when the pillow muffled his laughter.

It wasn't right that I wanted them to stop. It was so much fun, but it was so gross. I didn't want to see all that mushy nonsense when I was trying to enjoy myself with my friends.

"Hey Sidney! Where's that porcupine of yours?"

"Calc two final tomorrow morning. He's driving down after, though."

Everyone seemed to be hanging on my words. They were all looking at me. I had to say something else. "I—I'm super happy he's coming out to be here for me."

Silence. They were still waiting for me to say something witty or combative. But I was here for archery, not bragging about who was the better flirty tongue fencer. Sarah was also in a relationship. Why didn't they pick on her?

"I mean," I continued, "it's hard for him to jump right from the final and drive that exhausting fucking five hours, right?" That got a couple of noises. I smiled a bit again, but my heart kept beating. "Did my best to help. Got this grumpy old graying possum in the apartment next to his to bring him coffee and a card I wrote him early tomorrow morning before he leaves for class."

After another period of silence that lasted just long enough I thought I was going to have to start talking again, Anthony said, "That's really sweet!"

The rat chimed in, "Shit Marissa, he's showing you two up!"

I wished he hadn't said that.

Robin Hood was just swishing his bushy red tail seductively around Maid Marian in the movie. Marissa whapped her own thick tail on the bed and folded her arms with an overly exaggerated "harrumph!" She made sure all eyes were on her and Dan.

As the dashing movie couple slowly spun around with precision and elegance then drew in for a kiss, Marissa lifted Dan up to his feet, precariously on the springy bed. Then, she spun him slowly in a poor replication of the scene. The two beavers, of course, ended with a kiss that was even more exaggeratedly passionate than their last one.

The worst part was that when they finally broke the kiss, everyone turned towards me like I had to top that with some story of a sweet thing I did for Sid.

Fuck it, I'd top that during the competition. Dan, Marissa, and I scored neck and neck during the regional preliminaries. We were evenly matched during practice too. That's what this tournament was about. Not over the top tongue-fencing competitions.

"C'mon, Sidney, tell us what you got," Dan said with a hearty smile. I knew he meant well, but those words made me so angry.

I glanced over at Anthony. I had practice pretending to enjoy kisses. I could grab him right there, stuff my muzzle in his face, and force out a gross, awful kiss that would make the whole room so fucking uncomfortable. That's how I felt. They deserved to feel it too.

Everyone was still watching me. My heart pounded like the chugging of a train, but my breathing slowed it slightly. Every second that passed magnified the discomfort in the room. The team were my friends. None of them wanted me to bomb on this bit we were all doing, and they didn't want to give up on me either. But I was a second grader in the spotlight trying frantically to remember the lines to the school play.

I looked back to the room, but my eyes darted towards Anthony again quick. If I did it and kissed him right there just to spite Dan and Melissa, would his kiss be the one that I finally liked? Maybe Ken wasn't the right person. Did I need to experiment more? But I already experimented so much during my first two years of college.

Usually when I had anxiety about my love for Ken, I convinced myself by remembering one of our wonderful times we had together. We did love each other. I didn't have to feel it. My actions proved it.

This time, however, thoughts of those times didn't make it go away. Cold hands of dread wrapped around my chest until it was hard to breathe. My mind clouded and the room became fuzzy.

My memory of us having an amazing time strategizing an incredible comeback in a game of Pandemic that we had nearly lost usually helped me. When that failed, I tried picturing the time that I got him to sit backwards in a chair watching our favorite soap opera for four hours while I sanded the tips and barbs of each individual quill on his back.

He had complained about how expensive it was to get it done professionally one night while lamenting how I couldn't hold my arms around him very well. My sanding gave us a week of freedom and cuddling before old quills shed and a scattering of sharp new quills grew in.

The anxiety faded away, but I didn't feel better. I didn't feel like I loved him. Sometimes those thoughts convinced me that I did, but they never made me feel like I did.

"Hey uh," I said, "I'm saving what I got for tomorrow."

That wasn't funny. Luckily, the rat chimed in with, "That'll get you splinters in your muzzle, Sid! Maybe not a good idea."

Anthony asked, "Does our club even own a wooden bow?"

"Oh," said Dan. "Huh. Well, I'm sure Ken'll bring some wood."

Everyone cracked up. They piled jokes on each other until the source of them was forgotten, and so was the disgusting kissing contest.

I felt exhausted. I hated watching that. I hated having to be a part of it, and everyone expecting me to play into their stressfully gross and mushy competition on a night that was supposed to be relaxing.

I looked back over at Anthony, who was participating, if reservedly. My thoughts drifted back to the beaver's kiss. It was unsettling to me, but maybe that was just because I hadn't had the right kiss yet. Anthony was a good stoat—handsome too. Anyone would be lucky to kiss him.

He asked me once before about how he'd know if he was bi, since I usually wore my little rainbow flag lapel pin. After we talked, he said he'd follow up and that maybe I could introduce him to the gay bar all our friends talked about. He didn't though. I figured he was too shy. He never seemed like the type for a bar anyway, and Tail, with its jam-packed crowds, loud music, and aggressive flirtatious dancing, was not one he'd do well at.

What would happen if I put my paw on Anthony's? Would he smile? Would I feel my heart jump like it was supposed to? God, I wanted it to, and his paw was right there. His leg had crept up next to mine already. It wasn't a huge bed, but it still was there pressed gently to mine and it hadn't moved away.

If I put my paw on his, I didn't think Anthony would stop me. We couldn't fuck in the room. Everyone had made that clear as day to the two love-beavers tongue-fencing in the other bed. But hands were discreet, and I had years of practice being dead quiet jerking off by the computer, ears primed for any hint of my parents.

My stomach clenched. I shut my eyes. I'd lost all interest in the movie. I just wanted it to stop and for the lights to go out so I could curl up in the bed as far away from Anthony as I could. Ken was so good to me. How dare I even think about that? I couldn't hurt him and betray him that way. It made me queasy.

For a moment I thought my disgust had been something special—a symbol that I hoped meant I did in fact love Ken. It wasn't, though. I wanted to throw up.

***

I first took archery lessons back in middle school. I found out I had a decent knack for it at summer camp, and it turned out to be a lot of fun. My arm could barely hold the string back for a dozen seconds. After that, it would start to wobble, and then holding onto the string would become unbearable. I had to force myself to release it while still steadying my bow forward despite my aim going wide, since otherwise instinct led me to plant the arrow down towards the ground. A tiny instinctual mistake could have resulted in an arrow-sized hole in my foot.

Now, however, I had years of experience drawing bowstrings and holding them until I trusted my shot. My arm and shoulder muscles were toned and used to holding rock-steady while I shifted precise half-inches to adjust my aim.

The wind was proving difficult. Sometimes, a stronger breeze was actually simpler than a lighter one, due to a natural tendency to overcompensate for the angle you're shooting at. But the wind was just over that comfortable threshold as I stood alone out on the campground archery practice fields that evening. Pounding rain had discouraged most people from staying for more than a few ends of shooting. Rain didn't make the actual archery any more difficult, but it was miserable to practice in. No one wanted to slog through the mud to yank arrows out of targets or worry about their finger tabs getting water damage.

The last of those who had stayed to weather through their pre-tournament practice had already gone back to their hotels or other lodgings. The faint sun was setting behind clouds, and within half an hour it'd be too dark to reliably shoot. I had stayed behind though. I needed the extra practice. I had a twenty-two-point average goal for my three arrow barebow ends, but today I was coming in around eighteen. That wasn't going to cut it in competition tomorrow. So many of my arrows were going wide. Arrows always went wide in barebow since we didn't have sights, of course, but not to this extent. Competition didn't faze me. Crowds didn't faze me. But I just couldn't hold my focus.

"Sidney!"

I barely heard the voice over the constant thrumming of rain pelleting my coat, rattling against the band-aid style guard on my muzzle, and pounding the ground around me. I un-nocked my arrow, though, then carefully set my bow on the stand next to me.

Ken was closer than his voice sounded. I forced myself to smile when I saw him jogging across the field to reach me. He didn't have an umbrella. His quills had to be soaked. They were hard to cover unless he took time to put on his more complicated clothes. He only ever bothered in the winter, though.

I called out to him, "Hey! Ken! What're you doing out here?"

"Well," he said through an open-muzzled pant as he pulled up next to me, "I went to the hotel and luckily Marissa was in the lobby, because I sent you a text and all but you never answered. Which I can see why! It is really coming down. Anyway, I hoped I could catch you out here before you got back!"

"Why?" I asked. It was a serious question, but judging by the immediate drooping of Ken's muzzle and ears, the wrong one.

"I wanted to see you, Sid! I mean, I know I'm going to see you tonight when you come back to the room, but I just drove five hours to get here after the calc two midterm. So, I don't know, I just really wanted to see you!" He got this big dopey smile on his muzzle that highlighted his big porcupine front teeth. I couldn't help but smile back. He was a good guy. The eagerness and positivity brought a smile to my face like it always did.

I hadn't meant it in that way. I had just thought he'd meet me at the hotel, since I was going back soon myself. That's what we had planned when we talked on the phone.

"Right," I said. I still didn't quite know what to say. It would've been insensitive to tell him to go back to the car until I was done practicing in half an hour. But he'd just want to goof around. He'd gotten the focus he needed that morning. He didn't have me hovering over his shoulder bothering him when he took his midterm.

"I'm glad I came," he said. "Look at the sunset! I mean, it's just started and the rain is still really bad, but the clouds are thinning over there. It's so beautiful how the color shines through them. That and the rain. You know I love the rain. It's so romantic."

"Yeah, I know." I picked my bow back up off the stand and slid my thumb and forefinger down the bowstring. It didn't help with the wetness, but really the moisture wasn't a problem. I just did it because it felt comfortable—like it was the right thing for me to do.

I set my legs back into my stance. I drew an arrow, knocked the bow, then pulled the string steady to my cheek. It rested millimeters from my muzzle-guard.

Then I felt the pressure of Ken's chest up against my back. I shifted. My aim was way off now, irreparably so. I had been about to loosen the arrow again to redo the whole thing from start to finish when his arms wrapped around mine. He held me like a teacher guiding my paws into place.

His arm was positioned weird, too close to the bow. If I let loose the bowstring, it'd surely snag fur from his forearm, maybe even tear a chunk of fur out. It frustrated me to no end that I was stuck there now, waiting for him to finish his inane display of affection. The whole time, my arms ached from a long day of practice that I sorely needed with my lackluster performance.

There would be all the time in the world for affection up in our hotel room. Yeah, the sky was pretty. It did look really nice, especially with the rain. I'd love to admire it on a day that wasn't so important for me. I'd love to have his arms around me then. But not right now.

"Please, Ken. Don't," I said.

Ken let go of me. I didn't look at him, because I knew he'd be upset. I didn't need that right now. My aim was already off. I reset myself, taking a deep breath. I figured I had 10 seconds before Ken said something, but I gave myself 6 seconds like I would have in the competition.

One. Two. Three. Four.

"Sid, come on. It's so—"

The arrow let loose and hit the ground well past the target.

I was going to lose tomorrow. Everyone was going to be disappointed in me. I worked so hard for this, and I couldn't get my shit together.

"So what?" I said, twisting to face him. "So pretty? Yeah, sure, it is I guess. Look at all the colors coming from the sun that'll be gone in a dozen minutes. But that's alright. I'm sure I'll practice just fine with a porcupine bear-hugging me."

I breathed heavily. Ken's eyes were wide.

After a minute, he said, "Hey, Sid. It's okay, I'll just go then."

"Okay." I felt an awful pang of guilt, but couldn't he see that I needed this? I'd apologize back at the hotel room. I'd say that the stress of the tournament had me on edge and I was really glad he thought to come surprise me on the field even if the timing didn't work quite so well for me.

I'd tell him I loved him. The thought of that, though, created a lump in my throat.

"Okay?" he asked.

I needed every minute of practice time. I turned to him, and pointedly said, "Okay."

He stood there, like I was supposed to interject and say that I actually didn't mean it. My fists clenched.

"I drove five hours for you," he said, "I came out here to support you. I wanted to give you this nice romantic surprise. It's so beautiful out right now."

"I don't care!"

"There's no one around and the rain is so pretty and—"

"And you fucked up my shot!"

"That was one shot! You've been practicing all evening. I've been driving all evening!"

"Right. Because you couldn't wait to get out here and screw me up with all this lovey-dovey shit." My breath caught in my throat. My claws dug into my palm.

He clamped his muzzle shut and stared at me. He scratched the back of his neck, expertly rifling his claws through quills. "You're such an ingrate, you know that?"

"I'm an ingrate for you interrupting my practice and throwing me off my game?"

"What? Was my ghost here keeping you from practicing all day? Because you've had this field since morning, and I just spent five hours driving up because I was trying to do something nice!"

"Well, maybe you should do less of that."

Instead of getting all angry like he was supposed to, the porcupine just sighed. "You never cared about any of it anyway."

"You mean when you interrupt what we're doing for some soppy moment and I have to rewind the movie or miss my shot or lose my place in a book?" My voice rose to a shout, partially because a heavy sheet of rain slammed past, but mostly because Ken was just so infuriating. This was such an important evening for me. Ken could have just waited one hour. It was okay when I made time for it and was ready. But I was on edge. I needed to focus for the competition the next day. "It's obnoxious. You're obnoxious!"

Ken started shouting too, but it was the frantic kind. It was like he didn't want to be shouting, but needed to be at the same volume as me. "I bring you breakfast in bed! I surprise you with date nights! I get you flowers and wine! But you never cared about any of those things I do for you! You just shrug it all off like you expect it, or you give me some bland thanks like I didn't spend so much time in my life setting it all up for you."

It was my turn to gape. Did he really think that? I loved breakfast in bed with him, it was always really sweet. He also had excellent choice in wine and knew how to make a date night sail so smooth.

My lips stiffened. "Yeah? Well, they made you happy, so whatever."

He was sobbing. I realized that he probably started a while ago. "Sometimes I feel like you're faking it all and using me for sex."

I couldn't believe the words that were coming out of my mouth. I hated it, but I just wanted them to hurt like I was hurting. Like I was always hurting. I lied, "I am."

His words stuck in his throat and he audibly choked down a sob. "I love you, Sid."

"I don't."

I grabbed my bow and left. Everything was too much.

I thanked every God from every distant religion on the planet that we didn't have to drive back together. On my way to the hotel, I sent Anthony a text at a traffic light asking if I could stay in his room with the lovebeavers, even though right then I wanted to be as far away from those two as I could. Anthony said he didn't mind.

Those three dots popped up under that last text I sent, Thanks :), and hovered there for a minute. Then they went away. I knew what he was going to ask, and I appreciated so much that I didn't have to answer.

Nothing happened in his bed, of course. I had urges and I was furious at Ken, but I had always thought of myself as a good person. Even after fucking everything up and ruining my relationship with my loving porcupine, I wouldn't betray him that way—no matter what feelings I wanted to prove to myself that I could have.

***

I stepped off the podium. I wanted to tear the certificate in my paws in half, but I didn't. That would have been disrespectful and humiliating, not just to myself, but to my whole team. No one liked a sore loser.

I got smiles and hushed congratulations when I sat down with everyone else. They were happy for me, of course. That didn't help. I wasn't happy with myself. I ended up ranking top thirty-two—which was pretty good out of about eighty competitors—but it wasn't what I knew I could do. At our club practice, Dan, Marissa, and I were often neck and neck, sharing tips and advice. We used each other as goal posts to improve.

Marissa got third and Dan got eleventh.

Their muzzles stretched wide with smiles when they picked up their trophies—a two-foot tall, impressive beast of a trophy for Marissa, and a humbler half-foot one for Dan. I was happy for them. I really was, but I still had a pit in my stomach. I hated watching them kiss, and the way they posed for pictures together with their trophies, and how everyone giggled when Marissa whispered, "Mine is bigger!"

They had such a perfect, romantic relationship and it infuriated me that I couldn't. Why weren't they broken like me? Why did they get those wriggly looks on their muzzles when they caught each other's eyes? I just got annoyed when Ken tried to do those things.

Anxiety still had my stomach in knots. It was better than it had been that morning, but when my mind drifted back to Ken, everything would get hot and hazy until I refocused my thoughts on something else. I almost threw up during my second round of competition—I leaned over the toilet, waiting for vomit to come. It never did though. At least the tournament was over now. I didn't have to worry about that on top of everything else.

"Marissa?" I asked the bright-eyed beaver who was happily toting her trophy as we walked away from the outdoor stage.

She turned to me and tilted her head slightly. "Sidney? 'Sup?"

"Could I uh, ask you something? In private?" I added on quickly, "I mean, Dan could be around too—it's nothing he couldn't hear of course, but it'd be easier to just talk to one person, you know?"

After pausing as if unsure what to make of my request, she smiled and then nodded. "Hey man, sure. I'd be happy to. Wendalay Falls trail is right up there. Wanna veer off and chat?"

Without waiting for my answer, she turned to the rest of the team and gave them a big grin. "I gotta run off for a minute—stealing Sidney for some help! You guys go ahead and bask in how fucking awesome you all did!" Then, she took me by my forearm and marched me off towards the Wendalay Falls trail.

The falls themselves were a long was away, but the trail followed a slim ravine leading to the falls that was plenty scenic itself. More importantly, no one was walking it right then. The serenity of the lush green bushes and leaves all around us helped me calm down. It made it easier to talk.

"How do you and Dan do it, Marissa?" I asked.

"Huh? Do what?" She stepped off the trail, down a slight slope that led to the ravine. We were far enough down now that the voices of the other contestants and their family and friends leaving the awards ceremony were faint. Ken was with them. He hadn't approached me, but I saw him.

He was there in the audience for my elimination rounds, too.

"Dan went to all your rounds he was free for. I saw him running from his own round so he could make yours." That was a bad example. I had done things like that for Ken. But it clawed at the real point, and I desperately wanted to get there.

"Yeah, he's a good guy." She climbed up onto one of the big flat-topped rocks that clustered along the edge of the ravine.

I followed her, climbing up onto the same one and sitting on the opposite side. I picked up a pebble from its surface and tossed it into the ravine in front of us. It was only about five feet wide and shallow, the crystal-clear water barely distorting the rocky bed underneath it. Many of the larger stones broke the surface, and clusters offered a path across.

"Ken was watching me too."

"I'd figure. That's what people do in relationships, right? You support each other. But," She paused and gave me a look, "had a fight, didn't'cha? A big one. I hate to gossip, but that's what I've been hearing."

I nodded. "I was awful to him. He came to support me, and I blew up 'cause I was trying to get those last few shots in before the tournament. Felt like I was a complete failure, and I couldn't do it. Well, I guess the tournament didn't end up being terrible… but it was terrible for me and him. I just can't believe the things I said to him. I never imagined I could hurt someone like that."

Melissa didn't say anything. She just watched me.

I sighed. "That's not the root of it, is it? The fight wasn't just because of the tournament. It's 'cause, well, it's because I'm really fucked up right now. I don't know. I try to support him, but I—I'm just not doing it right. I can't love him right. No, I'm mincing my words here. That's not what I mean.

"You and Dan, I saw in the finals how he looked at you. He had those eyes that were just full of adoration and that smile that's supposed to come with butterfly-in-stomach feelings. I don't know! In the hotel room too. The way that you look at each other it's kind of," I paused, searching for a word. I wanted to say obnoxious or annoying, since that's how I felt—but that would sound like I was angry at Melissa, and I really wasn't. It made me upset that I didn't feel those things myself.

I sighed. I came out here to be honest, but I didn't need to be cruel like I had been the night before. There was a correct word to find. "It's kind of draining for me."

She raised an eyebrow. Her flat tail thumped on the rock. I knew her well enough to recognize that meant for me to continue.

"It's me feeling that everything, every fucking act of affection and dumb lovey-dovey thing I see is just, well, obnoxious, 'cause—because they make me feel nothing when Ken does them for me. No, it's fucking worse. I feel like I screwed up today when I was thinking about us! You

171

and Dan, you looked at each other and you did your best. Made each other better knowing you were there, but I was grinding my teeth and remembering Ken putting his arms out in the practice field and the resentment I felt there 'cause I just couldn't shoot when that's what I went there to do, not to look at the sunset and be romantic and... I'm sorry." I shook my head.

"Hey, Sidney, it's okay."

I put my muzzle in my paws and said, "It's not. I hurt him. I hate how I don't know what to feel. Just, I don't know what to do. Why don't I feel what I'm supposed to? It's like my love is broken."

"Maybe," she said slowly, "he's just not right for you. I mean, I've been with some guys before that didn't make me feel nothing. I'd watch these rom coms and get all those fuzzy emotions, then go out for a date with a boring slob who did none of them for me."

My fur stood on end. I raised my head from my paws to look at Marissa. "Ken's not a boring slob!"

"Shit! Sorry, I didn't mean that. I dated some boring slobs, wasn't calling Ken one. Anyway, I just mean that there's a good chance you're attracted to something different than what Ken is. He might not be right for you."

I sighed and leaned back. There was nothing to lean against, so I set my paws behind me on the stone and supported myself on them. "No, that can't be it really. Ken is the kind of person that feels so right."

"Are you asexual?" she asked.

"No! I mean, I don't think so? Sex is—can I talk sex stuff for a second?"

She grinned. "Sure. I mean, normally I gotta pay for that."

I snorted more than the joke deserved. I needed the humor. My paws were futilely and painfully squeezing down on the flat stone surface. My insides wanted to twist into an origami crane.

"I've been with a number of guys that just sorta didn't do it for me," I said. "Like sure, I'd get off just fine, and it felt good and it satisfied me, and I was attracted to them on a basic level, you know? But Ken works perfectly in tandem with me. Sex with him feels so right. It's like I hooked up with the guy in that perfect porn that just does it right away for you and you can rely on to always get the job done!

"When he's inside me, I struggle to slow my dick down and not finish at lightning speed. That's an exaggeration, obviously. Like, I last a normal amount of time usually, especially if I'd gotten off recently, so there's—"

"Sidney! The point!"

I blushed. "Right. Sorry. Just, I'm so fucking attracted to that porcupine. Can't imagine that he's not the right one for me. I'm not asexual, right? I just don't get it! I don't get why it doesn't work for me. It never has! Even with that amazing sex, people always talk about these fuzzy wonderful feelings they get. And like, my dick feels damn good, but I don't get those wriggly smiles and fuzzy feelings everyone says I'm supposed to."

"Sid, you know, sex and romance aren't the same thing."

"I mean, of course. I've had one-night stands before so—"

She cut me off, but I didn't mind. "No, I mean, Ken pushes all your sex buttons, but he might not push all your love buttons. Don't let Dan hear me saying this, but," she winked at me, "Ken's a looker."

"He is! God, that porcupine is hot. He's the best. He's considerate, thoughtful, amazing at sex, and absolutely my best friend. If I could fall in love with anyone, it should be him. I don't get it, I've tried so hard to be like him."

"Maybe that's the problem."

I thought for a minute. Maybe it was.

Of all my past relationships, none of them had been as wonderful as Ken and I. I had fun sex in most of them, made some good friends, and of course figured out that women just didn't do it for me, but those fuzzy feelings and romantic inclinations never happened. Honestly, they didn't even appeal to me. I wanted them because everyone else said I should. They were expected of me. Love was required to be happy.

That wasn't me though.

"Hey, Melissa?"

"Yeah?"

"You said sex and love are two separate parts of a person. Is there something like asexual, but for love?"

***

When I started my car, the audiobook His Auburn Tail began playing via bluetooth. Ken read it the week before. When we were home before the tournament, he couldn't stop talking about how adorable the scene was where the buck main character finally got to kiss the mysterious, handsome fox. His excitement infected me. Though I didn't care much for the kissing scene, or the romance in general, I knew Ken would love to talk about the book with me.

A smile spread over my muzzle. I didn't have to care about all the sappy romantic bits anymore. Even though they were a bit boring, I'd listen through those parts since I wanted to get back to all the juicy melodrama. That's what I'd be gushing to Ken about. I'd joke about how he sniffled when he talked about their love scenes, and he'd tease me about how my eyes lit up when I explained what Leone really should have done to counteract his estranged mother-in-law's newly discovered separated-at-birth twin who was plotting to wreck their relationship.

My blunt claws rattled against the steering wheel as I let the audiobook play for a minute. My running car sat in its parking spot. If my life were one of those melodramas, what advice would I give me? There was always some obvious solution I saw in the stories that the writers clearly missed. If Leone had just laid out the insane, evil mother-in-law twin plot to his partner along with all the good and bad that went with it, then everything would have been okay. He did bad things, but they had been for a good purpose—to protect his partner's feelings by not tearing him from his mother who unbeknownst to him at the time was being impersonated by the evil twin.

I took out my phone and hovered my thumb over Ken's contact information. I didn't know if calling him was a good idea though. Unlike Leone, I hadn't had a noble purpose for the horrible things I said during our argument. I did appreciate him. I wasn't using him for sex. There was no justification for those hurtful lies.

I sighed. I had said some serious relationship-enders, and I didn't know where to start to repair them.

But, the first thing I had to do was right there in front of me. If I started the call, everything else would follow, for better or for worse. Ken was my friend, and I hurt him. I wanted to make that right. I pressed call. My hand shook.

After five rings, Ken's voicemail played, then the beep told me to talk. I wasn't ready, but I didn't want to be the creep who left five seconds of silence, so I started talking anyway.

"Hey Ken." I cleared my throat. My voice trembled so bad I worried that he wouldn't understand his own name. I inhaled deep and then exhaled. "I said some awful things to you that I didn't mean. There's no excuse for what I said. Could I... could you call me back soon? Or text me? I'd really like to apologize, uh face to face if we could. I mean, a call's still okay. Or texting, I guess. Anyway, you know how to reach me.

Goodb—talk to you soon."

I leaned back against the car seat and breathed like I had just dodged a bus. Now I had to wait. His Auburn Tail was still playing. A moment of panic shot up my tail as I wondered whether it had mangled my words. I paused it, then pulled out my phone, about to call him to apologize for having it in the background so I could then say everything again, but I caught myself.

I shut off the phone's display and slid it back into my pocket. I needed to give him time and space. I'd never get the call right, if I tried to fix every mistake, I'd end up leaving a hundred voicemails in his inbox.

After a moment of consideration, I turned His Auburn Tail back on. I put the car into reverse, backed out of my spot, and drove onto the road. Halfway through the drive, my phone buzzed a few times in rapid succession, and Ken's name flashed on the screen. I forced myself not to read what he wrote. My rashness had led me to damage our relationship so badly. I could be calm and wait until I was home.

The initial burst of anxiety died down. I breathed normally. The evening mountains were so pretty with how they were framed by the oranges and yellows of the setting sun.

My audiobook was just wrapping up when I pulled in to the parking lot at my apartment complex. I switched it to my headphones and dragged my suitcase up to my apartment. When I got inside, I lay down on my couch and stared at the ceiling while His Auburn Tail finished. I waited a minute in silence after that, and then switched to my messages.

if I talk to you
Sid
are you gonna tear my fucking heart out again?

***

At first, I thought that Ken wasn't going to open his door when I knocked. I didn't have any classes on Monday morning, but he did. He likely spent all day finishing homework that he couldn't focus on during the tournament.

Three sharp raps echoed through the wood, the way I always did it. I wasn't going to try to mislead him. Honesty was a key part of our relationship. We told each other everything—except, of course, the big secret that had bored such a hole through my chest.

He cracked open the door to his small studio apartment. His headquills sagged, and the way he looked at me reminded me of my guilt. I felt terrible.

"Hey Ken. I uh, it's okay if I talk to you?" My voice quivered. He opened the door the rest of the way.

I clutched a small bouquet of three hyacinths; purple, red, and white, held together by a rubber band. They were Ken's favorite. He said the conical bunches of flower blooms at the top were like a dozen flowers in one. I hoped three would be like three dozen flowers to him. By the weak smile he gave, I figured they were. But that smile was accompanied by a choked sob that sunk my heart right back down.

Ken lived alone. He liked having an apartment to himself, even if he could only afford a tiny studio a few blocks from campus. I lived on campus, but somehow we ended up staying at his place more often despite the distance.

I sat down at his square plastic table in the middle of the room. He poured a cup of water, put the hyacinths in it, and set it on the table between us as he sat down across from me. There was a lump in my throat, but I knew I had to start this.

"First off, none of this is an excuse. I'm going to say some things, but it doesn't make what I said right, or what I did right. That was all me just breaking down and choosing to hurt you because I thought it would make me feel better somehow and I swear to god I never will again. I—" I stopped. My breath came short and quick. I just wanted to preface myself. I hadn't meant to dive deep into the shit pile I had stacked just yet.

He nodded.

Now it was time. I gulped. "You knew that this tournament meant a lot to me, but I never told you I felt like my performance was slipping this past month. I knew you wouldn't judge me for that, but 'cause I was in this whole spiral downward, these voices in my head told me you would, or that I couldn't burden you with it and stuff like that.

"And well—the tournament was part of it. I mean, the more important part is that I was fighting with myself. Lying to myself about my feelings. Those lies stacked on lies. I couldn't trust my love. I didn't know if I was a fucking loveless psycho or what. I'm not! By the way, I mean, I don't… Well, I'm fucking emotional and I think that's obvious."

I sniffled and reached over to pull a tissue from the tissue box next to the sofa. I dabbed under my eyes then blew my nose. Ken wasn't taking this great either. He had his own tissue clutched tight in his paw. It wasn't against his face, but I could see all his feelings just the same.

His mouth was scrunched together, and his ears were splayed flat as a prairie.

"The things I said to you weren't true. I promise. I like all the little things you do for me. Even when I get a little annoyed at having to re-wind our soaps, I know it's 'cause you care about me and I really appreci-ate that you want to share with me.

"I've been horrified at what I said to you since I left. I just—I know there's nothing that could make up for those words. They were so cruel. I'm so sorry."

My words hung in the air between us. He didn't talk for the longest time. When he did, his voice creaked like ancient hinges. "Are you?"

"I am. I really am. I'm so fucking sorry." I held a paw on the side of my muzzle. I wanted to bury my whole face in my paws, but I didn't dare look away from Ken.

He nodded. He clutched his paws together in front of himself and stared at them. "What feelings?"

"Huh?"

"You said uh, that you were lying about your feelings to yourself. And... love? Because of," he choked up, "because they were feelings about me, right? What feelings?"

"Ken, I think I'm aromantic."

He sniffled, but looked genuinely confused. He swallowed, then said, "But you, I mean, you always looked like you had fun when we had sex. I thought that you liked it."

"I did. I do! I really like sex with you, Ken!

"I," he paused. His paw wandered over to run fingers along the red hyacinth. Noticing that, I had the urge to do so too, but I didn't. I al-ready felt just plain awful, and that could have added awkwardness to the uncomfortable air in the room. "What do you mean, then?"

"It's uh, it's asexual that means you don't want to have sex. There's two ends to this whole thing though, sex and romance. Aromantic means I, well, I don't feel any romantic attraction to anyone. I just don't." I choked up again at the end there. Why was that so difficult to say? It was so hard to put those honest words out there to my best friend, the guy who made me so happy and who I'd hurt so bad trying to be some-thing I wasn't.

"I see," he said. He looked at the flowers, not at me. The tear streaks in the fur under his eyes stood out to me and I couldn't stop looking at them. I did that. I hated that I did that. I wanted to fill the silence so that I didn't have to look, but he was thinking, so I gave him time. Besides, I didn't come to his apartment to run away from the horrible shit that I had said.

Finally, he spoke again. "When you said you didn't love me, back on the archery field..."

He trailed off, so I finished for him, "Not just you, Ken. I've never loved anyone. Not romantically at least. I love you like I love my brother, or my mom and dad, and Jesus fuck I just realized how awful that sounds. I swear I don't do that with them! Honest!"

He laughed far too loud. I did too. I just wanted the emotion in the room to change, no matter how forced. "Damn. You know, I did not think there was anything worse you could say, but that was easily—" He stopped when he saw the look on my face. "I didn't mean worse like that. It was funny. And this is, well, this is hard, and I'm so glad you're telling me all of this. Although, I'm not sure how to handle it, Sid."

"I get it," I said, nodding. "It took me a bit too. You know, there are all these feelings that everyone expects me to have. I see the smiles you get for me and how you look at me. I just feel this awful anxiety when I know that I don't feel those things—not for you, not for anyone.

"The thing is, I only really want to feel them because everyone says I'm supposed to. People say that it feels good and will make me fulfilled and complete, when really I don't actually want any of them. I never did. I liked what we were, and I hated that I felt like we had to be more for it to work." I brought my paw to my muzzle to wipe away the tears that were getting into my fur. I wasn't afraid of Ken seeing me cry. I cried at sad stories, happy stories, and people being sweet to one another. He saw plenty of my tears. Yet, these tears were somehow different. I had been afraid of them for so long.

"So," he said with a long pause, "you like having sex with me?"

I almost laughed. That's what he wanted to ask? "Yes, Ken. I like having sex with you. I really like it. You're super hot, and you know just what I like. You're—" a knot was rising through my throat, but I fought to speak through it, "you're my best friend and I think you're wonderful. I just don't love you. I can't love you. And I know you love me, and I'm really sorry that I can't feel the same things you do!"

Ken nodded slowly. His voice cracked. "Do you like cuddling with me? How about when I touch your chest, or rub my fingers through your fur? Is that some of the romantic stuff you don't want?"

"No! Ken, I love that stuff. It feels great. I get all these tingles along my body and I just want to melt in your arms. Not even to mention the back scratches. You give back scratches like a fucking god!"

"And—"

I cut him off, cringing as I remembered lying about the cute things he did for me. "I don't really care for all the romantic gushy stuff that goes with these things, but I really appreciate it when you do caring stuff like bring me breakfast in bed. Also, you've got an awesome taste in wine, and our date nights are so much fun and I always look forward to them."

"What is it then? What don't you feel for me?"

"I—it's hard to explain. Like I said, those wriggly smiles that you get for me, or I see Dan and Marissa looking at each other with, I don't know, they're just kind of annoying to me. I haven't had my heart flutter like rom coms and romances describe it—unless that twisty feeling from anxiety counts and I don't think it does. I don't feel this big warmth for a person from a crush. I've never had a crush! I've found people hot—you're really hot! But never a swooning, wanting feeling. I, I'm sorry. It's hard to describe something that I don't have. I think I'm mangling it."

"No, Sid. I understand what you're saying, but it is…" he shook his head, "it's just weird for me. I can't imagine not having those feelings. I know exactly what you're talking about. And, like you said, you know I feel them for you. It's just so weird."

"I don't even want those feelings," I said. "I did, but that's just because I felt like there was something wrong with me for not having them. I've been doing a lot of thinking since the tournament."

I stopped for too long, since Ken had to prompt me, "Yeah?"

I'd been working this over in my head for so long. I took a deep breath. These words had to be perfect. "I want the feelings that I have. I like them. They're me, and I don't need all that other shit. But Ken, I do really like you. I'm not romantically inclined, though I know you are. If—if you still want me around, I'd like to keep what we have.

"You're such a loving person, and this may not be right for you. But I'd be really happy it if you wanted to give it a shot anyway. I won't," I choked down a sob, but kept going, "love you like you love me, but I love you as my best friend. Even if you stop having sex with me, and you decide you want to go out with someone who wants that sort of relationship, I'll be so sad, but I'll be happy with being your friend and happy that you're getting what you need. But I—I would like to try if you will."

Ken didn't say anything. His small ears were folded over. It felt like minutes passed, but I was sure it was less than that. I had to prompt him with a soft, squeaking, "Ken?"

"Sid, I—if you ever tear my heart out like you did on the practice field again, we are done. For good. Being aromantic isn't an excuse for what you did to me. You get that?"

I nodded slowly as I composed my thoughts. My heart was pounding again, but I gave myself the time to think of the right words. "It's not an excuse. I was awful, aromantic or not. Knowing why I did it doesn't mean it's excused or," my words creaked, but I forced them through anyway, "forgivable. But you're my best friend, Ken. I hope you can forgive me for how horrible I was."

"I can," he said. He looked like he had already decided. For a second, the thought that I didn't deserve him flashed through my mind, but I shucked it. If I could do better by him, I'd show that I deserved him. I vowed to do that.

"And," he continued, "you're getting therapy."

"Ken? But, I'm fine, I—"

He shook his head and spoke over me. "You're not fine. This is non-negotiable. Oh… Oh! No, it's not because of your, uh, aromanticism. It's because you let yourself spiral down and break apart, while never letting me know. You're saying words right now. I need to know that you mean them. You are going to go to therapy and make sure that the next time things start getting bad, we catch it before it causes the worst fucking weekend of my life again."

My chest clamped up. I nodded dumbly. "I'll call tomorrow morning. So, Ken, are we…" I trailed off.

"I think we can try," he said in a shaking voice. "Is it okay if I, if I say I love you?"

"Yeah it is."

"I love you," he said.

I leaned forward over the table, opening my muzzle just a crack. He looked startled.

"Do you even like kisses?" he asked.

"No," I said, "but you do, and I like making my boyfriend happy."

He leaned forward and kissed me. His tongue was slimy. It felt weird. I didn't like the taste of his spit and spent long seconds of discomfort thinking about everything we had been talking about, since I didn't want to focus on the gross kiss. But it ended, he pulled back, and the big smile on his muzzle was worth it.

He stood up. In his usual awkward way of initiating sex, he gave me a big grin and said, "It's uh, feeling really hot in here. Do you mind if I get rid of my shirt?"

"Of course not," I said.

He took a few steps over to his bed in the corner of the room and sat down. He started to undo the straps tied over his quills that held his shirt to his chest. Looking up, he said, "Hey Sidney, no pressure about this. I'm still shaking, and I don't know if you're ready to do something intimate so soon. Maybe I'm just being weird. I'm sorry."

I shook my head. "No! It's fine. I think. I need a break from all that heavy shit. I'd like this."

He slowly nodded. "Are you going to get the lights?"

I got up myself, and walked towards him, not the light switch. I placed a paw on his shoulder, gingerly smoothing down a few short quills, and another over the tent in his shorts. Warmth pressed against my hand.

"I think I'll leave the lights on this time."

To those struggling: you are loved.

FIRSTS

by TJ Minde

When the professor dismissed the class, the jackal slid his messenger bag over his lithe frame and joined the crowd milling out of the room.

A brick-red dhole slid beside him. "Have any plans for the Halloween weekend, Anthony?" He clapped the jackal on the back.

"None yet." Anthony smiled. "You were rather quiet today, Jude."

"Wasn't really paying attention. Brought my laptop and bounced around online instead."

The jackal shook his head. "You plan to just coast through college?"

"What can I say?" The dhole shrugged. "If it worked in high school, why can't it work now? Besides, some classes come easy to me. I mean, hell, most English classes are spinning bullshit anyway."

"Yeah, but the professor's trying to get you to look at the story from another perspective."

"Chill out, Mr. English Major." Jude smiled. "I mean, he can. But I've done this enough times. I'll just do what I normally do." The dhole raised his toned arms above his head and stretched. "Wanna hang out this weekend?

"You mean study together?"

The dhole blinked. "Do we need to clean your ears out?" He threw an arm around Anthony's neck and blew into his ear.

The jackal yipped, pulling away from the dhole. "Hey, not cool!" He reached a finger into his brown furred ear and rubbed the long, sensitive hairs inside before flicking it again and again.

Jude bent over laughing. "I didn't think you'd jump that much."

"That much? Every canid I know would." Anthony shook his head, grinning as he walked on. "Rude."

"I'm sorry," Jude said as he ran to keep up. "So, you don't have any plans? Halloween's Monday, you know."

"Just homework and studying. Nothing special."

"No costume parties or anything?"

The jackal shook his head. "My family never really did Halloween, so I don't see why I should."

"What?" Jude took two quick steps and stopped in front of Anthony. "Wait, wait, wait," he held his paws up. "What do you mean?"

Anthony shrugged. "I never did anything Halloween-related in high school. Why would I start now?"

"No way. I thought you always had plans?"

The jackal shrugged again. "We had plans, yeah, but they were always some church event or other. Didn't really do Halloween. Or trick-or-treating."

The dhole shook his head. "You know what? You're going to celebrate Halloween with me this weekend." He prodded Anthony in the chest.

"I don't know if that's a good idea." The jackal looked away. "I mean I have church on Sunday and Tuesday."

Jude put a paw on Anthony's shoulder. "I'll make sure we're at both services." He checked his watch. "Hey, I got to run. I'll pick you up tomorrow, okay?" With a wave, the dhole ran off.

Anthony stood there, blinking in confusion. *Well, I guess I have plans, now,* he thought.

***

A loud rap at the door pulled the jackal from his sleep. Rolling over, he looked at the clock: 8:27am. *It's too early for this.* Anthony slid out of bed and opened the door, peeking into the hall.

Jude, in jeans and a comfortable sweater, stood there with two insulated disposable cups, bright-eyed and full of energy. "Good morning, Sleeping Beauty," the dhole said, red tail wagging. "I was worried you wouldn't wake up."

"You realize it's not even eight-thirty, right?" Anthony rubbed the sleep out of his eyes and yawned. He stood up a little straighter and positioned the cross around his neck at the bottom of the chain.

"Uh huh," the dhole said with a nod. "That's why I brought you this." He raised one of the two cups. "We have lots to do and I wanted to give you a jump start before breakfast." Jude's gaze traveled along the stripe down the jackal's side. "But, while I like the cross-and-boxers look, I don't know if it works for the general public."

Anthony blinked before looking down. As he realized half his leg was visible, he yipped and hid behind the door. "Sorry," the jackal said.

"Give me twenty minutes?"

Jude chuckled. "Okay, I'll be in the common room." He turned with a wave and walked down the hall.

Lord, give me strength. That was embarrassing. Anthony sighed with his eyes closed and ears splayed, holding the cross around his neck. *Wait, he liked my look?*

***

The jackal walked into the common room fifteen minutes later in jeans, a scarf and coat. "You ready?" Anthony asked.

Jude looked up from his cellphone. "Dude, are you trying to over-compensate for the earlier show?" He chuckled. "It's like sixty out."

"Maybe I'm used to warmer weather," Anthony said from behind the scarf. "Besides, my phone said it was fifty-seven. Cold enough, thank you very much."

"Well, we're going to be moving today." The dhole stood from his chair, shoving the cellphone into his pocket, and stormed back down the hall with both cups in paw. "Leave the scarf and put on a sweater or something. I don't want you complaining later."

"But I like what I'm wearing now," Anthony protested.

"Trust me," Jude said as he stopped at the jackal's room.

With a sigh, Anthony unlocked his door again and walked in. "Fine." He made his way to the closet and hung up his scarf and jacket before slipping a sweater over his head instead.

"What type of Christian are you, again?" Jude asked.

The jackal turned around. "Huh?"

The dhole's paws were linked behind his back as he looked at a cross above Anthony's squat bookshelf. Jude's long-sleeved shirt bunched up around the top of his back, hiding the strong muscles that the jackal knew were there, but his jeans hugged his hips and rear tight. *Man, he has a nice—no. Stop staring.* He shook his head, lowering his ears a bit. "Uh, my family's Roman Catholic."

"Your family?" Jude looked over his shoulder. "You aren't?"

Anthony stood there for a moment. "I am. It's just odd saying it without my mother or sister around. I guess I never thought about it much." The jackal shrugged. "Part of why I wanted to get away from my family—so I can learn to be independent and speak for myself. Just don't tell my mom that." The jackal let out a wry chuckle.

"But," Anthony continued, "you're supposed to be introducing me to my first Halloween, not talking religion."

"You got it." The dhole passed Anthony a cup. "We've got a big day ahead of us. First stop, breakfast!"

***

"Oof." Anthony sat back in the seat and patted his stomach. "How the heck do pumpkin waffles fill you up so much?" He stared out the car window as the colors of autumn zoomed by.

"That's the magic of pumpkin," Jude said from the driver's seat.

"I need to learn these magic ways."

The dhole chuckled. "You might get the chance. Their coffee is pretty good too." He took a sip from his cup.

"Bleh." Anthony stuck out his tongue. "If I need a morning pick-me-up, tea is all I can do. Coffee's too bitter." The jackal sipped from his own warm cup.

Jude grinned. "Glad I grabbed one of each."

"I am, too." Anthony nodded his head with a grin. "So, how do you plan to introduce me to Halloween?"

"And spoil the surprise? Now, why would I do that?"

"Because I'm iffy on surprises?" Anthony replied in jest.

Jude smirked. "I know. But as the writer's mantra goes: show, don't tell. But if anything is ever too much, just let me know and we can head back to my place and find something else to do." The dhole flicked on his turn signal, exiting the freeway. "We're almost to our first stop." They pulled off the busy road, just out of town.

"Where are we? Looks really farm-y."

"Kinda cool that this is only twenty minutes from campus?" the dhole said. "First stop: the fairgrounds." Jude set his cup down and turned the wheel, pulling in to a parking lot.

A small sign sat beside the entrance of the parking lot with a "Saturday" and hours in bold, white letters. "A farmer's market?" Anthony asked, reading it aloud.

"Yup. But around this time of year, they mix it up a bit. Come on." Jude nodded his head towards the entrance.

"Do you need help getting veggies or something?" Anthony stepped out of the car and turned to the dhole with a tilt of his head.

"Almost." Jude smiled. "We're going to the back half of the fairgrounds; it's the real draw of the season." Jude hooked an arm around the jackal's and the two walked side by side.

I can feel how warm he is. Anthony almost didn't hear the dhole. With a cough he slid his arm free from Jude as nonchalantly as he could. "'The draw?'" Anthony asked.

"*That's* where we're going." He pointed to a billboard in front of the entrance with a massive pumpkin with the words "Pumpkin Patch" in bold orange letters with a swooping arrow.

The jackal raised an eyebrow in confusion. "Umm, we're picking pumpkins?"

"Yup." Jude nodded. "You weren't far off when you asked if we were getting veggies."

"And that's fun?"

"Oh, stop trying to be a stick in the mud. There are tons of things we can do with pumpkins. But I want to show you something else, first. Come on." Jude pulled the jackal onward.

Anthony let out a bark of surprise.

"Oh shit, are you okay?" The dhole asked, bracing the jackal.

Anthony planted his feet under him. "Yeah, just not used to being tugged on like that."

"Sorry. I'm just so excited." Jude let him go and instead stood next to the jackal, rubbing his own elbow. "I haven't been able to do this with anyone else before." His tail wagged enough to brush against the jackal's leg.

Anthony's ears warmed in a blush as his hip and tail were rubbed by the dhole's. *That's nice, but I should stop it.* The jackal coughed. "Uhh, Jude?"

"Hmm?" The dhole kept walking, head forward, tail wagging and eyes up.

Anthony took a step away from Jude and pointed to the patch. "Shouldn't we be heading over there?"

The dhole nodded. "Don't worry, we will."

"But what else is there to do?"

"Well, our first activity is right over there." He pointed to the edge of the fairgrounds.

Tall yellow stalks ran the length of the lot. "The corn field?"

"It's not just a cornfield, it's a corn *maze*. I help them set it up every year," Jude said, beaming with pride.

Anthony saw the dhole's eyes sparkle and he couldn't help but grin. "Sounds like it's special to you."

"It really is. And I can get in for free. Unless you don't want to. As I said, I won't make you do anything you don't want." The dhole looked to Anthony with an expression of reluctant hope.

The jackal sighed. "You're really excited, aren't you?" Jude only nodded. "Okay, let's go."

"Great, come on!" Before Anthony could reply, the dhole ran off.

"Hey," Anthony called, "wait up."

"Hi John!" Jude shouted to the ram by the field. "Jackal's with me!" He pointed over his shoulder as he bolted past the older man and into the maze.

Anthony chuckled at the dhole's exuberance and stopped by the ram. "Umm, thank you for letting us in."

John chuckled. "No need to thank me. Nice to see that pup with a *friend*." The ram winked. "Go on and have fun."

"T-thank you." Anthony walked in. His ears lowered as he thought on the ram's insinuation. *Was that what I think it was? Does he think Jude likes me?* His stomach began to flutter and his ears grew warm again as a grin crossed his muzzle. *No, no, no. I can't.*

Flat, golden stalks of corn crunched underfoot and brought him back to the present. A slight breeze rustled the dry leaves as the jackal followed the twists and turns of the maze. The deeper in he got, the quieter it became.

"Jude?" Anthony called out. "Where are you?"

"Come on, slowpoke. I'm just up ahead."

The jackal started to jog, trying to catch up. "You're not going to jump out and scare me, are you?" As he rounded the corner, Anthony found the dhole coming back towards him and jumped back.

Jude stopped right in front of him. "No. And you're taking forever. Come on We're almost to my favorite part of the maze."

"I'm coming, sheesh. Let me enjoy this place, okay?" The jackal chuckled.

"Fine," the dhole sighed. He stuffed his paws in his pocket and walked beside the jackal.

"You really like this place?" Anthony asked.

Jude closed his eyes and took a deep breath, nodding. "Yeah, I do." He reached out his paw, rustling the corn stalks.

"What makes it so special?" he asked.

"Man, so much. I love the smell of the air, the cool breeze that blows through. And this," he said, pointing to an opening in the maze. As they walked out, the two stood in a massive circle with three exits. Stalks were pressed flat to the ground with yellow hay mixed in, keeping them down. Square bales were scattered about.

Jude walked forward and sat on one in the center. "I feel," he paused, picking at the hay. "I feel so many things here." The dhole looked up at Anthony and patted the space beside him.

The jackal looked at the spot beside Jude. *Lord knows I want to. But… I shouldn't.* Instead, he sat on a hay bale nearest to the dhole, giving him his full attention.

Jude held his smile. "When its busy here, or when we're setting up, I feel such a sense of community." The dhole picked at the hay again. "Creating something like this is hard work but so rewarding. And on a busy day I get to see everyone running around," he sighed, "I feel such joy and belonging." Jude laid back, neck flopping over the edge of the hay bale.

"And times like this, when it's quiet and I'm by myself," he smiled with his eyes closed, "I don't feel alone."

Anthony sat in silence before moving beside the dhole. "You're not alone," the jackal said. "I'm here."

The dhole sat up, tail hitting the hay bale as it wagged. "Thanks." Their eyes met, happiness easily seen on the other's face.

Jude set his paw on Anthony's, causing the jackal to look. *Is he… Are we holding paws?* He coughed and moved his back to his lap, looking around. A new tension crept into the air.

"Okay," Jude stood and stretched back, "So, we have two ways out." He pointed to the paths ahead of them. "Left is point-to-point, like the first half. Right is more like a traditional maze." He looked back to Anthony. "Which way do you want to go?"

The jackal thought a moment. "Which do you like more?"

"With a friend?" Jude put a paw on his chin. "I prefer an activity." He grinned at the jackal.

"An activity?"

"Tag!" the dhole shouted, tapping Anthony's shoulder, "you're it!" He ran to the right path.

"Hey, I wasn't ready!" And the jackal chased after the dhole's wagging tail.

***

The jackal moved to the front of the house to admire their work. Into the flesh of the pumpkin he chose, Anthony had carved a large jackal-lantern with a crooked smile and triangular ears. Jude's was with rounded ears.

Anthony's tail wagged. "I'm happy with how it turned out. Especially for my first try."

"Oh yeah. They look great," the dhole said. "Hey, give me a sec, okay?"

After the jackal nodded, Jude ran inside. Standing there, Anthony watched the flames dance in the afternoon light.

A moment later, Jude walked back with two brown bottles. As he stood beside the jackal, he handed a beer to him.

Anthony looked from it to the dhole. "Isn't it a bit early to be drinking?"

Jude shook his head. "Special occasion. Besides, it's part of your education. It's a pumpkin ale." The dhole turned the label towards him. "This brewer only releases this style around this time every year. But you can say 'no' if you don't want it."

"Well, if it's seasonal." He took the cold bottle from Jude. "And your parents won't care we're drinking their beer?"

The dhole shook his head. "If I pay them back, they won't. Besides, they're out for the weekend. Got the place to ourselves. Enjoy the freedom."

"In that case, thanks." Anthony raised his to the dhole's.

"Cheers." Jude touched his bottle to the jackal's with a soft clink before they both drank.

Flavors of pumpkin and spices melded with the amber beer. "Wow, that's unique."

Jude smiled. "You like it?"

"Yeah. It's just so different. In a good way."

The dhole sipped his beer again. "I'm happy it's not that cold out." He walked up to the porch and returned with two plastic folding chairs in paw and set one on the lawn. "Still comfortable enough to sit outside," Jude said as he set down the second and flopped into it. He pointed to the empty one with his bottle. "Take a seat."

Anthony sat down and sipped his beer again. As he pulled the cross around his neck, the jackal stared at the pumpkins. The candle light moved and flickered, creating light and shadows along the edge of the faces carved into the squash. "Looks a lot neater than I expected; never really watched a flame move like that." His tail wagged.

"They look better the darker it gets," Jude said.

Anthony nodded. "Seeing the faces shine through the night must be really cool."

A comfortable silence set between the two. "So, you've never done anything like this before?" Jude asked.

"What, drink beer while watching a jackal-lantern flicker in the afternoon?" Anthony chuckled and shook his head. "Nah. My mom said it was all devil worship—the carving, not the beer. Though she wouldn't let us drink, either."

"That must have made watching TV tough with all the Halloween specials," Jude said

Anthony scoffed. "She wouldn't let us *watch* TV. Heck, books had to be snuck in and out of the house. The only ones I didn't have to sneak were my bible and school books. And even then I had to prove it was for a school assignment if she hadn't read it yet." The jackal sighed. "Which was often." He rubbed the bridge of his muzzle. "Safe to say I got real comfortable at the school library."

"Freedom to read?" Jude asked.

"Freedom in general." Anthony threw out his legs and arm. "I had books galore and internet access for research. And some personal use. I didn't have to worry about my mom checking my browsing history."

Jude grinned as Anthony sipped his beer. "Didn't want her to see the porn sites you were on?"

Anthony choked on the liquid. "No!" he said between laughing coughs. "The school's computers were firewalled, too. But I looked up sports information or theatre stuff. You know, so I could follow conversations with other kids."

Jude nodded. "I can understand that." He sipped his beer as another silence fell between them. "Is that why you're still trying to see your faith as your own?"

"Partially." Anthony shrugged. "I mean, I feel like a lot of fun things are, well, wrong. I heard stuff equating all fiction about magic to devil worship." The jackal sighed. "But then, I heard the pastor preaching about how God is love. Hearing both ends of the spectrum is hard." Anthony's ears fell and his gaze lowered.

"I can understand that," Jude said. "I mean, I went to a different church, of course, but I remember hearing some of that stuff, too."

The two sat in silence, drinking their beers. Jude tipped his head back, draining the contents of the bottle with a happy sigh.

"I really do hope you're able to come to terms with," the dhole waved in Anthony's direction, "whatever you are having troubles with." He set the empty bottle down. "And if you ever need help, I'm here." Jude placed a comforting paw on the jackal's shoulder. "For anything. Faith, school. Girls."

Yeah right, girls. Anthony scoffed. "Thanks, I'll keep that in mind," he said, trying to sound positive.

Jude's phone started to chime. "Time for more pumpkin magic." He turned off the alarm, grabbed the bottle in one paw and folded the chair with the other before carrying it back up to the porch.

Anthony sat there for another moment, watching the flames in the pumpkins dance.

"You coming?" the dhole called.

"Huh? Oh, yeah." Anthony finished his beer with a sigh and stood, collapsing his chair before setting it alongside the other, and walked back inside.

"Any issues with paprika or almonds?" Jude asked from the kitchen.

Anthony followed the sound of the dhole's voice. "None that I know of."

"Good to hear." Jude gave the bowl a shake.

Light glistened off the seeds and nuts. "Are the seeds shining?" Anthony asked.

"Olive oil," Jude responded. After a few more tosses, the dhole spread them out on the sheet again. "Twenty more minutes. Then snack time." He smiled as he washed his paws. "Hey, do you like musicals?"

Anthony scratched his head. "I mean, I saw a few in school, but not many. I like them well enough, I guess. Why, is there a Halloween-themed one you know of?"

Jude grinned. "A few, actually. Though one's more of a Christmas film in my mind."

Anthony checked his phone. "I'm not sure if I have the time for two movies."

"Well, I was only planning on watching one tonight. But if you're interested, I have a big bed and some extra clothes. Want to stay over?" the dhole asked, drying his paws on a small towel.

"I haven't had a sleepover before." Anthony wrung his paws in front of himself. "I didn't have any friends that Mom approved to spend the night. I'd like to stay, if you don't mind."

"Great!" Jude pointed the jackal to the living room. "Sit down and get comfy. I'm going to order us a pizza and I'll be there in a moment."

Anthony made his way out of the kitchen and sat on the couch. As he took another drink of his beer, a pleasant buzz began between his eyes and his body relaxed into the cushion. He heard the dhole chatter on the phone, and he closed his eyes. A smiled crossed the jackal's muzzle as he focused on the musicality of his voice, the lilt and lift of it.

With a sigh, he sat up and started at the movie collection under the TV. When he heard Jude end the call, Anthony spoke up. "What are we about to watch?"

Jude chuckled, walking back with a fresh six-pack and a bowl of seeds and nuts. "You'll just have to wait and see. I mean, if we're going to corrupt you today, we're doing this right." He grinned at Anthony before turning towards his entertainment center and squatting down again.

The jackal took a pawful from the bowl and tossed it in his mouth. "Oh wow, these are good." He took another scoop. "Everything crunches nicely, and you don't have to worry about the shells. And the flavor of the seasoning is subtle, too."

"So good, right? It's that pumpkin magic."

Anthony stared at the dhole's wagging tail and his eye drifted lower where his jeans became taut, cupping the dhole's firm rear. *His butt looks really nice in those jeans.* He shook his head, ears flapping against his head. *Wait, stop that!*

"You say something?" Jude asked over his shoulder.

"Nothing." Anthony flicked his ear. "Just chewing on some of the seeds."

"Okay." The dhole grabbed a remote and sat beside the jackal. "Now, I will say, this movie hasn't aged very well. But it is still a lot of fun. It's really campy and a hit with… unusual folks."

Anthony tilted his head. "What do you mean?"

"Let's just say your mother wouldn't have approved of this film."

"That doesn't surprise me."

"I think it might be better if I showed you instead. But if you don't like it, just say and we'll turn it off."

"Okay," the jackal said with a hint of confusion.

"Let the show begin," Jude said, starting the film.

As the production company's name rolled by, the screen went dark.

"A long, long time ago," Jude started with the music, "in a galaxy far, far away, God said, 'let there be lips,' and there were."

Anthony looked from the dhole to the screen as red lips appeared. "What was that?" the jackal asked with a chuckle.

"Audience participation. And it's only the beginning. Just wait," Jude's tail thumped against the couch.

And the film rolled on. Anthony's attention was split between the screen and the dhole as Jude not only sang along with it but added his own lines to the movie. Anthony laughed as the dhole hurled insults at the characters and replaced dialogue. Jude even stood at one point, dancing with the film. About twenty minutes in, the doorbell rang, and the dhole got up, returning with two pizzas.

As the movie ran, the two continued to drink and nibbled on food. From time to time, Anthony's mind wandered. *What would Mother think about this? Drinking with a cute friend and watching a movie she never would have approved of. Man, she would flip her lid.*

"Don't forget to turn off the globe!" Jude called, pulling the jackal back to the present. As the room on the screen went dark except for the blue-green sphere on the desk, he sighed. "Shit, he forgets every week."

Anthony laughed. "Every week?"

"Huh?" Jude tilted his head. "Oh, this show not only still plays in some places, but people will act it out at the same time." Jude smiled. "Where I saw it most, it was a weekly thing."

"And people would go to every show?"

"Oh yeah! It kinda became a safe place for the weird. I mean, look at Frank." Jude waved his paw. "He's at least some flavor of queer." As the dhole finished his statement, he placed his paw on Anthony's thigh. "What did you think of it?"

Anthony's head buzzed from the paw and the beer. "It was certainly different," he chuckled. "I mean the costumes alone were... Wow."

"Rocky was hot, wasn't he?"

"Oh, yeah," Anthony replied, flopping his head back. *Wait, did I just...?* His head shot up as he clapped his paws over his muzzle.

Jude smiled. "I thought you might enjoy that. I've always been partial to the floor show." He let out a deep breath and slumped against the jackal. "Have you ever said anything like that before?"

"Uhh, no," Anthony admitted. "I've never..." His eyes sank towards his lap.

"Thought about guys?" Jude asked, filling the silence.

Anthony's ears warmed. "I'd be lying if I said that. But I've never *said* anything." He took a breath and closed his eyes. "Out loud."

"Hey, another first." Jude said. "You're cute, you know that?"

"What?"

The dhole chuckled. "You're cute. Especially when you're flustered."

"Uhh, thanks." Anthony scratched his head in thought. "So, I guess that means you like guys?"

Jude sat up. "Some. And girls. It really depends on the person."

"So, you're bisexual?"

The dhole shrugged. "I don't like labels, personally. I just know I like certain people. And I like you."

"Well…" Anthony swallowed. "I think you're cute too."

Jude's tail thumped against the couch. "That makes me happy. Any other firsts you'd like to try tonight?"

As his face flushed, Anthony's spoke before his brain could stop him. "Can I… maybe kiss you?"

Jude smiled and cupped the jackal's cheek. "I thought you'd never ask."

Anthony leaned in, heart racing and ears warm and flushed—from the alcohol or his feelings, he couldn't tell. As he pressed his muzzle to the dhole's, Anthony closed his eyes and braced his weight on Jude's thigh. When he broke the kiss, he let out a breath. "Wow."

"You enjoyed that, I take it?" Jude smiled.

Anthony nodded. "Can I," he looked away, "kiss you again?"

"You can do anything you want," the dhole said. "But maybe move a paw to the couch?" he asked, patting the jackal's paw. "Might be more comfortable for us both."

"Sorry, sorry." Anthony said. He rested his arm along the back of the couch.

"It's okay," Jude chuckled. "And don't be nervous. Take it at your own pace."

The jackal nodded again. He twisted his torso to face the dhole and bent his leg in front of himself. Reaching out a paw to Jude's cheek, he leaned in for another kiss. As their muzzles met, the jackal's paw returned to Jude's thigh and squeezed.

Anthony broke the kiss and looked into Jude's bright and inviting eyes. He pushed the dhole back on the couch and braced himself on the arm rest, kissing him again.

Jude grabbed the back of Anthony's head and opened his muzzle, inviting the jackal in.

Their tongues danced against each other as Anthony's paw started to wander. He rubbed the muscles under Jude's shirt, and trailed his paw down the dhole's stomach. A soft moan escaped as his fingers teased lower, stopping at the waist of the dhole's jeans.

Jude broke the kiss. "You can keep going. If you want."

The jackal looked between the dhole's legs and watched as his paw cupped the warmth there. This time, Jude let out a soft whimper.

Anthony pressed his muzzle to the dhole's again, feeling the vibrations from the moan and adding his own to the music of their passion as he squeezed the dhole's growing bulge.

The jackal broke the kiss again. "Can we…" Anthony started, heat rising under his fur. "Can we move to the bedroom?"

Jude smiled. "We can."

Anthony moved to let the dhole up. As Jude stood, he took the jackal's paw and led him down the hall. Once in his room, the dhole closed the door behind them.

The jackal sat on the bed. "Can we do that again?"

With a smile on his face, Jude sat beside Anthony and guided a paw between his own legs and leaned in to kiss the jackal again.

As their tongues met, Anthony's paw danced along the dhole's growing warmth. And as the dhole's length grew, so did his own.

Jude's paw slipped down the jackal's chest to his belly and teased along his waistline.

Anthony broke the kiss for a moment. "Keep going," he said, and pressed his muzzle against the dhole's.

When Jude's paw cupped Anthony between the legs, the jackal moaned into the other's muzzle. The two stayed like that with paws groping each other and muzzles locked for what felt like ages to Anthony.

Jude finally broke the kiss. "My pants are getting a little tight. And I think yours are, too. Want to get a little more comfortable?"

The jackal's ear twitched as he felt a familiar feeling in the back of his mind, but he pushed it away. "I will if you do first?"

Jude smiled and slipped his shirt over his head as he stood. As his paws moved to his pants, he stumbled and caught himself. "Sorry, think I've had more than I thought." He smiled and stood up again and undid his pants and slid them and his briefs down.

Anthony couldn't help but stare. The cream fur under his neck ran down his belly, arms and legs. But red fur crept over his groin. His firm shaft sprung from his brick-colored sheath and a heavy sack hung below.

Anthony's own need pulsed in his pants, reminding him of his half of the bargain. When Jude sat back down, the jackal rose. With less grace and slightly more stumbling than the dhole, Anthony removed his clothes.

When he sat back on the bed, Anthony looked from Jude's erection to the dhole himself. "Now what?" he asked.

Jude slid his leg along the bed, pointing his shaft towards the jackal. "Want to go back to what we were doing?" Anthony's tail thumped against the bed in excitement as he nodded.

With a smile, Jude cupped the jackal's cheek and kissed him again.

Closing his eyes, Anthony let his paws wander down the dhole's arms to his chest. As his tongue explored Jude's muzzle, his digits wandered over the muscles hidden beneath cream-colored fur; first his chest, then his belly. The lower his paw moved, the more noticeable the warmth radiating from between the dhole's legs became.

Anthony broke the kiss and stared again as his paw trailed down Jude's side and caressed his thigh. The jackal glanced up to the dhole with a lick of his lips before sliding between Jude's legs, gripping the other's shaft. His own need pulsed as he slid along the dhole's length.

Jude let out a ragged breath and his paw rested on Anthony's knee.

Again, the jackal looked to the dhole, but then, this time to his own erect need. With his other paw, he set it atop Jude's and gently guided it between his legs. And when the dhole's paws wrapped about his flesh, he gave his own soft moan.

Jude pressed his forehead to the jackal's. "Do you want to finish like this?"

"Can we?" Anthony whispered.

The dhole nodded. "We can do whatever you want." He pressed his muzzle to Anthony's, kissing him again as both paws began a steady pace.

***

The incessant beeping broke through the jackal's slumber. *What in the world is that?* Anthony rolled over towards the sound and peeled his eyes open. As he started to focus, the jackal saw a wall of red fur. *Huh?* He blinked. The beeping grew louder, and his head warmed in pain.

"Damn alarm," Jude grumbled. He stumbled out of bed and walked over to the dresser, hitting the ancient looking clock with a thud.

Anthony blinked as he saw the dhole standing there in just his tight underwear. "Uhh, morning, Jude."

The dhole turned and smiled. "Morning. How you feeling?"

Anthony looked away and put a paw to his head. "A small headache and my mouth's kinda dry."

"Sorry about that. I should have had you drink some water before we went to bed." Jude began to move about the room, gathering clothes. "I wear a medium shirt, that fit you?"

"Yeah, it shouldn't be an issue." Anthony sighed and sat up, stretching his arms to the roof. He watched as Jude started to dig through his closet of clothes, tail wagging above his taut rump.

Stop staring at the nice view, Anthony scolded himself. Turning his head, his gaze fell to the mirror that sat above the dresser. His fur and cross was all that stared back. Reaching a paw under the covers he found the cross around his neck was the only thing he wore.

"Does this work for you?" Jude held up a button-down shirt.

"That's fine," Anthony said without looking and the dhole returned to his closet. Memories of the night before came flooding back; the kissing, the groping. "Jude?" Anthony started, pulling the blanket tighter around himself. "What happened last night?"

"We carved pumpkins, drank about two six-packs between us. Not a lot, but we didn't get as much food in as I thought, though. The alcohol may have hit you a bit harder than expected?" The dhole turned around.

Anthony's eyes were on the foot of the bed.

"You okay, dude?" He waited for a response. When nothing came, Jude crawled beside Anthony. "If it's about our state of undress, we didn't have sex," he said. "But, we were both paws-y."

Anthony sniffed. *Oh no.* A tear rolled down the jackal's cheek. *Oh no, oh no, oh no.*

"Hey, you didn't push me to do anything I didn't want," Jude said.

"But *I* wanted it, too." Anthony's voice cracked with emotion.

Jude nodded. "But that isn't bad."

"Yes, it is," the jackal whispered as another tear rolled down his cheek.

Jude put a paw on his shoulder. "Do you want to talk about it?" Anthony shook his head. "Okay, but I'm here if you change your mind. And I think talking about this may help you, buddy."

The dhole stood and grabbed a long robe, covering himself up. "I'll leave you to change while I get breakfast ready. If you want to shower, feel free. It's right across the hall." Jude pointed to the door.

Anthony nodded, not taking his eyes off the bed as the dhole walked out of the room, closing the door behind him. He took a breath and crossed himself, crying. *Oh my God, I am heartily sorry...*

***

Anthony stepped out of the bathroom and the smell of coffee and eggs hit him as he made his way into the dining room.

"Hey. Good timing." Jude smiled, but the spark that was in his eye yesterday wasn't there now.

"Hey." Anthony waved a paw. His tail hung limp and his ears were low.

"I just finished scrambling some eggs and making toast. And I found a few packets of tea; I could microwave some water if you want."

Anthony nodded.

The dhole filled a mug and set it in the microwave. While it heated, Jude puttered around the kitchen. As he set two plates on the table, the microwave dinged. "Dig in. Don't wait on my account." Jude hummed as he grabbed the mug for Anthony and poured himself a cup of coffee.

The jackal picked up his fork and pushed the food around his plate.

Setting the mugs in front of each place setting, Jude took his own seat and watched the jackal. "Do you want to talk about it?"

Anthony shook his head and pushed the plate back. "Sorry, I'm not hungry right now."

"Feeling sick?" Jude asked.

"No."

The dhole went back to the kitchen and drew a glass of water. "Maybe you're a bit hung over still. Food may help." Jude set the water beside the jackal's tea. "At least try to eat the toast."

Anthony nodded.

"Once the alcohol's out of your system, you'll feel better." Jude smiled.

"Thanks," Anthony replied. "But I don't think guilt works that way."

The dhole set down his fork. "I know I said I'd get you to church, but you don't look like you're in any shape to go. Do you want to stay here instead?"

Anthony shook his head. "I *have* to go. It's the least I need to do."

"Okay." He started to reach a paw out to the jackal but stopped. "If you change your mind, just let me know." Anthony simply nodded. "I'm going to take a real quick shower. I'll be back, okay?"

Again, the jackal nodded. From the corner of his eye, he saw the dhole walk past him and moments later the shower started. He sat there, with his mind racing. He replayed the night before and guilt flooded his body. *I'm going to burn in hell.* He fought back the tears and, before he knew it, Jude returned.

"Ready to go?" the dhole asked.

"Huh? Oh, yeah." Anthony stood, rubbing his eyes. "Should I do anything with the plates?"

Jude shook his head. "Don't worry. I'll get them when I get back."

Anthony nodded and followed the dhole to his car. Still lost inside himself, he sat in silence through the ride to the church. Absent from the present, he didn't hear the service. Muscle memory drove him through the motions, but when it came time to receive communion, he stayed seated.

Between his thoughts and personal prayers, he missed when the other parishioners started to shuffle out.

Jude placed a paw on the jackal's arm. "Hey, you there?"

Anthony blinked and looked at the dhole. "Yeah. Sorry. I'm just," he waved his wrist, "lost in thought."

Jude sighed. "Mind if I take you one last place?"

Anthony shrugged. "What more harm could it do?"

The dhole flinched but didn't reply. He stood, waving his arm for the jackal to follow.

As they got into Jude's car, Anthony kept his eyes on his knees, and they drove in silence. He didn't look outside the window until the dhole pulled into a parking lot.

"We're here." The dhole got out of the car.

Anthony looked around. "The farmer's market?"

"Yeah." He gave the jackal a weak smile.

They walked past the empty booths and strolled by the pumpkin patch. People were there picking pumpkins, but Jude ignored them. "I think we have about an hour and a half." The dhole checked his watch as they walked up to the maze.

"Sorry folks, not open yet," the ram said from a few feet away.

"I know, John. But it's important. Mind if me and my friend head in?" the dhole asked.

"Oh hey, Jude. I didn't recognize you. Bad eyes and that." The ram scratched his head. "Sure. Head on in." He shrugged.

"Thank you, sir," the dhole said, and he climbed the gate.

Anthony followed behind him head down, barely paying attention to the maze. Unlike their first trip through, Jude walked along with the jackal. The two canids made their way through the path as it twisted and turned.

When they reached the central courtyard, the dhole spread his arms out wide and took a deep breath. He exhaled and dropped his paws back to his side and walked around the perimeter of the courtyard. Anthony took a seat, watching the dhole.

After a full rotation, Jude stopped in front of the jackal. He looked down at him for a moment before muscling another hay bale in front of Anthony. Crossing his legs, the dhole sat on the bale across from the jackal.

Jude sighed. "You've been quiet all morning and you didn't take communion. I'm worried about you."

The jackal looked away. "I don't know if I want to talk about it yet."

"I completely understand that," Jude said, softening his voice. "But talking through your issues with someone who's been there can really help." He waved a paw around the cornfield. "It's private here and anything you say to me will stay with me."

Anthony didn't respond.

"Hey," Jude said, "you did a lot of other things for the first time yesterday that you weren't allowed to, right? The maze, the pumpkins, the beer. Did any of that feel bad or wrong?"

Tears began to dampen Anthony's cheek ruff. "No, but you kept reminding me I could say no." He glared at the dhole. "In some way, you gave me the chance to back out. But you never did *then*."

Jude nodded and looked down. "You're right. And I should have. I wasn't the most sober either and I made a mistake there." He sighed and met the jackal's gaze again. "But what about *that first* has you so upset?"

There was a moment of silence before Anthony spoke. "I'm scared," he whispered.

"Of what? Me?" Jude asked.

Anthony shook his head. "Are you really going to make me say it?"

"I can't help you unless I know what's wrong."

Jude tried to set a paw on Anthony's shoulder, but the jackal smacked it away. "Really? You want to help? Don't you think you've *helped* enough?"

The dhole furrowed his brow and tilted his head. "I caught the comment you made before. What was so wrong about being intimate with someone?"

"Are you serious?"

Jude leaned back. "Yeah."

"Really?" Venom dripped from his voice as his volume rose. "*Really?* Okay, fine. I'll spell it out. I'm terrified of going to Hell."

"Why would you think you are going to Hell?" Jude asked. "You're a good person." He set his paws on his crossed knees

"But last night!" Tears began streaming down his muzzle and he began shouting. "It's the same reason I didn't take communion; I'm unclean. 'A man shall not lay with another man as he does a woman, for it is an abomination.' I need to repent before I can accept His presence again and *you*—" he jabbed a finger at the dhole, "pushed me to a place you *knew* I wouldn't have wanted to know and now I'm going to burn in Hell."

Jude's jaw fell open and he tried to sit beside Anthony. "You're not going to Hell—"

The jackal sprang up. "You don't *know* that! You *aren't* God."

The dhole made his way over to Anthony and set a paw on his shoulder. "Hey—"

"Don't touch me!" He slapped Jude's paw away again. "This is all your fault." The jackal jabbed a finger to him.

"Anthony, calm down!"

"Why do you think you can tell me what to do?"

"Because I'm trying to help you."

The jackal threw his paws in the air. "How in the world do you think you're going to help me now?"

Without another word, Jude wrapped his arms around the jackal.

"No! Get your paws off me!"

"I won't." Jude shook his head.

"Let me go!" Anthony pushed against the dhole's shoulders, trying to free himself.

"I won't. I know I messed up, but I thought you wanted to. I'm sorry. I already said it and I'll say it again. I'm sorry." He tightened his grip around him. "I'm *so* sorry, Anthony."

"I don't care," the jackal yelled. "I don't care." Again and again, he shouted until the words morphed into cries of anguish and fear. Losing his will to fight—against both the dhole and his feelings—he pressed his head against Jude's shoulder, dampening his friend's shirt with his tears.

Loosening his grip, Jude continued to hold him, rubbing his back.

As Anthony's wails turns to sobs and sobs turned to sniffles, the dhole spoke up. "I'm really sorry. I understand your feelings and I know where you're coming from. But I really think you'll be okay. I mean, Leviticus has a lot of rules. Most of which are ignored today. Do you feel guilty eating shrimp or lobster? Do you feel you need to repent then?"

Anthony tightened his muscles around the dhole, trying to hold on to him like a buoy in the sea, clenched jaw and tears still falling down his cheeks.

"And do you check every clothing tag before you buy a shirt?" Jude continued. "A lot of shirts are mixed materials, which Leviticus forbids, too."

"But I heard how acting on feelings you have towards the same sex is bad so often growing up. Again, and again. It's been drilled into my core as true."

Jude pulled back, holding the jackal by the shoulders. "I truly believe that God loves every one of us. Every species, every nationality, every *sexuality*." As he said the last words, Jude squeezed the jackal. "Just because you're Catholic doesn't mean you can't be gay. Or love a man. You can be both gay and a person of faith."

As the dhole said that, a breeze rustled the corn stalks around them.

Jude looked around, taking a breath. "'The Son of Man has come to seek and save what was lost,'" Jude said from far away.

Anthony finally lifted his head, looking at the dhole. "And what's that from?"

Jude chuckled. "You really weren't paying attention in church today." He stretched his arms high above his head before dropping them to his side. "It was from the Gospel reading. I'm not equating myself to Christ, but I'll help you as I can."

"Didn't Shakespeare write 'the devil can quote scripture for his own purpose'?" Jude scowled.

"Merchant of Venice, Act 1, Scene 3. Touché. But I keep saying I'm not perfect," he said, "but I am confident in myself and God's love."

"How?" Anthony sat back on a hay bale, looking back at his knees. "How can you be so sure?"

"You remember how I said I don't feel alone here?" Jude asked. The jackal nodded. "I find this place just hums with spirituality and I always feel His presence here. I never feel judged; just safe."

"I don't know if I can feel that way," the jackal said.

"Well, you aren't alone, Anthony. There are churches that welcome an LGBTQ congregation, and so many people that won't care about who you love. And I'm here for you, too." The dhole held out a paw to him. "Start by putting one foot in front of the other."

Anthony put his paw in Jude's and stood. As their eyes met again, the jackal saw the spark back in Jude's eyes, and he finally broke down in earnest. Anthony wrapped his arms around the dhole's middle and pressed his face to his shirt as he let out heavy sobs of anguish.

Jude held on to him as he cried out the pent-up pain and denial he held in over the years.

When he started to calm down, Jude spoke again. "I don't think your issue is with your faith, Anthony. And here's the proof. It seems like you may need to come to terms with who you are."

"But I don't know if I can," the jackal said with his head pressed against his middle.

"Then let me help you work through it." Jude lifted the jackal's chin. "I really do care for you. As a friend, first and foremost."

Anthony nodded. The wind rustled the yellow leaves and stalks around him, calming him further. "Thanks."

Jude took a breath before continuing. "And I'm sorry about last night. I didn't mean to upset you or freak you out. We should have talked first."

Anthony shook his head. "I did what I wanted. I need to learn to live with the consequences."

"Well, you know I'll help you however I can, right?"

Anthony nodded.

"If you want me to take you home, I will," Jude said.

"Could I, maybe, stay with you a little longer? Maybe we could try to talk a little more?"

Jude nodded. "It would be my pleasure." He put his arm around the jackal's shoulder and started walking with him around the edge of the yard. "If you want, I was thinking of watching a movie tomorrow night while passing out candy for trick-or-treaters. You're welcome to join me."

"Candy?" Anthony asked.

"You'd be surprised at the number of college kids that trick-or-treat." Jude said.

"No way?" Anthony chuckled, rubbing his eyes on his sleeve. "Sounds like fun. If you won't mind me there."

"I'd be happy to have you." They started down the direct path out, side by side.

***

The jackal sat in the passenger's seat in a tie and nice pants staring at the door to the building. His paws were in his lap, but they shuffled constantly.

"You okay Anthony?" the dhole asked. "We can try to wait another week if you want."

Anthony shook his head. "No. I've already gone to confession. The priest talked a lot like you did. My sins have been absolved." He took a breath. "But I'm still scared." He rubbed the back of his neck.

"Why?" Jude set a paw on the jackal's knee, and Anthony held it.

"It's one thing to hear words and understand them here." He pointed to his head. "But it's different feeling them here." This time, the jackal pointed to his heart.

The dhole nodded his head. "There's another service in an hour and a half. Would you rather go to that one?"

Anthony squeezed the dhole's paw, closed his eyes, and took a deep breath. As the air left his lungs, he shook his head. "No, I think I'm ready."

"You sure?"

The jackal nodded. "Yeah. Time for my first service as a gay man." He opened the door and made his way in font of Jude's car and the dhole met him there.

"You ready?" Jude asked.

Anthony took another breath. "Yeah." He held the dhole's paw and took his first steps forward.

To all those just starting out in writing - keep at it! If I'm proof of anything it's that one day you can make it work.

High Sticking

by Ferric the Bird

I did my best to push away from the wall as that puck came zooming on by; where there were pucks there were usually giant bodies racing to get them. This time was no different as a blur of red and white rushed on by soon afterwards in heavy pursuit. Those two figures followed the black disk of rubber all the way behind the goalie's net, only to meet a matching set of red and white players coming in from the other side. With a few heavy hits between them both sides locked together in a heated battle over the small disc of rubber. Sticks and legs quickly surged towards the puck as each player desperately tried to knock it free of the sudden tangle.

It was times like this that I was glad I didn't have to try and muscle a polar bear out of the way anymore. I had some sympathy for the poor wolf that was trying to do just that as it certainly wasn't an easy task. A snarling tenacity, some serious core strength, and a great sense of balance were all things I once had in abundance. I was a young and spunky elk for sure back then, doing my best to play in the minor leagues and hoping to make it big one day. That was over ten years ago though, although I'd argue that I still had the balance down pretty good even now. The rest... eh, some things tended to mellow with age.

In fact, things were quite the opposite now. Instead of being the spearhead for every play and having all the eyes watching me, everyone simply did their best to avoid me and pretend I wasn't there. Not only did they avoid me, but they also did their best not to be seen by me either. It was quite a change of pace, but it was certainly less strain on my joints and body. Then again being a referee had its downsides as well, and I was about to be reminded of them quite loudly.

As that jostle began to get intense, I kept my eyes trained on each player as best as I could. I watched as the bear gave a firm kick to that puck with his skate, sending it rolling free of the small group of bodies and sticks pressed against the boards. A rather large snowshoe hare, who was perched right at the end of the little gathering, quickly gobbled up that puck and began to skate away from the pack with it on his stick.

He gave one powerful push to the ice with his thick and muscled leg, and he was just about in the middle of a second push before the wolf from the opposite team realized he had the puck. The canine reached out with his own stick, trying to lock it underneath the hare's to make him lose control. He tried to lift both sticks up and off the ice with a sudden flick of his wrists; however, his positioning was just a little bit off. As the wolf yanked up on his stick the blade quickly shot passed the hare's own stick, continuing even further past his paws. It flew towards his shoulder, and eventually gave him a grazing blow over his cheek, visor, and the side of his helmet.

It was just barely enough contact to ruffle the hare's white arctic fur, but his reaction to the contact told quite a different story. His head quickly snapped back as if he'd been literally punched in the face. The tips of his long ears, which were flattened and left dangling out of the back of his helmet, flopped back and forth throughout the whole exaggerated action. And as soon as the hare's head began to return back from its sudden snap, he lifted a gloved paw to his mouth, holding it tightly as if he was in sudden excruciating pain.

The whole thing was a ruse, and no one was really fooled by the display. The contact the hare got with that stick blade was barely enough to move his cheek fur, much less cause any pain. Yet at the same time I could feel my arm start to shoot up into the air to signify a penalty. I didn't have time to think about why, it just sort of happened, surging out of me as a straight up gut reaction. Ten years of reactive training had left me open to such gaps in my rational thinking at times, leaving me relying on instinct when I saw a reaction like that. This one was a slight shock even to me though as I felt my arm extending into the air. But, now that the signal was given, there was nothing I could do no matter how much I began to second guess myself.

The wolf, oblivious to my signal so far, reached out and touched the now free puck a moment later as the hare was still busy trying to sell the penalty. Upon his first contact with the puck I lifted my whistle up to my lips and gave a firm blow to stop the action.

Instantly I heard a loud rolling boo start to erupt from the crowd, with loud curses and downright evil shouts ringing out from those closest to the ice. This was a very important game after all. It was the

Stanley Cup Final, game five. The visiting team was already leading 3-1 in the series, and with one more win they would win the Cup. They were also ahead 5-3 in the current game with only seven minutes left. Now the home team had just taken a cheap and blatantly faked penalty. I was certainly not surprised that I heard those boos, but I did my best to push them out of my head as I slowly skated over towards the hare to check on his condition.

"Got any blood?" I asked quickly as I came to a stop in front of him. He was certainly not another one of those twinky rabbit boys that seemed to be everywhere. He was a big, muscled, cold-weather hardened snowshoe hare, and he was quite intimidating to have to look up at despite his cute and cuddly lapine appearance. His glove had fallen away from his muzzle at this point, but only after giving it a few final rubs in order to sell his discomfort just a little more.

"Nah, I'm fine," he said casually. He didn't even look in my direction as he said it before he began to skate back towards his bench without another word, pretending not to notice me like everyone else.

I slowly held up two fingers in the air to signify it was only a minor penalty while I skated over towards the timekeeper's box to let them know officially. I flicked on my microphone as I skated back towards center ice and said, breaking through the loud cacophony of boos still raining down at me, "Number 52. 2 Minutes. High-sticking."

The boos quickly surged in intensity as I did my best to keep a stern and steady face. I tried hard not to let them get to me, but at the same time it was near impossible not to. I was used to getting some negative feedback on my decisions, but this was one of the loudest I could remember hearing. It was a Stanley Cup Final game after all. The home team was losing and was about to be eliminated, and now they had two minutes where they had to play some serious defense for a silly, exaggerated call. But I'd made my call and now everyone had to stick by it. That was the power of being a referee. Everyone else certainly had the power to voice their displeasure with me though, and it seemed like they were going to shake the whole building down with their boos soon enough to prove it.

The boos didn't even stop as the puck dropped and play got underway once again. It took a few good saves from the home town goalie to finally shift the crowd's minds onto other things, although I still heard the occasional chant and shout directed my way as time ran down in the game. In the end the penalty didn't even really matter. All it did was kill two minutes off the play clock as nobody scored as a result. Even with the five minutes the home team had left they weren't able to get much done either. They surged and put in a good effort. They got in a few nice shots and made the goalie make some good saves. But, in the end, when the buzzer finally rang the score was still 5-3.

The crowd was mostly silent at the outcome, besides a few diehard fans for the visiting team that had made the trip all the way from the opposite coast. On the ice though there were sticks, gloves, helmets, and who knows what else flying up in the air in celebration as the final buzzer rang. I couldn't help but smile a little myself at the festivities, although I did my best to hide it as I slowly made my way off the ice. The game was over, my job was done. We refs didn't get to celebrate. We didn't win anything. We were simply there to make sure that someone else could.

Even though we couldn't be out there with all the excitement on the ice, the other referees and I still exchanged a few high-fives as we all slid into that tunnel. We might not have won the game ourselves, but we'd done a good job officiating the game, and that was worth some excitement between us. Only the best of the best got the honor to work at a Stanley Cup Finals game. I'd been making my journey there with many years of dedicated service and hard work, as had all of the others. We knew each other well at this point, and there was plenty of excitement to go around as we all were wearing rather large smiles.

We did our best to remain silent though as we made our way to the locker room. We quickly undressed and showered, trying to get everything done before the players started to come in. The best part was that us refs usually had to change in the visitor's locker room, so the place was empty while the excitement and ceremonies were still going on out on the ice. It was only when we were just about ready to leave that the first players started to walk in, offering up high fives and excited screams which we half-heartedly gave back. The sudden influx of players only made us want to get out of there faster to avoid the chaos that was to follow. Before most of the players could start filing in, we quickly slid out the back while we still could.

We made our way down a few hallways to the end of the locker room passage, and soon met up with our security guards. They were glorified rent-a-cops, but at the same time it was nice to have someone there to protect us. Some of the fans got rather rowdy at times, especially with a hometown loss. Thankfully most of the fans simply decided to go home and sulk tonight, although there were still a few small shouts as we began to walk outside and back to the nearby hotel.

We made it back without anything more than a few shouts directed at us and gave a friendly goodbye to our guards before making our way up to our rooms. Although once our stuff was dropped off, we quickly gathered back into a single room to break open the alcohol and start the celebration ourselves. It wasn't just the players that could party tonight after all, and we were prepared for a little referee party of our own! It'd been a long season for us too, and although we loved what we did we couldn't help but celebrate another completed season and another Stanley Cup given out. We were all a little older than most of the players however, so instead of loud music and raucous party antics we settled for a few small cups of booze and general conversation as we relaxed on the hotel beds.

We had a good time simply talking about the game, the series, and what next year might bring for us and the league. Not to mention just what all of us had planned for the upcoming break. A few vacations, a few wives and girlfriends to get back to seeing regularly, and a lot of just enjoying life and drinking in every moment we could.

It was a fun time shared by a few good friends as we all smiled and laughed along. We were up for a few hours drinking and chatting, but at that point the old man in all of us began to rear its ugly head. It started with Janus passing out on his bed, a half full cup of his special drink still clenched softly in his hand. By that point we all knew it was about time to say goodnight and part ways. So, with a few hugs, handshakes, and goodbyes my roommate and I slowly made our way back into the hallways of the hotel.

Once we were free of that stuffy room, I reached for my cell phone to check my messages. After scrolling through them I let him know that I wasn't completely dead yet, and I was going to go for a quick walk to get some fresh air. With a wave he wished me well, and with a short message sent off on my phone I began to head for the stairs.

I didn't make it down too many floors before opening the door and continuing along the 8th floor, casually looking around until I spotted the ice and vending room. The hotel we were in was pretty fancy, so the room was more of a lounge than just a little walk-in closet like some others. I carefully took a look around to see if anyone was watching, and with a deep breath I opened the door and stepped inside. I only made it about three or four steps before I suddenly felt two large arms push themselves around my rib cage and wrap tightly around my chest from behind.

I gave off a soft bleat as the air was forced out of my lungs with the tight squeeze. I could smell the alcohol on the male's breath behind me as he pulled me against his own muscled chest and slowly laid his chin down on top of my antler free head. (They were removed so my helmet would fit of course. It's the hockey player's look.) I did my best to try and push him off as my hands wrapped around his massively thick arms, but I wasn't as strong as I used to be. There was no moving those tree trunks off my body unless the person behind me wanted to move them, even as I gave off another strong yet playful squirm in his slowly crushing grasp.

"Mmmph, hey there... Mr. Stanley Cup Champion..." I added back, pausing in my squirms in order to focus on getting a good breath in through the pressure. "How's it feel?"

"Fantastic!" the hare behind me added with a soft and loopy chuckle, adding another firm squeeze that caused me to gasp once again.

"D...don't... kill me... Andy..." I added with another straining huff, now giving his arms a rather firm push and feeling his grip loosen on me just a bit. With a deep breath or two I slowly spun around to look up at him. The snowshoe hare's long ears were at full attention, although one was starting to droop just a little due to the alcohol. He had the widest drunk smile plastered over his face that I'd ever seen, and as he continued to stare back down at me, I watched his nose and whiskers twitch, adding to his surprising cuteness. Surprising cuteness for a six-and-a-half-foot beast of a man that is.

I could only imagine what he was feeling with everything that'd happened in the past few hours, and that smile of his was certainly quite infectious. I felt my own cheeks and lips start to grow into a nice and wide one myself, especially the longer I looked up at him. I caught it happening and gave off a soft chuckle before I simply said, "Congratulations." And then, as if I was continuing on in one smooth calculated movement, I slowly leaned up on my tippy toes and moved my smiling lips towards his.

He was quick to pucker up his lips and lean down into the kiss as well. Both of us closed our eyes slightly and just enjoyed the moment as I felt his large paws begin to slide up and down my back and sides. I did much the same to him as my hands traced along his muscular back. I felt every sore, beaten up, and bulging muscle underneath his shirt twitch as I ran my fingers along them, causing the large hare to squeak more than a few times into the deep kiss we shared.

We enjoyed the quickly deepening kiss for far too long before I finally began to tear myself away to catch my breath. I think we both gave off a little shiver at the passion still running through us as we filled our lungs once more with deep, slow breaths. There was nothing much to say really. We simply stood there smiling for quite a while before I finally had the sense to pull us away from the doorway and off towards the side of the room, hoping that would keep us safe from any prying eyes.

It was risky enough just being seen together much less actually kissing. That had made things quite difficult in the past, and in fact it still did. We'd been together for almost two years now and nothing had really come easy for us. The secret trips, the secluded meetings, the 'chance' encounters here and there… that's all we really had. During the season we were both quite busy, but on occasion we got to be in the same town on the same night. We did our best to make do when we could, but it was hard to even get a room together. If his name, or even mine had come up as renting a private room then questions would start to be asked. Questions we might not want to give answers to. Questions that might get us both suspended from the league, if not fined and all sorts of other stuff. It was certainly unethical, but then again… as I stared up into his large, excited eyes and felt his impressive arms and body squeeze tight around me again, I could say that the risk was well worth the reward.

"Mmmph, I'm really proud of you," I said back with another smile, gently giving his hips a few more rubs with the palms of my hands. "You played really well this game and the whole series. You guys earned it."

He gave off a soft smile at those words before leaning down and adding a nuzzle to my cheek and forehead. "Mmmm, thanks Jack," he said as he gave me a kiss to my cheek. "I couldn't have done it without you. Nice officiating."

"You could've and you did," I responded quickly to his attempt to be cute. I don't know why that comment always seemed to get under my skin, and it was certainly far from the first time Andy had said something like that. It always made me tense up a bit on the inside and feel like I was doing something I wasn't supposed to be doing just for him. But, on the other hand, I simply couldn't stay mad at the sexy hare. Especially when I looked up at that big, smiling face of his and the way his ears drooped just slightly at my sudden rougher tone.

Andy quickly leaned in for another soft rub against my chest and nuzzle against my head, before finishing it off with a rather strong hug. He did his best to be as sweet as a giant hare could, which was surprisingly sweet to be honest. "Mmmmph, I was just joking…" he added in with a small whimper under his voice, forcing a small crack of a smile to break through my stern lips, which were now pressed against his strong squeezing shoulder.

Something about being around the rabbit always tended to awake my inner youth. He made me feel many years younger than I actually was, and that was part of what I loved about him. That was the part that kept me coming back and taking risks. His soft apology was only the icing on the cake as I felt those words send a little loving shiver down my spine. Before I could stop myself, I gave off a soft grin and released one of my hands from his back. With a firm and directed swat I brought it right down on his sexy, muscled ass, letting the loud spank ring in the small room.

"Next time you have to work harder on your acting though," I said after hearing him squeak out from the sudden spank. It was meant to be more playful than anything, but I could tell I'd struck some kind of nerve with the rabbit. I knew that look on his face by now as he stared back, and I knew that he had enjoyed it a little more than I had intended.

Before he acted on anything though he had a challenge to respond to. A professional athlete could never back down from a challenge after all. With a rather cocky smile he looked down at me and slowly said back, "It was good enough to fool you at least!" I could feel his chest puff out just a bit, leaving his fur growing a few sizes around and underneath his shirt as he did his best to look confident and sure of himself.

I smirked at that and quickly slid both of my hands up to his chest to search for his nipples, giving each one a quick pinch to make him squeal and deflate rather quickly. I couldn't help but counter his childishness with my own as a soft chuckle escaped my lips at the same time. I felt like I was part of the team once again, twenty years younger than I was, and he and I were simply fooling around in the locker room. There wasn't any of this aching joint, straining back, old person stuff to worry about. When I was with Andy, I felt like we were both straight out of high school… except he actually was.

"Oh, I know just how much of a faker you are," I added in with a playful grin of my own up at him. Now I was on the attack since he'd gotten me slightly riled up with his response. The residual alcohol certainly helped with that as well, not to mention the sexy stud of a hare squirming at my touches in front of me. That normally large and powerful beast, a force to be reckoned with out on the ice, was already shrinking down in size and dominance as soon as I began to push back. It was cute to watch. Very cute. And it left me grinning nice and wide as I got more and more confident with each word.

"You're so much of a faker," I started again, although lowering my voice just a little bit in case someone was listening out in the hallway, "that I bet every orgasm you ever had from me was fake too."

He gasped suddenly at that accusation as another smile only grew firmer on my face. I could tell he was matching my playfulness with his reaction though. That was part of the reason I loved being around him. For some reason we just clicked, and although it wouldn't seem possible from the outside, we were quite the complementary pair, no matter the age difference. "How dare you good Sir!" he added back, reaching up a paw and very gently slapping it across my cheek as if a duel was just initiated.

It was barely a grazing blow, just enough to ruffle some of my cheek fur, and it made me grin a little more in the process. Then, after a good moment had passed by, I whipped my own head back in an exaggerated motion that sent my ears flopping against my head in the middle of the snap. When I returned back to my starting position, I quickly cupped a paw over my cheek and jaw, saying back with a gentle rub, "Owwww… that's a penalty right there!"

"Psh," Andy said back with a little roll of his eyes. "I barely touched ya! You're getting weak in your old age Grandpa…"

That comment made me grit my teeth and stare up at him with that firm officiating face I'd been working on for ten years. It almost zapped the fun right out of the hare's normal bounce and sway, but just as he was starting to transition from playful to serious, I made my move back to playful to keep him off balance. With a slow reach up of my own hand I extended out my fingers, casually brushing them up against the hare's cheek as my digits passed through his beautiful arctic fur. I made sure to use the same cheek that had been 'hit' with that stick only a few hours ago. I also made sure my caress was as sweet and gentle as I could make it to further prove my point.

"And that?" I added, focusing my glare a bit more into the hare's own eyes as a more evil and teasing expression fell over my face.

"Mmmm," he added with a little shiver in return. It was so easy to make such a big guy like him shake and go weak in the knees. I did love that power, and I might be guilty of abusing it just a bit. "I think that's a penalty too," he added with a few soft but deep breaths. "Teasing with intent to arouse! What's the signal for that on the ice?"

I chuckled heartily at that before letting my stern face fade. The rabbit had done it again. He'd broken through my defenses and left me vulnerable. I gave a few more soft touches to his cheek before finally sliding my paw down over his chin and to his chest. This was supposed to be a friendly meeting and a congratulations—at least that what the hare had told me in his message. But... in his presence I just couldn't help myself. He brought out all the bad parts inside of me. The parts that I'd worked so hard to repress and control.

Secretly I really loved letting my naughty side come out and break some rules on occasion though. It was just so liberating after being in a profession comprised of strict rule following. "Mmmm, I'd show ya," I finally responded with a little pressure against his chest, "but I have to take your pants off first."

"You have time to do that on the ice?" Andy added back without missing a beat. I think the alcohol, or maybe just the winning energy in the room made us both a little silly, because I couldn't help but laugh a good bit at that. And it only got worse when he continued with, "If you do then you should be *really* good at doing it quickly by now!"

He added in a quick wink himself that made me chuckle just a little bit more, and before I could stop myself, I felt my paws sliding down to the button and waistband on his jeans. I grabbed onto that denim firmly, pulling it away from those tight abs of his for just a moment, before threatening to open his pants up with a few more small twitches of my fingers. "You really need another demonstration?" I asked with a heavy grin, licking my lips to tease the now squirming hare even more.

I had been teasing up to now, and I thought that Andy had as well. But when the look on his face changed to a strong and needy whimper at my grasp, I could tell that something was up. "What's a matter?" I added with a smirk, not realizing that I should stop while I was ahead. "Can't take the teasing anymore?"

"It's just..." he started with a little gulp and shiver, "I've held back doing anything for more than a week, to keep my testosterone levels up. For a hare that's a week of torture!"

I barely had time to throw him a small smirk and watch him squirm a little more, finally feeling it was time to cut the teasing. But I found out it was a little late for that as those large lapine eyes stared down at me, burning heavily with more need than I could ever hope to control.

"P...please..." he said suddenly with a cute little whimper as he grabbed onto my sides rather tightly. "I want you to make this day so much more perfect." His large, pleading, and submissive eyes really fought against my own as I could feel my breath catch in my throat at that gaze. I knew what I *should* say, but at the same time...

"Right here?" I finally added back, looking up at him a little nervously as things had come to this point. I really had just meant to tease a bit. I knew Andy was pent up. I knew he needed some attention. But I didn't really want to get him going so far over the edge though. In a few weeks, once the media buzz around his win died down, we'd find a time and place to get in all the make-up sex we could ever hope for, and both of us would be too sore to even move. The problem was that we were here together at this moment, and that sexy rabbit staring down at me with those big, pleading, submissive eyes was making it very hard to think rationally about anything in our future.

He nodded a little to my question, not even daring to give back a vocal response, before I finally took a deep breath and slowly said, "I know we don't get very much time together, and I'm *very* happy to see you too, trust me. But you remember how we got in trouble last time when we tried something like this?"

"Y...yeah..." he added back as his breathing started to get heavy. "I know it's risky, but... it's late and no one will come by. Plus, neither of us have a room or anything, and I really want it. I *need* it from you Jack!" He continued to whimper up a storm as he let his hips thrust with some heavy need against my own belly and chest.

"You're just lucky that the passing cop knew who you were," I added with a groan, now trying my best to wiggle my way out of the situation as I tried not to grind back against the rabbit's growing need. "Back in the alleyway, a few blocks from the hotel, 2 am... seemed safe enough. Until that Mountie walked in on us. He was going to arrest us both, you remember? At least until he saw your ID and name. We were *very* lucky he was a fan Andy, and your autograph was enough to keep him quiet."

Andy gave a little nibble to his lip edge as he stared back through my lecture, slowly shifting from large foot to foot as he nodded and said, "Yeah, but that was one time... outside..."

"Then the other time in the arena restroom," I started with a groan, watching him squirm a bit more at the memory. "You remember that too? In the arena after all the fans had left? $250 later, after that janitor had peaked over the top at us… We're *very* lucky that he kept quiet for all I had in my wallet, and that he didn't recognize either of us."

"Yeah yeah," Andy added back, still squirming and quickly trying to brush my words off as he pushed his body against mine, letting me feel his throbbing need once again grinding into my belly. "Alright, twice," he said with a slightly frustrated huff. "How many times have we gotten away with it, huh?" He left a little pause for me to say something, but when I didn't, he quickly said back, "We don't have many other options. Ever."

I slowly shook my head, doing my best to wiggle out of the monster I'd created and his firm, horny grasp of me. But it was no use. The hare had me, and nothing I said would lead to him let me go. But I had one more card to play as I gave off a heavy sigh.

"In two or three weeks, we can head out somewhere quiet—just the two of us—and we can do whatever you want for as long as you want in complete privacy. I promise."

It was my last chance to convince him, and even though I could see his expression falter and consider it, those big needy eyes flashed back onto mine again after a moment to say, "I can't wait two or three weeks… I need you now."

Before I could even say anything back, I felt the hare lean in and squeeze my body against his one more time. His lips met mine in a deep, silencing kiss, leaving me squirming in resistance… but squirming against a mountain of muscle I had no hope of overcoming. I knew I could fight; I knew I could just simply say no, and have it end there. I'd have to deal with the hare's disappointment and frustration for a while, but in the end, we'd be better off for it.

That was never how it ended up working though. I was not strong enough of a person to do that. I couldn't just outright say no to him, and the longer we kissed the more I felt myself relaxing and falling into it as well. In the battle of need versus rationality need was beginning to win out—certainly on the rabbit's end, and after a moment I could feel my own desires start to creep up as well. Especially as those muscles flexed powerfully under my soft rubs over his shoulders and back.

As I pulled away from the kiss with an eventual heavy sigh, I couldn't help feel my hand start to reach for his button yet again. This time I didn't stop at just holding it. Instead I felt my hand slowly begin to tug his pants apart. "Mmmph, alright, something quick for now to hold you over." I added with a groan, feeling a little bad in my head for giving in, but at the same time knowing that I'd make the rabbit happy. That in itself was worth the risk. "But just something quick."

"Mmmph, thank you Jack," he added back with a heavy and relieved huff that only grew louder once I managed to slip his pants open. From there it was easy enough to slip underneath his underwear waistband and let my hand give a firm grope to his hard cock.

The first squeeze made him jump a good few inches as I could only smirk and hold on, loving the way the rabbit danced in my grasp already. His foot continued to thump down against the floor the more I squeezed and began to stroke, working him up into a good set of repetitive moans and squirms. I did my best to hide his large frame from view of the door with my own body, or at least the naughty parts of him that mattered, as my arm continued to slowly move up and down.

His gasps and moans grew heavier with each pass I made, but before long I could tell that he had some other thoughts beginning to surface as well. He certainly enjoyed each stroke I gave him, but at the same time I watched as his face twisted this way and that, knowing that he was craving more.

"Mmmph, Jack, please..." he added in with a heavy whimper shooting through his voice, making it quiver and shake much like the rest of his body was. "I can't just... have this. I need more. It's... not enough..."

"More?" I added back, a little surprised and thrown off myself at such a quick decision. I stopped my gentle pumps and just held my paw steady on his cock as I watched him whimper and nod a little in response. "I said we're only doing something quick."

"I want to go... all the way..." he added with a cute and needy smile. "Please... it's been so long since we have... and it'd be a perfect end to a perfect day..."

Sometimes the hare made me want to tear off my non-existent antlers. He'd played me. He'd played me well. He'd gotten me started, agreeing to get him off, and then dumped those cute whimpers and spine shivering sexy voice on me afterwards. I should've known. Then again, I'd always fallen for it in the past, so I wasn't exactly innocent for letting him go through with it.

He blushed just a little bit more to help get me on board, which was certainly a very cute thing to see. When I was still unmoved, he slowly lowered his muzzle down to one of my ears and almost whispered, "I want your dick inside of me. I want to suck your cock, and then I want it in my ass."

His needy tone simply made me shiver as he made no effort to hide his need. That deep breathing in my ear both before and after, as well as the heavy scent of aroused male quickly growing in the room, left me giving off my own little shiver at his desperate words. I hesitated just a bit before starting to say something and then stopping again. I was close to saying no, and that a hand job was all I could give him here, but... at the same time, the more I stared at his cute and needy face the more I felt my reaction begin to turn. With a defeated huff I finally felt myself say, "Get on your knees and get to work."

Those words felt wrong the moment I let them out of my muzzle, and I wanted to pull them right back as a sudden ping of rationality surged through me. But, at the same time, the smile that grew on Andy's face afterwards left a warm glow on my insides. I thought he might have been all out-joyed by now, spent from his various celebrations throughout the night, but it seemed that he still had plenty left as his body sunk down lower and into place at my groin level. I took a hold of his large ears and gave them a few soft strokes as his paws shot up towards my pants. With a few quick motions they worked my pants open and slid them down, as if Andy was already rather well practiced on the subject.

I didn't let them get too far past my rump cheeks though. I still wanted to be able to make a quick move if someone were to walk in and try to hide what was going on. But at the same time, I didn't resist as Andy pulled them a little lower, making sure my underwear hooked underneath my own cock and balls to frame and display them rather proudly. I was just as eager as the rabbit was to be completely honest, although I was certainly a little better at hiding it. I couldn't deny that I wanted to rail that sexy toned rump into next week. The rabbit had broken down my defenses, much like he usually did, and there I was... decent sized human-like cock out and being lead towards his lips.

He swallowed it like the hungry little thing he was, gulping down over it and pushing his lips over every inch with a flash of needy fury. I struggled to hold back a gasp as my member was engulfed by his warmth and wetness, but with a little grit of my teeth I was able to stay mostly silent. Not like it really mattered as the rabbit's slurps were far louder than I could be anyway. His head bounced eagerly back and forth, pushing my member into his mouth nice and deep. Already, after only a few movements, I could feel him starting to poke it down his throat as well.

I grasped his ears tightly, squeezing and pulling them in an effort to get him to slow down and stay quiet, but there was no controlling a horny hare. He was set on his course, and nothing less than a fresh load of cum would stop him now. He spread his slick spit all up and down my shaft, making it glisten brightly whenever he pulled himself back for a breath. Soon the slickness was dripping from his lips and onto his chin, matting down his fur in the process. His own poor cock, erect and throbbing between his spread legs and knees, continued to throb underneath his underwear's light covering. It was enough to leave him moaning and arching his back for more with each hungry slurp.

I could only take so much of that fantastic treatment before I finally had to pull him off, tugging back on his ears until he finally got the message and slowly withdrew. "I think… its slick enough…" I added with a few breaths to match the rabbit's own. "You want it in your rump still, right?"

That got a quick nod from him as I slowly let go of his ears, letting them bounce around a bit with each quick and eager nodding motion he made. "Well then," I started, looking around carefully to see what options we might have. Luckily there was a small counter space hanging out of the wall that was meant to hold your ice buckets and snack choices. It was well out of view of the door and just wide and high enough to work. So, with a little smirk I drew my gaze back down towards the hare and slowly said, "Alright then, up and on your ass here," with a soft pat to the counter next to us.

Andy took a quick look up at the counter and then back at me, looking a little unsure. But I continued to angle my firm officiating glare at him as I patted the counter space one more time. "Up!" I repeated, and with a quick hop the rabbit was up onto his feet and quickly pushing himself back onto the counter.

The large hare barely had room to keep his butt on the edge of that small counter, having to angle his back and wiggle almost uncomfortably into position as the weak plywood slowly bent and creaked under his weight. It held though, and that was all I needed as I slowly hooked my hands under his knees and began to lift his legs up, drawing his underwear around that sexy toned rump in the process. He had to adjust a little more, but soon his large feet were up by my shoulders, leaving me plenty of space to slowly wiggle in between them and spread his legs a little farther.

From behind it was hard to mask what we were doing at this point.

If anyone was to walk in then it'd be obvious what was going on. With the hare's large feet up in the air, my pants draped around my ass and thighs, and the scent of arousal and sex in the air... there was nothing I could do to even pretend we were doing something else. But, at this point, I knew neither of us would last long, so what were the chances that anyone would walk by in the next five minutes anyway?

I quickly pushed both his pants and his underwear up and over his upturned rump, bunching the wad of clothing onto his thick and powerful thighs. It gave me access to what I needed but left him able to pull everything into position should we need to abort fast. With a soft grin at the cute sight before me, and hearing the rabbit give off another set of needy whimpers, I quickly wedged my cock tip up against his ass.

I continued forwards right on through his pucker with an easy, slick push. He was a rabbit after all. He was a natural, and his large body size made it all that much easier to open him up. The spit he'd given my cock was more than enough lube as my shaft quickly disappeared inside and slid deep with a firm grind.

It was heaven for both of us as the needy hare got his filling and I had something warm around my cock once again. But it was more than that as we simply shared a rare moment of closeness together. I didn't even move my hips at all for what felt like a few minutes. I just kept myself stuffed inside that tight and muscular rabbit butt as I slid my upper body down for a kiss, feeling our lips and tongues intertwine once more.

Eventually we had to break the kiss for some air, leaving both of us panting before I slowly began to saw my hips back and forth. It was far from a straight up fucking though. It was more of a sensual grinding than simply thrusting into the muscled hare in front of me. As badly as I wanted to finish quickly, I also wanted to take my time and enjoy this rare opportunity as well—this rare opportunity to be so close and intimate with the hare I loved.

"Mmmmph, fuck..." I said back while still trying to get my breath back, "You... are such a bad boy... such a bad influence..." I gave off a little grin and grunt with those words as I shifted my grasp on the rabbit's legs, sliding him down just a little lower to get the angle even better suited for some more straight-up thrusting.

"Mmmmph, I am..." he agreed with a needy whimper, slowly squeezing around me as his powerful legs began to draw me in against him. I had no resistance against those powerful skating muscles as I simply let out a soft grunt, feeling my thrusts turn back into grinds as the rabbit just held me in deep for another moment. "Mmmph, but it's so worth it," he added with another hot moan up towards me. "God, I miss this. I miss you Jack."

"I miss you too sexy," I said quickly, leaning back down into a kiss as my hips continued to ramp up bit by bit. Soon they were flying at a good clip, smacking into the hare's rump forcefully and letting those loud smacking noises ring around the room.

It was pretty cute to watch him try to hold back as his body strained with each thrust, trying to keep his paws at his side and not rush to his needy cock to end the fun too quickly. Well, my hand beat him to it. I slid an arm from around his leg and reached down to grasp at it myself, knowing that we both needed to get off as soon as possible.

He gave off a hot huff and squirm at that sudden grip, and that only made me smirk as I added in a rather powerful squeeze to his hard member a second later. His reaction was priceless and gave me something to focus on to fight off my own orgasm for just a moment more. "I don't know how close you are, but I'm almost there… hot stuff," I forced out between a few of my heavy breaths.

"I can go, mmmph, anytime…" he added with a little bite to his lip, which usually meant he couldn't hold back much longer either.

With a smirk I slowly nodded and said, "Well then… lift your shirt up…" With a little grunt of my own I watched as that well-toned body came into view, those abs and pecs rippling with each thrust I gave him as the rabbit struggled to stay up and on the short counter. With a wide smile I kept my paw pumping over his member, trying to match the speed of my hips, only to lean down and wrap up his muzzle in one more deep, hot, passionate kiss.

That kiss took us through both of our orgasms, one after another. It was Andy who let loose first, sending his pent up load spraying all over his chest and almost onto my shirt too as he bucked hard with each shot. That sudden squeezing around my member and moaning into my muzzle, not to mention the tight squeeze from his legs and arms all over my back and shoulders, was all I needed to finish off as well. A few moments and some heavy thrusts later I was joining him, moaning into our kiss and pushing deep to send some thick and hot spurts of seed surging inside of him.

I slumped down just a bit as I wanted more than anything to land on the hare's chest and just lay there in my happy daze. I knew I couldn't though since 'evidence' would be everywhere then. I strained my back to keep myself up and off him, although I was more than happy to lean into that kiss for a few more moments before finally pulling back to gather my breath.

"Mmmmph, you weren't kidding..." I added with a soft smile. My mind was still a little loopy from the afterglow as I looked down to the mess he'd made on his belly. White cum and white fur didn't usually show much, but all the matted areas, not to mention some of the globs and strings spread out between fur follicle tips, really proved just how much he had needed this.

He could only smile and nod a little bit himself while catching his own breath from the rush he felt. "Told ya..." he said with a gentle smile. And with that he pulled me into one final quick kiss before pushing me away so he could get his feet back onto the floor.

It was only then that we both heard the strong throat-clearing cough come from behind us. Andy's large ears quickly snapped to attention as mine flicked up nervously at the sudden noise as well. I felt my body going stiff and taut as my hands raced down to the edge of my pants. I pulled myself back and out of the rabbit before quickly yanking my pants and underwear back up, trying in vain to hide any evidence of what we were doing. I didn't even bother to button or zip up either. I simply pulled my shirt down over my groin and hips, hoping that it would cover everything as I began to turn around and see just who was behind me.

Andy made his own set of quick movements as he slid his legs down and pressed his feet to the floor. In one fluid move he hopped up and quickly tugged his dangling pants up and over his groin. His frame, and especially his groin, were still mostly hidden by my body all the while. The person who snuck in didn't get to see much true evidence of what was going on at any point. There were no cocks flopping about or anything else that he could really snag a picture of. But, at the same time, hard evidence wasn't really required. A story and rumor could potentially be just as bad, especially from a good source.

Andy had already gotten a good view of who it was, and I just barely heard his soft gasp between my own struggles and noises to get presentable. But as I turned around and saw him with my own eyes, I instantly knew we were in trouble. I let out my own soft gasp as my eyes scanned up and down the large wolf standing there with a wide smirk on his face. It wasn't just any wolf though. This wolf was rather familiar. Stephan Sarzinski... one of the defenders from the home team. The same wolf

I'd called a penalty on with seven minutes to go in the game.

"H…hey there," I said suddenly, doing my best to put on my firm officiating face once more. It didn't seem to sway the wolf though as his rather wide grin stayed plastered on his face. He looked back and forth between the rabbit and I as Andy just stayed quiet, adjusting himself a little bit more as we both knew we were caught. He was probably the worst possible person that could catch us as well. I'm sure he was still in a grumpy mood from the loss, although that was hard to tell from his expression as he simply left us squirming for another long and silent moment.

"Just out for a little walk?" I added in eventually, using every last ounce of control I had left to try and make myself sound normal. "We were just talking here. Bumped into one another."

"Oh, there was definitely bumping going on," the wolf added in a firm tone of voice. He smirked a good bit at both of us and licked his chops as his arms stayed confidently crossed over his chest with each syllable.

"Look," I finally said with a quick and defeated sigh, gazing back up at the wolf with a softening and almost pleading expression on my face. "I don't know what you saw or how long you've been there, but… cut us a little slack? We'll owe you one for sure."

The cocky sway of the wolf almost made me shiver, and I could only imagine what the hare's expression behind me was like as well. "Owe me one, huh?" he added with a little whistle on top of it. That dominant, almost evil tone was thick in his voice, and it was only made stronger by his Eastern European accent. "I do like the sound of that…"

The way he said it actually did make me gulp a bit, especially as his tail casually and almost teasingly swished behind him. He had us, and I had a feeling things were going to get quite complicated rather soon.

"What to do… what to do…?" he added as another predatory grin flashed across his face.

"You could just say goodnight and catch up on some sleep," Andy added, although with a slightly more bitter tone than I think really helped the situation. Although, judging from the wolf's posture, he wasn't exactly thinking about letting us go easily for sure.

"But where's the fun in that?" he added, relishing his position of power over both of us as he seemed to grow ten sizes bigger, and both Andy and I shrunk down about the same.

"Come on Stephan," I added in, trying to take back some of the control over the situation. "You got us. I get it. Let's cut to the chase. What do you want to keep quiet?"

It was a tactic that had worked before when we were caught, but at the same time I was pretty sure that an autograph or some spare bills in my wallet wouldn't be enough to sway anyone this time.

"That is good question," he started back up, slowly rubbing a large paw over his chin before starting to focus down at me. "I see why you made that call today. Cause you were scared your boyfriend got hurt, wasn't it?"

No matter how bad it was for the situation I couldn't let that comment slide. I grit my teeth heavily as I nearly shouted back, "Don't you even think that! No fucking way in hell. I don't care what you do to us, but I will *not* have you leaving this room and thinking that! I called the penalty because it looked like a penalty. Stick to the face—high sticking. Yeah, I knew it was exaggerated, but the same call has been made all season. For ages."

"Not in Stanley Cup Finals!" he almost shouted back, leaving me time to adjust my pants as both of our shouts rung around the room for a moment. "It was bullshit call, and cost us the win."

"You know that's not true Stephan," Andy said back, for once trying to be the reason in an argument.

"Could be," the wolf added back with a huff. "You'll never know. So, I want you to take it back."

"I can't..." I said with a soft sigh, more frustrated at myself for losing my cool than at his stupid idea.

"Maybe not," he added with a huff, "but you can say just how bullshit it was, and that it might have cost us the game. I know how much you refs hate to say what you really think."

I kind of fell silent at that, wanting to shoot back with something snappy, but not really having anything that came to mind. It's true—there was nothing worse than a ref admitting he'd made a mistake. It never happened, at least not publicly. It was the most humiliating thing I could do, and my pride would be shattered to admit I'd made a bad call. While I doubt I could go on TV and say it outright, there were ways that I could 'leak' it to the press, and even if it wasn't a huge story outside the hockey community it'd still be quite the black scar on my record. Other plays, and especially other refs would look at me strangely all next season for sure.

At the same time, I couldn't exactly say no though. As I slowly turned to look at the nervous hare behind me, catching his large and unsure eyes about what to do, I knew I had to do it. I had to do it for him if for no other reason. Regretfully I turned back around to face the wolf and grumbled out a soft, "Fine, I'll make it happen."

The wolf smirked rather widely at that admission as he nodded his head, and then turned his gaze towards the hare behind me. "And you," he said as he pointed his fingers out towards him. "I expect easy assignment when our teams play next year. I want to clear the puck out of the zone easily. Even better if you tell your teammates to lay off too."

I didn't have to look back to see the hare gritting his teeth. As humiliating as it was for me to admit a mistake, it was even more painful to tell an athlete not to play hard. It wasn't in their blood. That's not how they became a professional athlete in the first place. To try and switch their effort off was just as shameful and embarrassing as anything he could've asked for.

I didn't really know what to expect out of Andy. He would be one to fight something like that, but at the same time here we were—stuck with very few options. The story of our combined lives so far. There was a moment of silence, but eventually I heard the hare almost whisper out, "Fine. I'll go easy on you."

Stephan gave off a wide smile as he gently nodded to both of us. "Good to hear. I expect you to follow through. If not, well…"

"Shut up," I said with an angry scowl right away, although I stopped myself from saying anything more. It was very unsportsmanlike to hold something like this over us like this. Most of the hockey playing community were all friends, and I expected something better if and when another player found out about us. But that smirking wolf got on my nerves as I just clenched my hands into fists, almost ready to throw them like back in the old days.

The wolf didn't seem phased by my interruption though, simply giving off a slight cock to his head as he added, "Oh, and I'll be sending you two a request for a donation to my charity as well. Make sure you pay the full amount when it arrives."

Whether that was a further bribe or not, or if he even had a charity, I couldn't tell by the way he said it. It made me clench my hands tighter though, but falling back on all my previous officiating experience I managed to hold out just a little longer and stay silent, watching the wolf's tail sway almost happily behind him instead.

"Anyway, it's getting late," he added with a soft fake yawn. "I'll leave you two to clean up. Just don't forget."

"We won't," Andy said through grit teeth, trying as hard as I was to hold back throwing some punches. But that would only make things worse. A physical assault charge is far more proof of wrongdoing than a rumor of something going on after all.

With a cocky grin the wolf spun and began to walk out of the room, giving us both a wave as he disappeared out of that door. We both waited for it to close before we could finally breathe again, each of us letting out a heavy sigh in a sudden rush of emotion.

I slowly turned around to face Andy, a defeated and sorrowful look on my face. But when I met his own, I couldn't help but feel even worse. Tears had started to stream down his cheeks, and before I could even say anything, I just wrapped him up in a hug, not caring what got on me in the process.

"Relax," I said softly, taking that fatherly tone I was destined to take. "It'll be alright. That was just a rush to judgement is all. We can try to talk to him later, in a few days or so, and see what we can do."

"What if it wasn't though?" Andy added, the large hare giving out a little sniffle and sob as his ears and muzzle gently drooped over my shoulder.

"Then we'll deal with it," I said back, adding a few pats to his back all the while. "But you know what?" I added after a little bit of simple deep breathing and squeezing. "I know I can deal with it with you, and you can deal with it with me. No matter what happens we have each other. And I'd do everything he said and more if that would protect you… and protect us."

"Yeah, me too," Andy added back after another sniffle. I could feel him squeeze me tightly enough to crack my back and stop my breathing dead, but I didn't care. I let him squeeze me as hard as he needed to as I worked on firming up my hug all the same.

"I love you Andy," I added back, reaching up on my tippy toes to plant a soft kiss on his chin and cheek.

I felt the rabbit lean in towards my forehead, giving me a matching kiss before pulling back and saying, "I love you too Jack."

"We'll make it through this together, I promise," I said one final time as we both nodded in agreement, letting the silence in the room overtake us for a long while thereafter.

To All the Bad Romances that Left Me Waiting

WAITING

by Tredain

Reyfus waited. He pulled his pocket watch from his vest to check the time, then compared it against the great clocktower that rose up from the city center. Still a few minutes. The rabbit stood on the sky dock and waited with the rest, all of them looking up to the clouds. He slipped the watch back into his pocket and settled his hands behind his back. He always felt out of place in the crowd, a little better dressed, a little quieter, and one of the few rabbits in the town. But he waited, as he always did, for the airship to come in.

He sighed a little to himself as he huddled near one wall. The crowds were thick that day, which usually meant shipments were coming in as they always did toward the end of the week. Merchants and servants filled the dock ready to take boxes down to waiting carts. Others waited for friends and family to arrive. Reyfus, however, waited for *him*. He checked his watch, then the great clock tower, again. Then, for what seemed to him, for the hundredth time, he pulled the small crystal from his other vest pocket. The little trinket glowed softly in his palm. Reyfus smiled and pocketed it again.

"There!" a kit pointed out with a raised paw. Dozens of eyes looked up. The unmistakable bow of a ship parted the clouds and it slid into view. A few children squealed, always delighted by the sight, while others stepped up closer to the dock. The ship, hanging from its great balloon and propelled along by dozens of small propellers and a good dose of enchantment, circled round and round the dock as it dipped lower and lower. It finally leveled off and gently drifted to the edge of the dock. Dockhands on and off the ship came out to lash it to the dock as a gangplank came down. The ship slowed to a stop and people began to unload everything as quickly as they were able.

Reyfus hung back as the crowds shifted up to meet the passengers and to collect their cargo. He hadn't come down yet. He was always too easy to spot, so the rabbit leaned against a wall and waited even as his heart began to pound a little faster.

His long ears perked as he caught a flash of orange. The fox crossed the threshold and began to descend to the dock with a hefty burlap sack slung over his back, though it didn't stop his usual swagger. Reyfus practically hopped his way through the crowd toward the end of the gangplank, his eyes never leaving the fox.

Alleo was dashing as ever in the rabbit's mind. That bright fur that stood out like a lighthouse amidst the sea of drab browns and greys of the ship and the other travelers. The black eyepatch clashed against it but seemed to make the orange look even brighter. His red cloak hung in tatters off one shoulder, freshly torn and apparently singe marked. With one paw carrying the sack, his other rested on the hilt of the sword sheathed at his waist. His thick boots thumped onto the gangplank with every step.

"Alleo!" Reyfus shouted as the few bodies between them parted and he could jump at the fox. The adventurer grinned widely, dropped the knapsack behind him, and opened his arms to catch the eager rabbit. The two hugged tightly.

"Hello honeybun," the fox whispered in his ear. Reyfus' heart skipped a bit. He wanted to kiss the fox right there. To hold him and take him, regardless of who saw. But that was hardly the proper thing to do, even if it was no true secret what the rabbit's preference was. This far out in the country, you kept your business to yourself. They kept pressed together for a moment more as the rabbit squeezed him close. The feel of his body, the spicy, nose twitching scent of him, his leather, his natural animal scent, Reyfus breathed it all in deeply.

"Gods I missed you," he whimpered before they parted. Alleo smiled widely and grabbed the burlap sack up again.

"Only been a few weeks," he said as he began to navigate the crowd with Reyfus only a step behind.

"Weeks, plural, where it was a week or two at most and only days before that," the rabbit reminded him. The fox tutted but smiled.

"I should have guessed you'd keep track. I'm sorry. These expeditions are, well, it takes quite a bit of time. But you know I always come back, eventually."

They made their way out of the airship dock and down to the cobblestone streets. Traffic was heavy, which was typical, as a steady flow of creatures big and small went to and from the dock and all the shops surrounding it. Several carts pulled by all manner of beasts trundled their way over the stones as drivers shouted at any that might get in their way.

Alleo paused to scan along the road, then took a deep breath. His nose wrinkled and he made a face.

"Ah this place never changes. Don't see why you stay here." The fox rubbed his nose with a little chuckle as they stepped down to one of the many waiting carriages looking for fares. Reyfus giggled and spoke to the driver before helping Alleo lift the heavy sack up top. The two of them climbed into the carriage together.

"It's out of the way, no one really bothers me," he explained, again, as they settled side by side onto the plush cushions. "And no one asks too many questions when you visit."

Alleo grinned widely and didn't hesitate to slide one gloved paw down the rabbit's backside. It slipped past the waistband of his pants and cupped one cheek as the two leaned in and kissed deeply. Reyfus let out a shivery little moan and pressed into the kiss. This was what he had waited for. This was what made it worth it. He pressed as close as he could, surrendering to the fox's tongue when it probed into his mouth, and slid a paw across Alleo's firm chest. They broke the kiss, hesitantly, and the fox tickled one gloved finger under the rabbit's little goatee.

"That's true, honeybun." He smiled, then leaned in for another kiss. It was quicker, but no less hungry, than the first. They rubbed whiskers as the carriage jolted them and began to plod down the road toward Reyfus' home. The rabbit smiled, his face getting warmer as his blush showed in his long ears. He traced his fingers over the fox's chest with little imaginary shapes and stroked his nose under the fox's chin. Alleo squeezed his butt firmly, his paw never leaving it the entire carriage ride, as they cuddled up against each other. Their lips and paws wandered and mingled together again and again. It always made the rabbit feel a little drunk being around the fox.

He had his paw stuffed down the front of the fox's pants and their mouths sealed together when the carriage came to a stop. Reyfus sighed a little as they broke the kiss and withdrew their paws. The fox winked and tickled the little pointed goatee again.

"As if you have to wait that long," he teased with a chuckle and got up first. The bunny took the moment to stroke his paw along the bushy tail, using it as a leash to tug himself to his feet as he climbed out after the fox.

The rabbit's house stood at the edge of town. Open grass dotted with trees stretched on into the distance with only a few houses nearby. It was a small two story built into the side of a hill. A thin plume of smoke rose from the chimney.

The two climbed from the carriage and took the fox's bag down as the driver took the payment, wished them well, and tugged the reins of his lizard steeds. The things hissed but clacked their way back over the cobbles as the carriage turned and trundled back into town.

"Never understood how anyone can stand being around those things," the fox remarked as he lugged the rucksack over his shoulder again.

"I prefer the birds, though they seem a little more finicky." Reyfus stepped ahead of the fox and waved a paw as they crossed past the threshold of the rabbit's yard. A little tingle passed over the two as they stepped into the rabbit's ward spell that kept the house safe when he was away.

"I prefer mammals, but I'm certainly biased," Alleo grinned and cupped the rabbit's ass again before he gave it a firm squeeze. Reyfus let out a little squeal of delight now that they weren't amidst a hundred prying eyes and ears, but kept walking to the door. He pulled the great brass key from his vest and opened the door for his lover. Alleo passed him but couldn't get by without pecking a kiss on the rabbit's lips. The rabbit huffed and ran his paw along the fox's bushy tail again as he followed him inside.

"No matter how long I'm on the road, I never get tired of coming back to you, honeybun." Alleo dropped the rucksack nearby and stepped out of his boots. As soon as the door closed, they pressed into another kiss with the fox pinning the rabbit to the door. The scholar moaned again but didn't resist, letting Alleo take him by the paws and press them to either side of his head. A little growl rolled up from the fox's throat. They broke the kiss and rubbed nose to nose, looking into each other's eyes with little smiles curling their lips.

"I have water on for tea, if you'd like a little bath while I get it ready," the rabbit offered, his fingers wiggling above the fox's as they gripped his wrists. Alleo leaned back, letting Reyfus' paws go, and peeled off his gloves.

"You're always too sweet to me, honeybun," he said as he tossed them on top of his boots and pulled off his cloak. He paused and looked through the fresh holes. "I'll have to have this fixed."

"Fixed? I don't know the tailor would take kindly to fixing a rag, you might be better off getting a new one," Reyfus teased as he went to the cupboards. Alleo gave it a little toss to land on top of the rest of his clothes and began to peel off his shirt.

"I suppose you're right," he answered as he began to undo his belt. Reyfus paused, watching the shirtless fox, the way the white from his chin ran down his neck and widened to cover his chest and dipped below to his groin, the way the soft fur didn't hide the well-developed muscles from years of training and adventuring. Reyfus gulped a little then squeaked when the fox caught him staring.

"Shameless thing you are," the fox chuckled as his sword sheath came off, followed by his belt. "But I do hate to get rid of something you gave me."

Reyfus paused as he fished through the great clay jar of his tea leaves then said "I did get you that didn't I? It does go well with your fur. Perhaps a new one just like it." He picked out the leaves, giving them a little sniff, good and potent, before he stuffed them into the infuser and set it inside the teapot and took the kettle off the warming stone. Steam still wafted up from it as it had when he set it on the stove to boil.

Alleo stood naked with his arms akimbo and muzzle perked in a smirk. He kept his eye patch on but nothing else.

"Sure you wouldn't care to join me?" he offered with a wry grin. His cock was already at attention, much as the rabbit's had stayed after all the kissing. Reyfus blushed deeper and bashfully rubbed at the back of his head. Alleo did not help matters by swaying his hips to make his dick wave through the air.

"So tempting love. But go ahead and wash the road from you, I'll get some food ready," he turned back to begin fixing the tea, though kept the fox in sight. Alleo kept grinning.

"Haha, suppose I have built up a bit of an odour, you might say," he chuckled and smacked one hip before walking into the bathroom, his dick bobbing with every step. Reyfus watched him go and couldn't help lick his lips at the sight of the fox's shapely cheeks beneath that big bushy tail.

"Ah!" he snapped as he accidentally grabbed the wrong part of the kettle. Damned fox was always distracting him, he chided himself mentally. Though what a distraction he was! He smiled to himself and continued prepping the tea, pulling some stored oat cakes and some meat and cheese. Alleo never took too long to wash when he was just trying to get clean, though when he wanted to, he could lounge for a solid hour, usually with a rabbit ass in his lap. Reyfus let out a happy little sigh at the memory as he set everything on the table.

The fox stepped out in just a towel draped around his neck. Reyfus chuckled and poured a steaming glass of tea while Alleo sat beside him.

"You spoil me honeybun," he said, pulling a saucer toward him and plucking a couple pieces of meat and cheese from the tray. The scholar smiled before he slid a paw along the fox's back.

"Just glad to see you," he leaned in and gave the fox a kiss on his cheek. Alleo smiled back, chewing his treats, and leaned in to nuzzle at the rabbit's cheek.

"Have something to show you." He bent down and pulled his rucksack to the table. A moment of fishing and the fox pulled something out to set it on the table.

"Oh my," Reyfus gasped and his leaf shaped tail gave an excited wiggle. The crystal glowed a soft blue and immediately began to float upright above the wooden table. He stroked one paw along his goatee and stared at it.

"Thoughts?" Alleo asked through a mouthful of tea cake.

"Mmm, third or fourth era draconian. Unmistakably draconian. They did love their floating trinkets," he reached for it and carefully turned it with a finger. Runes glowed faintly against the polished surface when they caught the light just right. He turned it one way, then the other, letting the light play over the runes.

"Can you read it?"

Reyfus nodded, turning the crystal a little more.

"It's a key. The manor of... it's a little hard to translate the title. High Magus, is my best guess, but draconian is a little... well, they liked to make something sound fancy, the fellow could have just been an enchanter."

The fox's ears perked, and he grinned widely. A couple claws drummed against the table while he chewed at another cake before saying "I had a feeling it was something worthwhile. More than a night light at least."

Reyfus gave a little giggle and let the crystal float on its own. One of the first trips back the fox had indeed brought a night light. The dragons liked their floating crystal trinkets, after all.

"So, are you going to go find the door it goes to?" The rabbit took a tea cake for himself before giving it a delicate nibble. The fox paused, his good eye glancing up and down the rabbit. He hesitated.

"Soon. Yes."

Reyfus nodded and didn't pause as he took a bite. The silence dragged on for a few moments before the fox reached one paw out to trail it slowly down the rabbit's back. It settled on the curve of one ass cheek and Reyfus let out a little moan through his mouthful of cake. Alleo smirked. He leaned in to kiss the rabbit on the cheek again, keeping his paw down below, and nuzzled whisker to whisker.

"Honeybun," Alleo whispered, then kissed him again. Another little moan before the rabbit was pressing back into it and arching his back to press his ass into that paw. Reyfus broke the kiss reluctantly but set a paw to the fox's chest and eased him back into his seat.

"Finish eating first, I'm sure you had a long day," he said, though did nothing to remove the fox's paw from his seat. Alleo chuckled.

"Spoil me," he said before he started on some more of the meat and cheese as the rabbit helped himself too. They finished it off and the rabbit picked up the tray, cups, and kettle to set them by the sink. Then he stripped off the fox's towel and gave it a little toss to the bin he used for laundry. He slid his paws over Alleo's shoulders and leaned down to nuzzle one of the pointed, velvety ears.

"Now we can go to the bedroom," he said before he closed his lips over the point and gave it a little suckle. Alleo never needed more encouragement. He rose from the seat and slipped his arms around the rabbit. His pointed muzzle stroked at the rabbit's cheek.

"You're overdressed," he said as he kissed the cheek, then let his muzzle rub higher up toward the rabbit's ear.

"I'll fix that, keep going," Reyfus chuckled and patted the bare furry rump. Neither quite followed the other as they kept themselves tangled together with paws sliding, stroking, mouths kissing and nibbling, but eventually they made their way up to the rabbit's bedroom, bits and pieces of his clothing coming off with every step. By the time they fell into the large bed together they were both naked.

Reyfus was the first to kiss. He leaned over the fox and pressed in as he slid one paw over the firm chest. He followed by straddling the fox's waist, their lips never parting, and sat atop of the male before he broke the kiss and looked down.

"Honeybun," the fox cooed and ran both of his paws up Reyfus' sides, rubbing up and down the lithe body until his paws reached down to cup the rabbit's cheeks. He kneaded them slowly around and around, letting one thumb stroke at the leafy tail, and grinned up at the bunny.

"Can't get enough of that, can you?" the scholar asked as he bumped nose to nose. He shivered a little as those deft paws kneaded over his cheeks to spread them and press them together repeatedly with one blunt claw dragging along his crack. The fox rolled his hips in response and gingerly tapped his hard maleness against the rabbit's cheeks.

"I do call you honeybun for a good reason, I like to think," the fox smiled and tapped the rabbit's butt a few more times. Reyfus felt his face getting hot again. He leaned in and pressed into another kiss, rolling his own hips to grind his stiffness into that silky soft vulpine belly fur. The two of them groaned into the kiss as their tongues played against each other. Reyfus let his paws stroke across Alleo's chest as he rocked on top of him.

"Are you ready?" the fox asked, breaking the kiss and punctuating the question with a firm squeeze to both cheeks before spreading them wide apart.

"Ah, ah, almost," he pecked the fox's lips, then reached over to the nightstand beside the bed. He snatched one of many little vials and pulled the stopper out with his teeth.

"Ooohh," Alleo cooed as the oil drizzled over his waiting cock. The fox pressed his head back into the pillow and sighed happily when the rabbit's paw wrapped around him and stroked the slick oil into his hot flesh. Reyfus took his paw away, only to smear the oil inside his crack and against his hole. Alleo couldn't help but muse "Always prepared."

"You have to be, with foxes." The rabbit set the vial back and ran his clean paw through the fluffy chest fur again. He sat back until the warm cock pressed up between his cheeks and slowly ground up against the stiff rod. Alleo bit his lip a little.

"Mmm, I want to take you from behind," the fox said, smiling up as he curled one paw around the rabbit's cock. He squeezed.

"Ah, any... oh." Alleo squeezed again "Any way you like." Reyfus leaned down to kiss him again, then carefully rolled off so the fox could get up. Alleo rose and climbed off the bed, slowly stroking his oiled cock in one paw and taking in the sight of the rabbit as Reyfus moved to all fours and presented to him.

"Spoiling me," the fox chuckled. He reached one paw up to stroke along one spread cheek, letting his fingers sift through the white fur. One thumb ran down the slick crack and tickled at the tight pink hole within. It tensed once, then relaxed, the rabbit giving his tail an impatient little wiggle. Alleo stepped closer and aimed his cock at the waiting valley. He swabbed his purple head up and down the crack before kissing it against the hole.

Together they sucked in a breath as he pressed in. Reyfus let out a little groan when the familiar pressure opened him up and the fox's hard cock slid inch after inch inside him. Alleo gripped himself in one paw, grunting as he eased in, and teased the rabbit's tail with his other paw, his thumb slowly brushing it back and forth.

The fox hilted inside and took a moment to admire the pert buns pressed flush against his lap. Both paws slid along the rabbit's side and stroked up and down as he slowly withdrew, then pushed back in, taking his time to work the rabbit open. Reyfus clutched at the sheets and didn't hold back any noises, groaning every time the slick maleness probed deep inside or pulled out nearly to the tip. The fox sawed his hips back and forth until he worked it to a slow, steady rhythm.

"Harder," the rabbit groaned and started to rock on his knees in time with the fox's thrusting. The fox took the cue and began to speed up, pulling out faster and thrusting until his groin slapped lightly against the rabbit's round cheeks. A little faster and the noise became audible, the rabbit grunting with every thrust inside him.

"I can take more," Reyfus gasped as he splayed his legs wider to press back into the steady thumping.

"Don't want to hurt you honeybun," the fox cooed, but sped up a little more, raising one leg up onto the bed while he gripped the rabbit at the waist and started to thrust in again and again with a faster pace. The two of them were panting harder and faster, every thrust making one of them groan while the fox's nuts smacked into the rabbit's cheeks. He gripped down and pressed the rabbit into the bed, keeping himself inside as he thrust harder and harder, the slap slap slap becoming a steady tattoo filling the room. Reyfus hung his head and let out one long, low groan. He reached one paw below to stroke and tug himself. They were both getting closer.

The fox put his leg down and began to take full strokes, rolling his hips and slamming into the rabbit's wanting ass, hilting with every thrust then withdrawing all the way until the pink hole was gaping wide before stuffing himself back inside.

"Oh honeybun," the fox gasped and pressed in close, his fingers curling in against the black mottled fur as his thrusts grew quicker and quicker. He bent forward, his eyes squeezed shut, and growled into one of the rabbit's long ears. One hard thrust sheathed him as deep as he could go, followed with a quick withdraw, one sticky spurt splashing the rabbit's tail, before another roll of his hips slammed the meat back to the hilt and the fox let out one long growl as everything tensed up. Reyfus stroked himself faster and faster, nearly whining. He felt the fox's cock swell inside him before a wet heat blossomed and the fox began to cum inside him.

The two of them shuddered, the rabbit's seed releasing into the sheets while the fox emptied inside his lover. They gripped tightly against each other, keeping themselves locked in that warm embrace until finally the fox withdrew. His swollen cock kept drooling seed as it flagged toward the floor from its own weight, looking red and angry now. The rabbit lay in a heap on the bed with his chest to the sheets and his ass stuck up in the air, the hole wide and already starting to drool with the fox's cum. Alleo gave it a little pat and traced around the open hole. Reyfus shuddered again.

Then he yelped when the fox took a nearby cloth and wiped the rabbit clean, attending to his own messy lap afterward. Alleo chuckled a bit, climbed in beside the rabbit, and slipped his arms around the narrow shoulders to pull the rabbit close to his chest. Reyfus was still breathing hard, a smile on his short muzzle, and nestled up against the fox. They pulled a sheet up and over them as they settled against one another.

Reyfus laid his head against the fox's chest then slipped his paws around the adventurer's slim middle.

"I love you," he muttered, settling his cheek to the fluffy chest and listening to the fox's rapid heartbeat.

"I... m-my honeybun," Alleo kissed the rabbit's spotted forehead and squeezed him against his chest. He slowly stroked up and down the rabbit's back and the quiet stretched on. Reyfus drifted off, listening to the fox's heart and letting the heat lull him to sleep.

The light filtered in past the curtains and Reyfus took a deep breath as the fog of dreams lifted and he began to wake up. He stretched out under the thin sheet and let out a little groan as his muscles woke up too. He pressed into the pillow to let out a happy little sigh. Alleo's scent still filled his nose so he breathed deeply. He reached one paw out to find... empty sheets. He felt around slowly. One eye peeled open, then the other.

Reyfus sat up to find he was alone in bed. He gave another sigh, this one decidedly less happy. He crawled off of the bed and stood, then let out a light groan when his knees buckled a little, his ass still a little sore from last night. Perhaps the fox was just downstairs getting a little bite.

He rubbed one cheek and carefully made his way down the steps, walking past his discarded clothes along the way.

His heart sank a little at the sight of the familiar parchment on his table. He padded over to take a seat, wincing slightly at the feel of the hard, wooden chair against his sore bottom, and pulled up the letter.

Dearest Honeybun,

I am sorry to steal away once again as a thief in the night but I cannot delay a moment more lest I lose my advantage. That key could lead to a very valuable find. I have taken the first airship back to the islands. Know I will miss you, but I will return, eventually. Be safe, I will signal as always.

Sincerely yours,

Alleo

Reyfus set the letter down with a small gnawing in the pit of his stomach. Again. This would mark the third such letter the fox had left him, again disappearing before he had risen for the day. He sighed a little and sat there, naked in his kitchen while he stared into space.

"May as well have expected it," he admitted to himself. The fox excited him in ways none could, but he could disappoint him in ways none could either. He sat up, wincing once more, at least thankful to have seen the fox for a night. He slowly stood and began to pick up his clothes to start about his normal chores for the day, to include a long, warm bath. He took the little crystal from his vest and set it in his study, a little pedestal on his desk made just for it, to wait for when it might glow again and show when the fox would reappear.

A week passed. Reyfus waited. He kept busy, as he always did, studying the tomes he had collected and checking the local merchants for more when they came in. He kept the house clean and practiced his warding spells. But nonetheless, he waited, always stealing glances toward the little pedestal to find the crystal dim and lifeless.

It was on the seventh night the rabbit couldn't stay inside the house anymore. He couldn't focus on his tomes, his wards merely shimmered before winking out, and cleaning seemed tedious and unnecessary. He paced the floor and climbed the stairs once or twice before he realized he needed to get out and perhaps head into town.

"What the hell should I do?" he asked aloud as he glanced out the window. The sun had already dipped past the horizon with twilight setting in soon. He looked at the dim crystal. The tavern, he considered. It's where he had met the fox. He had frequented it now and again when he wanted something to break the tedium of his studies. He tried to think of the last time he had gone out.

"Well that's decided then," he muttered and pulled on his vest. He paused and looked at the little crystal again. Still dim. It could light up at any moment. But it also might not. He lingered, then turned without taking it.

The trip to the tavern was short, a simple walk into town and near the sky docks. There were plenty of taverns, pubs, and bars that scattered the streets. Any town worth its salt knew to cater to all the travelers that filtered in and out. Adventurers set for the sky islands were always willing to throw down for a little drink and food.

The Posh Hog was a popular such tavern. It wasn't too far from the docks but not far from the edge of town either. He stepped inside to be greeted by the familiar scents and sounds of a couple dozen beasts getting drunk and unwinding after a hard day's work or a long journey. Reyfus settled at a small table off to the side from the bar.

"Any food hon?" a rather buxom ferret asked as she passed with a tray of mugs. Reyfus smiled and pulled a coin from his pocket.

"Just an ale, please," he answered politely. She gave him a smile, slipped the coin into her apron, and sashayed past. Reyfus gave a small sigh and propped up on one elbow onto the table so he could set his cheek against his palm. He scanned over the room. Several dock workers, some sailors, a few merchants. One group near the bar were unmistakably adventurers. He idly wondered how they hadn't been asked to give up their weapons yet. A cheetah in a tattered green cloak and a crossbow strapped to his back smiled and sipped a drink as he listened to a very large bear drunkenly talk to a white wolf with striking purple eyes and a golden mask slung on one shoulder. The latter two had large mugs of something frothy they kept sipping at.

"Oh, you want a real arsehole, Benjamin the Ninth Wind! That egotist will barely lift a paw to get a treasure then take all the credit," the bear complained. "Nevermind you all he's good for is blowing that namby pamby little gust of his when he *does* bother."

The three of them chuckled.

"Ran with him once, never again. Doesn't listen for spit," the wolf said. He sat back on his stool and took a long pull from his mug. "I'm all for charging in if you have the chops, but it's still a team effort."

The other two nodded in agreement.

"His brother is nothing special either. Worse in the sack even," the cheetah snickered.

"Oh, ye wanna talk about *boning*," the bear finished with a loud belch before pounding a fist at his chest. "Oh, sorry, hehe. No, ye wanna talk about the sack. Y'know who was just in town eh?"

"Oh, you don't mean…" the wolf started.

"Aye, *him*. The Hurricane!" the bear let out a big bellied laugh that made most of him jiggle. Reyfus' ears perked up.

"Mm, can't say I've heard of that one," the cat admitted. The bear clapped his mug down to the counter and grinned widely.

"Oh, so he's a fox, see. Tries to charm just about anything on two legs, comes into town, works his magic, gets what he wants, takes off."

"Not sure I understand the nickname then," the cheetah's tail slowly flicked back and forth.

"Aye, cuz he leaves everything wet and devastated in his wake!" the wolf chimed in. The three of them burst into loud laughter. Reyfus felt his stomach drop out of him. They continued to talk but everything seemed drowned out as he stared off into nothing.

"Here's your drink hon," the ferret had returned and sat the mug right in front of him. He barely noticed until it clacked against the table.

"Oh. Oh, th-thank you," he muttered and stared down into the frothy golden ale. He suddenly didn't have any appetite. He pushed off from the table and got up.

He didn't remember the walk home. He didn't remember stripping down and climbing into bed. He could only remember waking up the next day, where he stayed in bed the better part of the morning. He replayed the trio's words in his head over and over. The Hurricane. It could be a coincidence. It was certainly a coincidence for him to walk in on the exact night they'd be discussing it. He could have just stayed home, he could have studied, practiced his spells. He had a hundred such conversations in his head over it.

Did it really matter, he asked himself. Alleo wasn't his, exactly. He excited the rabbit in ways no one else did but they weren't a formal couple. They really didn't spend much time together, even if what they did had felt fantastic. But Alleo was his own creature. It didn't really matter if he slept with others.

The hours crawled by as Reyfus contemplated all of this. The hours turned to days, which turned to weeks. The rabbit settled back into his usual routine, even the occasional glances at the small crystal on the pedestal, but that grew less frequent. He continued to study his tomes, practice his warding magic, and keep his house up. His heart, however, still skipped a beat when he walked into his study to find the crystal lit up.

He rushed to the airship dock in town, dressed as before. He waited with the others expecting an arrival that day. He did not check his watch, but still he waited. The ship appeared and pulled into the dock and he still pressed up toward the gangplank to meet the fox as he disembarked.

"Alleo," he greeted, that familiar thrill running up the base of his spine as the fox came into view.

"Honeybun!" the fox hugged him tightly. As before, they walked from the docks and took a carriage. He didn't hesitate when the fox kissed him, he didn't pause as the familiar paw felt over his bottom. They kissed their way into his home. The fox stripped and took a bath while Reyfus fixed a few treats.

"So, what did you bring this time?" the rabbit asked as the naked fox settled back to the table. It was the fox's turn to blush a little.

"Honeybun, am I getting predictable?" he asked, a sly, teasing smile perking his muzzle. But Reyfus simply waited. "Ah, suppose I am."

Alleo reached over and pulled something from his rucksack. The golden disc had a great square hole in its middle and several runes inscribed along its rim. The rabbit couldn't help but perk his ears and let out a surprised 'ohh.' The fox's smile widened.

"So…?" he asked after he gave the rabbit a few minutes to study.

"Was this from the manor? Did you find it?" he asked as he turned the disc over in his paws, lifting it up to look through it and turning it back to inspect the runes.

"I did! A few good traps. Nothing I couldn't handle, mind you," the fox grinned and huffed against his claws, rubbing them against his bare fluffy chest.

"It does say its the property of the high magus. It's another key. Well, sort of. It's more of a… well, a code cypher. The dragons were fond of these things. Hidden messages and the like." Alleo nodded eagerly, his tail even beating against the chair.

"Wonderful news, I think I know exactly what to do with it now," he reached out and tried to gently take it from the rabbit's paws. Reyfus held on though. "Er, something on your mind… honeybun?"

He glanced at the disc, the fox's fingers on it, then up at the single golden eye.

"I could use this," he said, then realized he needed to say more. "That is, I mean. I could use this better than you could. I mean, if I…" his stomach knotted a little. He had considered the next words very carefully. "If I came with you."

The fox's ears and brow perked up high.

"Oh! Oh. Oh honeybun I…" he paused, letting the disc go suddenly. Reyfus kept looking at him. "I… I couldn't take you. The islands, they're… well for adventurers, people used to traps and monsters and others trying to steal their findings. I… I couldn't bring you into that." It was the first time the rabbit had ever seen the fox even the slightest bit flustered. He gave a quiet nod.

"Well, I… I understand. I wouldn't want to be in your way," he said, though his shoulders and whiskers drooped a little. Alleo smiled and patted the rabbit's shoulder.

"I'm… I am flattered, honeybun. I do always say you need to get out of here but… I couldn't put you in harm's way." His fingers squeezed the rabbit's shoulder and gently traced down it. Reyfus just nodded. The fox tickled a finger under his chin and lifted his muzzle up before he leaned in for a kiss. The rabbit didn't resist, his tail even twitching a little. Nor did he hesitate as the fox got him upstairs and in bed again.

They made love with the rabbit riding the fox's lap. It all still felt amazing, feeling Alleo against him, inside him; it felt wonderful curling up beside him, sore and sticky, and drifting off to sleep inside his arms.

It still felt as hollow to wake up alone and worse to find a note again. Reyfus barely read it; he knew what it said by now. The Hurricane had come and passed again. He sat at the table holding the letter for several long moments before he set it down and stared at nothing in particular as he thought. He glanced up at his mantle. His old fencing rapier from school still hung across it. He smiled a little to himself.

***

Days turned to weeks turned to months. Reyfus settled into a new routine that kept him busy enough. He even found time to visit the Posh Hog on occasion when he needed something different to do, though he never saw the three adventurers again. He still glanced at his crystal, but it laid quiet and dim on its pedestal. He wondered idly if Alleo had finally moved on having gotten everything he needed. Then, one day, it began to glow.

Reyfus waited at the dock. He met the fox, as he always did, and they took a carriage to his home.

"So, what did you bring this time?" the rabbit asked in the middle of the ride. The fox smiled a little, his paw already cupping Reyfus' bottom.

"Eager, are you? Well we'll have to wait to get my sack down, but I think you'll find it very interesting honeybun. I think it's some scrolls from the high magus, or whatever he was. I think I know where more are, but I wanted you to see them first, to see if they're valuable."

Reyfus nodded. He leaned in against Alleo and nuzzled his cheek, letting his muzzle rest against the fox's neck.

"So, you won't be staying," he said plainly. Alleo's paw stilled.

"Ah, no. Not... not long, honeybun," he admitted. The rabbit stroked a paw across his chest and kept rubbing up against him before arching his back to press his butt into the groping paw. The fox let out a little murr into the rabbit's ear and gave his ass a squeeze.

"I've been thinking," the rabbit said as the carriage slowed to a stop.

"Yes?" the fox asked while they climbed out. He reached up for his rucksack, then yelped when his fingers stopped a few inches from it, a crackling, solid shield of light blocking them. He turned to the rabbit.

"Well, I've been practicing a few things. I've gotten better, faster with my wards." Reyfus smiled and snapped his fingers. The shield popped like a bubble.

"I can see that," the fox pulled the sack down, hefting it over his shoulder. "Very impressive honeybun."

Reyfus gave a mock bow before he gave the driver a couple coins and ushered the fox into his house. They kissed again against the door and the rabbit helped to undress the fox.

"You are eager tonight," Alleo chuckled as Reyfus peeled his pants off. Reyfus smiled and fondled his cock before kissing him again, just a quick little peck.

"Always eager to see you," he said, which was still true. Even then the familiar excitement tickled the pit of the rabbit's stomach. He stroked his muzzle along one pointed ear and walked the fox into the bathroom where the great tub was filled with steaming water. He even squeezed the fox's round, pert ass as he helped him into it, though still didn't join him.

"Oh. Oh, always feels so nice. Sure you won't join me?" he grinned and wiggled his hips, making his stiff cock wave under the water. Reyfus smirked.

"Still very tempting. I think I'd like to see these scrolls though, if you don't mind?"

Alleo's ears perked.

"Oh, no no, feel free honeybun. I'll just soak for a little bit," he answered and sank into the warm water with a content sigh. Reyfus returned to the kitchen and fished the scroll tubes out, taking his time to read them while the fox bathed. They were, in fact, of the high magus, a series of journals detailing the dragon's activities running a school and dealing with a royal vizier. The dragons were quite the backstabbing lot, he mused as he continued to read.

"So?" Alleo asked into his ear before nuzzling along it. He leaned into the damp fox's naked body and reached a paw up to stroke along his side.

"They're what you thought. Probably some historical information the Archives would find valuable. And there's more?"

Alleo grinned widely and gave an eager nod.

"Many more. I think I found his personal library. Might even be some spells he developed. Could be a major find." The fox's tail beat about excitedly. Reyfus nodded, then steeled himself.

"Well, if you know where they are... I could help you collect them."

The fox's tail paused, and his fingers held still on the rabbit's shoulders.

"Oh, honeybun, I... I thought I explained last time..."

Reyfus nodded.

"I know, it's dangerous. That's... well, I've been practicing with more than just my wards," though he made one appear in his paw for effect, a crackling, spherical shield above his palm. He stood slowly and drew the rapier from the chair he had rested it on. The fox's ears and brow went up again, his golden eye wide in surprise.

"Oh, honeybun. I... for me?" His tail gave a flick. Reyfus smiled.

"For you," he said, laying the blade back down on the table. Alleo looked down, his ears back a bit. He seemed to consider his words carefully.

"It's just... I... it isn't just that I don't think you couldn't watch out for yourself, but... well, I'd have to be watching you, and you me and... well, we might... distract... one another. And if you got hurt I... I couldn't forgive myself."

Reyfus' shoulders drooped a little, but he nodded. It wasn't an unexpected answer.

"I understand, love." He let the silence drag a moment, then reached out and pulled the fox close. Alleo tensed, but relaxed as he realized the rabbit was kissing him again. They ate some stew the rabbit had already prepared then retired to the bedroom.

They made love again. There was no hesitation, no reluctance, just raw, unbridled lust, as always. Reyfus rolled on his back and let the fox mount him with his legs on Alleo's shoulders. He looked in heaven as the fox bucked into him again and again, filling the bedroom with fleshy slaps and moans. They finished together, each leaving a mess in the other's fur, before curling up as they always did with the rabbit's head on the fox's chest.

Reyfus waited.

***

Alleo woke suddenly, as he always did. Time to go, he thought, staring up into the darkness. The sun was still hours from rising. He shifted slowly, only to find the rabbit not entangled with him. That made it easier, he considered, and carefully sat up as he let his eye adjust to the darkness. No. He felt over the sheets. Empty.

"…Honeybun?" he asked the darkness. Perhaps the rabbit had gotten up to drain water. But that was unusual for him, he was quite the sound sleeper, especially after a solid pounding. He felt over the bed to confirm it was empty. Carefully he climbed out of the big bed and scanned around for the rabbit. Alleo was alone in the bedroom. Walking on the tips of his toes, the fox crept down the stairs, careful to make as little sound as he could.

Something was glowing in the kitchen. He made his way down the stairs and paused in the doorway.

The little blue crystal hovered over the table top and emitted a soft glow. The night light he had taken from so long ago. He smiled a little at the thought that the rabbit had still kept it rather than selling it or donating it. His heart stopped, however, when he spied what was beneath the crystal.

Alleo unfurled the parchment slowly and stared down at it, just able to read it by the crystal's light.

My Dearest Hurricane,

I am sorry to steal away as a thief in the night, but you were right that I cannot stay here anymore much as I cannot wait for you either. I care for you deeply, but I cannot keep this up. So, I am changing. I have taken the first airship to the islands. I've also taken your scrolls. Chase after me if you wish or you may stay there, the house is warded to allow you, and only you, to stay. I may return, eventually.

Sincerely yours,

Honeybun

A Farewell to Swords

by Starvix Draxon

Gaius Lucius Umbatzu, the great lion general of the twelfth legion, stared out into the horizon at the top of a hill overlooking a vast plain, grim faced, mounted on his war horse, his armor glinting the rays of the noon sun. Below him on the flat plain stood his infantry, armed with pila-spears, shields, and gladius swords. A tension hung in the air. Gaius could smell it. His whiskers twitched in agitation. They would be here soon.

A great, draconic roar resounded. Gaius gripped the reins on his horse. A series of sharp, reptilian roars echoed out. From the depths of the forest emerged the Darukai, the drakes, dragons with no wings, horns sharp, ridge-manes fierce, scales fire-bright. Their armor had basic padding, but what they lacked in armor they had in strength, ferocity, and a bloodlust not even the lion gods had. The Darukai bared their fangs, snarling, their reptilian eyes striking fear into Gaius's troops. The general could feel the angst among his soldiers. A bead of sweat trailed down Gaius's furry cheek. The lion's breath shallowed. He could not find their leader. He could not find *him*.

Suddenly a chilling, bloodthirsty roar boomed from the forest. The soldiers twitched in fear.

"Hold steady!" Gaius shouted.

A great drake came galloping out by horse. Gaius's heart skipped a beat. He squeezed his reins. Azakhra, the mighty drake of the Darukai, stood dressed in plated armor and traditional Darukan warrior garb. His muscles were like that of the lion war-god Shangorus: bulky, slender, and bulging with bloodlust. His ruby-red scales sparkled like flaming god-fire in the sun's rays; his fire-red eyes glared a monstrous bloodlust; and his obsidian black horns pierced sharply as a gladius. Gaius's heart cringed. The gods were cruel to him today.

Azakhra roared at Gaius and his army from afar, and his drakes bellowed their malice at the Luxoron army. Azakhra seemed to glare directly at Gaius. The drake had made his choice. Despite all of Gaius's pleas from the night before when they had… It was too late. Their fates were sealed.

"You damned fool," Gaius muttered bitterly under his breath.

The great lion general galloped down to his army, down to the front lines, strutting proudly as a general should. He eased his anxious troops with his commanding speech.

"Fellow felines, you see before you the Darukai. Armed with spears and swords, their numbers are great, their battle prowess extraordinary, their bloodthirstiness unquenchable. It seems as if the gods would cast our Fates poorly tomorrow," Gaius began.

The crowd of lion, tiger, leopard, cheetah, and jaguar soldiers shifted in unease.

"But who is it to say that the gods will cast our fate unfavorably? Who's to say we cannot beat these vile lizard scum? After all, they are barbarians, vile, emotionless slaughterers. They want us to fear them, to believe that their barbarousness is what makes them strong. But that is what makes them weak!" Gaius roared.

The soldiers looked up at him, eyes filling with hope.

"They may outnumber us, but do not forget that we are the superior intelligent beings compared to these barbarous skinks." Gaius twitched at that proclamation. "We are the lions and felines of Luxoron, the largest Empire in the known world. We move as one unit; they move as individuals bent on their own glory for bloodshed. They have no cohesion; we have strategy. After all, did we not win the battle of Carnassus?"

The felines roared in agreement.

"Did we not win the battle of Phillipai?"

The felines roared.

"Did we not win the battle of Gormenghast, the battle of Mac Kullan, the battle of Augustus, and the battle of Kadesh?!" Gaius roared.

The felines bellowed from their lungs.

"Then do not forget as we go into battle that we are the lions and cats of Luxoron. We will slay the Darukai, and we will bring these wretched skinks into submission! We will be victorious!" Gaius roared triumphantly!

The lions and the other cats roared, cheering their general on. Morality was restored. Gaius nodded to his generals; they shouted their commands. The troops roared and began marching to battle. Gaius turned to face the Darukai. There Azakhra stood, glaring a vile glare. The humongous drake roared, and the Darukai charged into the field. Gaius's heart sank. He could hear the words from the night before echo in his head. "This is goodbye."

***

Three days before the battle.

The sun beat down on Gaius as he discussed military strategy with his commanders. Throughout the encampment soldiers trained for battle while others worked on sharpening weapons, building fortifications, and setting up tents.

A horn sounded. The scouts had returned. Into the encampment sprinted three cheetahs. The lead cheetah scout approached Gaius, panting harshly, his eyes wide and frightened, a grim expression on his face.

"You have news I take it?" Gaius said.

"Yes my lord, and not happy news at that," the cheetah said.

"How many?" Gaius asked.

"Seven thousand," the cheetah answered. "They have camped just beyond the woods north of us. Azakhra is preparing to attack three days from now when the sun reaches the middle of the sky."

Gaius frowned. His legion was only six thousand soldiers, two thousand of which were velites, and two thousand cavalry. It would be a push to fight the Darukai, even with their skilled tactics. After all, the Darukai have managed to outwit Luxorian legions before. They could call for aid from a nearby legion. No. There was no way for another legion to reach his in time. They could retreat and fight another day. That way he could avoid… No. It was time to face him. It was time to end this conflict once and for all.

"Did Azakhra say anything else?" Gaius asked.

The cheetah's eyes darted nervously, glancing at the other generals. Gaius understood. He gestured towards his commanders to leave; this message was for him only. When the commanders walked away, Gaius nodded to the cheetah.

"Azakhra, leader of the Darukai, requests an audience with you on the night before the battle. He wishes to… to wrap up all final personal conflicts before the battle takes place. He told me… he wishes to say goodbye," the cheetah looked at Gaius, quizzically.

Gaius nodded; his face grim. "I guess it's time to settle the score." He looked at the cheetah. "Speak of this to no one. Send a bird to Azakhra. Tell him that I agree to settle the score."

The night before the battle, Gaius checked both ways outside of his tent. Two patrols had just passed by. It was time to go. Under the starry sky, Gaius crept through the encampment wearing only leather armor and a brown hooded cloak. Soon he snuck out of the camp and into the adjacent forest that bordered the right of the encampment.

Gaius soon arrived at a clearing. In the clearing a large stone with ancient symbols carved into its flesh stood leaning next to a clear pond where fairies, sprites, and willow o' wisps fluttered about, chirping merrily. The stars sparkled, and the moon shined down a calm silver light. In that moment Gaius felt all his worries, fears, and struggles evaporate from his heart. No war-tension hung in this serene clearing. Yet not all of Gaius's worries evaporated on the spot. One still held him down, a growing angst, a fear that he would not show.

A soft wind blew gently, rustling the tree leaves and shrubs, the small grass blades whispering soft secrets, the pond's water waving with the wind. Gaius sighed a hefty sigh.

"I knew you'd come," a deep, rough, scraggly voice echoed from the other side of the pond.

Gaius turned. From the shadows of the forest emerged a mighty drake. His ruby-red scales and obsidian black horns shone a luminous silver gleam under the moon's moonbeams. His fiery-red eyes seemed soft tonight. His muscular form stood tall and proud, yet the drake's head tilted, looking down at the ground. Then the drake looked up at Gaius in a wistful manner. Gaius's heart lurched and twisted. He gulped; his throat swollen.

"Azakh," Gaius said stiffly.

"Gaius," Azakhra answered.

For a moment there was silence between the two, and all that could be heard was the sounds of the fay and the frogs and the crickets, the occasional water droplet plopping into the creek. So long had Gaius not seen this drake, not since that bitter conflict when tensions swelled and left fraternal bonds broken.

"It has been a long time, old friend," Azakh spoke first.

"Indeed it has," Gaius replied.

"My scouts tell me your army is looking quite fierce, yet they tremble in fear of us Darukai," Azakhra said.

"What may seem as fear can be fierce resolve to fight to the death," Gaius stated.

Azakhra snorted. "Cats may hiss and swipe, but even wolves have been known to make them screech and run away like cowards."

"Watch your tongue, drake! You forget that you betrayed our legion to the Darukai," Gaius growled.

"A righteous cause, considering how your kind has treated my people, overworking them in the Kaverkoron mines till they drop dead from exhaustion and poisoned air. We will not bow down to tyrannical cats who deny us our freedom," Azakhra snarled.

"Have I ever treated you ill, Azakh? We fought together side by side. We had each other's backs. We fought as one. If I ever was in trouble, you'd rush to my aid. And now you turn your back to me, to our legion, to the Empire. Have you forgotten our brotherhood, our comradeship?" Gaius spoke, his voice trembling with emotion.

Azakhra snorted and glared narrowly at Gaius, his tail flicking. "Come now Gaius. You know very well that we did not come to meet and reminisce on past grievances and hurl insults at each other." The drake slowly strutted towards the lion. "The past is past. We cannot undo Saturn's path. There is only the future, only now." The lion stood his ground as the drake approached him. "So, let us remember how the gods toyed with our hearts."

The two beasts came to each other. Gaius looked up at Azakh, their bodies inches away from each other. They gazed into each other's eyes, each one assessing the other, searching for some kind of lost connection that had been fractured long ago.

Suddenly each other's paws grabbed the other's neck. Lips smashed together. The two embraced in a fierce kiss. Gaius's heart fluttered, beat faster. A reptilian tongue fought with his rough, sandpapery tongue and dominated it into submission. Soon paws were caressing leather armor and padding, and the kisses became fiercer, more urgent.

Gaius pulled away. The two beasts panted into each other's faces, their hearts racing, heat flushing in their groins, an aching lust and desire, ragged and damaged emotions re-tethering to each other's anima.

"I've missed you, Aza," Gaius breathed.

"As have I, Gaius," Aza hissed softly.

Soon they tore off each other's armor until a naked lion and a naked drake, both muscular, equally ferocious, and proud with Imperium, stood before each other, golden fur and ruby scales glistening with a silver sheen from Luna's Light. Gaius gazed up into Aza's fierce eyes as he stroked his reptilian face with the thumb of his paw. How he missed that hostile, cold, yet tender face. It had been those defiant eyes that struck Gaius with Eros's arrows. He was untamable as the nature gods, feistier than any wolf. When Aza turned his back on the Empire to join his kin, Gaius thought he'd never see him again. Now here he was gazing lovingly at Gaius with those same wild, defiant, daring eyes.

The drake leaned in and kissed the lion, softer this time. The lion savored those sweet reptilian lips. It had been so long. If only he could freeze Saturn's scythe, halt Time in its tracks, and savor this sweet moment, treasure it, bury it into the earth, and let it never stop repeating, over and over, forever eternal. But hands started to stroke flesh, pluck nipples, squeeze pecs and asses, caress scaly and furry flesh. Time moved forward. They grabbed harder, kissed fiercer, beginning their ritual. And that was how Gaius knew how powerless he was against Kronos's cruel verity.

Aza tossed Gaius to the ground. Gaius laid there, his legs opened and inviting, his arms curled, paws dangling in a flirtatious, submissive way, his whole torso exposed. His mind was fogged, glazed over with lust. Aza stood over him, broad chested, muscles ripped, a stance of domineering aggression. He squatted down, landed on his knees, fell forward, and engulfed Gaius, radiating masculinity. The two teased each other, brushing nose against nose in soft, graceful touches. Their cocks touched; they sucked in their breaths.

Then Aza kissed Gaius with a passionate rough yet tender kiss. Then the drake moved down, dragging his tongue along Gaius's bulky pecs. His tongue twirled around Gaius's left nipple, licking lightly, teasing. Gaius quivered. Aza bit down. Gaius groaned, his cock jerking. Aza did the same to his right pec, that same twirling teasing motion, before he bit down and made Gaius purr and groan, just like he used to when the two of them made love.

Aza slithered down, kissing bulky arms and rock-hard thighs, calves, and toes, making Gaius purr. Then Aza grabbed Gaius by his ass, gripped tightly, wrapped his rough, reptilian tongue around Gaius's erect cock, and sucked it. Gaius let out grunts and moans, pleasureful sparks coursing through his body. He grabbed Aza's horns and shoved his head down, engulfing his cock. Over and over Gaius shoved his cock up Aza's throat. He took pleasure in hearing his drake occasionally gag, overwhelmed by his ferocity. Gaius was almost there, his cock pulsing, almost at the precipice. But Aza pulled away, Gaius groaning, aching for more. Aza wiped precum from his muzzle, smirking with greedy eyes.

"You were always too eager to get off fast," Aza chuckled.

"Hmph. You weren't fast enough. Sometimes a slave needs coercion to please his master." Gaius smirked.

"As if you could ever coerce me," Aza snorted, grimacing. "Slaves don't have free will. Not that you ever noticed."

Gaius stared at his lover. He opened his mouth to counter what he had said, but both he and Aza knew the truth of how they first became acquainted. He remembered first seeing Aza at the arena, where the drake fought as a gladiator, slaughtering enemies in a bloody sport. He was known as Azakh the Mighty. Impressed by the drake's skills, Gaius bought Azakh from the arena's owner. For a while Azakh served Gaius as a bodyguard and nothing more. But as time grew, he let Aza train with him, then fight with him. From that they bonded in war. Repeatedly Aza would save Gaius from being killed. Whenever an enemy injured Gaius, Aza leaped to action, slaughtering the foe. Then one night, Aza came to Gaius's tent and presented him with a sword he had crafted himself. The two shared a bed that night, and Eros took the reins from there. From then on out, Gaius always treated Aza as an equal, but apparently that wasn't enough to erase the fact that Gaius still owned Aza as a slave.

Gaius shook his head trying to restore the mood. "Well get on with it." He smiled. "Or are you too superior to lay with your lover?"

Aza snorted, his eyes glaring sarcastically at the lion. He mounted Gaius, forcing the lion's legs up back. Gaius's tail flipped with anticipation, his hole exposed. It didn't take Aza long to find and mark Gaius's gaping hole. Aza slid in his cock with ease, and the two beasts gasped. Lion and drake embraced in that moment and kissed. Oh how long Gaius had waited to feel the drake's thick cock in him again. Only in secrecy did he ever let a young infantry lion pierce him like that, which happened rarely. More often it was Gaius who topped the young male, dominating him with his Imperium. Now he was with his lover, kissing him passionately.

They moved.

Aza slid out and thrust again, his torso towering over Gaius. He thrust a couple of times, teasing Gaius. But then he thrust hard. Gaius groaned. He thrust hard again, even deeper this time, hitting that magical spot.

"Ah!" Gaius purred.

Aza's leg muscles tightened, thrusting harshly, pleasuring his lion lover. Aza grunted as the moistness of Gaius's hole massaged his member, squeezed his cock, rubbing it in ways that no drake could ever truly satisfy him with. It had been long for him too. Domineering other drakes got old. They never felt the way Aza wanted them to feel. It was just aggressive sex. They did it because he was the alpha and they submitted to him. But Gaius wanted him this way. The feelings were mutual, understanding, unified as one love. And yet Aza took pleasure in having Gaius submit to him. It gave the drake a sense of power that he always felt he lacked.

Aza leaned down and hissed into Gaius's ears, "This is what it feels like to be dominated, my cat." He thrust harshly in that pleasure spot.

Gaius moaned. Aza nipped him on the neck. "I have you right in my grasp. I have you right where I want you. So vulnerable, just like your army."

Gaius almost missed that. But then the lust faded, and instantly Gaius looked at Aza, his face hard with concern.

"What are you talking about?" Gaius said.

But Aza silenced him with a kiss and continued to fuck. Gaius grabbed Aza's paws and tried to shove him off, but Aza fought back, pinning the lion's paws down and thrusting repeatedly, filling Gaius's heart with lust. Several times Gaius tried to recall what Aza had just said. But each time he fought back, Aza fought back harder with his kisses, his love-bites, and his thrusts, erasing the concern from his mind. Perhaps Gaius let it slip away on purpose. After all, he didn't want to think of the battle now. He just wanted to be with Aza, to forget all the betrayal, to forget all the pain of losing the only one he ever truly loved.

Aza sped up his thrusts as Gaius squeezed his pecs, egging him on to thrust harder, to strike deeper into his hole, like a sword piercing through armor. Aza grunted; his body glazed with sweat. He pounded Gaius, growled aggressively, licking the side of Gaius's throat as Gaius licked his. Then Aza lifted Gaius, supporting the lion's back, and fucked him with sharp thrusts, fiercely kissing, caressing flesh. Gaius grunted. "More."

Aza laid him back down, but soon Gaius forced Aza over onto his back, their bodies tangled. Gaius rode him hard, making Aza gasp and hiss and grunt in ecstasy. He squeezed Gaius's abs, his pecs, flicking his thumb-claw over Gaius's nipples. He worshiped his lion, praised his body, his might, his masculine bravado, his honor and valor, his courage, his lover's pride, his Auctoritas.

Aza was getting, close. He flipped his lion over onto his back and ravished his lion's flesh, making the lion cry out as he rammed his cock into the lion's pleasure spot until the lion roared, his cock spewing its seed. Aza thrust deeper, harsher, faster into Gaius. His cock swelled with blood, beginning to pulse. He leaned into Gaius's head as he thrust harshly, biting down on Gaius's throat, snarling. A feeling of ecstasy coursed through Aza as his cock spasmed, seed spurting into Gaius's ass. This was victory. This was triumph. The lion was all his.

The two beasts cried out, grunting each time one's cock spasmed. The drake slowly pulled out of Gaius, making the lion purr uncontrollably.

"Do you want to submit to me now, lion?" Aza hissed.

"Ha! I'm just getting started," Gaius growled and toppled Aza, straddling the drake. "You are mine to pleasure," Gaius said, his own venom hidden within the words he spoke.

Gaius kissed his drake, then kissed his pecs, biting down. Drakes may not have nipples, but all animals have pleasure spots somewhere on their chests. Aza hissed with pleasure, his cock springing to life again. Gaius nipped near Aza's collar bone, and Aza cried out. He nipped it again, and he felt Aza's cock jerk near him, prodding around Gaius's cum filled hole, seeking reentry. But the lion would not have it.

Gaius slid down and pleasured each muscle, worshiping Aza's reptilian body. Gaius then reached Aza's thick, slender cock. He gave it a kiss.

Aza sighed.

He gave the tip a lick.

Aza hissed.

Gaius gave the reptilian cock a nice long lick.

"Ah!" Aza cried.

Then Gaius sucked on the drake's cock. It was fiery hot, like molten rock, already leaking precum. Gaius felt strong claws tug at his mane, massaging his fur, rubbing tender areas that had longed for such affection. No young lion soldier ever understood Gaius's needs, but Aza always knew he liked his mane fondled when he performed oral sex.

Gaius straddled the drake, prodded the hole, and sank his cock deep into the drake. No lion ass felt as good as a drake's. Aza's hot hole massaged Gaius's cock, keeping it warm and moist.

259

Soon Gaius thrust deep, and made Aza groan. He thrust again. Groan. Again. Groan. Again! Hiss and groan. He hit and struck the pleasure spot within the drake.

"You like that don't you," Gaius purred.

Aza purred in agreement.

"How about this?" Gaius thrust harshly.

"Ah!" Aza cried out.

"Hurts a little doesn't it?" Gaius growled softly.

Aza grunted both in pleasure and in irritation. "You thrust as if you were trying to inflict pain on purpose."

"Well then. Let me teach you a little bit about pain, Aza." Gaius suddenly latched his claws into Aza's chest, drawing blood. Aza yelped in pain, then snarled and glared at his mate.

"What are you doing, Gaius?" Aza growled.

"What makes you think you can just say goodbye like this? One night, Aza. One night is all you give me? After everything you've done, you expect me to forgive you?" Gaius bared his teeth. "If I am to make love to you, then I want you to know exactly how I feel."

Aza sniffed, scrunching up his snout, smirking. "Go on then, oh mighty lion. Show me what you've got!"

"Allow me to demonstrate." Gaius grinned malevolently.

He thrust hard, causing Aza to cry out.

"This is for betraying the Empire."

He thrust hard again. Aza snarled.

"This is for betraying our legion."

Thrust. Yelp!

"This one's for siding with your kin instead of Luxoron."

Thrust. Roar!

"This one is for betraying *me*."

Gaius shoved his cock up Aza's ass as harshly as could. Aza let out a cry, tears forming in the rims of his eyes. Then the drake started to laugh. He looked at Gaius grinning a daring grin.

"Is that the best you could do?" Aza taunted.

Gaius snarled. Clearly, he hadn't learned anything about betrayal. Aza just stared at him with those defiant eyes, the same eyes that gazed upon Gaius as the Darukai ambushed them that dreadful day, when Azakh became Azakhra. The army was marching to the battlefield when suddenly the Darukai emerged from the forest nearby and charged from the side. Hundreds of Luxorian infantry died that day.

But the thing that haunted Gaius most was when he saw Azakh pulling out his blood-stained sword from a Luxorian soldier. The drake looked up and stared at Gaius, his eyes fiery, cold, and cruel, as if to say 'you brought this upon yourself,' and with that he trudged away, never to be seen again. Now here his drake lay beneath him, defiant, cruel, and alluring. This drake knew nothing of betrayal.

"I'll show you what betrayal feels like then." Gaius growled.

Gaius pulled out and tried to turn Aza over, but the drake fought back and slapped the lion away. The lion roared, the drake roared back. The two swiped at each other, snarling and roaring, but Gaius held the upper hand, turned Aza over onto his chest, pinned him down, and mounted the drake. He sank his cock back in. He thrust rapidly, making the helpless, lust-glazed drake grunt like a bitch.

"This is what it feels like to be abandoned by your lover!" Gaius snarled into Aza's ear.

The two beasts growled, completely one in erotic ecstasy. Gaius thrust as hard as he could, growling, snarling, wielding his Imperium over Aza. But it was a false Imperium. No matter how much Gaius got off fucking Aza like an animal, it only hid the fact that it was always Aza who was the stronger of the two. Aza defeated Gaius more times in sparring practice than Gaius ever did. It was Aza who first ignited the spark of Eros that one tent night, by initiating the first kiss. It was Aza who convinced him over time to take the female role in their lovemaking, who opened him up and dominated him like Gaius was doing now. In reality, the drake had already gained Imperium over him the moment Gaius fell for him that night in the tent. Aza had stolen his heart, and now he was ripping it apart, and Gaius could do nothing to stop him.

Gaius fucked his drake with wild abandon. Then he felt it, that urge of closeness. He knew it when he started licking Aza on the throat. Gaius thrust harder, the barbs in his cock beginning to protrude, making the drake growl in pleasurable pain. Soon Aza went over the edge and roared in ecstasy, the reptilian cock pulsing, spewing seed. Gaius thrust as deeply as he could, roared, and bit down into his drake's throat so hard he tasted draconic blood. His cock spasmed wildly, spurting seed into his drake's ass, barbs tearing into flesh. Gaius grunted, squeezing his mate, filling his drake up with his seed, a pulsing pleasure. When it was over, he slowly pulled out and collapsed upon his mate, almost crying, licking his drake on the cheek, whispering half mumbled words that sounded like "Never leave my side."

The two beasts lay naked on the ground, snuggling, Aza embracing Gaius from the back. The night was calm. For a while it seemed to Gaius that nothing could jar this serene feeling.

"Do you still have it?" Aza asked.

Gaius looked back at Aza. "Have what?"

"The sword I made you. Your gladius?" Aza said.

Gaius chuckled. "Of course I still have it. It's never left my side."

"It hasn't failed you?" Aza asked, trying to hide a hidden fear.

Gaius nodded faintly, sensing the fear. "Not once." He wish he hadn't spoken.

Aza gave him a squeeze. The two of them gazed at the quivering pond, listening to the fay chirp and buzz. The stars twinkled. The moon glimmered. Gaius held on tight to Aza's arm, afraid that his beloved would let him go and disappear forever. He savored every second, every kiss Aza gave him on his neck, every bit of remaining love making they shared.

"I wish we could stay like this forever," Gaius croaked, throat full of emotions.

"I wish we could too," Aza cooed.

Gaius tried not to feel stung by that comment.

"If you really felt that way, we wouldn't be fighting each other right now," Gaius grumbled.

Aza growled. "Don't start, Gaius."

"You were the one who betrayed my army."

"I did it for my kin."

"So those skinks are more important than our friendship?" Gaius asked.

With that Aza pulled away, growling. "You know nothing about them. You and your kin have fed off of the livelihood of my kind. All your jewels, goblets, gold and silver, come from the sweaty broken backs of my people! And what do you give us in return? The flail! The whip! You lions lounge about in chairs drinking wine and fucking whores at your stupid symposiums while my kind toils in disease and starvation as we slave away in those wretched mines."

"What do you expect me to do? Beg the Council to change everything? You knew I couldn't do that? Or did you forget that I was the one who treated you with respect," Gaius spat.

"You bought me as a slave," Aza murmured.

"And yet I treated you as my equal!" Gaius shouted.

Aza said nothing.

"I let you train with me, fight by my side, and this is what you have to say for it, by stabbing me in the back? Gods be damned, Aza, I love you!"

The words came out stronger than he had intended. They carried all the pain and emotion in the world. The lion's heart was completely exposed. Even Aza looked surprised. It made Gaius wonder if he had ever actually said those words to him before everything went to the Badlands.

Aza looked away, frowning. Gaius growled in irritation and grabbed the drake's snout, forcing him to look at him directly in the eyes.

"We shared one bed at the camp. We slept one sleep. We were a force to be reckoned with. Our enemies feared our wrath. We were one, Aza."

Aza looked mournfully at Gaius and shook his head, "No Gaius. We were never truly one. We were not equals."

Ranks and social class always fuck things up.

Gaius looked wistfully at his lover, held his face in his paw. "Don't fight me, Aza. Please… I love you." He could feel the tears in his eyes rising.

Aza laid a kiss gently on his soft lips. A cold tear touched Gaius's finger. He looked into his drake's watery eyes that still glimmered like a campfire's flame.

"I'm sorry, Gaius. What's done is done. The gods are cruel," Aza said.

"Aza," Gaius croaked.

"This is goodbye, Gaius," Aza said, kissing him once more. "Let's just enjoy the moment, while we can, my Eromenos."

So, Gaius let him kiss him and make love to him once more, letting his drake take him one last time. This time the love making was gentler, softer, expressing each other's vulnerability. When it was done, they snuggled together, holding onto a memory doomed to never last.

***

The war began. The Darukai clashed with the infantry, the velites having retreated. Roars and howls echoed. The infantry struggled to hold the Darukai back, their bloodlust unquenchable, their ferocity infinite. Slowly the drakes ripped their ways through the centuries and squads.

It was time.

"Cavalry, with me! For Luxoron!" Gaius roared.

Gaius Lucius Umbatzu and his valiant cavalry charged down the hill at rapid speed. Gaius felt the air rush by him. Courage in his heart could not fully overcome his fear, but he held on for honor of his homeland, for the Empire. He channeled his feelings of anger and betrayal, and roared a lion's roar as he speared his first kill.

The cavalry trampled the drakes in droves. Gaius swung his gladius sword, hacking off heads, slashing through chests, thrusting into hearts, trampling them with his horse. Valor and bravery coursed through him as he slayed his mighty enemies. But something seemed off. The Darukai seemed smaller in number, even though many had died. That's when he heard it. Another set of reptilian roars came from the forest to the right, where he and Azakhra…

"I have you right in my grasp. I have you right where I want you, so vulnerable, just like your army."

Gaius cursed himself for his foolishness. He had planned this all along. Ambush them from the side. He should have known Azakhra would attempt such a trick, just like he had when he first betrayed Gaius. This ambush would charge right into the infantry's weak point: its side, for the shields cannot protect the entirety of the soldiers' bodies.

All hell broke loose. The infantry's formation began to collapse. The cavalry soon lost its formation and took heavy blows. The Darukai broke the legion's ranks, causing a chaotic whirlwind of swords and a rainstorm of blood.

Gaius fought ferociously, but then he saw Azakhra roaring, slashing open a lion soldier, his snarling snout drenched in blood, his frenzied reptilian eyes turning to glare directly at Gaius.

It was time.

Gaius charged at Azakhra, but Azakhra dodged his charge with sleek swiftness and sliced open his horse. The horse cried out and crumpled to the ground. Gaius flew off and tumbled to the ground. The impact knocked the air out of his lungs, an aching pain in his back. But Gaius forced himself up, sucking in air, took his stance, and unsheathed his gladius sword. Azakhra turned to him, stood in his war stance, arms open.

"The time has come, Gaius Lucius Umbatzu, to meet your doom. Face me mighty lion!" Azakhra roared a gut-wrenching roar.

Gaius roared back. The two charged and their swords clashed, sparks flying. Lion and drake fought, the glares from the sun glinting off their steel blades. Around them drakes and felines fought, blood spilling to the earth. The cacophony of clangs and roars reverberated in Gaius's ears, surrounding him and Aza in a war dance.

Soon Aza got the better hand and struck Gaius at the leg. It was not a deep cut, but Gaius felt the blood trickling down his calf. Then Gaius got the better of Aza and slashed at his arm, inflicting a kindred wound. Azakhra howled, enraged. The two circled each other, snarling.

They clashed once more, and though they fought equally, Azakhra was indeed the better warrior. Soon enough, Azakhra had walked Gaius into his trap, parried him, tripped him with his tail, buffed him with his shield, and slashed his chest with his sword.

Gaius roared in agony. Blood splashed. A raging burn sheared across his chest. He tasted his blood. Then he felt claws swipe at his face, taking fur and flesh with them. The lion crumpled to the ground. Azakhra then kicked him hard in the ribs. He heard a crack. Then Azakhra struck him hard with his foot in the stomach. Gaius puked, suffocating. Azakhra grabbed him by the throat and punched him hard in the snout, the helmet flying off.

Gaius laid on his back, gasping in pain. Azakhra stood over him like an ominous shadow, a shade of doom, a bringer of death, his eyes glowing with blood-rage, like embers in the forge. He smiled as he snarled, sharp fangs bared at his lover.

"This is for my people. I will no longer be a slave to the Luxoron Empire. I am a free drake! This lion I kill for my freedom!" Azakhra roared.

Aza's sword came rushing down only to clang against the flat side of Gaius's sword. Gaius growled, pushing against Azakhra's force, the drake's blade inches away from splitting his head in half. Gaius filled his heart with rage and used every ounce of energy in his bloodied body to shove away Azakhra's vile weapon. Gaius rose despite the searing pain in his body.

"Traitor to Luxoron, your time has come!" Gaius roared.

"Then let's end this," Aza hissed.

The two charged, roaring their lungs out. They clashed! Silence! Gaius found his sword deep inside Azakhra's chest. Aza stood there, stunned, shock bright in his eyes. The two beasts had a war-grip on each other. Gaius panted. Aza only could cough. Gaius slid his sword out, sucking blood out with it. He raised his gladius sword and slashed down Aza's chest. A crimson splash splattered on Gaius's armor. It felt like the world had slowed, as if Kronos had retracted his scythe and cut Time in half, forcing Gaius to take in every second of Aza's fall to the earth, how he gurgled blood from his snout, how the drake painted the sky with blood. The irony of it, a gladius blade stained with the blood of its maker. A traitor that was once a comrade and a lover crumpled to the blood-soaked soil.

Gaius summoned all his strength, and let out a lion's mighty, triumphant roar! It resounded throughout the battlefield. Soon warriors froze in place and turned to see Gaius standing over Azakhra's broken body, triumphant.

"Followers of Azakhra, lower your weapons, for I have slain your leader. He lies before me, broken by my sword. Your leader has fallen. The Luxoron Empire is victorious!"

The lions and felines roared triumphantly, yet Gaius, underneath his triumphant snarl, looked at his sword, its maker's blood oozing down the bright steel blade.

Surrender did not come easily. Most Darukai fought on, but they fought with a broken morale. Those who fought lost their lives, slaughtered by brave lions and felines. Those who surrendered were whipped, beaten, bound in chains, and sold into slavery to be dispersed throughout the Luxoron Empire, primarily in the mines where their muscle was needed most.

After several days of healing, Gaius was in shape to walk again. His fellow lions and felines greeted him with praise, roaring triumphantly for their mighty leader, patting him fiercely on his back. He would be granted much Imperium when he returned to Luxoron's capital. The council would grant him a profuse amount of land that he would distribute to his fellow soldiers. He gave a stirring and laudatory speech praising his army and their courage. Then, when no one was looking, Gaius slipped away out of the encampment.

Gaius trudged up to the hill and gazed upon the grim battlefield where ravens and crows feasted on decaying corpses, the soil stained with blood. All the felines had received proper burials. The drakes were left to rot. The pungent smell of death made Gaius's nose scrunch up. He wandered through the battle-grave, almost in a trance like state, searching for something precious. Then he found the decrepit body of Azakhra, flies swarming around his rotting flesh, emitting a foul stench, eyelids open, drooping. Gaius grimaced, a rage boiling within. He shooed away the flies, gently closed Aza's vacant eyes, picked up his lover's corpse, and carried him away.

On a distant hill, as the sun began to transform into the evening sun,

Gaius gently laid the corpse on clean soil. It took him hours to dig the grave, sweat pouring down his body, dirt sticking to sweat. Both stung his still healing wounds, yet the lion dug on, disregarding the pain. Physical wounds were nothing to him. He had gathered battle scars since he was a youth. He wore them honorably as a sign of prowess. But the scars he gained from this battle would not inspire in him honor, valor, or even Imperium. No. These wounds would tear at his heart and inflict damage that cannot always be seen in the warrior's eye.

Memories can be the cruelest things to bear in the heart, for as Gaius recalled all the joyful memories he shared with Aza, his throat swelled up, making it hard to swallow. He had to fight back feelings that would break him if he let them out.

When he finished digging, he looked over at his fallen comrade, the drake who had betrayed him. He looked like he was just asleep, almost at peace. Gaius grunted, his throat swollen to where he thought he couldn't breathe. He scooped Aza up, cradled him in his arms. The lion's face softened as he gazed mournfully at his lover.

"You were always too cocky for your own good, my friend," Gaius croaked. "If only we could have died on the battlefield together, having each other's backs."

This time he could not hold back. He tried to keep himself from crying, but the tears dribbled down his sweaty cheeks in torrents. All the sorrow in his heart poured out of him. He let out a wretched, howling roar, screamed it to the sky. A soldier rarely has the time to mourn his comrades whom he bonds with in training and in battle. Each battle nullifies the mind into dullness and hardens the heart. How else can a soldier carry on to fight and kill? But every now and then a soldier breaks down, and must let out his sorrow, let it overflow lest it consume him with madness and insanity.

Gaius gently lowered Aza's body into the grave. Then he unsheathed the sword Aza gave him so long ago. Gaius gazed at its pristine beauty, the sun glinting off the rim. Yet Aza's blood still stained it. No matter how hard Gaius had tried to clean it, a remnant still remained. He looked down at his lover.

"I am not worthy of this sword, Aza. It should belong to its maker. You were the better fighter after all," Gaius said wistfully, then gently laid the sword down on Aza's corpse.

When Gaius finished burying his lover, he found some rocks and laid them over the grave. He then took a large rock and carved Aza's name with an epithet into it: *Azakhra – Valorous Leader of the Darukai and Lover of Gaius Lucius Umbatzu.* After finishing the shrine, Gaius sat there, and said nothing for a long time. Then he spoke.

"You were the greatest friend a lion could ask for." Gaius paused for a moment, sniffing. "I hope that you can one day forgive me. I hope that in the next life, we can reunite." He paused, stared at the grave for a moment and spoke again, "I love you, Aza. I will forever miss you until the end of Time."

Gaius wiped his tear stained face, stood up, and began to trudge away, but before he left, he turned back to face the shrine. A sublime feeling befell Gaius, for as the wind blew against him, he thought he saw the proud drake standing there gazing towards the evening sun.

"Aza," Gaius said wistfully. He trudged towards him, reaching out his hand. It seemed as if Aza turned to face him, to gaze upon him with his sun-bright eyes. But then he vanished, and Gaius fell forward upon the grave. The lion looked up. He watched the sun set beneath the horizon. He was really gone. The lion let out a tearful howl and hugged the grave like how a mother would for her dead child. After some time passed, Gaius sniffed, kissed the grave, and looked out to the empty sky. "Goodbye, Aza," the lion said. And with that, Gaius trudged down the hill back to the camp, emotions put back in check, so he could continue the workings of the ever expanding Luxorian Empire.

With gratitude to Laura "Munchkin" Lewis &
Rechan, who have always sent positive energy my way.

QUIPIS

by Bill Kieffer

The Cat stood quietly on the street corner as the sun set.

Pervert. Blasphemer. Desecration. These words reverberated in his skull as fresh and as raw as they had been that afternoon. Because they were true, he could find no relief.

Jinx's tears had stopped an hour before. It was more dehydration than healing.

He'd texted everyone else. Word had spread quickly. Teddy told him to call the Alligator he never expected to take his call. Yet, the phone was answered. Hearing the man's gruff, deep voice nearly broke his heart.

He couldn't even bring himself to say hello. "I need some place to sleep tonight," Jinx choked out. The lump in his throat seemed about to strangle him.

"Where are you?" Cecile asked without hesitation, managing to sound rough and gentle at the same time. "I'll come get you."

Minutes later, his Phorde Corsair pulled up. It was a van popular for Repts with shorter limbs and extra thick tails. The Cat sniffled and stood up as straight as possible, trying not to think of it as the fuckmobile. A drizzle of rain started as Jinx wondered how it had all come to this. He switched the ratty gym bag from one silvery blue hand to the other, aware of how shitty he must look.

The 'Gator popped the lock open on the passenger door with a button on the steering wheel as he gave what Jinx thought must be a measuring look. Cecil didn't emote much with his face, but the young Feline knew his ex-lover would be fantastically curious about his situation.

Jinx tossed his gym bag over the seat into the back of the van, the "playroom" as they'd once called it. He tried to greet his old lover and express his gratitude, but the weight upon him only allowed the Cat to whisper, "Thanks."

Cecil glanced into the back. The gym bag was obviously far from full.

"Is that all you have?" Not judgment, but concern.

The Tonkinese's ears swept back in shame and a few other mixed emotions. He nodded and concentrated on buckling his seat belt. The tears began blurring his vision again and he felt his tail trying to lash in agitation under his clothes. He said nothing.

Cecil's eyebrows raised up to a comic height for an Alligator, not that most Mammals would ever notice. One did not generally need to pull a story from a Tonk, much less this one. "We can go back tomorrow and get the rest of your stuff."

The Tonk gasped something and shook his head frantically. The van did not roll forward. Jinx looked forlornly at the greenish wedge of a head that stared at him. The stillness was unnerving, but the Cat had learned to read Alligators long ago. "This is all they will let me have."

Cecil started with surprise, a subtle ripple of muscles that crawled from his toothy jaw and then across his face, until a second later his thick tail thumped twice behind his seat. "What do you mean, that's 'all they will let you have?'" The 'Gator's outrage colored his voice.

It pleased Jinx to hear it. Yet, he was still too raw to tell his tale. "Can we just go, now? The further away we get from here, the better."

Cecil nodded and put the van into gear. After a few miles, Jinx began rubbing his black palms into the rough upholstery of the passenger seat. The texture and the vibration from the road began to soothe him. The touch of it gave him hope… but then his erection let the shame return.

***

"Yes, please." Jinx held his bowl out with both hands. Cecil poured them tea from a clay pot with a hint of ritual to it. They sat at a small table that featured a rainbow of tiles in an abstract pattern that hinted at the old Homeland glyphs. The Alligator, the Cat knew, was not a practicing Chromatic, but he still maintained many of the traditions he'd been raised with.

Jinx looked about the house, wondering how much of his own religion that he himself would maintain now that he'd been shunned. Everything was so different from his own. Here, there were a lot of macramé tapestries that may or may not have different meanings to the 'Gator. Cecil had always been good with knots. The Tonk felt a fleeting smile on his face, recalling Cecil's skills. He wondered how many of the decorations his rescuer .

He'd never been invited into the Rept's home before. They'd only had sex in the van. There were a lot of questions he wanted to ask. Instead, he lapped at his tea delicately. He waited to be berated. He'd hurt Cecil when they'd last spoken. He hoped that Teddy was right, and that Cecil could give him at least the one night.

After they both finished their second round of tea, the 'Gator sighed. "Jinx, honey, I've never heard you stay so quiet for so long. So, I'm going to assume you don't want to talk yet, 'kay?"

The Cat nodded and kept himself from letting loose a relieved sob.

"I never bring my lovers home, you know that. That's because I do take in strays and I don't have sex with my charges. So, as long as you stay with me, we can't have sex."

The Tonk gave him a slightly betrayed look.

I never said that I wanted to have sex.

But, Jinx knew, the denial was false. When had he stopped wanting to have sex? Cecil had been his first. Cecil introduced him to such pleasures. Every lover since then had been compared to Cecil. Because he had never stopped wanting the rough skin of the Rept under him.

The 'Gator barely acknowledged Jinx's dark look. "I don't want to take advantage of anyone. When things get sorted, we can hook up again, if that's what you want. I do not want you feeling like you have to whore yourself to have a safe place. You shouldn't have to become a hustler to get by, okay?"

Sulkily and somewhat satisfied, Jinx nodded and stared back into his empty bowl.

"I've a big house," Cecil continued. "And a nicely sized larder. I eat 'normal' food. The milkman brings fresh lox and chicken eggs every morning. I assume fish is okay with you?"

The Cat nodded. He'd spent much of his hour standing on the corner wondering if he'd be eating out of the dumpsters in the alley by week's end. Smoked salmon would be much more than he deserved.

"You can stay as long as you want," the Alligator said, lifting a huge weight from the Cat's mind. "I work from home, but I need to keep my van handy. There's a bus stop two blocks over that goes right past where you work."

Jinx shook his silver-blue head and closed his eyes. "I don't have a job anymore." He failed to fight down a sob.

Cecil went still with that focused Rept attention until the Cat took a breath and opened his eyes. Yet, he would not look at his older friend.

"Your parents threw you out because you lost your job?" There was the thump of Cecil's thick tail on the carpet, punctuating his disbelief. "I know Darwinists can be... demanding... of their children. But that seems severe."

Jinx shook his head and looked for a tissue box. Of course, Repts didn't usually leak body fluids all over the place. He wiped his nose on his sleeve instead. "No... they... walked in on me... when I was... masturbating." A silver-blue tail slipped out from his shirt and darted about in agitation until the Cat grabbed it.

Cecil stayed patient and still, the Alligator's default setting. "My understanding was that Darwinism was copacetic with jerking off. Wait... were you at work?"

Jinx laughed despite himself and shook his head no. "No, I was home."

"Then I don't understand what happened," Cecil said. His rumbling voice was calm; comforting. "You can tell me, Jinx. I won't judge."

The Cat looked at his friend and wondered, not for the first time, how the Alligator really felt about him. They'd hooked up while Jinx had been a high school sophomore. Technically underage for the older man, but both of them were ill-prepared for guessing the age of the other's species. Jinx was the man's first Cat and Cecil was his first 'Gator.

Cecil was his first Rept, his first man, his first lover, his first time, his first obsession, and his first break-up.

He'd awoken so many things within Jinx, things that the older and colder man could not possibly know about. His palms tingled just thinking about the almost smooth belly of the Rept, laid out like an organic chess board. It was never as dry as he expected, never as dry as it looked like it should be. Jinx loved the feel of it, especially where the scales gave up their attempt at order below his waist.

He loved the smooth coolness of Cecil's penis. That had been a surprise; Jinx could never believe it was quite the real thing. It felt too much like the perfect dildo, always erect and ready. It was almost the polar opposite of his slender instrument, hot all over and abrasive when erect.

He wanted, even now, to reach over and run his palms along every inch of the large Rept's cool, rough hide. The soft pliable webbing between his fingers called out to Jinx while the raised diamond ridges of Cecil's neck and shoulders made promises of their own. The 'Gator's body was a buffet of different textures for his fingers and toes to explore.

Despite his misery, just even looking at that snout full of braided, interlocking teeth made him hard. Cecil had never used his teeth on him. He wondered if he could talk his friend into letting him finger his mouth as if they were a keyboard of an ancient and priceless miniature piano.

It wouldn't count as sex, if I jerked off with his left hand and caressed his head with my right, would it?

But Jinx caught himself, pressing a sweaty black palm into his crotch, and he knew the answer would be yes. Yes. Yes, of course. It would be sex.

Of course, it would be.

He shook his head. No.

After a moment, Cecil patted his back and then rested his huge greenish hand on Jinx's shoulder for a moment. The Cat looked down at the thick, ribbed fingers and the creamy smooth claws that the 'Gator kept long for typing on his computer. "When you're ready," the Rept assured him, and it was all the Tonk could do to keep his tongue from licking and exploring the fingers that had opened so many doors for it.

He began to sob as the taste of Cecil's body came back to him in a sudden wave.

The Alligator left him, alone, to mourn his losses.

***

With the run of Cecil's two-story house, Jinx spent the first few days silently haunting his friend's house. He wasn't ready to look for a job yet. He was barely ready to look out a window. Yet, on the third day, Jinx found himself staring at a display case in what Cecil had called the family room. It was mounted atop a four foot tall cabinet. Four rolled up rugs in shades of green were nested in the cabinet's deep cubes. The Cat had seen enough Chromatics to know what the prayer mats were, but he didn't know why Cecil might need four. Or what the different shades might mean, if they meant anything at all.

It was the little knotted pieces of string and yarn in the case that held his attention.

They were obviously pieces of art, but too small to be called macramé. They were also obviously something religious, being mounted on top of the cabinet that held the prayer mats and books of and about Mosaic. Not to mention the inset clock and bell that tolled the times of prayer that Cecil had studiously ignored. No doubt the cabinet was set so that he was facing Homeland even as he studied the little trinkets.

Jinx had opened and closed the case three or four times so far, re-sisting the urge to finger the knots and explore their textures, but he'd already been caught committing sacrilege once. He could not let himself get thrown out of Cecil's home, too.

Instead, he comforted himself with just tracing the pieces on the cool glass lid. The textures of the cabinet would have to be enough.

The Tonk was guiltily rubbing his bare palms against his pants when the 'Gator politely cleared his throat. With a thick, serrated tail dragging behind him, Cecil wasn't known for his ability to sneak up behind people. Jinx looked over his shoulder and their eyes met. Jinx couldn't read much into the Rept's features or pose, except for the incredible patience the Cold always seemed to have.

As a 'Gator, Cecil could play the silence game so much better than Jinx ever could. Even if Nature hadn't designed the Alligator for calculated stillness, chattiness was a trait that even the Darwinists hadn't been able to breed out of the Tonk.

A part of him wanted to talk about what happened… he just didn't know how. Cecil had already rejected him once when he had discovered *The Truth*.

"What are these?" Jinx looked back for a glance at the case. Almost the size of a pizza box but not quite square, it housed a dozen pieces. There were little green badges the size of a match book to long unknotted tassels that were mostly that strings around a core of rainbow colors. Each of these started with a little brass circlet that reminded him of an earring.

Cecil strode over and gave the Cat a slow blink. It was an affectation that he knew the Rept saved for him, a Feline smile that Cecil could emulate in his often inexpressive face. Jinx blushed despite himself.

"These are all Tzitzits," Cecil said softly but factually. The voice of someone not sure why he kept a thing. "These are ritually knotted badges that have different meanings. The ones on the top row are all mine. My birth band, my first name, my father's name, my mother's name, my first word."

Jinx could see the knotwork varied with each piece, yet each small piece held roughly the same shape. "I've never seen Quipus like this. Do your folk come from South America?"

"No." Cecil laughed, amused at the thought. "We are Amerinds but not that far south. Floridae, I believe. What's a khrip-us?"

"Quipis. They are talking-knots. Used in the Andes and ancient cultures to keep inventories and stuff." Jinx closed his eyes and imagined running the knots between his black finger tips. His neck fur lifted in gentle waves. He licked his lips and forced his eyes open. "I did a report on braille in school and I came across them."

"Tzitzits are from Homeland. The ancient Middle Easterners were always big on math so I wouldn't be surprised if the knotwork had a mathematical component. Chromatics today are really more interested in the images and meanings the knots evoke. And, of course, the traditions."

Jinx wondered if he made a mistake by reminding Cecil of their age difference. The Cat wanted to say that he hadn't learned much about the Chromatic traditions in his school. Darwinists were big on science and biology, but they tended to ignore the trivia of other religions. Silence seemed the wisest choice, but it felt awkward just standing there.

After a moment, the 'Gator opened the case and took out a green badge with a column of knots in the middle that reminded Jinx of the collar of a noose. Some darker green threads showed in the design and Cecil allowed the Tonk to touch it while his thick fingers held it delicately out. "This is my first adult name, Sea Isle Pine. We are supposed to pick an image that we hold of ourselves... but the truth is, I picked the name because of a rapper that was in the news at the time."

Jinx closed his eyes and barely heard the story. His sense of touch overwhelmed all else, even limited to just the one finger tip. Goosebumps ran up his spine, lifting his blue silver fur the wrong way against his cotton shirt. As he stroked the badge, another image came to his mind's eye... and it wasn't a pine covered island. Suddenly, his naked palm was running over the big, cold hand and the goosebumps invaded his ears.

Jinx gasped and jumped back, feeling guilty. He clutched his offending hand to his chest and bit his lower lip.

Cecil gave him a Rept's passive look that might have meant anything. He merely put the little badge back into the case and left the lid up.

"These two," the Alligator said, waving a claw over the unbraided rainbow tassels. "These two are my parents.' When a Chromatic dies, the family will undo the knots of their Tzitzit."

"How come they had rainbows in theirs and yours don't?"

"There's a rainbow inside of most of these. A rainbow is the Creator's Promise. When we untie the rainbow, we help guide their spirits to Heaven, The Rainbow in the Dark brings them home. Yet a part of them stays behind, transmogrified."

Cecil blinked another smile for the Cat. Jinx allowed himself to step close again as he nodded, thinking it a sweet image, trying not to think like a Darwinist. He stared for a moment longer at the little badges, sensing that his Cold friend was waiting for him to say something. "What are the little brass rings for?"

The 'Gator barked his richly textured laugh, a little murmur of surprise. The sound tickled the Tonk's ears.

"That's where they go into our skin, like a piercing."

That earned a look of such disbelieve that Cecil snorted and waved a short green hand at the ear holes on the side of his long head. "Not there. Here." He pulled up his shirt, revealing his quilted yellow-white chest and belly. He took the Cat's silver-blue hand and placed it on his right pectorals. A firm long-clawed digit moved his fingers across the silky flesh until he felt a series of tiny pinprick perforations. "My dates kept touching them, making jokes wondering if I had a Prince Albert or other piercings. Sometimes they even pulled at them, trying to get a reaction from me. As a Chromatic, we are only supposed to touch them with reverence."

Cecil let his hand fall away.

Jinx did not.

He brushed at the tiny, invisible scars with his fingertips. The little bumps and blemishes sent Morse code directly to his dick. He remembered all of the times he'd touched the older Rept's chest and was fascinated that he'd never explored these inches of the Alligator's body. The world fell away as he stroked the chest, finding a dozen holes, each one a mystery and an image that his first lover had never shared with him.

"Reverence..." Cecil said, almost breathy. "Yes... like that."

But then the cold body snapped and Jinx's wayward hand was snapped back in a powerful green clawed hand.

Cecil released him after a moment with a look that the Cat decided must be a glare. They had a no sex rule. He hadn't forgotten. He had merely forgotten himself for a moment. Jinx stared back at the case, feeling that was the only safe place that he could look now.

"What do you know about Darwarnists, Cecil?"

"I know you're 'poly-cannibals.' I know you believe in evolution of some sort. I know you have a sort of secular religion, but you believe in reincarnation. I know you work all the holidays." Jinx heard Cecil shrug next to him, the rough ridges of his normal-sized shoulders rubbing against his wide, thick neck. "I know what most people know."

Jinx nodded and gathered himself. The Darwinists thought of themselves as rather pragmatic and flexible, but they were more complicated than that. He'd spent many hours trying to think how best to open up to Cecil and explain his crime, yet at this moment, he still felt woefully unprepared.

"Did you know that we use Our Dead?"

"I know some of it besides the Wake and Final Feast." Claws touch and pull at the cotton smock that Jinx wore. "I know your clothes are often spun from your own fur. And, I know you didn't bring any of that with you."

"It isn't just the fur." Jinx swallowed a sob and pushed onward. "We use our hides, too. We make leather. We make suede... from the dead we revere."

"I know. I made the mistake of looking for Alligator shoes on the Internet once." Cecil let the silence hang for a moment and rubbed the Cat's shoulder encouragingly. "It's not the memorial I'd choose for myself, but... to each their own."

"Like your badges... these are all supposed to be treated with a certain reverence."

Jinx closed his eyes as Cecil began to gently stroke his arm encouragingly. The result was a hard-on that made him feel terribly ashamed, so he moved a half step away. Silence—and an air of acceptance and concern—eventually pulled the words awkwardly from the Cat's soul.

"I like touching things, Cecil. Doraphilia. I really, really like feeling stuff against my palms... my belly... my... anywhere there isn't fur. I don't care if it's rough or smooth... You... had a really big impact on me. You were... were my first. You were my best..."

"They didn't kick you out because you liked Repts, did they?"

"I was shunned because they walked in on me... playing with a suede..." He choked on his words as the soft sensation of the dead hide on his genitals suddenly returned to him.

"Oh."

Jinx waited for the words of condemnation to spill out of this man as they had three years ago when he'd been caught in a lie.

And then short arms pulled Jinx to the older man, and where his arms could not reach, he draped his throat and chin. The thick tail of the Alligator coiled around and under the Cat's now flailing tail.

Covered in his friend's protective armor, Jinx began sobbing in release.

***

Jinx had always loved to touch things with his little black fingertips. It wasn't until he tried to explain to his friends what sex had been like with Cecil that he began to understand that not everyone felt that way. Even the ones who liked touching, didn't feel about it the way Jinx felt about it. Not even close.

On that awful day, however, Jinx had been between men. Jinx had slept with a lot of men by even Darwinist standards and enough women to know his future would be exclusively with men. He had already slept with anyone in the Cattery that he had wanted to. He had also slept with some Repts, but they'd never be more than trade to him. They weren't anything like Cecil. He was unlikely to ever meet anyone at his Uncle's business.

He was laying naked on his bed. The comforter had been made with his parent's shed fur, making it a pretty silvery color similar to his own coat. The overhead fan caused dust and shed fur to dance in the sunbeam that fell on his shaved groin. The feel of sunlight on his naked sheathe and balls, made him drowsy and yet aroused. There was a box of scraps near his right hand. When he was done, he'd have to hide it back deep in his bookcase. The box of tissues would stay on his night stand, within reach of his left hand. His dark-furred right hand idly stirred the contents of the box. Most of the scraps of materials had names written on them, but Jinx studiously avoided looking at them. He stared up at the ceiling and concentrated on feeling only what brushed up against his black fingertips.

He began to purr as he found a large piece of suede. It was soft and expertly worked and Jinx might have guessed who donated it if he let himself. He slipped it down on his balls for a bit. When he was done flexing his sack with it, the Cat wrapped the hide around his aroused member, pushing the sheathe down until the ring of thorns at the base of his cock brushed against the material.

The Tonk had played this game any number of times. He knew it was a tad distasteful, but most of these pieces were too small to be used for anything. As long as he came in to tissues, Jinx was convinced, there was no harm. No foul.

The piece felt almost like Cecil's belly. It was the same room temperature that Cecil usually was. The suede piece wasn't exactly the same yellow of Cecil's belly. But then, it had been three years since he'd last seen Cecil undressed. He might be wrong. With his eyes closed, it was all the same, wasn't it? And the Alligator's belly was soft… Jinx purred a sigh and wondered what it would be like if the Alligator had forgiven him.

If only his bed was harder, he could imagine they were in the Pforde fuckwagon.

Jinx imagined Cecil's large body over his, his hands free but his legs tied.

I have to buy some hemp rope, he thought, feeling the ghost sensation of the rough cord on his furry ankles. He didn't like the restriction, but the feel of the knots titillated him.

His body was ready to release its load, but Jinx was not ready to give up his idyll just yet. Darwinists' idea of sex education hadn't stopped with mere biology. Although they'd never been able to get him to like girls, his instructors had taught him control.

It was such a sweet torment, in this day dream with Cecil.

If he heard the gentle rapping, he dismissed it as the imaginary thumping of Cecil's tail.

Right until the moment his mother walked in, Jinx had thought he had locked the door of his bedroom behind him. His sat up and instantly his control broke as he tried to cover himself and hide the box of scraps all at once. Cum shot up, shattering any illusions his mother might have had about what her son had been doing.

The screaming started before her laundry basket even hit the floor, the box of contraband spilled across the bed splattered by tiny drops of Cat cum.

***

"I'm nervous." Jinx said as they walked into the bar. It was a Tea Dance Sunday and all the lights were up. "What if he doesn't like me?"

"He'll like you, Jinxy. What's not to like?" The 'Gator's voice was gentle rumbling thunder, somehow comforting.

"I talk too much. I'm unemployed." Back to his chatty self, the Tonk rattled off all his faults, spilling out his nervous energy. "My tail is too long. Did you tell him I was a Cat? I heard some Dogs don't like Cats."

Cecil laughed and stroked the fuzzy question mark of a tail that followed Jinx to a table. No longer a Darwinist, the Cat felt free to let his tail do what nature had designed it for. "You have several job interviews at places the Darwinists have no power. Which, as I keep reminding you, is many, many more places than they'd have you believe. And he's just looking for a flatmate for now; not a soul mate. 'Kay? You'll find something before your unemployment runs out."

They took a low table where Cecil's frame would be more comfortable. Jinx chattered non-stop but paused at all the right places to allow the 'Gator to reply. They'd gotten very comfortable with each other again, old friends and nearly polar opposites. They'd avoided sex, although it was sometimes awkward. The sight or touch of Cecil's hide almost always made him painfully hard. It did not help knowing that Cecil was always ready, his white pole hard but hidden in his body.

A dark, short-furred Dog entered wearing a pale cowboy hat with a forward brim long enough to provide shade for his long, narrow muzzle. Jinx noticed something right off that he didn't have ear holes cut into his hat, so assumed that he was one of the Dogs that had long floppy ears.

Floppy ears could be fun to play with.

The newcomer noticed the lone Rept in the bar and waved as he walked over.

Cecil mugged a Mammal's smile and Jinx knew the 'Gator didn't know the Dog very well. Or that the cowboy was worse at reading Cold expressions than Jinx was. He didn't like the idea that his friend might be pawning him off on a stranger to get rid of him.

"Thank you for coming to meet us, Raul." Cecil shook his hand and waved the other arm towards the Cat. "This is my friend, Jinx Tonka. Jinx, this is Raul Xolotl. He's also a former Darwinist."

Jinx glared at Cecil even as he stood up from the low table and reached out a hand to shake. He wasn't really sure that he wanted to live with anyone who could understand the depth of his shame. He thought the 'Gator knew him better than that. However, before he could ruin the moment with words, hot fingers wrapped around Jinx's outstretched hand. Startled, the Tonk looked at his hand and the brown fur-less hand it held. It was a strong grip, fever hot.

Naked brown skin, with interesting wrinkles and folds, extended all the way to the white cotton sleeve with jade buttons. Jinx could see his veins under the Dog's skin on the wrist. His eyes followed the arm up and stared back at the jade eyes in the brown Canine face. This close, he saw that he'd been mistaken about Raul being dark furred. The Dog's face was completely naked, save for three whiskers on each side of his muzzle.

"Howdy, Janks," Raul said with a soft, but confident Tejas accent. He gave the Cat such a warm smile, that Jinx could feel the heat on the fur of his face and ears. Or maybe he was just blushing beneath it all. "Ah'm guessing you never met ah Xoloitzcuintle before?"

Jinx shook his head and was barely aware he was holding Raul's hand with both of his. It wasn't an illusion. The Dog's hand was fever hot. He suddenly wanted to explore the Dog's every inch and it was an effort to sit himself back down. His screaming hard-on made it even more awkward.

Cecil chuckled but it sounded slightly forced. "I think he likes you, Raul."

"He's a pretty kitty, Ah'll give you that." The Dog squeezed Jinx's sleek blue-silver hands after he sat down, not hesitating at all to rub his naked blunt thumbs into the Cat's fur on the back of his hand. "Ah think Ah like him, too."

Jinx purred and closed his eyes slowly, giving a silent thanks to Cecil. The Alligator looked back with the stillness that Repts were famous for. The Cat found himself not able to read the man.

Are you giving me away?

Are you just letting me go?

Cecil remained still, as if he could not sense Jinx's silent plea.

Raul moved closer and clasped the Cat's right hand under the table. They spoke of many things, but not about why Jinx left the Darwinists. Raul left because he was not interested in fathering children; not even via donation. They didn't talk about his past with Cecil, although Jinx got the impression he'd never seen the inside of the Corsair fuckmobile.

They all had drinks, even the normally sober 'Gator.

Jinx wasn't at all certain how he had ended up in Raul's bed, or even if he had said a proper goodbye to his rescuer. The events of the night were as fuzzy as his new lover was not.

Jinx found his gym bag the next morning on Raul's door step. It was stuffed with his old clothes and the few thrift shop finds Cecil had paid for.

Jinx turned it inside out. He checked all the pockets of his clothing. There was no note.

***

"I got the job," Jinx announced as he put his phone back on the charger. "We should celebrate."

The Dog's jade eyes darted to the clock on the television, which the Tonk had muted to answer his phone. "Ah've got time for ah quickie," he drawled. The Dog leered as he placed his hat on a wall peg so it wouldn't get crunched.

Jinx took off his boxers with a purr.

Raul was casual about sex, and willing to have it anywhere, under almost any condition. Raul was almost lazy about sex, taking it slowly when he could get away with it. If Jinx asked him to go faster, he went harder, deeper. The heat that Jinx first noticed was not some one-time thing. The bare-naked Dog was hot all the time. When Jinx bottomed for his new flat mate, it was like having a freshly grilled sausage shoved up his ass. It was an odd analogy, but the Cat had no complaints. Except for the man's knot. If he got trapped by that, Raul would want to snuggle quietly until it went away.

The Tonk didn't like to be hushed.

Jinx had quickly learned to top Raul to avoid 15 minutes or so of boredom. Raul did not seem to have a preference. The second Raul got his pants down around his legs, Jinx grabbed the Xolo's naked tail and forced him to bend over the room dividing bookshelf. Raul was already slick under his tail with his sweat.

The Tonk was rigorous and vigorous, letting Raul's panting be his guide to his rhythm. Soon, he was on edge, ready to spill his load into the hot ass he was pounding. The Cat practiced his control as reached around to Raul's own sheath. The Xolo was casually stroking himself without any rhythm. A black palm rested on a brown back as Jinx used the other hand to slap the Dog's right hand away. Happily, Raul used both his brown arms to brace himself against the couch. Jinx licked the sweat off the Dog's back. His friend had already lubed himself up. Lube was just something Raul had all over the apartment.

It was a point of pride for Jinx that they almost came together.

Raul stood, scooping up the wipes that were also all over the apartment. The Dog took some out and passed the tub to Jinx, who collapsed onto an ottoman. They cleaned up in a content silence that they both knew would only last until the Tonkinese caught his breath.

"We should go out to dinner and celebrate. My treat."

Jinx then proceeded to name the top five places he could afford, but Raul cut the list short.

"Ah can't Pretty Kitty, Ah got a date tonight."

Jinx tried not to feel deflated or used. Raul had always been clear he was only interested in a roommate. A friend with benefits was a nice bonus, but that was it.

"That's all I am to you," Jinx said. He tried not to sound bitter. Indeed, he didn't even feel bitter about it, now that he gave it some thought. He tried to say more, more curious about his own apathy than Raul's reaction. "You're never going to love me."

Raul gathered up his clothes and tossed them into a hamper in the bathroom. He looked thoughtful, as he dived back in recover his wallet and toss it on his bed.

He leaned in the doorway, a perfect wood stained Canine body—if you didn't mind the missing body hair. He smiled shyly, almost sadly.

"Let me put it to you this way. Ah'd be right happy with someone like you. Right happy. But Ah'd be a darn fool to fall in love with ah Cat who is already in love with someone else."

Then the bathroom door was closed.

Jinx licked his wrist thoughtfully, tasting Raul all over him.

He felt very stupid as he realized that the Tejian was right.

***

Several weeks later, Jinx brought himself back to Cecil's house. He rang the doorbell, knowing the older Rept thought texting that one was at the front door was somehow rude. He did a quick self-exam to convince himself that he'd figured things out correctly as he waited for the 'Gator to drag his tail to the door.

Cecil seemed surprised, in a happy way, to see him on the doorstep without his gym bag. "Come in! I was about to have tea."

Jinx came in. "I wanted to thank you for everything. Taking me in and not judging me and finding a place for me to stay."

With a casual ceremony, the tea flowed into their bowls. The slight scent of Catnip came from the tea and it made Jinx smile. It seemed a good omen.

"How is it working out between the two of you?" The Rept voice was suddenly flat and neutral, and that made Jinx smile, too.

"Raul's a good guy and he never complains that I shed everywhere." Cecil flinched a little but said nothing as Jinx prattled on. When his bowl was empty, he helped himself to another serving. Cecil raised his eyebrows and Jinx caught the subtle expression now. He'd learned more than a few things living with the older man this past spring.

He watched Cecil as he spoke, and he felt confirmed in his assessment of the situation. When he finished his second cup, he stood up. "So, do you want to have sex in your bedroom, or do we need to go outside to your van?"

Despite his uncanny ability to stay still, Cecil's tea did slosh and spill a bit in his hands. "I'm sorry, what?"

"No, Cecil. I'm the one who's sorry. I'm sorry that I ever misled you about my age. By the time, I realized that the age difference was important to you, I was already in love with you. I misled you—first by accident—but after that, it was on me. And when you broke up with me, I tried to convince myself that we had no future together. I have a pedigree. I was expected to be a breeder. But I was wrong about that, too. I was wrong about so many things. But mostly, I'm sorry that I did not realize that you were worth fighting for."

Cecil's long head followed Jinx as he came around the table. Otherwise, the Rept stayed perfectly still and passive as Jinx's bare fingertips slipped under his robe. "What… what about Raul?"

"We've fooled around, but it's not the same. You said it yourself, he's not looking for a soulmate. Besides… he's hot and sweaty and he doesn't know how to use his tongue." Buttons came undone and the cool, quilted broad chest appeared. He touched the tiny scars that littered Cecil's chest. "Seriously, apparently it's a Xolo thing. Nevermind the Dog. I love you. I have always loved you and it's time I told you the truth. I don't want to wait for you to forgive me. I was a stupid young Tom, but I thought you loved me. I still think you do. I think that's why you were so hurt. And now that I'm not living with you, we can have sex now. In the van or upstairs?"

"Shut up, Jinx," Cecil said, a climbing excitement in his rumbling voice. He stood and let the robe fall from his many-faceted body. "We'll split the difference and fuck here."

Jinx laughed and moved Cecil's hands to his belly. It was now as bare as a cue ball. He giggled as the 'Gator's hands explored all that he'd shaved. "I thought you'd like a little skin to skin contact, too."

"You feel so smooth," Cecil cooed. A tiny voice from such a huge mouth.

"I also brought a little lube and some condoms."

"So, very smooth… oh, you didn't shave down here." His big right hand had slipped into the Cat's pants.

"I can shave there for you, next time."

"Next time," Cecil agreed. He stood still, but squirmed a little as the Cat explored his body with his smooth, naked palms, with his little satiny lavender nose, with his hot, rough tongue. "You said something about someone knowing how to use their tongue…"

A ripple danced on Cecil's cobblestone groin as the Cat pulled at the wide business slacks. As soon as the pants were cleared, the massive erect penis popped forward out from the unfolding fleshy pocket where it had waited patiently. It was easily seven or eight inches long but as wide as any four of Jinx's fingers for most of that. Cecil gasped with joyful surprise. It was larger than he remembered, although that might just be seeing it under good lighting for the first time. The silicon filled member certainly seemed whiter than he recalled, yet there were also hints of pale pinks, yellows, and oranges below the surface.

How did I ever get that thing into me?

Jinx was intent, taking it in visually before closing his eyes and leaning forward with the tip of his tongue leading the way, His mouth watered as he recalled the step by steps of what they'd done before. Carefully, slowly, knowing Cecil would never lose his erection, the Cat worked his spit across the member.

The tea table rattled as the larger man was directed to the floor so that the Jinx could take all of that day-glow whiteness into his mouth. It tasted as sweet as he remembered, but saltier. He'd caught the 'Gator by surprise. He liked the natural taste of it over the clinical, tar soap the Rept had always used when he was cruising. Carefully, he allowed a small length of it to touch the back of his throat. To distract himself from choking, Jinx rubbed at the fleshy tiles of hide along the Rept's groin area. With his mouth full of maleness, Jinx began to purr.

Just like riding a bike.

I'm just… a little out of practice.

Cecil's dick had its own bulges and knots. It was softer here… firmer there. Gentle pressure applied just here, made it twist ever so slightly. Jinx was careful with his small sharp teeth, but his rough tongue was reckless. The 'Gator did not complain.

Against him, his lover moaned in sync and welcomed him back.

"I do love you," Cecil gasped, surrendering to Jinx's intense explorations.

To the trepidatious romantics: may they seize opportunity and happiness

Timeless

by Mog Moogle

The cheetah came up behind the red panda and peered over his shoulder. Large earmuff headphones covered his triangular ears. He was focused on his book, ignoring the world. The cheetah walked around into his field of view and cleared his throat. It only earned the briefest of glances before the red panda went back to reading. He cleared his throat again and added a polite, "Excuse me?"

The red panda looked up at him again and brought his paw up to push back one of his headphone muffs. "Can I help you?"

"Yeah," the cheetah said then looked at the empty spot on the bench beside him. "Would you mind if I sat next to you?"

The red panda looked down at the bench then back up at the cheetah. "Uh, yeah. That's fine, I suppose."

He gave the red panda a smile and moved over to the empty space. "My name is Antonio, but everyone calls me Tony."

"Oh," the red panda replied. He glanced down at his book then back at Tony. "I'm Augustus."

"Good to meet you," Tony said and smiled. "I take my break in the park. I've seen you over here and I thought it'd be nice to talk to you."

Augustus chuckled before pushing the other muff off his ear and settling the headphones around his neck. "I'm pretty sure you don't want to get to know me. I won't be in town long."

"Why would you say that?" Tony asked as he cocked his head. The red panda's expression dropped. It was subtle, but enough that it was still noticed. "You moving? Here on vacation?"

"No, not exactly," Augustus said with a head-shake and then chuckled. "It would be fun to play tourist, I guess. Eat some pizza, visit the Creative Writers House…" The red panda noticed the cheetah looking at him. "It's not really important."

Tony blinked then scratched his head as he looked Augustus up and down. "I think you're cute."

"Oh?" Augustus paused. "Oh," he said as he realized Tony's meaning. "Yeah, that's really not a good idea."

"Don't tell me; you're not into guys?" Tony sighed. "Sorry for coming on to you."

"What? No, it's just…" Augustus shook his head. "It's not that."

"Did I do something wrong?"

"No, it's not that either." Augustus' long tail dropped between his legs. He looked out over the pond at the other side.

"Augustus?"

The red panda looked back at the cheetah and shook his head. He smiled and said, "You can call me Guss."

"Guss, did I say something to upset you?"

"No. I just have a lot on my mind."

Tony frowned and shook his head. "No pressure. Maybe do something simple. Grab that pie or go for coffee?" Tony watched to see if the red panda's expression changed. "Maybe we could keep in contact? I spend a lot of the downtime at work chatting on the Internet anyway."

Guss looked over the pond again, taking his headphones off and then tapping his phone screen that the wire was jacked into. "I suppose that I don't have anything to lose," he said, though his tone was pensive. "I just don't want to disappoint you."

"Well, we'll just see how it goes," Tony said and smiled. "So, would you like to get coffee, get dinner, or see a movie?"

"Coffee is fine. Did you want to go now?"

"Ah, I actually need to get back to work," Tony said a little embarrassed. "Get off at five though. You want to meet somewhere?"

"I can be here," Guss said as he looked at the book in his paw. "I got another one after this, and my schedule is free."

"Okay," Tony said and stood up off the bench, "I'm actually going to be a little late getting back. So I gotta run, but I'm glad you took me up on my offer. See you a little after five, yeah?"

"I'll be here," Guss replied then looked back at his book.

***

Tony pushed through the revolving door of his firm. He crossed the street and headed into the park. The shades of oranges and yellows on the pond reflected up as Tony walked up the path to the bench where Guss was sitting. It was early spring, and the few hours they had before sunset made the park even more scenic. He saw Guss glanced over at him as he approached.

"Half expected you to bail on me," Tony said and then chuckled. "Glad you didn't."

Guss cast his glance down then looked back up at the cheetah. "I guess I did come off as a little cold, didn't I?"

"Can't blame you. Probably not asked out by a random guy in the park every day."

"Did you get in trouble for being late from lunch?" Guss asked.

"Ah, no. Not really." Tony chuckled and shook his head. "Maybe a little. Third time this week I got back late."

"Third time?"

"I like watching you. Sometimes I let the time slip."

"Oh, uh," Guss paused as he looked at the cheetah with surprise. "I see. I didn't know I had an admirer."

"I should have said something sooner, I guess. Sorry about that. Sometimes it just takes a while for me to get up my courage with cute guys."

Guss frowned for a moment but it was brief. He giggled and then shook his head. "So, where's this coffee shop?"

"Just down the street a ways," Tony replied. "It's where I get my lunch most days; they got really good paninis."

"Panini," Guss corrected.

Tony cocked his head a bit and looked at him slightly confused.

"Panini is a plural of panino," Guss explained.

"Wait, my name is Tony, and you're schooling me on Italian food?" he asked facetiously.

"Well, English Lit major until a month ago," Guss said and smiled.

"Yeah? Did you graduate, change majors, or what?"

"Dropped out," Guss said and shook his head.

"Ah. Sorry."

"Don't be. Just didn't see the point in going to class anymore."

"You know this whole vagueness thing is making me more curious about you and not less, right?"

Guss smiled and extended his arm toward the walking path. "Lead the way."

Tony sighed as he walked on the path and the red panda came abreast of him. They exited out of the green onto the gray of the Manhattan sidewalk. The foot traffic was heavy as the white-collar professionals flooded out of the office buildings on their treks home. The increased crowding slowed their advance, but the half-block walk to the large bank plaza didn't take long.

Tony opened the door on the near corner of the building that housed the trendy coffee shop and held it for Guss. He watched as the red panda entered. His tail sashayed with his step, and as they walked past the high tables to the counter, Tony fixed his view below the red panda's waist. It wasn't until he stopped at the counter and turned around to catch him staring that Tony pulled his eyes back up.

Guss give him a little smirk before he turned back to the cashier and ordered green tea. When Guss tried to pay, Tony stepped up and told the husky in the apron behind the register that the orders were together. Guss looked surprised at first but then smiled at the gesture.

After they got their drinks, they settled in at one of the tables near the door. Tony watched as Guss pulled out his chair. His hoodie and shorts were loose, but the fabric hugged his hips below his waist. The red panda stopped before he sat down and Tony looked up at his face. Guss' ears perked and his expression was mildly perplexed.

"I, uh, guess you do think I'm attractive," Guss said.

Tony looked away. "Sorry, I know it's rude to stare."

"It's flattering," he said and smiled. "It's just not something I'm used to."

"Really? That I find hard to believe."

"Well, I wasn't out in high school. Rural upstate is kind of reserved in that way. And I was only in college for about two years before I dropped out."

"You never got hit on in college?"

"Oh, I did. Some. I haven't been actively looking for the last few years."

"Why is that?"

Guss looked back up at Tony with his ears still splayed. He nervously bit his bottom lip then shook his head. "I'm sorry," he said as his ears perked back up. "I'm not used to talking about things like this."

"Okay," Tony said after a moment. "So, uh, you're always reading. What do you like to read?"

"Oh, well, it'd be easier to list what I don't like to read," Guss said then chuckled. "I've been reading since I was little. My mom didn't have cable, and she'd only let my sister and I watch TV on Saturdays, but we could read all we wanted."

"Ah, so not the typical American household then?"

"Probably not so much. Because of that, it's rare that I find a TV show I actually like. We would go see the kid's movies every now and then, though." Guss looked up at Tony and flashed a smile. "So, what do you like to read?"

"Uh…" Tony splayed his ears as he glanced around the red panda. "If it doesn't have to do with forecasting Asian markets, I usually don't read it."

"So that's what you do? You're a stock broker?" Guss chuckled as the cheetah looked back at him. "I mean, we're quite a way from Wall Street."

"No, I'm an analyst. It's pretty boring, but it pays the bills."

"Manhattan can be pretty expensive."

"No kidding. Good thing I live in Queens."

"Yeah? I don't actually live in the city." Guss looked out the window at the skyscrapers.

"Quite a commute from outside the city to the park, ain't it?"

"Well, I'm actually staying off Fifth, so I can see the park from my window."

"I thought you didn't live in the city."

"It's just a temporary thing," Guss said and smiled.

"I couldn't even imagine what it'd cost for an apartment that over-looked the park."

"More than I could afford, I'm sure."

"So, what do you do for work then?"

"Nothing," Guss answered.

"You don't have a job?"

"No," Guss said and then smiled at Tony's confused expression. "Well, like I said, this whole gig in the city is just temporary. Not much point in looking for employment."

"You remember what I said about that whole vagueness thing, right?"

Guss smiled and nodded. "Maybe I like being the interesting but mysterious type." He paused as Tony chuckled. "What is it about me that made you want to talk to me?"

"You're cute," Tony replied.

Guss feigned a cough and cleared his throat. "Is that the only thing?"

"'Bout all you've given me so far." Tony's tone was more jovial than chiding.

"Well, what is it you look for in a guy?"

"Hmm," Tony paused and looked the red panda up and down from what he could see over the tabletop. "Without trying to sound like a personals, I like to have fun. I like an outgoing guy. I'm an affectionate kitty, so cuddles are nice. You spend your afternoons in the park, so got some common ground there. If you're talking something more long term, then I would say…" Tony trailed off as he saw Guss shift in his seat. "You okay?"

The red panda's ears had flattened and he looked at steam rolling up from his tea. After a few moments, Guss looked back up at Tony with stern determination. "Let's say you had one night to spend with someone you found attractive, and only one night. What would you do?"

"This a hypothetical?"

"Yeah, something like that."

"Well, I'd invite him for coffee; get to know him."

"No, that part I already know." Guss shook his head and sighed. "It's silly, forget I asked."

"It's fine, I don't mind answering. It'd be more up to him, honestly. I would probably ask if he wanted to go for a walk, or go back to my place and watch a movie, or maybe—"

"Your place," Guss said, cutting him off.

"My place?" Tony asked.

"Mmm. Let's go."

Before Tony could say anything else, Guss grabbed his shoulder bag off the floor and was tugging the cheetah's shirt sleeve. Tony looked down at the red panda in confusion as he was led out of the store and onto the sidewalk. Guss was pulling him toward the subway stop. After descending the stairs below street level, they stopped at the turnstiles as Guss was pulling out his prepaid card.

"What train do we need?" he asked as he looked up at Tony.

"We take 'C' to Downtown and then the 'E' to Queens."

"Sounds easy enough," Guss said as he swiped his card through the reader.

"Yeah. Bit of a ride, but not terrible." Tony followed suit with his transit card and they walked down the final set to the platform.

***

The lines moaned and clattered as the train wormed its way through the tunnels. The car wasn't crowded when they started, but as they continued, more and more commuters crammed in. Before long, Guss was pressed up against Tony.

The cheetah blushed as he felt Guss' tail brush against his slacks. "Almost there," Tony said as the speaker announced the stop at Kew Gardens. "Not that I mind the change in attitude, but it kinda caught me off guard."

Guss looked at the floor of the train and shuffled his feet. He kept his eyes fixed downward until the doors slid closed and the train lurched forward. When he finally looked back up at the cheetah, he was met by another concerned expression.

"You keep worrying me that I'm doing something wrong," Tony said.

"I'm sorry. I don't mean to. I'm glad you talked to me."

"Would it bother you if I asked why the sudden change, then?"

"It's just…" Guss paused as his ears flattened. "I, uh, think you're attractive. I've never been in any kind of relationship, so I don't know how this is supposed to work."

"Well, I'll just ask what you'd like to do when you get to my place?"

"You suggested a movie," Guss replied.

"Yeah, I got a few movies and a comfy couch to sit on." Tony saw Guss nod in response as he kept his eyes down. The cheetah let out a sigh; it was a subconscious thing and he didn't mean it to be offensive, but he noticed Guss wince. "Sorry."

"No," Guss said and looked back at the cheetah. "I keep getting this feeling that this won't work."

"Why don't we just start with the movie and see what happens?"

Guss smiled then chuckled. "You do seem like a really sweet guy."

"So do you," Tony said as he leaned into the red panda. Tony felt Guss ease against him and then he rested his cheek against his shoulder. He could smell his shampoo from the red panda's headfur. Tony assumed it would be fragrant with a conditioner mix, but it was neutral.

The ride was quiet between the two before it made its stop at Jamaica-Van Wyck platform. They got off the train and made their way back to the street level up the stairs, both of them squinting as they left the fluorescent lights and walked out into the oranges and yellows of the setting sun.

"My place is a few blocks down," Tony said.

"Okay." Guss looked at the small storefronts and shorter towers than the big buildings in Manhattan. "I've never been to Queens before. It looks kind of nice."

"I was born in Brooklyn, but I've been really happy here," Tony said as he started walking down the block with Guss beside him.

***

Tony unlocked his door and held it open for Guss, then followed him in. The finished basement had plush carpeting, a love seat along the wall with a flat panel TV on the opposite. There was a doorway to a small office and the bedroom beside the entertainment center. The kitchenette was attached to the living room. If it weren't for the windows by the door being so high, it would have been hard to tell it was a basement.

"This is a nice place," Guss commented as he looked around.

"The couple upstairs owns it. Got a really good deal."

"What's a really good deal?"

"Eight-fifty."

Guss turned around and looked at the cheetah and blinked a few times. "Uh, yeah. There's no way I could afford to live here."

Tony chuckled a bit then motioned his paw at the shelves under the TV. "The movies are right here. Pick one out."

The cheetah walked over to the love seat and kicked his loafers off before he settled down on the cushion. He watched the red panda bend over to scan through the spines of the movie disc cases. His long tail lifted a bit and gave Tony a view of his rear as the khaki shorts he was wearing tightened around the curves of his backside. When Guss turned back around with a movie case in his paw, Tony tried to look away quickly to hide his staring.

"This one," Guss said, pulling the cheetah's attention back to him.

"That's a kid's movie." Tony chuckled as he looked at the cartoon characters on the cover.

"Yeah, but I haven't seen it in years," Guss said. "And besides, if it's a kid's movie, why do you have it?"

Tony blushed and shook his head. "Yeah, okay. I like it."

Guss giggled as he opened the case up and popped the disk out. He turned around and bent over to the disc player under the TV and opened the tray. When he did, he lifted his tail a higher.

Tony was sure that it was intentional. The red panda swayed his hips a bit as Tony felt his ears heat; that left no doubt. He squirmed as his slacks tightened and crossed his legs.

Guss turned around as the disc tray swallowed the movie and he smiled at the cheetah on the couch. He walked back toward Tony with a knowing smirk, but then stopped suddenly before he sat down. Guss looked around the apartment. "Bathroom?" he asked as he looked back at Tony.

"Oh, uh, little room there by the kitchen."

Guss nodded and hurried away, closing the small door to the bathroom behind him as Tony looked on with confusion.

The cheetah sighed and rubbed his eyes with his paws. *What am I getting myself into?* he thought. *He is cute, though.* He dropped his paws and picked the TV remote off the small table by the couch and turned it on.

By the time Guss came out of the bathroom, the animated title screen was looping and waiting for the cheetah to press play. The red panda settled in on the seat but kept some distance from Tony. His expression had once again shifted. He looked uneasy, and even a little somber.

"You don't have to do anything you're not comfortable doing," Tony said in the most understanding tone he could muster.

"I know," Guss replied. "Are you going to start the movie?" The red panda forced a smile.

"Yeah," Tony said as he returned the smile and then picked up the remote.

The opening credits rolled with the song that made the children's movie iconic playing over the home theater speakers. Guss began to drift over to the cheetah. As the stereotypical villain disrupted the characters' idyllic lives, the red panda was pressed against the feline. By the time of the hero's return, Tony's arm rested on Guss' shoulder and the red panda's head was laying against Tony's chest.

"I remember when this came out," Guss said. "My sister and I had a lot of fun seeing it with mom."

"Yeah? You know they still do the Broadway show. We could go see it."

"My sis and I always wanted to." He nestled in. "Despite living close to the city, I've never been here before about a month ago."

"Kinda like living here and never seeing the Empire State building, huh?" Tony chuckled and squeezed the red panda with his arm.

Just before the confrontation with the villain, Guss nuzzled Tony's chest and looked up at the cheetah. "I remember why I liked this movie when I was little," he commented, "but I don't know if it aged very well."

"You can still appreciate it for the timeless quality. It's a modern classic," Tony offered with a smile as he looked down, nearly muzzle-to-muzzle with Guss.

"Timeless…" Guss' eyes shifted away from the cheetah and he swallowed so hard that Tony felt it. "Nothing is timeless; everything fades."

"Guss, I'd be more than willing to talk if something—" the cheetah was suddenly silenced as the red panda's lips pressed against his. Tony let a surprised murmur escape as he looked at Guss with wide eyes. He lifted his right paw from the couch arm and moved it to Guss' shoulder, but stopped short.

Guss' tongue pushed into Tony's muzzle and he moved his body against the cheetah. He lifted his leg and eased atop the cheetah while his fingers balled in fists and gripped the fabric of Tony's shirt.

Tony let his arm continue around the red panda and his eyes fluttered closed. He pulled Guss close to his body, his arms wrapped around him. Their tongues mingled as the kiss grew deeper.

The cheetah's slacks tightened as the red panda pushed down against him. Tony lifted him up and pulled Guss completely into his lap. Their thighs rubbed together as the smaller frame of Guss slid into a straddle. Tony bucked his hips up against him as he pulled his head back and forced a separation from the kiss. Guss whimpered but it shifted to a long moan when Tony put his muzzle in the nape of his neck and started kissing up the side.

After a few moments of kissing, grinding and panting, Tony moved his muzzle back to Guss' lips and planted a few small kisses before easing back again. Guss chuckled and rested his nose against Tony's. "I should probably let you know that I've never done this before."

"It doesn't show," Tony said before kissing him softly again. "We'll go a little slower, then."

Guss nodded and sat up. He moved his paws to the zipper of his hoodie and started to pull it down. Before much of the dark fur on his chest was exposed, Tony's paw cupped his and stopped him.

"Not here," Tony said as he moved his paw pack around to the red panda's rear and lifted him. He eased Guss back off the love seat and lowered him to the floor and stood up in front of him. "This will go a lot easier on the bed."

Tony took his paw and led him through the door by the TV. He turned left into the small bedroom and guided Guss to the edge of the bed. The room was still dark as Guss sat down on the comforter while Tony walked around him. The cheetah turned on a small lamp and a soft incandescent glow illuminated the nook.

The bed stretched almost from wall-to-wall with a path up the left side. At the head was a nightstand with the lamp on it. Tony walked back over to him. He took Guss' zipper and slowly pulled it down until it came unclasped and it fell open.

Tony rubbed his paws on the soft fur of Guss' chest as he moved his arms back and slipped out of the sleeves. When his hoodie fell behind him, Tony knelt down and kissed Guss' stomach. He trailed down to his waist and then stopped to work his shorts open. After he pulled the zipper down, Guss lifted slightly as he hooked the waistband of the shorts and boxers.

Tony got his first look at the bear-cat's exposed arousal. His length was modest but proportional to the smaller male. It had a small tapered tip that bulged up near the middle and was covered in small spines. The thing that caught his attention the most was that they all seemed to point backwards. He took his thumb and slid his pad along the spines and Guss gasped.

"Sorry," Tony said as he looked up at the red panda. "Didn't know you had spines. I got a few myself but, wow. I've never seen anything like yours."

Guss panted and cracked an eye open, looking down at Tony. "I never had anyone touch me before. It's intense."

"You better brace yourself, then," Tony said before he leaned forward and took the tip between his lips. He heard another gasp as his muzzle descended past the taper and over the spinescent bulge. His tongue brushed the top of the rearward facing spines and then he lightly dragged against his tongue on the way back up.

Guss' tail flicked and thrashed against the bed as he moved his paws to the top of Tony's head. Tony began to suckle the length as he pulled up and he felt Guss grip his headfur tightly.

"No," Guss said aloud as he bucked his hips up. "No, it's—ugh!"

Tony's eyes went wide as a warm jet of the red panda's seed shot into his mouth. It was thick and coated his tongue almost entirely, but was rapidly followed by a second, then a third. He had no choice but to swallow, though it wasn't a chore. The thick and creamy jism was slightly sweet and slid down his gullet as he swallowed with Guss' member pulsing in his mouth.

The cheetah pulled his muzzle back and gave the tip a small lick to get the rest of Guss' cum. Tony looked up at Guss as the red panda's paws released the top of his head and fell to his sides. He saw Guss crack his eyes open as he struggled to regain control of his breathing.

When his gaze caught Tony's, he flattened his ears and frowned.

"I'm sorry," Guss said with a pout. "I didn't want to finish so fast."

"Heh, I don't think I did any better my first time," Tony replied then smiled. "Besides, you taste really good." He saw Guss shy away at the comment, but there was a small smile across his muzzle. "You up for some more?"

"You want me to do the same?"

"Only if you want to," Tony said as he slowly rose to his feet and started unfastening the row of buttons on his shirt. "I was thinking something else, if you're up for it."

"What do you mean?" Guss asked and cocked his head a bit as he watched Tony peel the half-unbuttoned shirt off over his head.

"I never had anyone with spines, you know, inside me."

Guss blinked as he looked up at Tony then shook his head. "I don't know if I'd be any good." He paused as he looked down at the dressy slacks and the obvious bulge behind the cheetah's fly. "Besides, won't it hurt?"

Tony unbuckled his belt and unclipped the tab on his fly while Guss looked on. "Don't worry about me," he said as he took down the zipper with deliberate slowness. "I practice." He pointed at the nightstand and Guss looked over his shoulder at a small dildo beside the lamp.

"Oh," Guss said and turned back when he heard the clatter of Tony's belt on the floor. He saw the bulge in Tony's white briefs and swallowed hard. "But what about the spines? Won't they hurt?"

"Don't know, but I want to try." Tony smiled and winked.

"I, uh, I would kind of like to try blowing you." He blushed as he looked up at Tony's face. "If that's okay, I mean."

"I sure won't turn it down," Tony said and chuckled. He stepped out of his crumpled slacks and closer to the naked red panda. He noticed Guss look down at his briefs and then back up at him. "Just pull them down, then do what you would like."

Guss sighed then took a deep breath. He extended his fingers to the waistband of Tony's briefs and started to tug them downward. He was again wide eyed as he saw another male's arousal in person for the first time.

Guss looked at it for a moment, taking in the features. The tip sort of looked like his own, but the spines were more pronounced and there were fewer of them. He eased his muzzle forward and opened his mouth to give the tip a tentative lick.

Tony groaned as the texture of the bear-cat's tongue teased his opening. His hips swayed forward and his member bumped against Guss' nose. He saw the red panda jerk back, but he shook off the surprise as he took Tony's head between his lips. He felt the warmth of his tongue brush the underside of his glans as he summoned all his willpower not to push into the virgin's mouth.

Guss took it slow, easing down on him until half of the length was inside of his mouth. It was about all that the short muzzle would accommodate. Then Guss closed his lips and moaned, causing his tongue along his flesh to vibrate. Tony raised his paws to the red panda's cheeks and stroked his tufts with his fingers and then rubbed the inside of his ears with his thumbs. Guss giggled softly at the touch. Guss pulled his head back and then pushed it forward again.

"Oh yeah," Tony groaned. "That's good, keep doing—ow! Teeth! Watch the teeth."

"Sorry," Guss mumbled around the cheetah cock.

"It's okay, you're doing fine. Try sucking a little," he instructed.

Guss' lips clamped around the spines of the feline malehood and a lewd slurp echoed in the small bedroom. Tony took Guss' cheek tufts between his fingers and gently guided him up and down his length. The cheetah's hips started to gyrate, meeting the red panda as he descended toward his sheath.

After a few more moments, the rhythm built as the inexperienced Guss grew accustomed to the task. Tony looked down at him as his breathing increased in speed. It filled him with a bit of pride to see Guss' recently spent arousal standing at full attention with an occasional throb. He would have been content to keep going, but the prospect of those backward spines was just too appealing.

Tony pulled back and the tip slipped from between Guss' lips. The bear-cat whimpered a little as he pulled out and Tony chuckled softly. "You liked that?"

Guss looked up at him as his ears folded back over Tony's thumbs that were still rubbing his ears. "I did," Guss said with a note of embarrassment. "I didn't think it would feel so good, just in my mouth like that."

"Just wait," Tony said as he moved his paws off Guss' cheeks. "I think you'll like this next part even better." He finished pushing his underwear down to his ankles and kicked them to the side. He crawled onto the bed toward the pillows on all fours and lifted his long tail. Looking back over his shoulder, he gave Guss a wink. "Come on. It won't bite."

Guss shifted around on the bed and eased up behind Tony. "I, uh, I'm not sure what to do."

"It's okay," Tony said as he reached over to his nightstand and opened the drawer. "Just use some of this on yourself and on me, line it up and push in." Tony pulled out a bottle with a flip cap that was half-full of a clear liquid. He handed it to Guss and the red panda looked at it for a moment. "It's lube. Water based. It's good stuff."

Guss shrugged then flipped the cap up. He poured some on his erection and gasped as the cool liquid trickled onto his length. He then upturned the bottle and poured some between Tony's cheeks.

"Now," Tony began, "spread it around on yourself then me, and you'll be able to slip right in."

"Okay," Guss said. He took his paw and smeared the lubricant along his length. After a few strokes with his paw, he moved his fingers to the pink textured pucker between Tony's cheeks, rubbing the glob from the cleft of his rear over the outside of the opening. Guss capped the bottle and handed it to Tony. He eased up behind the cheetah and took a deep breath.

Tony spread his legs as he felt Guss' paws rest on his cheeks. Then Guss pushed his hips against Tony's backside, and the cheetah lowered himself down a little to help. Guss' tip slid up the cleft of his rear and then back down as he rocked his hips.

"Guide it in with your fingers," Tony instructed. He could feel Guss move his paw off his rear and then felt his lithe fingers push against his cheeks as he worked his tip against his tailhole. Tony didn't expect there would be a problem, but he put his face in the pillow just in case he had to grunt so as not to discourage Guss.

The tip pushed against his tailring, then the resistance gave way and half of the red panda's length was inside of him. Instead of his feared grunt he moaned into the pillow and heard Guss share it. He looked back at his lover. Guss' expression was a mix between perplexing and ecstasy. "You okay?"

"This is amazing," Guss said and opened his eyes, locking them with Tony. "I had no idea it was like this."

"Mmm," Tony confirmed and wiggled his rear back against him. "Don't be afraid to go all the way."

Guss nodded then closed his eyes as he rocked forward. His whole body shuddered as his sheath nestled against Tony's opening. He stayed there for a moment then started to pull his hips back. When he did, his spines raked Tony's walls and the cheetah gasped. "Am I hurting you?"

"Mmmnf," Tony muttered with a quiver.

"Tony?"

"Wow," Tony managed between pants and looked back at Guss. "Don't hurt; just never felt anything like it."

"It's," Guss paused and rubbed Tony's rear in his paw, "It's good?"

"Yeah," Tony replied between pants. "It's good. Keep going."

Tony felt every small movement of Guss as he withdrew. Then, as the red panda pushed back inside of him and the spines folded down, the sensations of being penetrated felt amplified. After a few thrusts, the near sensual overload wore off and he started to push back. The red panda behind him took it the hint and picked up his pace.

As the sounds of Guss' thighs hitting his rear echoed in the small room, Tony slipped a paw between his legs and stroked his bobbing erection. Then the big cat began to purr, and he heard Guss grunt as the deep reverberations teased the exotic cock in his rear.

"Kitty," Guss said as he panted. "Keep purring. Wow..."

Tony let a soft chuckle escape before a long and sultry moan, affirming that he would do just that. Guss' paws clawed at his rear as their bodies slapped together. Any virgin awkwardness there was initially had faded in the lust fueled frenzy. Tony could feel Guss' member throb inside him and that made the spines flare out a bit. The red panda's hips started to quake and it left no doubt about what was coming.

With a high-pitched twittering yowl, Guss pushed as deep as he could and warmth radiated inside of Tony's backside. The big cat kept purring as he felt Guss filling him with his orgasm. Guss eased his body down against Tony's back, keeping most of his length inside of him as his flood subsided. He slumped down a bit but kept his hips raised while he tweaked his own erection with his thumb and index finger.

The cheetah's purring ceased as his muscles tightened, eliciting a grunt from Guss as the waves of his own orgasm swept over him. His pent-up seed from the incredible buildup of pleasure splashed against the comforter underneath him. Tony held himself up as long as he could before he collapsed to the bed, the last little bit of his member draining out into the thick puddle he'd made below him.

They lay on the bed, Guss on top of Tony, each panting in the afterglow of Guss' first sexual encounter and their first shared experience as lovers. Tony let a smile creep onto his muzzle as he hoped that they could repeat the process at least a few more times before Guss moved away.

Tony shifted his body over and Guss slid off his back onto the bed. He rolled over to face him and wrapped his arms around the red panda to pull him up to the pillows. He looked at the white, black and red fur on his face as he lay beside him. He pushed his muzzle forward and locked lips with him, sharing a deep kiss before softly pulling out of it.

"Glad I finally decided to talk to you," Tony whispered.

"Me too," Guss replied as he rested against Tony's side.

Tony held Guss close as the sticky couple drifted off to sleep.

***

Tony's eyes fluttered open. The first thing he saw was the back of Guss' head. He wasn't sure how long they'd been asleep, but when he moved his leg he felt the dried remnants of their tryst tug and pull his fur. With a contented sigh, he rolled over toward the small pathway and swung his legs off the bed. The alarm clock on his nightstand read 5:37. It would be going off to wake him up for work in less than an hour. He'd gone to bed earlier than usual, so he figured that getting up then wouldn't hurt.

Sitting on the edge of the bed with a yawn and a stretch, he reached over to the small switch on the lamp and turned it off to let Guss sleep more soundly. Tony knew his apartment well enough to make his way around it with just the ambient light from the few windows he had.

As he got up and walked into the living room, he pressed the button on the side of the TV to shut off the looping movie title screen that had been running since the previous night. He continued to the small bathroom and flipped on the lights. His eyes squinted as the overhead lit up the nook that was little more than a small shower, toilet and vanity sink. He opened the glazed door of the shower and turned it on and stepped under the stream.

After he got out of the shower and dried off, Tony opened the medicine cabinet and pulled out the cotton swabs. As he dropped the used swabs in the small waste bin, he noticed a perforated piece of plastic. Tony bent over and fished it out of the trash. He turned it over in his paw and saw that it was a hospital ID band.

"Fornwell, Augustus J," he read aloud. "Mount Sinai. Dr. W. Friendly." He looked at the yellow tab stuck through one of the perforations. "Fall precautions." Tony felt his heart sink. He tried to swallow the lump in his throat as he turned the wristband over in his paw, but it wouldn't go down. Tony looked at the door to the bathroom, back at the wristband, and then back at the door. "God damn it."

***

Tony heard his alarm buzzing. He sat on the love seat and looked blankly at the doorway to the bedroom. He hadn't bothered to go back in after he got out of the bathroom. He'd just sat there for the last half hour staring into where Guss had been sleeping and turning things over in his head.

"Tony?" he heard weakly. "Tony?" he heard a little louder.

The cheetah didn't move. He couldn't bring himself to move. His legs had been numb ever since he plopped down on the cushion. Guss wandered through the door rubbing the sleep from one of his eyes, holding his unbuttoned shorts up with his other paw,

"Tony, your alarm is going off."

"Time to get ready for work," he said while he maintained his stoic expression.

"Ah. Well, do you want me to turn it off?"

"No."

"Okay," Guss replied and stepped toward the cheetah. He stopped when he noticed the blank look on his face. "Are you okay?"

"I'm fine," Tony replied.

"Okay," Guss said with a note of concern. "When you go back into work, can I ride the train with you?"

"Yeah, I imagine you need to be getting back to the hospital."

Guss winced as Tony finished his sentence. He looked at the floor and folded his ears. "I'm sorry," he said.

"For what?" Tony asked.

"What I did was incredibly selfish. I told you that I'd be a letdown."

"Guss, what exactly are you in the hospital for?"

"Malignant tumor," Guss said as he looked back up at the cheetah then pointed to the left side of his head. "Inoperable. My 'two weeks to live' was up almost three weeks ago."

"Three weeks? You've been on borrowed time for three weeks?"

"Yeah," Guss replied as he brought his paw down to his eye and wiped away a welling tear. "I feel like I roped you into something that I shouldn't have. It was very selfish, just because I thought it'd be my last chance to try anything."

"Three weeks?" Tony said as his expression shifted to confused.

"Three weeks!" he yelled, causing Guss to step back.

"Tony, please—"

"No," Tony interrupted. "You don't understand. I saw you in the park two weeks ago, and I wasted that. You were on borrowed time then, and I wasted it."

"I, but, I—"

"I'm so angry right now," Tony said and hung his head.

"Tony?"

"I wasted two of those weeks."

"What are you trying to say?"

Tony looked up at Guss and shook his head. He covered his face with his paws. "This is bullshit. It's not fair. The only thing I can think about is how little time I have. I don't..." Tony trailed off as his emotions swirled like a torrent. "Nothing is timeless."

"Everything fades," he heard in his ear and felt the red panda's paws wrap around him. "Well, maybe not everything."

He lowered his paws and saw Guss looking into his eyes. His cheek tufts were damp.

"Where we go is up to you," Guss said. "I made a mistake when I didn't tell you up front, and I won't blame you if you want to stop this right n—"

Tony's muzzle locked tightly against Guss' and his tongue pushed into his mouth. His arms wrapped around Guss and pulled him into his lap. They stayed in the moment for a while before Tony pulled away and nuzzled his cheek against Guss'.

"I should probably shower," Guss said softly. "It'll give you some time to think things over." Guss eased out of the cheetah's arms and stood up out of his lap. "And, I'm sorry, again." He gave Tony's paws a small squeeze before turning away and walking into the bathroom.

Tony shook his head and wiped his eyes. The distant buzz of the alarm clock rang a little louder in the cheetah's ears. He sighed as he stood up and headed to the bedroom to remedy it.

He eased over to his nightstand and shut the alarm off. On his way out, his foot brushed against his crumpled slacks on the floor. He looked down at the pile of fabric for a moment then bent over and fished the phone out of his left pocket.

With a button press and a thumb swipe, he unlocked the home screen. Tapping his contacts, he scrolled down to his supervisor's desk phone. After a few rings, the voicemail echoed through the speaker, then the tone.

"Chris, it's Tony. I won't be into work today." He paused as he looked out of the bedroom door and into the living room where he could hear the water running in the shower. "Something came up, and if I don't fix it now, I won't get another chance." Tony looked at the screen, ended the call and then turned off his phone.

"Everything fades," he said to himself. His thoughts turned to the gentle paw squeeze Guss gave him before he went to go shower. He lifted his paws up and looked at the pads as his chest warmed at the memory of his touch. "Well, maybe not everything."

The cheetah walked out to the living room then stopped in front of the bathroom door. He heard the water cascading in broken streams disrupted by the red panda. He rapped a knuckle against the door. "Guss? You decent?" He turned his head and cocked his ear but heard no response. "Guss?"

"I'm in the shower," the red panda replied after a pause.

"I know that," Tony said and chuckled. "Mind if I come in?"

The only sound for several seconds was the water in consistent patterns to the shower floor, indicating Guss wasn't moving. "Okay," finally broke the silence.

Tony realized he had been holding his breath before his friend answered. He turned the handle and opened the door to the shower nook. Through the foggy glass he could see Guss' silhouette. "I thought it over," Tony said as he hooked a thumb in the hastily tied knot and pulled his towel down. "Can I join you?"

Guss went silent again. He shifted under the streams and then leaned against the wall.

"You okay, Guss?"

"Yeah, I…" He wrapped his arms around himself. "I'm sorry. I'm not used to anyone seeing me naked." Guss shuffled back and forth. "I mean, I know that we did it last night, and there's a lot of that at the hospital, but I—"

"Guss, it's alright," Tony interrupted. His tone was understanding. "You can say no." The cheetah put his paw on top of the shower stall. He saw Guss step forward and felt the red panda's paw against his. "Like I said, you don't have to do anything you don't want."

"Okay," Guss said as he eased back and pushed the door open a crack. "I want you to."

Tony smiled and pulled the door open. Guss was standing under the water, withdrawing his paw from the top of the stall, with his other still crossed over his body and covering his genitals. The sight of the water-soaked cheek tufts hanging down made the cheetah chuckle. He stepped in the small shower and up against Guss.

"It's a tight fit," Guss commented as he nestled close to Tony.

"You think so?" Tony laughed as he wrapped his arms around Guss. "Maybe, if you're up for it, I can find out later tonight, huh?"

The embarrassment on Guss' face was obvious. His ears tucked back and his tail sagged. Nevertheless, he looked up at Tony and smiled. "You're okay with this, right?"

"Wouldn't be here if I wasn't." Tony canted his head and pressed his lips against Guss' lips. His tongue met the red panda's and they kissed as the water cascaded through their fur. When their lips separated, they held their embrace. "Need help with your back?"

Guss giggled and nodded with his cheek against Tony's chest. He eased away from the cheetah and turned around. The confined space barely allowed room for the maneuvering, but he picked the shampoo bottle from the rack and passed it to Tony.

The cheetah popped it open and poured it between Guss' shoulder blades. He worked his fingers into the wet fur and started to lather the shampoo. As he was rubbing the fur, he noticed the streams of water washing it away. "Switch places with me." He moved his paws down to Guss' waist and eased him around.

Tony guided the red panda out of the stream and slid his paws back up to his shoulders. The cheetah resumed his work, lathering Guss and working the suds into his fur. When he was down to the middle, Guss braced himself against the stall and eased against his paws. Tony chuckled as the red panda gave a contented murmur. "You like that, huh?"

"I've never had anyone wash my back before," Guss replied as the cheetah's paws went lower. When they were at his rear, his tail hiked and he spread his legs for the cheetah.

"Lots of firsts, huh?" Tony said as he rubbed the pert cheeks in his palms. "Mind another first?"

Guss looked over his shoulder as Tony adjusted the shower head to rinse his fur. "What do you mean?"

"You'll see." Tony rubbed down his back until the soap had been washed out. Afterward, he turned the water off and knelt on his knees. He looked up at Guss' confused expression and gave him a wink before he parted his cheeks with his thumbs.

"What are you—" Guss' query was cut short as he yipped in surprise. The cheetah's tongue brushed his virgin opening in long, broad strokes. He gripped the top of the stall and squeezed as his legs spread wide. It didn't take more than a few licks for his knees to feel wobbly. "Tony…"

The big cat responded with a huff before probing with the tip of his tongue. He pushed against the texture of Guss' pucker, teasing for a moment before sliding inside. Guss gasped and his muscle ring instinctively squeezed against Tony's tongue. The cheetah waited for him to relax before snaking his tongue in as far as he could.

Tony caressed Guss' rear while he withdrew his tongue. When he was almost out, he pushed it back in. The pace was deliberately slow, and the bear cat under his ministrations panted and moaned. He continued until he felt Guss start to go slack against him.

Pulling his tongue out, he looked up and saw Guss hanging on to the shower stall with his legs barely able to support him. "You okay?"

Guss responded with quivering gibberish between deep panting.

"Guss?"

The red panda's eyes fluttered open as his raised tail settled down over Tony's shoulder and draped over his back. "I'm okay," Guss said when he could control his breathing. "So intense…"

"You sure?" Tony's tone was concerned.

"Yeah, just a head rush. I've never felt anything like that."

"You need me to stop?"

"God no!" Guss quivered and then giggled. "Wow. Please, more."

Tony chuckled before obliging.

***

Tony and Guss took turns toweling each other off. They laughed at the frizzy fur, shared caresses, and kissed several times until it turned into a full makeout session. Their towels crumpled at their feet, their tongues melding in each other's muzzles, and their arousal brushing against one another's bodies.

Tony was the first to pull back. He and Guss were both panting, their lust at the point of boiling over. When the red panda tried to kiss him again, Tony put his finger on Guss' nose and stopped him. The red panda whimpered against the cheetah's finger.

Tony chuckled and shook his head. "Save it for tonight," he said as he stepped back. "Get dressed. Got places to be."

"Places?"

"Don't worry about it."

Guss pouted but grabbed his shorts off the top of the toilet tank and they left the small bathroom nook. He and Tony made their way to the bedroom and he sat on the bed and watched while Tony pulled his wallet, keys, and phone out of his dress slacks. "Why did you decide to keep this up?"

Tony's ears flattened and he looked at the floor. "Don't really know, if I gotta be honest." Tony slid his closet door open and pulled a t-shirt off a hanger and picked up a crumpled pair of jeans from the floor. "Maybe that whole bit about everything fading. Maybe I don't like that."

"Maybe not everything," Guss offered warmly.

"Maybe not everything," Tony echoed. "Need to get Midtown 'fore the rush."

"Can you tell me where we're going? I'd like to know what to bring."

"You can just bring me." Tony chuckled. "You staying at the hospital tonight? Can't imagine they liked you going AWOL."

"I'm going to check out today," Guss said as he fastened the button on his shorts. "If I can stay with you, that is."

"I'd like that." Tony smiled, but it faded. "You need anything from there? They doing something to…" Tony's mind knew the question, but a tugging in his chest made him not want to ask.

"It's all research, I'm afraid." Guss had answered the question many times. "Just tests and such at the neuro unit. They can't fix me. It's always just been a matter of time."

"Just don't want to lessen—"

"You're not." Guss shook his head. "This means a lot to me. I don't want to impose on you more than necessary, though. I'll get ahold of my mom and make arrangements to head home after the weekend."

"Stay as long as you want, Guss."

"Thank you, but I don't have any way to repay you for that."

"Been doing fine so far," Tony said and laughed.

Guss smiled and shook his head. "I'm glad you think so."

"Me too." Tony pulled the shirt over his head and walked over to the red panda, leaning in for a quick kiss. "Now get a move on. We got things to do."

They made the walk to the subway and headed back toward Manhattan. Unlike the previous trip, Guss was much less tentative about being close. The train lurched and rocked, and the couple swayed with its motions. Their tails brushed one another, and Tony entwined his with Guss' as he put an arm around him and held him.

"It's strange," Guss said as he looked at the other passengers that paid them no mind beyond an occasional glance. "My hometown, two guys could never do this."

"Used to be worse, but things change."

"It's just not what I'm used to. Guess I'm not much of a city boy, huh?"

"I'll teach you." Tony rested his cheek on top of Guss' head. When the speaker announced 5th Avenue, Tony nudged the red panda. "This is us."

They got off their train and made their way to the street level. The late morning bustle of the big city was lessened before the white collars took to the streets for the lunch rush. Tony led Guss along the south end of the park, then down 6th, pointing out the Ritz, the Modern Art museum, and the music hall. He stopped at a large public plaza surrounded by the feel of old New York. In the middle was a golden statue.

"Rockefeller?" Guss asked as the stood looking down at the activity.

"They got the big video game store over there, and they got all the shops over there on 5th. Or we could go up on Top of the Rock."

"The observation deck?"

"Yeah. Haven't done that since I was a kid."

"Okay." Guss hooked his arm under Tony's and chuckled. "I haven't explored much past the park."

"We can fix that."

Tony led him into the lobby and bought two passes at the desk. The elevator wasn't crowded and the couple stood close at the back of the car on the ascent. Tony took the opportunity to slide a paw around Guss' waist as the cables pulled them skyward. When they reached the top level, the stepped out into the cooler air high above the streets.

The wind whipped around them as Guss went up to the glass. He looked across the skyline around the tower. Blue sky with wispy clouds was the backdrop for the iconic New York landmarks. The spires of the Empire State, the Chrysler building, and the Freedom Tower stretched skyward.

Tony walked up to him and looked at the cityscape. He waited while the red panda took it in. "Nice view," he said as he looked at the Empire State building. He felt Guss brush against him and he looked over to see the red panda holding out his phone.

Tony chuckled as Guss nudged him and turned around. When Guss held out the phone, he saw the screen with them on the display and the Empire State between them. The shutter sound effect coincided with the frame of the shot flickering.

"One more," Guss said as he adjusted the angle of the phone.

Tony leaned in and kissed Guss on the cheek just as he snapped the shot. The red panda giggled and quickly took another picture before Tony pulled away. He looked at Guss' screen when he clicked over to the picture. Even with the slight tilt of the phone, the image of the two with Tony kissing Guss while the red panda giggled, one eye closed, and the backdrop of the city was perfect.

"Send me that one," Tony said as he put his arm around Guss. "That's a memory worth keeping."

***

The streets were getting crowded as the noon rush approached. Guss stayed as close to Tony as he could so as not to get lost in the crowds. They had moved a few blocks from Rockefeller and were approaching Times Square. Before the intersection of the cross road, Tony ducked in to a door on the corner and Guss followed him in.

The small, crowded building no wider than a city alley on the inside was lined with tables and chairs. The air was full permeated with the scent of baking dough, melting cheese, and sauce warming in the ovens. There was a line to the counter almost to the door.

Guss moved closer to Tony as more started to file in behind him. "We're getting pizza?"

"We're getting a couple of slices," Tony corrected. "Figured you'd be hungry. I know I haven't eaten since yesterday."

When Guss brushed against Tony to make room for the line as it spilled out the door, the cheetah wrapped his arm around Guss' shoulder and coaxed him in front.

"Not so good with crowds, huh?" Tony said as he gave the red panda a buffer.

"Rural upstate is a little less crowded." Guss watched as the line in front of him moved through the queue with surprising speed. "I'm just not used to it."

One after another, the line dwindled as locals and white-collars filed through. The red panda was taking in the atmosphere of the small pizzeria. The spartan decorations and inexpensive chairs gave the impression of a dive. The crowd however, indicated that there was more than met the eye.

"Ta stay a ta go?" the rotund hedgehog in the flour stained apron asked Guss, speaking quickly with singular intent.

"What?"

"To stay," Tony said before the hedgehog could dismiss them and serve the customers behind them. "Two plain slices."

The speed of the exchange was dizzying. Tony handed the hedgehog a bill, was handed his change, quickly followed by two flimsy paper plates with pizza slices that drooped over the edge, and a fist full of napkins.

Tony made his way back toward the door with Guss in tow. He sat the plates on a table near the door, taking one of the napkins and wiping it down as Guss settled in opposite of him. He sat down and took the shaker from the edge of the table and sprinkled red pepper flakes on the pizza.

When he looked back at the red panda, he saw him looking at his food with an expression of curiosity. "You okay?"

"It's big," Guss said as he examined it.

Tony chuckled and picked up his slice and bent it in half. "It ain't right if you can't fold the slice."

Guss watched the way the cheetah held his food, folding the crust in the middle and supporting the end with his other paw. "I usually like pepperoni on my pizza."

Tony swallowed his half-chewed bite. "Gotta do it plain, first."

Guss nodded, picked up the slice, mimicking Tony's hold, and took a bite. It wasn't until it was half-chewed that he noticed Tony had sat his slice down and was staring at him. "What?" he asked around the food in his mouth.

"Good?"

"Mm-hmm," Guss replied as he resumed chewing.

***

Another subway trip skipping several blocks beneath the streets. They came to the surface at 6th and 14th. A few blocks down, Tony stopped in front of a three-story brick house and looked up at it. Guss' eyes followed his. It looked nice with its nineteenth century charm, with white trim on the door and windows and intricate plate glass, but was otherwise unremarkable.

It wasn't until Guss noticed the brass plaque on the brick by the steps that he realized what it was. Fifty-eight west 10th street. Guss jogged up the stairs to the plaque and read aloud, "New York University Creative Writing Program."

"You wanted to see it," Tony said as he walked up behind him. "Glad my phone led me to the right place."

"I don't believe it," Guss said as he reached up and touched the plaque. "Do you know how many giants of literature have stood, right here, before they went through that very door?"

"Can't say I do," Tony said and chuckled. "You said you wanted to see it, so here we are."

"Thank you." Guss looked at the simple stairs with the iron rail. "Can we go in?"

"Don't know. Let's find out."

They walked in and the old, polished hardwood creaked under their steps. They looked to a room off the foyer. It held bookshelves, rustic furniture, and a crowd around a podium. There was a student behind the podium reciting a poem. They made their way to the crowd and listened as a slender wolf with half-rimmed glasses read with inflections and emphasis on certain words and phrases.

Tony listened, but his focus was more on the red panda. He watched as Guss would cock his head, twitch his ears, and furrow his brow at irregular intervals. The cheetah couldn't help but chuckle, and Guss glanced his way. Tony wrapped his arm around him and finished listening to the speaker.

At the conclusion there was mild applause from the crowd. Everyone in the group started to disperse and a vixen wearing a skirt suit turned around and noticed them. She looked at the two with a curious glance.

"Oh, are you gentleman new students?" she asked.

"Us?" Guss looked up at Tony.

"No ma'am," Tony answered. "Just tourists, today."

"Oh, I'm afraid that this particular reading wasn't open to the public."

"I'm sorry," Guss said as he looked back at the vixen. "I just always wanted to see the house, and—" he cut himself off and studied her face. "I know you."

"Me?" she said in a half-knowing manner. "We may have met before. Maybe on a signing tour. I'm—"

"Betty Racer!" Guss finished for her as his eyes lit up. "You wrote *Ruins of the Ancestors*. And, and, and, *Sailing into the Darkness*."

"Yes, and a few others." She chuckled and waved it off with a paw.

"Oh yeah! I have all your novels, and…" Guss trailed off as he reached for his shoulder bag only to find it missing, left behind in the cheetah's apartment. "I'm sorry, I don't have any of them with me. I'd love to get your signature."

Tony stepped back from the two as they talked. He watched the red panda, his bright eyes and wide smile between gushing praise of particular scenes and descriptive prose. He bounced, swayed, and waved his paws in animated gestures. His eyes stopped on his tail, which Guss was swaying with unconscious gusto.

"I love meeting fans," she finally said. "But I'm afraid I have to join the students in their critique circle, and you and your boyfriend aren't technically allowed to be here."

"B-boyfriend?" Guss asked as he was pulled from one reality to another.

"Sounds right to me," Tony said as he wrapped his arm around Guss once more.

"I'll tell you what," Betty said as she ushered them toward the door. On the raised counter by the entrance, she picked up an overcoat and pulled a paperback from one of the deep pockets. "This is an advanced reader copy of my newest release. I would love to hear what you think, and I'd be willing to send you a signed copy when it's released." She extended it to the red panda. "The contact info is in there."

"I…" Guss looked down at the book. "I'm not sure I'll have time—"

"Thank you," Tony said as he nudged the red panda.

Guss took the novel and looked at its cover for a moment, then looked up at Betty with a smile and a nod.

"Pleasure to meet you, Ms. Racer," Tony said as he squeezed Guss with his arm.

"It's Mrs.," she said. "I don't want you getting any ideas, slick." She winked at the cheetah and turned away to attend to her students.

At the base of the stoop, Guss tugged on Tony's sleeve and stopped him. "Boyfriend, huh?" he asked as the big cat looked back at him.

"Yeah," Tony said and turned to face him. "If you'll have me."

Guss giggled, shook his head, then wiped an eye with the back of his paw that still clutched the novel. The cheetah pulled his body close lowered his muzzle toward his, he canted his head and received the kiss. When Tony pulled away, Guss sighed in contentment as he looked into the cat's golden eyes. "You always ask a guy out after you sleep with him?"

"First time."

"Lots of firsts, huh?" Guss asked, mimicking Tony's tone from the morning.

"Lots."

Guss eased back and chuckled. "Well, let's see what other firsts we can get up to, slick."

"God, don't let *that* stick."

The red panda chuckled and looped his arm under Tony's.

***

Tony waited in front of the hospital shifting his weight from one foot to the other. The pristine building stretched skyward. It was a center of healing. But like a coin, it had an opposite side. One that took all the hope and healing of the ages and turned it upside down. It was the sense of loss that made the cheetah uneasy.

Tony saw Guss walking out of the sliding doors with a dufflebag over his shoulder. It was a relief to see him, but his unsettled feeling lingered. "You sure about this?" Tony's query was as much for his own sake as Guss'.

"Yeah." Guss turned and looked back at the building. "Been here for two weeks straight. It will be nice to sleep in a comfortable bed." Guss turned to Tony. "With a handsome boyfriend. At least until the weekend is over."

"Like I said, long as you want."

"I know. But I think I should head back after the weekend." Guss glanced around. "Not because of you, but…"

Tony put his paws in his pockets and splayed his ears back. "You know, I'm worried about you checking out of the hospital for good." When he looked at Guss, he saw the red panda canting his head. "I mean I don't want to take away a chance you'll get help."

Guss smiled and scuffed his toes on the ground in a semicircle. "No. It's not." He stepped close to the cheetah. "You are helping me."

Tony slipped his paw under the strap of the dufflebag and lifted it off Guss' shoulder. "Let's head back."

They were quiet in the tunnels as the train wheels clacked and moaned. Tony held Guss, one arm around him as he had many times that day. Guss rested his head against Tony's chest. The normal tedium of mass transit was made into a shared moment.

Tony felt the soft breaths of the red panda. He watched his triangular ears occasionally twitch and his chest rise and fall. The cheetah nuzzled the red panda's headfur. He took in his scent; the neutral of the hospital soap now absent. It was a mix of Tony's own shampoo and Guss' aroma; a sign of their shared time.

When the train stopped at their station, they got off and made their way up to the street. The sun was setting, and much like their first walk to Tony's apartment, the sky painted in the twilight with the twinkling of the crowded buildings in front of them. This time however, Tony and Guss held paws with interlocked fingers.

When they got into the apartment, Guss rushed to the couch and fell on it face first with a long and exaggerated sigh.

"Long day?" Tony asked and chuckled.

Guss rolled over onto his back and looked up at the cheetah. "I haven't walked that much in years."

"Guess I wore you out, huh?"

"Not yet," Guss said and rose to a sitting position on the couch with his legs crossed on the cushion. "You implied this morning that we would be finishing the night with more *firsts*."

Tony felt his ears heat as he looked at the red panda. "Yeah, if you want. I understand if you're tired."

Guss looked down at his lap, rubbing his thighs and his knees with his paws. "If it's anything like what you did last night, I pretty much just have to be still, right?"

Tony coughed and rubbed the back of his head. "Yeah, I suppose. It ain't like it don't take effort. Still wears you out."

Guss laughed as he looked back at Tony. "I can't tell if that's a compliment or not, but I'm taking it as one."

Tony smiled as he walked over in front of Guss. He held out his paws and the red panda grasped them. Lifting Guss up to a standing position on the couch, he looked up at him as he stood about one foot taller than him with the boost. Tony saw him bend down, and he closed his eyes and canted his head.

Guss kissed him. It was soft and light. Then Tony's paws slid up Guss' back while Guss put his paws on Tony's cheeks. The kiss deepened, their tongues lashed against one another and their pulses raced.

The cheetah felt one of Guss' legs lift and wrap around him. He slid his paws to the red panda's rear, and Guss lifted his other leg. Tony held him off the couch as their kiss continued. His paws squeezed the red panda's rear through his shorts as Guss' arousal pressed against his stomach.

When Guss finally pulled his head back, panting and murmuring, they stared at each other for several moments. Finally, the red panda cleared his throat. "Should we take this to the bedroom, slick?"

Tony rolled his eyes then nodded in response. He felt Guss shift around, expecting to be sat down, but Tony held him tight. He carried him to the bedroom and sat eased his back on the bed. Tony straddled him, rubbing his body and kissing up his neck.

Guss replied in kind with heavy petting, but it soon turned into tugging at clothing. They peeled off their clothes in a midst of kisses, licks, and loving nips. The nervous foreplay was absent, washed away by the simple kiss on the couch that turned into burning desire. Guss panted as his naked body rubbed against his lover's. "I want you, Tony. I *need* you."

Tony lifted his head and looked at Guss. Despite the darkness, he could see every detail. His eyes drank in the features of the bear cat's face. Warmth radiated from his chest, enveloping him like a warm blanket. "I…" Tony looked at Guss' chest, then back up the lines of his mixed colored fur past his neck, over his muzzle and back to his eyes. "I need you, too." Guss' chuckle pulled the cheetah out of his daze. Tony narrowed his eyes at Guss. "What?"

"You laid it on thick in the shower," Guss pointed out and then giggled. "I'm just wondering if you're going to do more than stare."

Tony's arousal throbbed at the red panda's insistence. He lifted off Guss and grabbed his hips. With a lift and some coaxing, Guss rolled onto his stomach. The cheetah pushed his hips forward and his member slid between Guss' cheeks.

He moved back and forth, letting his flesh slide against Guss' fur. His paws rubbed the red panda's cheeks; spreading them apart and pushing them back together to enhance the feel. Tony was content to keep going until a shaky exhale in the form of a twittering moan pulled his attention back to Guss' face.

"Get the lube," Tony said as he accented his words with a long squeeze of the red panda's rear.

Guss steadied his breath as he reached for the night stand. His fumbling paw knocked over the dildo and lamp as he felt around. "I'm sorry!"

"Screw it," Tony said as he roughly ground his hips against Guss. "Doesn't matter. Lube now."

Guss felt around until he found the bottle. He held it back toward Tony. "Please go slow."

Tony chuckled as he took the lubricant and flipped the cap up. "You were being all impatient." He used his thumb to spread Guss' cheek as he upturned the bottle and drizzled it along his shaft and head, letting the flow drip on the red panda. He capped the bottle and tossed it away, thrusting his hips and spreading it around with his penis.

He heard Guss whimper as he smeared the viscous fluid over his opening. Tony smiled as he continued to rub his lover's backside. "Don't worry, I'll go slow. Just you got me so riled the way you were begging."

"I'll try and curb my enthuse—" Guss let out a sharp gasp as the spiny head pushed against his pucker. His fists balled and grabbed the comforter in tight wads.

"Let me know if it hurts, yeah?" Tony rocked forward and his tapered tip pushed in until the spines brushed the texture of his opening. Guss' warmth radiated around Tony's head. Holding the cheeks apart with his thumbs, he closed his eyes and tilted his head back with a moan as the spines slipped forward.

Guss gasped at the feel of the nodules rubbing the sensitive opening. His muscle ring expanded as the girth of the cheetah pressed against it. His inhales were small gasps and his exhales short pants. "It's…" Guss looked back at the cheetah; his eyes still closed and his muzzle pointed to the ceiling. "It's different than I expected."

Tony murmured in agreement as he continued pushing inside the bear cat. "Fuck," was his long, drawn out, and near breathless response. He slid his paws around Guss' hips and pulled him up as he sank to his sheath inside.

Guss' muscles squeezed and released him over and over. The silky walls rubbed his shaft and head as the red panda's breathing and heartbeat made subtle movements. All of the emotions that swirled in his chest and surrounded his being were amplified by the intimate connection of their bodies.

Tony began to purr. He didn't intend to do it, but it was uncontrollable. He heard Guss moan as his body—and his ensconced cock—vibrated. "Guss, I…" Tony moved his arms up and eased his body down against the red panda's back. He held himself there as he rubbed Guss' sides. "I want more. You okay?"

Guss' response was unintelligible at first. A serious of animalistic and lustful twittering coupled with moans. After several moments of enduring the natural vibrator with the soft barbs in his backside, he drew in a deep breath to steady himself. "It's so much."

"Does it hurt?"

"Some," he managed. "More, just... wow."

"Can I move?" Tony asked as he restrained every instinct that told him to rut his red panda then and there.

"Yes."

It was more than enough for the big cat. He moved his hips back in a subtle motion and then slowly pushed back inside. Guss gasped underneath him and Tony stopped when his sheath butted against the opening again. His purring hadn't ceased, and he deliberately kept his movement slow.

After two more repeats of the process with Guss' muscles squeezing and his walls tugging his spines, he felt the red panda begin to relax. Tony let out a deep sigh as he tucked inside his lover and nuzzled Guss' cheek. "Can't hold back."

Guss looked back at the cheetah as best he could. His body quivered and he forced his breathing to calm. "I think I'm okay. I trust you."

Tony's heart fluttered and he caressed Guss' flanks. He pulled out until his spines tugged Guss' tailring and pushed himself back to the hilt. The red panda cried out, but it was less strained. Tony's thrusts gradually increased in speed while the big cat still kept himself under as much control as he could muster.

As the pace increased, Tony was surprised to feel Guss start to push back against him. His thrusts had been gyrations, letting his body linger against the red panda's backside. "Doing better?" he asked with caring while keeping his movements going.

"It doesn't hurt so much now," Guss replied and let out a long moan. "I think I can take more."

Tony slid his paws to Guss' hips as he repositioned himself. His knees moved up to straddle Guss' and their thighs rubbed together. He pulled more of his length out in the new position and slid back in with more force.

Guss gasped as Tony's body impacted him. The increased force threw off his rhythm of pushing against the big cat's thrusts, but the deep purring from the cheetah implied he didn't mind. The sound of the impacts with the spines and length filling him over and over made his erection twitch and throb. "Go faster," Guss insisted.

Tony pulled Guss against him as the thrust in and pushed as he withdrew. The bed creaked and thudded against the wall. As he squeezed Guss' hips, the tips of his claws pricked the flesh under the red panda's fur.

With a sudden intense wave, Tony felt his orgasm rush forward. It caught him completely off guard. He tried to stave it off, but it was too sudden, and he pulled the red panda tight against him as he thrust as deep as he could.

Guss moaned as Tony's member throbbed inside of him. The cheetah grunted as he tried to steady himself, but he collapsed on top of the red panda. Guss was pushed further down, but Tony managed to lessen the impact on his body by catching himself on his elbows.

"Sorry," Tony said as he panted. "You okay?"

"Better than I have been in a long time, kitty." Guss giggled, but stopped when he felt Tony trying to lift up. "No. Stay there." Guss felt Tony ease more of his weight on him. "And please, don't stop purring."

Tony dry chuckled at his lover's request. His breathing was calming but he was still seeing stars from the unexpected climax. "Got an idea," Tony said as he shifted to the side. He worked an arm under Guss and rolled to his side. Holding the red panda close to him, he kept his spend member firmly lodged in Guss' rear.

"This works," Guss said as he nestled as close as he could to Tony. He moved his paw to his erection and stroked it. "This works well," he said with a long-contented exhale. The big cat kissed and licked his neck as he worked his length at a frenzied pace.

Tony's member began deflating and slipping out. It was withdrawing of its own volition, but when the spines tugged the red panda's tailring, he felt the muscles tense around it. The stimulation on his orgasmically sensitive head caused him to gasp.

At the same time, Guss moaned as his ministrations coupled with the big cat in his rear pushed him over the edge. His seed shot on the comforter in thick ropes. He panted as he rode out his orgasm and gasped when his flexing muscle ring in his backside finally released Tony's member.

The cheetah flinched as Guss' cheeks gave his head one last squeeze. He hugged Guss close while the red panda laid in his afterglow. "Sorry," he whispered to his lover.

"For what?" Guss asked in a tired tone.

"Kinda lost control there. I, uh, went a little rough and came a lot quicker than I thought I would."

"I'm not sorry," Guss said as he nuzzled his cheek against Tony's arm. "I'm glad my first time was with you. Thank you for everything."

***

Tony had his arm around Guss as the subway moved toward Manhattan. The morning commuters boarded and disembarked but it was background noise. The cheetah pressed his lips against the red panda's. Their tongues mixed in each others' mouths. Disgusted glances and leers alike went unnoticed.

It was a new comfort for both of them. They had a reckless disregard of the perception of others. The train stopping at their station was what separated them, and they held paws as they went up to the street.

Tony looked up the sidewalk toward his firm and then across the street at the park. "Gonna be okay by yourself 'til lunch?"

Guss nodded as he fished around in his shoulder bag with his free paw, pulling the advanced copy of Mrs. Racer's novel out. "I have a book to read, and a review to write. I'll be fine."

Tony chuckled and hugged Guss. "See you at lunch, yeah?"

"I'll be here, slick."

Tony broke the hug and playfully rolled his eyes. He gave Guss' rear a light swat as he sent him off and went toward his office. He settled into his cubical and idly shuffled the memos left on his desk from the previous day as he waited for his computer to log in. He felt aimless and distant, and his chest felt like there was a gaping hole in it.

"Come on," he said out loud to himself.

"Log in trouble?" he heard behind him.

Tony swiveled in his chair and saw a wolf in slacks and a button up shirt with a tie that matched nothing else he was wearing. "Nah, Chris. Just thinking."

"We had trouble with the network yesterday," Chris said as he picked a rubber band up off Tony's desk and stretched it between his fingers. "You picked a good day to skip work."

"Wasn't like that," Tony said. "Important issue. Personal."

"I'm not trying to pry, Tony. Hell, I think that's the first time you called off since I been here. Just worried about you." Chris pulled the rubber band back with his finger and flipped it at Tony's monitor as his desktop loaded in. "Maybe you just wanted to skip hump day, eh?"

"Didn't skip that," Tony said quietly.

"What?"

"Wait, it's Thursday, isn't it?"

"Yeah." Chris turned to finish his morning stroll through his section. "Which means you need to get me the Seoul projections before you leave."

"Yeah, you'll get them," Tony said with disinterest. "After I take care of something more important."

He opened his browser and typed, 'Broadway tickets.'

***

Tony walked the path to the bench where Guss was sitting. As he approached, he noticed the red panda looking in the distance. The book was in his lap, his phone was face down on top of it, and his headphones were around his neck. His posture and expression were pensive.

"You okay?" Tony asked.

Guss looked suddenly at Tony as if he was pulled from a distant thought. "Oh, yeah. Sorry."

"Something wrong?"

"I called my mom after we had lunch. She's not very happy."

"What happened?"

"I told her I checked out of the hospital. She thinks I'm giving up."

"Should you go back?"

"No." Guss shook his head and sighed. "My mom was convinced that this would be a way to save me. It was grasping at straws. She didn't want to accept that there's nothing that can be done."

Tony felt his heart sink and his stomach knot. He nodded his head. "I can understand."

There was a long moment of silence before Guss laughed and waved off the tension. "Nevermind that. Ready to head back?"

Tony smiled and shook his head. "Nope."

"No?"

"If it's okay with you, I thought we might make a quick stop on the way." Tony pulled his phone out of his pocket and brought up the electronic tickets. He showed the phone screen to Guss.

"Seriously?" the red panda asked with excitement in his voice.

"Seriously." Tony tucked his phone away and offered his paw to Guss. "Little more than an hour to get over to Broadway. Better get moving."

Guss smiled and put his things in his shoulder bag. He took Tony's paw and the big cat helped him to his feet. As his back straightened, his knees buckled, and he grabbed Tony with both paws to catch himself.

Tony reflexively wrapped his arms around him to catch him and hold him steady. "Guss! You okay?"

"Yeah," Guss said as he straightened himself and stepped back from the cheetah. "I probably just sat too long. It happens sometimes."

"You sure?"

"Mmm." Guss waved it off and slung his shoulder bag. "It's no big deal, really. Let's go see the show."

***

They stood under the marquee in the line filing in to the theatre. Young parents with kids chasing the magic of their youth and sharing it with the next generation, nostalgia seekers, tourists, and even the odd couple holding paws.

Tony's fingers interlocked with Guss' as they entered the lobby. The gold gilded lights and decorations sparkled. It was a few moments before Tony realized that he had stopped, and the other patrons were making their way around them. He looked over at the red panda and saw that Guss was taking it all in as well.

"First time?" Tony asked.

"Yeah," Guss replied as he continued looking around.

"Mine too."

"A lot of firsts," Guss said and chuckled.

Tony squeezed his paw. Guss looked up at him and their eyes met. The noise of the crowd, the bright colors, and the scents of the popcorn form the concessions stands dropped away.

The cheetah's pulse raced. His chest swelled with warmth and his ears heated. Nothing mattered in the moment except the red panda looking back at him with the same emotions reflected in his expression.

They moved closer and Tony wrapped his arms around Guss. Their heads canted as they closed their eyes. Just as their lips touched, they heard someone clear their throat. Looking in the direction of the noise, the setting around them came back into sharp focus. Tony and Guss stepped back from one another as they looked at a father holding his daughter's paw.

"Sorry," Guss said and looked away.

"I'm not," Tony said as he moved his paws to Guss' and squeezed them.

Guss shook his head and smiled. "Let's go get our seats."

They folded into the crowd and made their way into the performance hall. Guss looked around at the architecture. Trimmed in gold with acoustic indentations along the walls. The floor sloped down with row after row of theater seating. The balcony and boxes stood out like ornate sculptures. Farther down was the orchestra pit, and finally the stage.

Tony led Guss down toward the front. Five rows from the pit, he cut down the row, excusing himself with those already seated. When he got to the middle he sat down. As Guss was passing in front of him, Tony brushed his tail.

Guss giggled as he sat down. "Didn't we just get the stink-eye for that sort of thing in the lobby?"

"Still not sorry," Tony replied. Guss leaned over and put his head on the cheetah's shoulder. Tony shifted to move closer and took Guss' paw.

"Thank you for this," Guss said softly.

"You act like I don't want to see it."

"I didn't say that. You've done a lot for me." Guss sighed and nuzzled Tony's sleeve. "More than I thought I would ever have."

Tony felt his heart flutter. "Me too."

The house lights dimmed, and Tony felt Guss perk up as the curtain opened. The opening theme played as the elaborate backdrop mimicked the rising sun over a savanna. Colorful cartoon characters were replaced by their Broadway counterparts in bright costumes and professional singing voices.

The audience sang along, and Tony smiled when he caught Guss doing the same. Despite the quality of the show, the cheetah found himself watching the red panda more than the performers. All through the first act, Tony's glances and his thoughts were focused on Guss.

As with the animated feature, the story progressed with only minor deviations for the Broadway adaptation. The second act ramped up to the big musical number, and the red panda nestled against the cheetah. They were both singing along.

At the climax of the song, Tony noticed something change. He felt the weight on his arm grow heavy. There was a short exhale from his lover and then stillness. Looking over at the red panda, Guss appeared asleep but something was off. He nudged Guss with his elbow, but the red panda was slack. "Guss?"

He didn't respond. Guss' eyes were closed and his mouth slightly agape. The appearance still very much that of sleep.

"Guss?" Tony leaned over and gently shook the red panda. "Guss, answer me."

The sound of the play was distant. The musical number with half the audience singing fading from Tony's perception. The only sound the cheetah wanted to hear was the red panda stirring awake. It made everything else superfluous and his mind closed it all out.

"Guss. Wake up. You're... missing the show." Tony's voice was becoming a plea. "No. No. No, you're going to wake up. We're going to finish the play and go home."

No answer.

"Guss!" Panic was starting to grip the cheetah. He grabbed the red panda by his shoulders with both paws and shook him. Guss still didn't respond. He looked up at the people around him. The younger ones looked confused, but one father caught his gaze with a realization of what was happening. "Call 911," Tony told him.

"Guss, c'mon. Open your eyes. You need to open your eyes. I *need* you to open your eyes." Tony felt his stomach knot and his chest tighten. "Give me this weekend, Guss." Tony pulled Guss against him and cradled him. "One more day. Give me one more day," he pleaded. "This... show. Give me this last show with you."

Guss remained limp in Tony's arms. He didn't move, he didn't breathe, and he didn't speak.

"One more hour. Don't go yet. I..." Tony realized the culmination of his feelings over the last few days at that moment. The light had gone. Guss wouldn't smile. He wouldn't reply. "I love you."

The dam broke, and the cheetah cried.

***

Tony hadn't made many trips out of the city. Spring was giving way to Summer, and the hills of northern New York were green and alive. The car driving him pulled under the wrought iron arch on the narrow road. The fields on either side were lined with granite, marble, and limestone markers in neat rows. The oldest were weather faded and moss covered. The car stopped and Tony opened the door.

"You need me to hang around?" the driver asked.

"Don't know how long I'll be," Tony replied.

"Not like there's a lot of fares in small towns like this." The driver did his best to give a sympathetic smile. "I'll be here awhile."

Tony nodded before he added a tip to the fare and closed out the app. He walked up a small slope toward an old maple tree. Three stones from its base and one row back was a flat black granite marker. He stopped at the headstone and looked at it for a while.

Birds in the tree chirped and sang. He ventured a glance up at the branches. The leaves obscured the blue sky and wispy clouds. "A lot like the park, huh?"

He wiped away a tear welling in his eye and looked back at the marker. It was the first time he had seen it. The simple stake with a paper nametag was all that was present the day that Guss was lowered into the grave.

"You're Tony, right?"

Tony turned around to see a red panda walking toward him. It was Guss' mother. He had seen her at the funeral but hadn't spoke to her. He hadn't spoken to anyone. "Yeah. I…" Tony shook his head. "I'm sorry."

"He told me about you. The day he—"

"I'm so sorry, Ms. Fornwell."

She stopped beside him, looked down at the marker and then up at Tony. "Call me Elizabeth. Please. Guss would want that."

Tony's ears flattened as he looked at the stone.

"He told me that he was happy. I was furious that he left the hospital to galivant around with someone he didn't even know. Our last conversation was… an argument."

"I can't begin to apologize."

"Because you shouldn't."

Tony looked at her and cocked his head.

"Guss sounded so happy. He described you as the sweetest person he'd ever met. I… shouldn't have been angry." She sniffled back her tears. "He wrote a letter. It was in his personal things. It went into more detail about what—about who—you are. Who you are to him. I didn't read it until after the funeral. I'm sorry."

Tony sighed and started to turn away.

"Wait," Elizabeth said, grabbing Tony's sleeve. "I want to give you my phone number. I would like to get to know you better." She knelt and ran her fingerpads on the carved inscription on the stone. "Nothing is timeless…" she read aloud.

"…but not everything fades," Tony finished as he looked at the phrase carved below Guss' name. "I would like that, Elizabeth." Tony held out his paw and helped her to her feet. "You ever in the city? Know a great pizza place."

The trip home was less solemn than Tony expected. The train took him in the city, the subway to his neighborhood, and his feet to his apartment. He opened the door, went to his bedroom and started to dress down for the night.

He looked at the nightstand by his bed, and the new addition adorning the surface. A framed picture, taken from a cell phone, of Guss and Tony. The angle slightly tilted, the red panda giggling with one eye closed and Tony kissing his cheek, and the Empire State building behind them in the distance.

ABOUT THE AUTHORS

Skunkbomb lives in McLean, Virginia making a living as an office assistant in D.C. When he's not writing, he enjoys going to the movies, playing board and video games, and visiting amusement parks. He needs to add roughly 1000% more skunks into one of these stories for FANG. His other erotic work can be found in FANG Volume 7, FANG Volume 8, and CLAW Volume 1. He is on FurAffinity as Skunkbomb123 and on Twitter as @Skunkbomb123.

Quincy Connally studied music at the University of Maine at Farmington. He currently resides in central Maine.

Slip Wolf hops worlds with the help of his trusty damaged attention span and forwards little notes once in awhile about fun stuff happening there to editors moonlighting as therapists (whether they know it or not) He's now in his seventh year in the fandom and still finding stuff to rant about out of other animal's written mouths. Keep tabs on him on the blue birdy app @ Slip_Wolf

MythicFox discovered the fandom via an anime magazine's letter column 20 years ago. While he'd been writing before that, mostly trying to shamelessly mimic Stephen King, finding the fandom helped focus him. His biggest influences are, in no particular order, the aforementioned Mr. King, William Gibson, S. Andrew Swann, and Kyell Gold. Within the fandom, his work has

*appeared in ROAR and FANG. Outside the fandom, he's
an avid tabletop gamer and his writing has appeared in
a number of RPG books, most of them about werewolves
and involving handfuls of d10s. He can be found on
Twitter @mythicfox, and as "MythicFox" on FA and
SoFurry.*

Jaden Drackus, *or Jay Dee is a dragnox from
Maryland. He has been writing furry stories since 2010.
He counts joining the greater furry writing community in
2016 as one of the best decisions he has made. A historian
by training, he was inspired in his youth by science fiction
and fantasy, he tends to work in those genres as well as
historical fiction when he writes.*
*A video gamer, builder of model airplanes, reader,
and keen observer of Life's little ironies Jay Dee lives in
Baltimore with his boyfriend and 3 cats.*
*In addition to stories in FANG Volume 8 and Dogs
of War 2: Aftermath from FurPlanet, he can be found on
FurAffinity as JadenDrackus. His silly observations on life
can be seen on Twitter:
@JadenDrakus.*

Reverie *frequently writes but is often reluctant to share
his work. He has been taking steps to fix this however,
and is taking on more projects. He lives in Central Texas
with a rat.*

NightEyes DaySpring *is a known troublemaker who
is rumored to have a penchant for coffee and an interest in
dead, ancient civilizations. He has been actively writing
furry fiction since 2010. His stories have appeared in
Werewolves vs. Fascism, Seven Deadly Sins, and FANG,
along with other anthologies. He also co-edited Dissident
Signals, an anthology of dystopian furry literature with
Slip-Wolf. Currently, NightEyes resides in Florida with
his boyfriend, where in his spare time he masquerades as*

an IT professional.
For updates on his writing, visit nighteyes-dayspring.
com, and for day-to-day nonsense, follow
@wolfwithcoffee on twitter.

A small-clawed otter born in Waukesha Wisconsin
in 1994, **SignificantOtter,** *also known as John Kulp,*
has steadily moved Southeast his entire life. After at-
tending the University of Pittsburgh for a double degree
in Computer Science and Japanese, he relocated to
Philadelphia to work at a start-up as a full stack web
developer.
John currently resides by the Schuylkill River, where
he's evaded several attempts by the coast guard to remove
him. He enjoys playing the board game go, running along
the shore, and imbibing impossible quantities of tea. His
weekends are spent in a flurry of board gaming and
tabletop role-playing. You can follow him on Twitter at @
RunningOtter.

TJ *found the furry fandom after moving to Ohio*
almost ten years ago. It is there, he picked up the pen—or
grabbed a keyboard, as it may be—and started creating
characters and worlds. TJ is incredibly grateful for the
community of artists, writers and friend he found; they
helped him discover something that he cares about—writ-
ing. TJ has grown to become more passionate about the
craft of writing and enjoys creating new worlds and aiding
others with projects of their own.
TJ's other works may be found in ROAR, FANG,
and other anthologies both in and out of the fandom. For
thoughts, comments and replies in bite-sized chunks, he
can be found on Twitter
@TJMinde.

Ferric *has been writing short stories for over ten years,*
and furry stories for about seven of those. Most can be

found on Sofurry and FA, but recently he's started to get a few published whenever possible. He enjoys writing in his spare time as it allows him to be creative, and his head is full of too many crazy things to ever stop.

Tredain *is a furry author writing mostly gay erotica, sci fi, and fantasy fiction that has been with the fandom longer than he'd like to recount but it rhymes with 'schmecades'. While this will be his first officially published short story in an anthology, his work includes comics in Radio Comix's "Genus Male" series and Rabbit Valley's "Spooo Presents" series. He's been writing fiction and burying his nose in books since he was a kit and not likely to stop anytime soon.*
Currently living somewhere in the land of Fruits and Nuts where he most often disguises himself living among the normal folk, he spends most of his time working his day job, writing, or leisurely enjoying games and books. A large body of his work and commissioned art can be found on his FurAffinity page - http://www.furaffinity.net/user/Tredain while his random musings and thoughts can be found on his twitter - http://www.twitter.com/Tredain

Starvix Draxon *is a dragon who discovered the furry fandom roughly three years ago and has been reading its books and viewing its art ever since. His poems, "The Dragon's Lament," and "Moonlight Howl" have appeared or are forthcoming in Typewriter Emergencies and Wolf Warriors respectively, and his other furry story, "The Great Camping Adventure," has appeared in Breeds: Wolves. You won't see him often as he is a rather skittish and shy dragon, and often likes to keep to himself, curled up in his cave with his book-hoard, movies, and video games. Under his real name, his articles, reviews, and poem have appeared in places such as Threshold, Fantasy Scroll Magazine, Sirius Reviews, and Glass Mountain.*

He also wrote a play about a dragon. When not writing, he's reading (and researching) mythological, ancient, and medieval texts, listening to Celtic or Dream-pop/Electro pop music, or playing Kingdom Hearts games for the fifth hundredth time.

When he is not looking in the mirror, **Bill Kieffer** is actually a 6 foot tall gray anthropomorphic draft horse that types as Greyflank. He is a member of the Furry Writers Guild and has recently published short stories in several Furry anthologies as well as The Goat: Building the Perfect Victim, a rather dark and adult novella which won a Cóyotl award.

Jinx and Cecil from "Quipis" also appeared in Roar Volume 9—Fang's more PG sister publication. "Qibla" is a sequel to this story, taking place about a year later than the beginning of "Quipis."

COLD BLOOD: Fatal Fables, a collection of his furry noir, was recently released by Jaffa Books.

Mog has been writing for over a decade, with his first printed works appearing in 2016. When not doing furry stuff, he's usually trying to figure out how to do more furry stuff. Feel free to contact him and let him know what you think of his work.